"Angela Elwell Hunt has created a powerful story, rich with historical detail and filled with compelling characters. Jocelyn is a light in the wilderness!"

Francine Rivers, *award-winning author*

"Based on the historic voyage and mysterious accounts of the first Virginia colonists, Angela Hunt takes readers on an unforgettable journey back to 1587. Although no one is sure what really happened to these brave settlers, the heartaches, joys, and challenges Hunt brings to life will certainly intrigue and encourage!"

Beverly LaHaye, *president, Concerned Women for America*

"Angela Hunt has a God-given gift for storytelling. Her historical characters brim with life; her settings resonate with authenticity. Roanoke evokes a world of passion and treachery where only the characters' faith in God can sustain them. Compelling, heartbreaking, thought-provoking. Don't miss it!"

Catherine Palmer, *best-selling author*

KEEPERS
OF THE RING
1

ROANOKE
THE LOST COLONY

Angela Elwell Hunt

Tyndale House Publishers, Inc.
WHEATON, ILLINOIS

Library of Congress Cataloging-in-Publication Data

Hunt, Angela Elwell, date
  Roanoke : the lost colony / Angela Elwell Hunt.
    p. cm. — (Keepers of the ring ; 1)
    ISBN 0-8423-2012-1 (SC : alk. paper)
    1. North Carolina—History—Colonial period, ca. 1600-1775—Fiction.
2. America—Discovery and exploration—English—Fiction.
3. Roanoke Colony (N.C.)—History—Fiction. I. Title. II. Series:
Hunt, Angela Elwell, date Keepers of the ring ; 1.
PS3558.U46747R63   1995
813′ .54—dc20   95-37575

Printed in the United States of America

00 99 98 97 96
 7   6   5   4   3   2   1

It happened many years ago,
The memories still haunt you, though.
And who's to blame, you really don't know
You're just locked all alone in these chains.

Sometimes it's hard to live at all,
The pictures of your history call,
Your mind's a decorated wall,
But the Lord has a cure for your pain.

You've had your little victories,
But perfection's pretty hard to please.
And guilt is an annoying breeze
That blows all that's peaceful away.

And life is too short to go on living like this,
Or to brood over who's done you wrong.
If the years pass you by, look at all that you'll miss,
You've been walking in shadows too long.

It's time, come back to the land of the living,
Come home to the land of forgiving,
Jesus will be faithful to the end.
It's time to break the tangled webs that bind you,
Let the grace of God unwind you,
Give the Lord your broken heart to mend.

It's time.

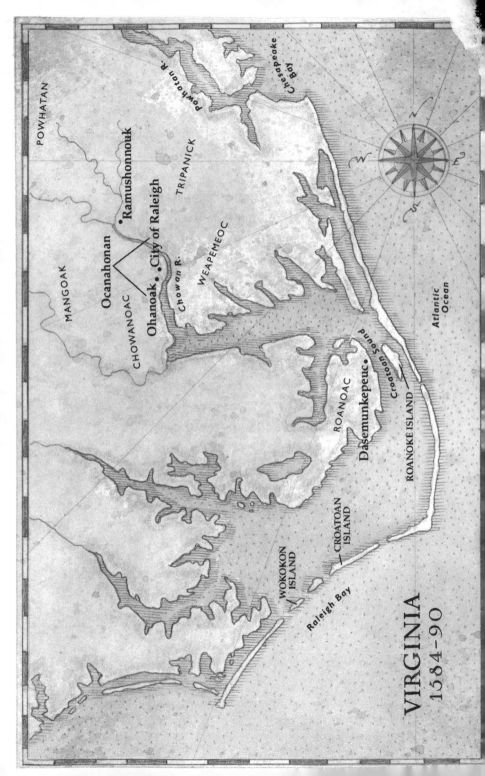

VIRGINIA
1584–90

THE NAMES OF THE VIRGINIA COLONISTS AS RECORDED BY JOHN WHITE, 1587

The names of all the men, women and children, which safely arrived in Virginia, and remained 'to inhabite there, 1587.
Anno regni reginae Elizabethne, 29.

Households of the Gentry:

John White, Governor
Thomas Humfrey, cabin boy
Roger Bailie, Assistant
William Clement, servant
Ananias Dare, Assistant
Eleanor Dare, wife
Virginia Dare, daughter
Agnes Wood, servant
Christopher Cooper, Assistant
James Hynde, servant

Thomas Stevens, Assistant
John Sampson, Assistant
John Sampson, Jr.
Roger Prat, Assistant
John Prat, son
George Howe, Assistant
George Howe, Jr.
Rev. Thomas Colman
Jocelyn Colman, wife
Audrey Tappan, servant

Households of the Common Folk:

John Jones
Jane Jones, wife
Joan Warren, servant
Dyonis Harvie
Margery Harvie, wife
Sylvie Harvie, infant daughter
Jane Pierce, servant
Arnold Archard
Joyce Archard, wife
Thomas Archard, son
Margaret Lawrence, servant
Ambrose Viccars
Elizabeth Viccars, wife

Ambrose Viccars, son
Emme Merrimoth, servant
John Chapman
Alice Chapman, wife
Jane Mannering, servant
Edward Powell
Wenefrid Powell, wife
William Wythers, nephew
Thomas Smart, servant
Henry Payne
Rose Payne, wife
Elizabeth Glane, servant

Unmarried Men:

William Willes
John Brooke
Cutbert White
John Bright
Clement Tayler
William Sole
John Cotsmur
Humfrey Newton
Thomas Gramme
Nicholar Johnson
Thoms Warner
Anthony Cage
John Tydway
Edmond English
Thomas Topan
Henry Berrye
Richard Berrye
John Spendlove
John Hemmington
Thomas Butler
John Burden
Thomas Ellis, his son
Robert Ellis
William Browne
Michael Myllet

Thomas Smith
Richard Kemme
Thomas Harris
Richard Taverner
John Earnest
Henry Johnson
John Starte
Richard Darige
William Lucas
John Wright
William Dutton
Morris Allen
William Waters
Richard Arthur
Robert Little
Hugh Tayler
Richard Wildye
Lewes Totton
Michael Bishop
Henry Browne
Mark Bennet
John Gibbes
John Stilman
Robert Wilkinson
Peter Little

John Wyles
Brian Wyles
George Martyn
Hugh Pattenson
Martyn Sutton
John Farre
John Bridger
Griffen Jones
Richard Shaberdge
James Lasie
John Cheven
Thomas Hewet
William Berde
Henry Rufoote
Richard Tomkins
Henry Dorrell
Charles Florrie
Henry Mylton
Thomas Harris
William Nicholes
Thomas Phevens
John Borden
Thomas Scot

Savages That Were in England and Returned Home into Virginia with Them:
Manteo and Towaye

For Him whose grace is greater than our sin

Grace comes into the soul,
as the morning sun into the world;
first a dawning; then a light; and at last the sun
in his full and excellent brightness.
THOMAS ADAMS

AUTHOR'S NOTE

Much has been written about the lost colonists of 1587, and I am indebted to the work of David Beers Quinn, perhaps the definitive authority on the Roanoke voyages, and to David Stick, William S. Powell, Karen Ordahl Kupperman, and, of course, the journals of John White himself. I owe a special thanks to the helpful present-day inhabitants of Roanoke Island, who have done their best to ensure that the lost colonists will never be forgotten.

My readers often want to know how much of a book is fiction and how much is fact. Be assured that I have tried my best not to contradict the extensive historical record. And while no one knows exactly what happened to the lost colonists of Roanoke—their disappearance has been attributed to such unlikely culprits as tidal waves, sea monsters, and plagues—there is strong anecdotal and historical evidence to support the premise and conclusion of the story as presented in these pages.

The people of this book are a very real part of American history. John White's trials at sea were documented in his journals, and the exploits of Ralph Lane's soldiers have been preserved for us through other publications and letters.

From White's list of colonists we know the names of the people who set out for Roanoke, but names do not tell us as much as we'd like to know. I have had to invent characters and qualities to enlarge upon the slight historical evidence we can glean about these individuals. We do know that the colonists were devout and courageous people who were determined to take the gospel of Christ to an unexplored land. And we know that they were willing to pledge their lives in an uncertain and risky venture.

All in all, they were people well prepared to make their homes in the land of the living.

TABLE OF CONTENTS

Prologue

Jocelyn White

Thomas Colman

George Howe

Ananias Dare

Regina

Richard Taverner

William Clement

Ocanahonan

Gilda

Epilogue

PROLOGUE

Anno Regni Reginae Elizabethae, 28.
Her Majesty's Virginia, June 1, 1586

The hard fist of fear squeezed John White's stomach as the aroma of an Indian woman's breakfast stew wafted by on a breeze. *What are we doing here?* A bird warbled in the brightening treetops; the tinkling sounds of children's laughter rose through the ghostly morning mist of the forest.

The man to his right stepped forward, and John felt the rigid slap of his leather scabbard on his right leg as he followed his fellow soldiers into the clearing. *If Sir Walter Raleigh had named me governor instead of Ralph Lane, we'd be sitting down for a peaceable meal instead of running to war.*

At the sight of the uniformed English emerging from the woods, a gaggle of naked children scattered from their games to join their mothers. The circle of warrior-counselors around the aging chief's fire stilled their voices and gazed impassively at the approaching white men.

Ralph Lane stepped briskly forward to face Pemisapan, the chief of this and many other Indian villages. The white man wore the full uniform of Her Majesty's Governor of Roanoke—a uniform expressly designed to intimidate—and determination lay in the jut of his sharp chin as he faced the Indian leader.

Pemisapan kept his face expressionless under Lane's hot glare. "Hear me, Pemisapan," Lane bellowed, addressing himself more to the camp than to the chief. "Last night your men fired upon us."

Pemisapan did not answer but folded his arms across his bare chest. One of the Indian counselors spoke: "In the night, four of our warriors were killed by the long guns."

Lane ignored the comment. "Hear me, Pemisapan, and know that we have learned of your dire conspiracy. We will not be driven into the sea; we will not vacate this land. We will not sit idly by while you and your fellows scheme to murder every Englishman and servant of Her Majesty Queen Elizabeth."

At the mention of the queen's name, Pemisapan lifted his hand as if he would speak, but Lane never gave him that chance. "We will not surrender because in the queen lies our glory, and in *Christ, our victory!*"

The signal! Lane's words rang through the camp with the force of a cannon, and the thirty Englishmen drew their weapons. White fumbled with his unwilling sword and pulled it from its dark leather sheath as the keening wail of women and children rose around him. The arm that held his sword rose stiffly; his feet took a troubled step forward.

Before him, a dark-haired woman snatched her child up, holding the small one protectively to her breast. White looked past her to the governor and felt his mouth go dry as Lane raised his musket to his shoulder and fired directly at the chief. A cloud of white rose in the confusion, and a bright flower of red bloomed in Pemisapan's chest. Without a word, the chief crumpled like parchment in tongues of fire. The war council members by his side rose, too late, to gather their weapons.

The woman in front of White ran for shelter, and he whirled and held his sword toward a fiercely painted warrior who grasped a battle club. For an instant their eyes met, and White felt himself pleading wordlessly, *Please. I don't want to kill you.* The warrior swung his club in answer, filling the air with his bloodcurdling death song. White parried the blow with his sword and obeyed the soldier's instincts bred into him years before. His sword bit into the unprotected target of the warrior's chest, and White looked away as the man fell to the ground, still rasping his eerie song.

Around White the other English responded as one with

swords and muskets. Several fired in the heat of the moment as women and children bolted toward the woods. "Don't shoot the Croatoan!" Lane's voice cried above the din. "We have promised Manteo that his brethren would escape unharmed!"

The Indian warriors who did not resist were quickly stilled by English muskets. Within ten minutes the dreadful sounds of gunfire and pain had faded to be replaced by the mewling wails of children and the dry sobs of grief-stricken women.

White sheathed his bloody sword and surveyed the damage. Pemisapan the chief lay motionless on the ground, still surrounded by aged counselors who sat mute in the paralysis of astonishment. Governor Lane, swaggering in victory, handed his musket to his servant and moved toward the prone body of the chief. White felt a sudden quickening of his heart. Was it his imagination, or did Pemisapan stir?

"Hold there, Governor," he called, stepping forward. "The man lives."

"Nay," Lane answered, grinning over his shoulder. "I shot the savage myself, and at close range."

A log suddenly shifted on the smoldering fire in front of the fallen chief, and a dense plume of smoke rose like an angry cloud amidst the carnage. The sight distracted Lane's attention for a moment, and in that instant the wounded chief leapt to his feet and crouched, his hands upraised like the curved talons of an eagle.

Lane took a step back and motioned to his servant. The boy, an Irish lad of thirteen, dropped the unloaded musket and fumbled with the heavy revolver tucked into his belt. Pemisapan's dark eyes shifted from Lane's outstretched hand to the revolver, and after a moment of hesitation, the chief wheeled and flew toward the woods. Lane's Irish boy, the revolver now in hand, cocked the governor's gun and fired at the Indian's back. Pemisapan flinched; his back flowed with blood, but still he ran.

Two of Lane's soldiers roared in frustrated fury and sprinted after Pemisapan. Lane watched them go and frowned. "I fear we will lose those two today," he muttered to no one in particular.

"This savage Pemisapan's barbaric warfare holds the advantage in the woods."

"The result will be as God wills, but I wish we had not resorted to bloodshed," Thomas Hariot answered, frowning at the bloody scene before him as he leaned upon his weapon. Hariot possessed one of the most scientific and mathematical minds of all Europe, and, as always, he offered a rational opinion. "For it is possible," Hariot went on, glancing to White for support, "that Pemisapan did not conspire to wound us, but merely strove to protect his own people."

Lane cut Hariot short with a harsh glance. "There was a conspiracy against us, I can assure you," he insisted, his index finger forcefully punctuating his words in the air. "The Indian boy we hold hostage told me of the plot against us."

Hariot did not answer, but glanced again at White as if to ask, *"How do you reason with the unreasonable?"* White knew he ought to say something, but he was less skilled even than Hariot in dealing with people. As long as Ralph Lane was governor, there was no proper way to protest the bloodshed they had wrought.

He turned from Hariot's gaze and looked around. Several Indian women clutched their frightened children and cried softly while others knelt by the bodies of their warriors and tore handfuls of hair from their heads. One group of Indians stood unmolested in a knot, but stared at the scene around them with bewilderment and a vague sense of shame in their eyes.

Croatoan, White thought. *Manteo's friends, probably, and therefore our friends. But how long will they be friendly to us now that they know we are capable of such harshness?*

One tall brave among the Croatoan looked familiar, and after a moment White remembered that the warrior was the son of a chief from Manteo's village. Months before, White and Hariot had left the English fort on Roanoke Island to live among the Indians and learn their language. They had spent weeks among the Indians, searching out native plants and medicinal herbs, and they had come away from the experience with a profound respect for the Indian culture and simple way of life. The Indians, White knew, understood vengeance and war. They did not understand conspiracy, for each tribe looked after its own affairs.

White walked toward the Indian brave, raising his hand to show that he intended no harm. "Governor Lane wishes you to go in peace," he said, nodding gravely to the warrior. "You are Manteo's people; you are our friends. We wish you no harm."

The brave turned and spoke to the others grouped behind him. White waited while the men of the group conferred.

"I fear some of our company have showed themselves too fierce." White jumped at the low voice in his ear, then turned to see Thomas Hariot by his side. Hariot had learned well the Indian technique of soundless movement.

"What if they ask the reason for this?" White asked, keeping his eyes to the ground. "How can I explain that Lane fears a conspiracy?"

Hariot stroked his beard as he studied the conferring Croatoan. "Our governor's foretelling of an uprising may be but a self-fulfilling prophecy. We have slain some people in some towns for offenses that we might have easily borne. Perhaps this is the worst we have done so far. Verily I tell you, John, we may yet see the villages banding together to rise against us."

"Let us pray it is the worst we shall ever do," White answered, glancing at the dead and dying around him. He lowered his voice: "For if those in the interior of this land hear and believe that white men cannot be trusted—"

"Hallo, Governor!" A joyful cry echoed from the woods, and White recognized the Irish accent of Edward Nugent, one of the governor's servants. "Look at what we have brought you!"

The man with Nugent held something aloft as the men entered the clearing, and White felt his gorge rise. From the man's hand dangled Pemisapan's severed head.

Jocelyn White

I cried unto thee, O Lord: I said,
Thou art my refuge and my portion in the land
of the living.

Psalm 142:5

England, 1587

The March wind whistled through cracks in the sealed windows of her uncle's coach. Jocelyn White nestled closer to her father and the warmth of his heavy frieze cloak.

"'Twas lovely for Uncle John to send his carriage for us," she said, wriggling her gloved fingers to resist the numbing cold. "Though I think the only reason he's bringing us to Portsmouth is to find a new audience. Does he never tire of talking about his adventures in America?"

"John does like to talk, but a girl like you shouldn't judge her elders," her father replied easily, his voice muffled by the heavy cloak and the wide starched ruff around his neck. His dark eyes twinkled over the crisp collar, but she felt the gentle rebuke behind his words, and her heart softened. For years he had done his best to mold her into a gentlewoman, and for all those years she had done all she could to resist him. Motherless since the age of six, she was doubtless responsible for more than a few of the silvery strands in his dark hair.

"I'm sorry, Papa," she said, resting her hand on his arm. "I'm ungrateful, I know. I should be happy that we could leave London at this dreary time of year."

Her father wagged a finger at her. "You are forgetting the important things. How many people do we know who have personally visited the camps of the American savages? Who have stood on the shores of that dark land and confronted dangers unknown—"

A coughing fit cut short his words, and Jocelyn's blue eyes deepened with concern as her father jerked away and coughed into his handkerchief. When at last his spasm ceased, he took a quick, shallow breath, folded the handkerchief into his palm, and gave her a tentative smile. "Enough talking." Only a whisper remained of his voice. "We should rest until we reach Portsmouth. I believe John will talk enough for both of us."

Jocelyn's eyes filled with tears, and she made an effort to steady her voice. Robert White did not want pity. "All right, Papa," she said, pretending to look out through the hazy shade covering the window. "But I know Uncle John will try to convince you to join him on this next expedition to Virginia. And since you are scarcely well enough for this journey to Portsmouth, I don't see how you could even think about going to America."

He lifted his hand as if he would argue with her, but another coughing spell seized him. Jocelyn felt her heart tighten with anxiety again as she pretended not to notice that the handkerchief into which her father coughed was stained with blood.

He had become ill several months before. Many times she had urged him to stay in bed and rest, but Robert White, proud philosopher and scholar, had refused. "My students are waiting; my books demand my attention," he had told her one morning as he pushed the breakfast tray she offered out of the way and swung his thin legs over the edge of the bed. "When death comes to me it will find me busy, Jocelyn, unless I am asleep. If I thought I was going to die tomorrow, I should nevertheless teach my classes and do my reading today. A faithful Christian life in this world is the best preparation for the next."

His coughing filled the carriage now, and Jocelyn clenched her fists under the lap blanket as she obeyed his unspoken wishes and said nothing. *The doctor says he ought to be home in bed,* she told herself, *no matter how much he wants to hear these tales of Uncle John's.*

Once again she turned to stare out the window, though she saw little of the scenery. Her attention was focused inward, not toward the dreary winter landscape. A faint frown of concern creased her forehead as she pondered her father's insistence that

they make this journey. *Why?* she wondered. *Why was it so important for us to come to Portsmouth in the dead of winter?* But she had
no answer . . . save a slight chill of apprehension.

▼▲▼▲▼ Since his return from Virginia in the fall of
1586, John White had taken up residence in Portsmouth with his
daughter, Eleanor, and her husband, Ananias Dare. Despite Jocelyn's reluctance to leave London, she found herself peering
through the shades of the carriage as they entered the port city.
Much smaller than London, Portsmouth nevertheless exuded an
air of self-importance, for Her Majesty's America-bound ships
departed from either Portsmouth or Plymouth.

While her father lifted the window shade and braved the
chilly March air for the sight of an oceangoing galleon on the
English Channel, Jocelyn peered through the window facing the
city and wondered what sort of house her cousin Eleanor had
chosen for her home. Nearly two years older than Jocelyn, Eleanor was a gentle lady and the daughter of an important man, but
at her wedding last year she had seemed as giddy and frivolous
as the average maid.

The cousins had a great deal in common, yet much kept them
apart. Both were motherless; both had been reared by their
fathers with only a maid for feminine companionship. Eleanor's
father had engaged the dour-faced Agnes Wood to serve and
restrain his high-spirited offspring; Jocelyn's father had hired
Audrey Tappan, a pretty Irish maid a year younger than Jocelyn.
John White had found a chaperon for his daughter; Robert White
had sought a friend for his.

Jocelyn had to smother a grin as she thought of the many
times Eleanor had succeeded in vexing Agnes. Vain and pretty,
Eleanor had been given to harmless flirtations and romantic musings, and the entire family had breathed a sigh of relief when she
accepted the proposal of Ananias Dare, a modest bricklayer and
tiler from Portsmouth. What sort of wife had Eleanor become?

The coach turned onto a narrow lane muddied by freezing

winter rains. After urging the horses through the mud, the driver halted the carriage and jumped down from his perch. He flung the door open and bowed as Robert White struggled to extract himself from the depths of the carriage. Jocelyn helped her father up, then held his elbow as she followed him from the carriage.

Her eyes widened as they walked. Why, Eleanor's house was lovely! Ananias Dare must be a prosperous man.

A stream of mild complaints reached Jocelyn as Audrey dismounted from the top of the carriage, but she blocked the girl's whining from her mind as the door to the house opened and a tall, spare man came out to greet them.

"Robert!" John White called, his voice echoing in goodwill. "Thank God you have arrived safely. I wondered if I would ever see your devilishly handsome face again!"

As her father laughed and embraced his elder brother, Jocelyn stood quietly aside and studied her father and uncle. The two men shared the same pronounced cheekbones, thin, expressive lips, and wide, pensive foreheads. Even their eyes were strikingly similar: dark, eloquent, intelligent. But there the resemblance ended. John White's tanned skin had been etched by the sun with fine lines; the grayish pallor of illness underlined Robert White's countenance. Of the two, John was taller and more robust, with a fine, full head of white hair. Robert's thinning hair hung limply from his skull, and though it had once shone with the same shimmer of sable as Jocelyn's, illness had dulled it to a muddy gray.

John pulled out of the embrace and regarded his brother with a stern expression of disapproval. "I take back my words about your good looks. You look like death, Robert. You should have written me."

"Nonsense." Jocelyn watched her father shake off his brother's arms and concern with a shrug. "I have a cough. If God wills, I will get better." He turned to Jocelyn and Audrey. "Go inside, girls, and stay warm. John is sure to have a roaring fire in his hearth, for I see by his bronzed face that he is unaccustomed to our English winter."

John opened his arms toward Jocelyn in a gesture of welcome. "Forgive me, Jocelyn dear. How pretty you are! Certainly, go inside and warm yourself. Eleanor is waiting and eager to see you, so go reacquaint yourselves while I have a talk with my brother. I've taken a little room in the back of the house until we depart again for Virginia, but I'll be around to talk to you directly."

John White threw a protective arm around his brother and led him away. "Are you absolutely determined to go?" Jocelyn heard her father ask as they walked toward the rear of the house.

"Nothing can deter me. Did I not tell you in my letter? Eleanor and Ananias are coming, too, to live with me in Virginia. Two hundred colonists, Robert, and this time we cannot fail."

▼▲▼▲▼ "Jocelyn!" In a flurry of satin and lace, Eleanor appeared in the hall and hugged her cousin earnestly. "I was so delighted to hear you were coming! Such news I have to tell!"

"I hate to disappoint you, Cousin, but I believe I already know your news," Jocelyn replied as the two pulled apart. "I overheard Uncle John telling my father that you and Ananias are planning to go to Virginia."

Eleanor laughed gaily and pinched Jocelyn's cheek. "'Tis only half my news, little one. There's more to tell. But first, give Audrey your cloak and come nearer the fire. There's a good girl, Audrey. You'll find Agnes in the kitchen. Jocelyn, come here and let me have a look at you."

Audrey took Jocelyn's cloak and left for the kitchen while Jocelyn pirouetted neatly before Eleanor, who laughed again and clapped her hands in delight. "How very pretty you are, Jocelyn! Your hair is quite lovely, and that gown! I'd give anything to visit a London sempstress before we depart for Virginia."

"Whatever for?" Jocelyn asked, sinking onto a bench near the fire. "The savages of Virginia won't know a ruff from a frill."

"Oh, my dear, but our fellow passengers will," Eleanor answered, sinking onto a low stool. "And Ananias is to be made one of the gentry, have you heard? He's one of the thirteen assistants for the new colony. So I'm to be a gentleman's wife as well as a gentleman's daughter."

Jocelyn smiled in silent congratulations and knew that Eleanor had to be relieved at this turn of events. Jocelyn herself had been surprised when John White had agreed to marry his daughter to an untitled bricklayer, for the gentry and middling folk did not usually mingle, let alone marry. But Eleanor had boldly announced that she and Ananias the bricklayer had fallen in love . . . whatever that meant.

Eleanor murmured something about fetching tea and left Jocelyn alone for a moment. Taking advantage of the silence, Jocelyn removed her gloves and held her chilled hands before the warmth of the fire as she looked around the room. The house appeared tidy and prosperous, and the blazing fire bore eloquent testimony to Ananias's success, for wood was very expensive.

In a moment Eleanor returned and twirled delicately beside the hearth, the hem of her skirt billowing about her dainty slippers. "I suppose I should let you have a look at me and see if you can guess my news," she said, smiling impishly. "Look, Cousin, and see what a difference marriage makes."

She twirled again, slowly this time, and Jocelyn studied her carefully. Eleanor seemed as giddy as ever, but her style in clothing was definitely more matronly. She wore an expensive-looking gown of watchet and rose-colored camlet lined with white silk and embroidered generously with sprays of tiny blue flowers. Double epaulets graced the shoulders over long, thickly quilted sleeves, and a starched, lace-edged ruff set off her face and delicate features. A long rope of pearls hung from her neck, and a blue feather fan dangled gracefully from the belt at her waist. For all her complaints about being far from a London sempstress, Eleanor certainly dressed the part of a fine lady.

Jocelyn felt a small dart of jealousy. Though her own simple green taffeta gown was elegant and attractive, it was far from new or stylish. Once her father had spoiled her with new dresses, furs, and jewelry, but due to his illness, in the last few

months her father had not been able to fulfill his duties at the
school where he taught. Thus there had been no money for visits
to the sempstress, and Jocelyn had quietly sold her few jewels to
pay household expenses.

"Well?" Eleanor's tone changed from wheedling to demanding. "Can you guess my secret?"

"You have commandeered the queen's sempstress."

"You are being silly. Try again."

Jocelyn shrugged. "You have married a rich man."

"Not really." Eleanor giggled, then rushed forward and knelt
on the ground at Jocelyn's feet, clasping her hands tightly over
her cousin's. Her eyes were surprisingly clear and direct. "I am
going to have a child. In August, if God wills. Mark me, Coz:
Not only are Ananias and I going to Virginia, but our child will
be born there."

Jocelyn took a quick breath of utter astonishment. "You would
travel to Virginia in such a condition?"

"Yes." Eleanor's sweet face showed no signs of concern.
"Papa has said the journey will be difficult, but we should make
good time and establish the City of Raleigh well before June. In
less than four months . . ." Eleanor's voice trailed away as she
considered happy thoughts.

"You will be . . . ," Jocelyn offered hesitantly, uncomfortable
discussing such a delicate subject, "very large with child."

Eleanor smiled and her eyes misted. "Yes. But Papa will be
with me, and Ananias will not leave my side. Papa has promised
that I will receive the best of care and attention. And if you will
come, too, dear Cousin—"

Jocelyn laughed and pushed Eleanor's outstretched hands
away. "I'faith, *I* go? To Virginia? Dear Coz, have you lost your
mind? My father is ill, and he is in no condition to venture on
such a journey."

Eleanor pulled herself up to sit on the bench next to Jocelyn.
"Have you never considered," she said carefully, her voice a
husky whisper, "that perchance your father might wish you to
go with me? You are seventeen, Jocelyn, and should have been

married before this. There are many eligible young men preparing to go to Virginia, most of whom are eager to take a bride."

"To what?" Jocelyn snapped, forgetting herself. "I am not ignorant of Virginia, Eleanor. I have heard of the difficulties faced by Ralph Lane's men. They were attacked by savages, nearly killed by starvation, shipwrecked, and oft abandoned. Go to Virginia? I would as lief go to Spain and serve their Catholic king."

Eleanor shook her head, then went on, unruffled. "You don't know what you are saying. Papa has said that this expedition will be different. The first venture failed because 'twas a military endeavor. But this, Jocelyn, will be an outpouring of families: men, women, and children eager to establish new homes in Virginia. Ananias and I are keen to go. Agnes, my maid, is coming as well, and surely your father would allow you to take Audrey if it would please you. You could stay by my side, Cousin, and help me when the baby arrives. After that, you could make a life for yourself, far from that stuffy university where you fill your head with useless books—"

"Stop." Jocelyn raised her hand to halt the flow of words, wishing she could politely clap her hands over her ears. Such sincerity shone from Eleanor's eyes that Jocelyn found it difficult to answer. "I would gladly offer my help for your baby," she said finally, twisting her hands in her lap. "But marriage? I do not want to be married. I am not ready."

"Bah!" Eleanor playfully waved the objection away. "Every girl is ready when the right man comes along. A hundred men will be on our ship, Jocelyn! Many born gentle, and all brave souls. You could have your pick from the lot of them. I believe there are ten, no, twenty who would know how to move your heart if you would but give them the chance to woo you."

Jocelyn lowered her eyes. "I cannot go," she said simply, shaking her head. "Nothing can be done about it, Eleanor. My father is very ill, perchance dying. If he does not rest, his strength will fail him altogether."

Eleanor reached out and squeezed Jocelyn's hand. "Mayhap

God has brought this opportunity to you in his divine wisdom," she whispered. "If your father dies—"

"No!" Jocelyn jerked her hand away. "I will stay with him, I will make him rest, and he will not die. He needs me, and as long as I am there to make sure he takes care, he will remain strong."Eleanor did not answer for a moment; then her hand moved to shield the slight bulge at the waistline of her gown. "I admire the strength of your love, Coz," she whispered, staring into the fire, "and hope that my child will feel as strongly attached to me when he is grown. Do what you must, and I will pray God to preserve you and your father. But Ananias and I will be departing within two months, and it may be a very long time before you and I meet again. I had so hoped that you would join us. . . ."

Eleanor's voice cracked, and Jocelyn felt a wave of compassion flood her heart. Despite Eleanor's careless confidence, she had to be frightened. At least a little. She was leaving home, kin, queen—everything she knew and held dear—for the untamed wilderness of Virginia. Indeed, it was only natural that she had wanted her closest relative to join her.

"I am sorry. Truly sorry," Jocelyn whispered, slipping her arm around Eleanor's shoulders. "I would go with you if not for Papa. I know you must be frightened."

Eleanor shook her head, but her eyes remained locked on the fire. Jocelyn embraced her briefly and felt wet tears upon her cousin's cheek.

▼▲▼▲▼ "I did not know that you were so ill. What does the doctor say?"

Robert White sat on the narrow bed in the small but tidy chamber. His brother sat on a threadworn chair facing him. One tiny window allowed only a small stream of light into the room, and the darkness magnified the shadows of Robert White's face.

Robert squared his shoulders defensively in response to his

brother's question. "I am not so ill. Perchance I am only growing old."

"Nonsense. I have seen dying men, Robert."

Robert coughed softly. "A plague on your tactlessness, John! If you are to be a governor, diplomacy is a skill you should develop."

"Beshrew diplomacy. There is a time for speaking plainly, and 'tis now." He leaned closer and placed his hand on his brother's knee. "You have a bloody cough. Is it phthisis?"

"So my doctor says."

"How long?"

"Not very."

The two men sat in silence for a moment as John struggled for words. Robert had never been one to ask for or accept sympathy, not even when his young wife died and left him with a daughter to raise alone. Then, three months ago, at Christmastide, John had heard that Robert had lost his teaching position to a witty would-be poet called Shakespeare. He regarded his brother's face and smiled slightly, fairly confident that Robert had read little more than two lines of the condolence message he had sent.

Even so, the situation was not to be borne! Assistance must be offered. "Can I help?" he asked, fully expecting a proud refusal.

"Yes," came the surprising reply. Robert's hand trembled as it rested on his knee, and his lips quivered as he spoke. "I came here to talk with you about this, John. Something must be done for Jocelyn, and since you are leaving England there is no one else to see to her welfare."

"I'll do whatever I can."

Robert twisted the handkerchief in his hand. "I would like her to go with you to Virginia so you can act as her guardian. I have set aside a certain sum which should more than adequately pay for her voyage—"

"Forget the money, Robert. I myself will provide for her."

Robert coughed again, then wiped his chin with the stained handkerchief. His eyes narrowed in pain. "I pray you, keep her safe, John. Protect her, for she has been sheltered and knows little of the world—" Robert's voice broke, and John placed his hand upon his brother's bony shoulder.

"If you wish it, Robert, it will be arranged." He managed a smile. "Safeguarding her will not be easy, for she is a pretty girl and a lady, and the ship will be loaded with unmarried men, most of whom are common folk. But if I assign a man to look after her—"

"Find her a husband." Robert barely managed to utter the words before a coughing spell seized him, and John sat helplessly while his brother coughed into his handkerchief for what felt like an eternity. When at last Robert could catch his breath, he leaned toward his brother, his dark eyes large and fierce with pain. "Find her a husband," he repeated, his voice a thin whisper in the room.

John leaned forward. "What sort of husband, Robert? The father customarily arranges a marriage, so if you wish to do so—"

"I leave it in your hands," Robert said, clearing his throat of rumbling phlegm. "Only do not tell Jocelyn anything of this. She won't want to go, and I fear I will have to resort to subterfuge to bring her onto the ship." He paused and took a weary, rasping breath. "Find a man who will love her, John, a man who loves God above all. A gentle man, a kind man, one in whose strength she can rest. She has done too much for me. She deserves a better life than . . . this."

In that moment, John White caught a glimpse of his brother's future: the expressive, sensitive face would grow pale and shrivel like an old orange; the hands that rested now on his knee would soon be little more than bone and tough sinew. If nothing were done, Jocelyn would watch her father crumple and die. Her youth and beauty would be spent on his decay. . . .

John clasped his brother's thin shoulder again. "I will see to it," he pledged. "Have no fear, Robert, she will be well wed. And she will prosper in our new City of Raleigh. Lane failed because he affronted the Indians, but we will succeed because we are families. Just like the Indians, we want nothing more than to live and work in peace."

Robert's eyes closed in relief and weariness, and John softened his voice. "But now, Brother, take your rest on my mattress. I will wake you before supper."

Robert silently nodded his thanks.

▼▲▼▲▼ Audrey Tappan was defrosting her chapped hands by the blazing kitchen fire when she felt a rude nudge on her hip. "Move out of the way, dearie, or I'll burn you with this 'ot soup," warned Agnes Woods, Eleanor's former maid and now servant to the Dare family. Audrey had met Agnes at Eleanor's wedding the previous year, and the powerful woman with the bones of a man had only grown more dour with age. The woman had to be nearly thirty, but any signs of gray in her hair were covered by her cap, and her face was too plump for wrinkles. Yet, in spite of her stern face and quick tongue, Agnes was well beloved by the Dare household.

"A wee bit pushy, aren't you?" Audrey remarked mildly as she stepped out of the way. "Are you as brash with your mistress?"

"'Bout as cheeky as you are with yours," Agnes answered, placing a heavy iron pot over the fire. She straightened and grimaced over her flushed cheeks. "I saw you alighting from the carriage and 'eard your complainin'. I might be cozy in my mistress's confidence, but you won't 'ear me complainin' within 'er 'earing, that's for certain."

Audrey shrugged and held her hands up to the fire again. "Miss Jocelyn doesn't mind me. We're friends, we are."

"So you say." Agnes turned to the chopping board, where a handful of onions awaited her knife. "Just how friendly are you and your mistress?"

"Friendly enough. I've been with her for nearly four years now, since I was twelve."

"And are you thinking of going with 'er to Virginia?"

Audrey forgot about warming her hands and turned to gape

at the older woman. "Och, and where'd you hear an eejit thing like that? Virginia? Miss Jocelyn's not going *there.*"

Agnes lowered her voice and winked conspiratorially. "Aye, I overheard Master John talking to Master Robert 'bout taking Miss Jocelyn to Virginia. Seems they want her to find a 'usband."

"'Tis not so," Audrey answered, but her brain hummed with the idea. Virginia! Such stories she had heard about savages who ran through the forest half-clothed, long hair streaming down their backs. Virginia was Paradise, people said, but one had to endure the very devil himself to thrive there. Perhaps no one could. Indeed, perhaps no one was meant to. Audrey pursed her lips. If Miss Jocelyn was truly thinking about going to Virginia, it was time to start praying that she'd change her mind.

"You'd better be packing your own trunk," Agnes said, chopping the onions with relish. "Mine are packed with wot little I 'ave. The ship sails from the port 'ere in about a month, Master John says, and will arrive in Virginia before summer."

"Virginia!" Audrey sank onto a stool in amazement, then turned wide eyes to Agnes. "But I know Miss Jocelyn. Her father's ill, and she won't be leavin' him."

"I tell you, the plans 'ave been laid," Agnes said, smiling in the calm strength of knowledge. "Pack your bag, then write your mummy and daddy, and tell them good-bye. You are as bound for Virginia as I am, or else you'd better find a new master and mistress."

"Och, I could never leave Miss Jocelyn," Audrey murmured, her head still crowded with the image of a long-haired, dark-eyed savage. "But—Virginia!"

"Not all the news is bad, dearie." Agnes winked at the younger girl and rapped the knife on the table. "Master John says there are over a hundred unmarried men goin', and not many maids. Be glad, girl, for you'll catch a 'usband easily, and I'll be right behind you with my own if God is willin'. Serving women like us would never get married if we stayed 'ere, but in Virginia there's no gainsaying that we'll be wanted as wives."

"Imagine that," Audrey finished numbly. "But I believe I'd

rather be single and alive in London than married and—goodness me, I can't say it."

"Boiled by the savages?" Agnes volunteered, tossing the onions into the kettle hanging over the fire.

"Sure an' that thought did get into me head," Audrey murmured.

The lights of London houses made yellow rectangles on the thin snow that had fallen in their absence, and Jocelyn smiled with relief when the carriage driver pulled up outside her own small house. She helped her father from the coach and supported his arm as they went inside while Audrey thanked and dismissed the driver. After leading her exhausted father to his room, Jocelyn made her way to the hall and removed her traveling veil. As she unfastened her cloak, the slightly perfumed fragrance of the pine boughs that had adorned Eleanor's house rose to remind her again of her cousin's parting plea to join them in Virginia.

Jocelyn's farewell to Eleanor had been bittersweet. Her happiness for her cousin's prosperity and great expectations was tempered by the knowledge that her only other relatives were leaving for another world. It was too much to comprehend. If her father died after Eleanor and Uncle John departed, she would truly be alone in England.

The click of the door latch broke the silence in the hall. Audrey tossed off her bonnet and fell onto her cot, too tired to remove her cloak. Jocelyn let her sleep and moved through the house in the pattern she had established long ago: hang up the cloaks, check the fire, fetch a log. She mumbled under her breath at the thought of having to step out again into the numbing cold; then the touch of a hand on her shoulder made her gasp in surprise.

Her father stood behind her, weariness etched into every line on his face. "Don't go out, my dear. I'll bring in a log."

"No, Papa," she answered, sorry that she'd complained. "You should be in bed. 'Tis no trouble for me. Just lie down and rest, and I'll have a fire soon, then something warm for you to drink. Eleanor gave me a small bag of tea before we left—"

"Sit down, Jocelyn; never mind the fire. I want to talk to you."

She had not heard her father speak so firmly in years. Reflexively, she sat on a stool while her father stood before her. Had she done something wrong?

Her father forced a smile to his tired face, but the effort could not lift the lines of weariness and exhaustion that surrounded his eyes. "I have spoken with your uncle," he said, folding his hands across his chest. "We both agree it's best if you accompany Eleanor to Virginia."

So that was it. This firm determination was only for her benefit. Well, she could be resolute, too.

"No, Papa, I will not go," she said, lifting her chin stubbornly. She met his eyes and smiled. "Think you that I could leave you behind? I would rather remain here."

"This is not a choice, Jocelyn Marie. This is my wish. I command you to go with your uncle."

"Command what you will, Papa, this choice is not yours to make." She knew she walked the dangerous ground between rebellion and the independence he had always encouraged her to exhibit.

"'Children, obey your parents in the Lord . . . ,'" he began, wagging his finger at her.

"'Honor thy father and mother,' Papa," she answered. "'Love thy neighbor as thyself. In honor prefer one another.' And, 'Little children, let us not love in words, but in deed and in truth.'"

He let his hand fall to his side, defeated. "I should know better than to throw the Scriptures at you," he said, the corners of his mouth lifting in a weary smile. "Whatever possessed me to allow my daughter to read? She now knows more than I do myself."

"Pray do not tell me to go away," she whispered, lifting her eyes to the ceiling so she would not have to look at the pain in his face. "You are all I have in the world, Papa, and I cannot leave you."

"If I insist?" His voice cracked, and Jocelyn knew he found it hard to command such a difficult decree. He had reared her to think for herself, to weigh right and wrong in the balance of truth and God's Word.

She lowered her eyes squarely into his. "I do not wish to go to Virginia. I will stay here in England with you."

He raised his hand and stroked her cheek with the back of his fingers. "If I cannot command you, Daughter, can I—" He broke off, coughing slightly. "Can I *beg* you? Will you go so my mind and heart may rest in peace?"

It may have been his choice of words that provoked the image, but she suddenly knew with pulse-pounding surety that her father was dying. Swift tears stung her eyes. He no longer had the strength to fight his illness or even command her obedience; her proud and intelligent father had been reduced to begging so he could die in peace, with no worries about Jocelyn's future. Uncle John wanted her to go to Virginia, her father wished it, Eleanor wanted her by her side . . . perchance God himself wanted Jocelyn to make the voyage.

No! She could not do this thing.

She spoke softly, her voice thick with emotion. "I could not bear to leave you, Papa," she said, catching his fevered hands tightly in hers. "Pray don't ask me again. It is impossible, and I have told Eleanor so. My place is here, with you, until you are better."

"I will not get better." His words were a rasp from a torn soul. Though she knew they were true, still Jocelyn hated hearing them.

"I will not leave you."

Despite the cold ashes in the fireplace, the room seemed to grow warmer as her father looked down at her. "It's settled, then," he said, his eyes large and luminous. And yet as she met his eyes, she fancied a secret lurked behind his dark pupils. But he only smiled and whispered, "You are a good daughter, Jocelyn Marie."

She pulled his hands to her lips and gently kissed his fingers. "You are my only father. How could I leave you?"

"I am tired," he said abruptly, pulling his hands from hers. He took two steps toward the back chamber, where his bed waited, then turned toward her. "Will you ask the apothecary to visit me tomorrow? I have a boon to ask of him."

"I'll go as soon as I have lit the fire," Jocelyn answered, glad to see that for once her father seemed eager to take the apothecary's advice. Maybe he had been worried that he would be left alone and so had resisted measures that would only prolong his death. But now that she had promised to remain, he could regain his strength. If she could only convince him to rest.

"Good night, Jocelyn," he called from the doorway. "Do not forget the apothecary."

"I'll go now." She threw on her cloak and left the house, hurrying for the apothecary's house on the next street. The fire would wait.

In his office near the docks of Portsmouth, John White sat at his desk and interviewed a new group of prospective colonists for the City of Raleigh. It had required all of Sir Walter Raleigh's considerable persuasive powers to convince Queen Elizabeth to grant the charter for the Virginian city. That she did so at all was a miracle, given Ralph Lane's disastrous attempt, and the charter spoke remarkably of the Virgin Queen's devotion to the handsome and articulate Raleigh.

The grant of arms allowed for the establishment of the "City of Raleigh" in Virginia, with John White, of late from Virginia and Lane's colony at Roanoke, as governor. Twelve assistants were also appointed to act as White's council to ensure the development and prosperity of the city. The queen would not allow Raleigh to leave her side long enough to make the trip, so Raleigh invested his rapidly dwindling fortune and allowed White to set about the task of enlisting colonists for the venture.

White gazed out to sea and scratched his chin as he recalled his impassioned boasting that he would have no trouble enlisting one hundred fifty willing colonists. Within the first month of his recruiting efforts, he realized he had spoken prematurely. Eleanor and Ananias had signed on readily enough, and nine of the assistants pledged their lives and fortunes to the venture. The three remaining assistants had decided to remain in England and vowed to do all in their power to accrue supplies and the required financing for the colony's sustenance.

George Howe, one of the Virginia-bound assistants, signed on with his eleven-year-old son, but his wife refused to join the expedition, saying only that she would join her husband and son when she had received word that they had arrived safely and had not "been swallowed by the sea." Despite the success of English ships in the great Western ocean, many of Her Majesty's subjects were still not convinced that giant sea monsters—or worse—did not arise from the deep periodically to swallow ships whole.

As the departure date began to draw close and more families had not signed on to the venture, John White sent letters to prisons, villages, estates, and the homes of gentlemen. Commoners, middling folk, the second or third sons of noblemen who would inherit nothing in England, all were urged to sign on and thus discover riches and wealth in Virginia. Those willing to invest a bit of capital to outfit themselves for the harsh terrain would be guaranteed five hundred acres of virgin land outside the City of Raleigh.

Gradually, one by one, the prospective colonists came. By mid-March John White's list included the names of scores of single men who had little to leave and nothing to lose by journeying to Virginia, as well as two prisoners released from Colchester Castle. These two, jailed for stealing, had agreed to become lifelong indentured servants for the privilege of life in Virginia. But John White needed families to make his colony survive.

Last month he had posted a notice that families who emigrated to the City of Raleigh would receive five hundred acres *per person*, up to two thousand acres per family. And, he was pleased to note, the notice had apparently worked. In England, where both land and employment were increasingly scarce, the prospect of unlimited land and forests was undeniably appealing.

Fifty men now stood outside the small building that served as his temporary office, and John noted with satisfaction that quite a few were dressed in the richly embroidered attire of gentlemen. If any of them represented England's fine families, the success of the venture would certainly be assured.

▼▲▼▲▼ By three o'clock that afternoon, John White and his clerk were hard-pressed to contain their enthusiasm. Among the forty men who had signed their names and pledged their capital were twenty heads of families. Seven families, including Ananias and Eleanor Dare, had reserved a place for their maidservants as well. Women, White knew, stabilized a community, and the more women on board his ships, the more solid his city would be.

White looked at his watch and nodded to his clerk, who shut the door and pulled the parchment blind over the window. It had been a good day's work, and Raleigh would be thrilled with the news. "Take a letter, I pray you," White said to his clerk as he stood to stretch his long legs. "To Sir Walter Raleigh, London."

A rap at the door interrupted his thoughts, and White frowned. The clerk paused, his quill poised over the parchment, and White was tempted to ignore the knock. But if yet another prospective colonist stood outside, perchance it would be folly to refuse him entrance. . . .

White strode to the door himself and threw it open. A tall and straight man stood there, clothed in black hose and a somber black doublet, a cloth cap in his hand. He was a well-favored young man, handsome in appearance with a strong, narrow face, a broad pair of shoulders, and a reserved, guarded manner. Despite his unkempt hair and less-than-elegant clothing, an air of unmistakable dignity clung to him.

The man blinked in surprise at the sight of White in the door. "Begging your pardon, sir, but I am seeking the Honorable John White."

The young man's voice was striking, White thought. Deep and resonant, it caught one's attention immediately, despite the man's somber and somewhat off-putting expression. For a brief moment, White had the fleeting impression of proud humility; then he remembered his resolve to recruit colonists and forced himself to nod pleasantly.

"I am John White. What business brings you to the docks, sir?"

The man pointed over his shoulder with a long, elegant finger.

"The notice, governor. I would like to journey to this City of Raleigh, if God can find a place for me there."

White opened the door farther and lifted his hand in welcome. "We shall see what God can do, my friend. If you will just give my clerk your particulars, all will be arranged."

The clerk sighed noisily and set aside his parchment as he pulled forth the register. "Name?" he asked, visibly annoyed at the impertinence of the latecomer.

"Thomas Colman. Reverend Thomas Colman."

From his desk against the wall, White raised a finger. "You are an ordained minister?"

"Yes."

"Anglican?"

"Precisian."

"Ah, a Puritan."

The young man cleared his throat with a cautionary lift of his hand. "We prefer to simply be called the godly. We follow the Bible and no earthly creed except it be of God."

"I see." White smiled and tented his fingers, thinking. Every settlement needed a man of God. Of course, it wouldn't do to have a Catholic priest in the City of Raleigh—at least half of Elizabeth's court supported the idea of Virginian colonization simply to balance the influence of Catholic Spanish settlements in Florida and New Spain. An Anglican priest would be ideal, but none but an aging cleric had signed on for the journey; most were too caught up in the politics of the English church to venture into the unknown. White's eyes settled on the man before him. This independent Puritan minister might well be an ideal choice for the spiritual leader of the colony. He was young, certainly not over twenty and nine or thirty, and could be molded to suit the colony. . . .

He nodded for the clerk to continue.

"Are you married, Reverend Colman?"

"Widowed."

"Children?"

"One son. But he will remain in England." The minister

shifted uncomfortably, then ventured a quick glance at White. "I'm not irresponsible, sir. My son lives with his aunt."

"Quite understandable, Reverend. But I can assure you that many children are making the journey. Though it may be indelicate to speak of it, my own daughter is with child and plans to give birth to my grandchild in Virginia."

The minister shook his head. "My son will remain here. My wife's sister has agreed to rear him."

"Your age, sir?"

"Thirty."

"Are you of gentle birth?"

"No."

"Have you skill in a trade, sir?"

"I am a minister of the gospel."

White waved a hand to interrupt. "I don't mean to discredit your holy calling," he said, shifting his weight on his stool, "but we are in need of men with skills. Are you familiar with farming? Brick making? Woodworking?"

Something akin to a pale blush crept along the young man's cheeks. "I have been called of God to save the souls of men, sir. Surely there is no greater calling, nor one which requires greater skill. I do not know what God would have me do in Virginia, but I stand ready and willing to minister to the souls of all men."

White sighed and nodded for the clerk to continue. Though the colony would certainly need someone for spiritual guidance, he would have preferred that the man be able to build a house or fire bricks as well.

"What vices have you?" the clerk went on, reading questions reserved for men and women of the working class. "Gambling? Drinking in excess? Fornicating? Have you run away from any master or army?"

"I have none of those vices and am not running from any man," Thomas Colman replied firmly. White noticed with approval that a flash of steel rang in the man's voice. The questions had offended him. Good.

The clerk glanced over his notes, then looked up. "There only remains the matter of your subsidy," he said. "You are required to deposit two hundred pounds or its equivalent to pay for your portion of the journey. You will also be required to bring certain tools and articles of clothing with you when you report to the ship."

The minister shuffled his feet uneasily and looked at the floor. White leaned forward in curiosity and lifted an eyebrow. Surely the man had not hoped to journey to Virginia without investing something of himself to ensure the colony's success.

"I do not have two hundred pounds," Colman said finally, his voice brimming with conviction. "I pray you will make an exception since I may be caring for the spiritual needs of my fellow travelers both aboard the ship and in the colony."

"There are no exceptions," White said, rising to his feet. It was too bad. But if the minister had no skills and no subsidy, well . . . too bad, indeed, for he would have made a fine addition to the group of colonists. And Eleanor would certainly have welcomed the prayers of a clergyman as her baby's time approached.

Thomas Colman remained rooted to the floor in front of the clerk's desk and gestured toward the clerk. "Hold, sirrah, don't cross my name from your list. I must go to Virginia. Surely there is some way . . . perchance I may serve on the ship's crew. I should talk to the captain."

"No, you wouldn't want to work among those seamen. They'd eat a man like you alive, Reverend," White answered, nodding in grudging admiration for the man's persistence. "They're a rough lot and bound to their mistress the sea, not to God."

He came closer and studied the young man intently. Tall and straight, Thomas Colman was lean but powerfully built, his face marked by serious dedication. Intelligence and an aloof strength lay upon him like a protective shield, and John White sensed that this minister was an honorable sort, gentle in spirit if not in birth, tenacious, the sort who would make a good husband and father—

An idea whipped abruptly through his thoughts, and White

felt himself grinning. Surely this was a heaven-sent opportunity. He looked away for a moment to smooth the triumphant smile from his countenance, then turned back to Thomas Colman with a suitably grave expression on his face.

"As God has willed, Reverend Colman, a sponsor is willing to outfit and subsidize one godly and worthy man on this journey. If you meet with his specifications, he will pay your subsidy price and outfit you with whatever you need. He had not anticipated that we would recruit a minister, but perchance God knows that we will have need of you."

A gleam of interest flickered in Colman's dark eyes, and White had to suppress another smile. Ah, like a moth to a flame, he is drawn. . . .

"This patron . . . what are his *specifications?*"

"Very few." White dismissed the question with a wave of his hand, determined to dangle yet more attractive bait in front of this prospective catch. "If you are the young man he seeks, in the City of Raleigh, you will own a house, one thousand acres in your name, and as a clergyman you will be recognized as one of the gentry. The royal Garter King of Arms will confer a coat of arms upon you even before we leave port."

Ah, the fish was nibbling at the bait. This young minister would never have such treasures in England, not if he lived a thousand years and accomplished ten thousand mighty deeds.

"What must I do?" The man's voice gave away little, but White noted the way his knuckles whitened slightly on the cap in his hand.

"Our patron has specified that the recipient of his gift be a man of honor and virtue. He must be kind, gentle, and follow God with all his heart, as I believe you do. And he must take as his wife a very lovely and sensitive girl, the daughter of a gentleman in London."

The light in the minister's eyes flickered and died. He replaced his cap upon his head and bowed slightly. "Thank you, sir, for your time, but I cannot marry."

"Why not?" White slipped from his stool and hurried to block

Colman's exit from the office. "You, sir, are too quick with 'I must' and 'I cannot.' Listen to what I have to offer before you make your decision." White placed his hand on the minister's back in a fatherly gesture and lowered his voice so the clerk would not hear. "The girl is my own niece, seventeen years old, beautiful in every way and virtuous. If you will promise to woo and win her, without divulging our conversation and your promise to me, we can conclude our agreement. I ask only that the marriage take place before the ship lands in Virginia."

White held his breath for an answer as the minister's eyes deepened in speculation. "And if I fail? If she will not marry me?"

White reflected. He knew his unconventional niece. It was very possible that she could harden her heart against marriage. His gaze rested again on the minister's face. Surely the girl could be won by this handsome man!

He smiled. "She will marry. Her cousin and I will convince her it's best."

"No." The minister held up a hand. "She will not be trifled with. She must make her own decision and choose this marriage of her own free will."

"If she refuses, my patron's offer is withdrawn, and you, sir, will be on board my ship without having paid for your passage. Would you then have me throw you overboard?" White leaned against the door and thrust his hands behind his back. A pox upon him! This was a most strange and deliberate minister! The man should have been a merchant, for he drove a hard bargain.

Colman lifted his dark brows. "I must go to Virginia. Hence, if the girl will not marry me, or if you judge that my efforts have been less than sincere, I would be willing to give my service in whatever capacity you choose."

White moved toward his desk. "Agreed. If the girl will not consent to this marriage, you shall serve fifteen years as my indentured servant." He pulled a sheet of parchment from the desk. "And after fifteen years you will walk away with nothing but your freedom. No land, no wealth, no wife."

Thomas Colman's brows rushed together in a brooding knot over his eyes as he considered the stiff penalty for failure; then he nodded soberly. "Draw up a document, and I will affix my signature," he said, his voice surprisingly toneless for a man who had just agreed to win a beautiful wife and vast fortune. "I will do whatever I must to leave England."

The apothecary paused outside the door of Robert White's London house. The man inside had been slowly dying for nearly a year, and the apothecary knew both the local surgeon and physician had given up hope for his recovery. Through countless bleedings and purges, the man had rallied, then failed again as the consumptive disease ran its bloody course.

The wizened druggist knocked at the door, then made pleasant conversation as White's lovely daughter led him back into the bedchamber where the frail scholar reclined upon tattered pillows. The stench of death lay heavy in the room. White's bony hand waved the daughter away, and when he spoke, the apothecary had to lean close to hear.

"I want a mixture to make me sleep," White said, phlegm rumbling in his lungs and throat. "A deep sleep, mind you, with no waking for at least five hours. Something that can be stirred into a drink and swallowed easily."

The apothecary nodded. "Is the pain so great?" he whispered.

White made a brave attempt at a smile. "Immense," he said, his eyes shining like dark globes in the narrow sockets of a skeleton. "Pray deliver it tomorrow and place it into my own hand, not my daughter's."

"It will be done, Master White," the apothecary answered, struggling to hold his breath so he would not inhale the thickened odors of the room. He bowed, then hurried out of the house.

▼▲▼▲▼ "Supper is ready, Papa," Jocelyn called, carrying a bowl of pottage into the bedchamber. She lay the bowl on the bed while she arranged her father's pillows so he could sit upright, then held the spoon and fed him the watered-down pottage. She tried to smile and keep her voice light as she chatted about the day's events in their part of the city, but after a dozen spoonfuls her father's frail hand pushed the spoon away.

"Enough, Jocelyn. I am not hungry," he said. The sight of his weary smile through cracked and bleeding lips brought tears to her eyes.

"Would you like me to read to you?" she said, turning away. "Something from Aristophanes? Sophocles? Marcus Aurelius?"

"No Greeks or Romans today," he whispered, his head falling upon the pillow. "But if you could find something in the Scriptures . . ."

His eyes closed, and Jocelyn fumbled for the leather-bound Bible by his bed. The Bishops' Bible, as it was called, was a beloved translation of the Scriptures authorized for the Church of England. Jocelyn let the book fall open to a well-worn page and began reading:

> "And you, who were dead in trespasses and sins;
> wherein in time past you walked according to the curse
> of this world, according to the prince of the power of the
> air, the spirit that now worketh in the children of disobe-
> dience. . . . But God who is rich in mercy, for his great
> love wherewith he loved us, even when we were dead in
> sins has quickened us together with Christ, for by grace
> you are saved."

"By grace," her father murmured on his pillow, the words barely distinguishable. "Only by grace, Jocelyn. 'Tis what Martin Luther fought for."

"I know, Papa." She paused to see if he would say anything else, but he lay still. She kept reading. "'And has raised us up together, and made us sit together in the heavenlies in Christ Jesus: that in the ages to come he might show the exceeding riches of his grace in kindness toward us through Christ Jesus.'"

She paused as an image came to her mind: her father sitting in a heavenly golden chair among white-robed saints who lingered in a sea of misty clouds and could see down to earth. In the days to come he would watch her to see how she lived, what she did, where she would go. . . .

"Grace," her father murmured again from his pillow. "Unmerited favor. God knows I do not deserve the goodness he has bestowed upon me."

She sobbed, and his eyes flew open at the sound.

"Weep not," he said, struggling to catch his breath.

"I'm sorry, Papa; I can't help it."

Robert White reached across the pages of the Bible in her lap and held her hand. "Don't worry, girl. I'm in no pain."

"Yes, you are, and you don't deserve to suffer like this, Papa! If I could take the pain for you, I would! I could—"

He squeezed her hand and stopped the angry flow of words. "I deserve worse than this, Jocelyn, but God in his grace stooped down to redeem my soul. I will suffer here for a few days more, then I will go to my undeserved reward. When I go, God will send his grace to comfort your heart. But, before I go—" he released her hand and struggled to sit up—"I have something for you."

He fumbled for a moment under the blanket on his bed and brought forth a small wooden box. Jocelyn recognized it; the box came from a trunk of her mother's things. "Papa, you shouldn't have risen from the bed to fetch that," she scolded, thumbing tears from her cheeks. "Why didn't you let me bring it to you?"

He ignored her protest, opened the box, and pulled out a slender gold band. "This was your mother's wedding band," he said, the words thick in his unwilling throat. "I placed it on her hand on our wedding day and removed it as we buried her in the churchyard. I want you to have it, Jocelyn."

She protested weakly, and he caught her right hand and pressed the ring into her palm. "It is yours," he said, allowing his hand to fall. "Always remember the words engraved inside, Daughter."

He paused to catch his breath, and Jocelyn opened her palm and held the band up to the glow of candlelight in the room. *"Fortiter, fideliter, feliciter,"* she read, grateful that he had insisted that she learn to read and speak his beloved Latin. "Boldly, faithfully, successfully."

He nodded and sank back on the pillows. "Such must be your credo in life, Jocelyn Marie. Wherever you go, go boldly. Go faithfully, following the loving God you serve. And go remembering the words God spoke to Joshua: 'This book of the law shall not depart out of thy mouth—'"

His voice rumbled and failed, and she caught his thoughts and finished the Scripture for him: "'But thou shalt meditate therein day and night, that thou mayest observe to do according to all that is written therein: for then thou shalt make thy way prosperous, and then thou shalt have good success.'"

"Yes." He closed his eyes. "Boldly, faithfully, successfully. As your mother lived, so must you."

"As my father lived," she whispered, leaning forward to kiss his forehead. He lay motionless in his exhaustion, so she slipped the ring on her finger, cleared the supper bowl, and left him to sleep.

▼▲▼▲▼ Sleep did not come easily to Jocelyn. She tossed fitfully in her bed that night. For some unexplained reason the accumulated memories of her life chose to march across the stage of her memory, unsettling her with their vividness. So many images . . .

Her father teaching her to read from the Bible. His big feet supporting hers as she clung to his fingers and learned to dance in the small hall of their house. Her father had taught her about love and life and God and man at a very young age.

"Look here," he had said one afternoon as they worked on her Latin lesson, "the word 'believe.' Do you believe in me, Jocelyn?"

"Of course, Papa," she giggled, looking up at him.

"Ah yes, you have seen me. You know I put you to bed at night. That is the Latin *noticia,* 'to observe the facts.' Now, Jocelyn, do you believe I always want to do what is best for you?"

She stopped giggling and looked down at her textbook. The day before her father had made her come inside and study instead of playing with the other children, so did she really believe he wanted what was best for her?

"Yes, Papa," she said, more soberly.

"Good," her father answered. "That is the Latin *assentia,* 'to agree.' Now, Jocelyn, do you believe in me so much that you know I would risk my life—even give my life—to save yours?"

She stopped moving altogether. This was a new concept. Would her father, a teacher who regularly acknowledged respectful greetings in the street, give his very important life so that she might live? Her eyes flew to his face to search for the answer, and in his loving eyes she found it.

"Yes, Papa," she said, delighted in her discovery.

His broad palm brushed her head. "Good, Jocelyn. That is the Latin *fiducia,* 'to hold in confidence and trust.' And now I'll tell you a secret: as you believe in me, my daughter, so you must believe in God. And though you can trust me with your life, little girl, God holds your life even more tenderly."

Jocelyn turned on her mattress and pounded her lumpy pillow with her fist. If God had held her life so tenderly at age seven, where was he now that she was seventeen and in desperate need? Gazing toward the rough ceiling of her house, Jocelyn mouthed a silent prayer for help and strength as tears flowed from the corners of her eyes and mingled in her hair.

▼▲▼▲ The next morning, Robert White read a letter from his brother, then waited for Jocelyn to leave for the marketplace. When he was sure she had gone, he rang the bell by his bedside to summon Audrey. The girl had always been shy about coming into his sickroom, but with Jocelyn out of the house, she had no choice.

"Yes, Master White?" Audrey asked, peering from behind her apron as if the thin fabric would shield her from his contagion.

"You must do three things for me," he said, struggling to strengthen his voice. He chose his words carefully so that he would not waste his precious breath with explanations. "Pack Jocelyn's trunk with her clothing, and pack your things as well. Say nothing to her of this."

"Yes, Master White." She turned as if to go, but Robert called upon inner reserves of strength and commanded her to stop. She halted in midstride and turned timorous eyes toward him.

"An herbal remedy will arrive from the apothecary today. You are to take it and secretly mix it into your mistress's breakfast drink on the morrow. The drink will make her sleep. A carriage from Portsmouth will arrive at midmorning. You will have Jocelyn placed aboard, with her trunk, and you will board as well. If she wakes on the journey, you will give her more of the drink so that she sleeps again."

Audrey's blue eyes flew open at this unusual request, but Robert believed she intuitively knew the reason for this less-than-forthright means of transporting his daughter. "Will we be stayin' in Portsmouth for some time, Master Robert?" the maid finally asked, curiosity overcoming her fear.

Too tired to speak, he nodded. She did not need an explanation. John would handle things once the girls had reached Portsmouth.

▼▲▼▲▼ That night he dreamed of his schoolroom, then awoke with a start in the gloom of dawn and waited impatiently for the sun to rise. He heard movement in the front chamber—Jocelyn and Audrey had risen, and soon Jocelyn would drink the apothecary's potion. He had said his farewell to his daughter as he gave her the ring, but he worried that Audrey's devotion to her mistress would undermine his plan.

Within an hour after sunrise, Audrey rapped lightly on the door, then opened it and stood with her hands folded and her eyes downcast. "Jocelyn is sleepin', Master White. She is dressed, and the trunks are by the door."

"Help me dress, then, Audrey," Robert called, pulling himself out of bed. He swung his thin legs from the mattress to the floor and felt his courage leave him for a moment as he tried to stand. *God, give me the strength to do what I must to aid my stubborn child.* Audrey timidly held a loose robe open for him, and Robert fought his way to a standing position, then let her enfold the robe around him.

Audrey did not offer her arm but scampered out of his way, and Robert clung to the walls as he made his way into the front room. Jocelyn lay on her mattress, her long hair askew, but she had dressed for the day and looked presentable enough to travel. "She will need shoes on her feet," he pointed out to Audrey, "and a veil for her head. If perchance someone sees you, it must appear that she is a lady asleep, not a captive hostage."

"I understand, sir," Audrey answered, scurrying to get her mistress's shoes.

Robert lowered himself onto a stool and coughed gently into a handkerchief as he stared at his only child. She was so beautiful, so like her mother! Her dark blue eyes, fringed now in sleep with a thick row of sooty lashes, could change his mood from melancholy to merriment with a single twinkle. Her nose was slender and fine, and her delicate mouth the perfect punctuation point for her lovely and graceful features. A fallen ringlet of her hair threw her brow into shadow, and he resisted the impulse to run his fingers through her curls one last time.

He was sending her away to live. Though she would be angry and possibly heartbroken by his treachery, she would not waste her life in sorrow mourning his death. John had already made arrangements for Jocelyn. His letter held glowing words about a suitable candidate for her husband.

Carriage wheels churned the gravel outside the house and

Audrey leapt to her feet. "I'll see if the carriage is here," she said, eager to end her observation of the uncomfortable leave-taking.

Robert nodded, then rose and stood over his sleeping daughter. The slender gold band shone on her right hand, and he held her palm to his heart and breathed a prayer for her happiness as a veil of tears obscured the lovely vision from his eyes.

Jocelyn was moving, rolling, flying, floating, sinking on a dark
bed that had neither form nor substance. Muffled noises reached
her ears and faded away: the pebbly clatter of wheels upon a
road, a murmur of voices, odd windborne sounds. Her lips and
throat were parched; then someone placed a cup to her mouth,
and she drank thirstily until blackness surrounded her again.

A soft breeze blew past her cheek. She slowly became aware
of the sound of men's voices, the creak and groan of wood, and
the flap of canvas. She felt rough wool beneath her hands and
linen against her cheek. Her eyelids were heavy, unable to open,
and a palpable unease enfolded her. Was she ill? Was she dead?

In time the fog lifted, and Jocelyn opened her eyes. She lay on
a straw-stuffed mattress in a small room with open windows in
one wall. Audrey sat on a stool near the door, her head buried in
a book.

"Audrey?"

The maid jumped. "Och, Miss Jocelyn, how you gave me a
start! How are you feelin'?"

Jocelyn sat up and raised her hand to block out the bright sunlight as a sharp, stabbing pain ripped through her head. "Oh!
My head hurts. Where are we?" She lowered her hand to look
out the windows, but from the edge of the windowsill to the horizon there was nothing to see but water and blue sky.

Audrey lowered her book and took a deep breath. "We're
aboard the *Lion*, Miss Jocelyn, your uncle John's ship. He put
you in his cabin till you woke; then we're to join Mistress Eleanor with the other passengers."

"Passengers? Surely we're not—"

Audrey didn't answer, but she didn't need to. The truth hit Jocelyn like a slap in the face, and her blood rose in a heated rush. Her father had betrayed her! Uncle John, Eleanor, Audrey, the lot of them! They had placed her on a ship to Virginia regardless of her wishes . . . and if her sluggish tongue and aching head were any evidence, they had drugged her in order to accomplish their treacherous deed.

She rose to her unsteady feet and staggered to open the cabin door. "Uncle John!" she screamed, not caring who heard her on the deck beyond. "John White! Where is he?"

A grizzled sailor passing by the doorway gave her a lecherous wink, and Jocelyn was suddenly aware of her loose hair and disheveled appearance. What must the ship's crew be thinking? Had she been brought aboard in a sailor's arms like a drunken strumpet?

"Oh!" she cried, humiliation stinging her. She darted back inside the cabin and slammed the door, then covered her scarlet face with her hands. "What have they done?" she cried, angry tears scalding her fingers. "Audrey, why did you let them do this to me?"

"Nobody's done a thing to you, so I can't imagine what you'd be thinkin'," Audrey protested, lifting her chin at Jocelyn's accusation. "Your father is dyin', Miss, and he wanted you to leave him in peace. Your uncle sent his carriage, and he carried you aboard himself early this afternoon. You've been sleepin' like a baby, with no one to bother you. We're goin' to Virginia, we are, with Mistress Eleanor and a fine group of folk, and I've been sitting right here by your side, though I'm fair perishin' with hunger and dyin' for a little company, if you take me meaning."

Jocelyn listened in amazement to Audrey's speech, then fell back on the mattress as her thoughts raced. Maybe they had succeeded in bringing her aboard, but they couldn't keep her drugged until they reached Virginia! If the ship put in at any other port, or if any other passengers were to come aboard, then surely she could find a way to leave!

She sat up abruptly and smoothed her dress. "Have you a

brush, Audrey?" she asked, coiling her unruly long hair with her hands. "Help me look presentable, will you? I'm sure you don't want to stay in this tiny cabin any longer than you have to."

"Well, now, I knew you'd come around, didn't I say so to your uncle?" Audrey answered, leaping up. "Sorry, Miss, I don't have a brush, but I'd be glad to braid your hair or something—"

"Beshrew my hair, let it hang," Jocelyn snapped, moving past her maid toward the door. There had to be a way to leave this ship, and she intended to find it. Just because she was a girl, and only seventeen, did not mean she could be shipped to Virginia like a bundle of excess baggage.

▼▲▼▲▼ When she and Audrey made their way from John White's cabin to the main deck, Jocelyn was surprised to find the ship under full sail. A crew of able seamen worked the sails and climbed the rigging, and the ship slipped easily through the blue-green waters of the English Channel. The blinding dazzle of the sun's path on the quiet sea held many of her fellow passengers enthralled on the deck, but Jocelyn slipped carefully among the collected knots of strangers as she searched for her uncle. She would demand to be set ashore at the first opportunity. He had to see her point of view.

A seaman finally told her John White was "aft, on the poop deck," and she found her uncle on an elevated deck at the stern of the ship. He did not acknowledge her when she and Audrey climbed to meet him, for he was engaged in a heated argument with a small, dark-haired man with an unmistakable Portuguese accent. Deliberately ignoring all she had been taught about respect for her elders (for how had stowing her aboard this ship shown respect for *her?*), Jocelyn marched boldly between the two men and turned to face her uncle.

"Uncle John, I would speak with you," she said, steeling her voice with resolution. Her uncle gave her a distracted "not now" look and pointed a finger in the small man's direction, but Jocelyn would not be ignored. "Uncle John, I *demand* to know where we are going. If we are making a stop, I insist that you put me ashore. I want to return home. You had no right to bring me here without my leave."

She heard the Portuguese snicker behind her as her uncle's face clouded in anger. In that moment she realized how she appeared to him: a mere upstart of a girl, a penniless niece who had dared to swagger into the midst of an argument and command his attention. Then familial affection gleamed in his eyes, and he patted her shoulder. "Jocelyn, my dear, go find Eleanor and keep her company. I'll talk to you later."

"But, Uncle John!" She felt silly stamping her foot, but she did it anyway. "I must go home!"

From the corner of her eye she saw the Portuguese lean forward to glance at her face; then he turned away to allow her a moment of privacy with her uncle.

"Jocelyn, you can't go home. Today we cross The Solent to the Isle of Wight. I have business at Cowes with Sir George Carey, who wants to use our new colony as a privateering base."

"After that, can I go home?"

"No, child." His glance softened as he looked at her. "We'll return to Portsmouth to pick up a few late-arriving colonists and more supplies. But you cannot go home. Your father wishes you to remain with me."

"If we're returning to Portsmouth, I want to go home."

"That is impossible. Now be a good girl and go find your cousin."

"It is *not* impossible." She nodded in conviction, but her voice quavered as she thought of the resolution in her father's eyes when he had placed her mother's ring in her hand. He had known then that he would send her away!

She clutched at her uncle's sleeve and injected a note of pleading into her voice. "I want to go home, Uncle John. Papa needs me and I cannot leave him. By all that's merciful, Uncle, you must let me go. Papa is your brother, and he has no one to tend him. If it were Eleanor dying or even having the baby," she intensified her whisper, "would you not want to be at her side? Have mercy, Uncle, and let me go home."

"Your devotion is most praiseworthy, madam," the Portuguese said, turning to face her. His grin was an open and shameless confession of his eavesdropping, but he turned to John White, and Jocelyn felt hope rise in her heart. "Let the lady return to her father if she chooses."

John White's expression gentled, and his eyes searched her face for a moment. "If you still want to leave us when we return to Portsmouth," he said finally, his voice heavy with disappointment, "I will not stop you."

▼▲▼▲▼ Far from satisfied, Jocelyn followed Audrey into the bowels of the ship through a series of steep and narrow stairways the sailors called "companionways." There were at least four decks under the main upper deck, Audrey told Jocelyn. The upper deck was reserved for the seamen who worked the ship. The deck under that was for the passengers. Below the passenger deck was a deck for cooking and the storage of cargo, and at the bottom of the ship, the orlop deck, water barrels, food, and stone for ballast were kept.

Jocelyn did not care to tour the ship, for she had no intention of remaining on it for more than a voyage to Cowes and the return to Portsmouth. When Audrey led her to Eleanor, though, Jocelyn felt her anger soften. She could not be angry at her uncle and cousin once she saw how badly Eleanor fared.

Her vivacious cousin lay curled on a stuffed mattress, her skin a sickly gray-green. Agnes Wood sat staunchly beside her, her expression screwed into a sour snarl, but her face cracked into humanity as she tried to explain Eleanor's condition.

"Seasickness," Agnes said when Jocelyn looked at her cousin in horror. "Master Ananias said 'twill pass once we reach the open sea. 'Tis only the harbors that are so choppy."

Jocelyn didn't have the heart to remind Agnes that they would be in the harbor for many days to come, so she sank onto the wooden floor next to Eleanor. "I don't know which of us is sorrier to be here," she said, trailing her hand over her cousin's glistening brow. "Mayhap you should come off the ship with me when we return to Portsmouth. Let your father and husband go to Virginia without you."

Despite her weakness and nausea, Eleanor's pale blue eyes flew open in protest. "Leave?" she croaked, struggling to raise her head. "Why, never, Cousin! I couldn't leave my husband. Ananias isn't—well, I won't leave him. This is only something to be borne, and I bore the sickness gladly enough when I was first with child. It's just—" She paused and gestured frantically toward her maid. Agnes expertly pulled her mistress's head toward a low basin while Jocelyn turned away.

Why had her father put her aboard this living purgatory? She could not wait to be rid of it.

When Eleanor lay quiet again, Jocelyn looked down at her cousin and was surprised to find a brave smile on the elder girl's face. "Ananias was granted a coat of arms before we left. Did you know that?" she whispered. "All of Papa's assistants were given them by the royal Garter King of Arms. My children will be gentlemen and ladies, not middling folk."

"I thought all men were to be equal in your new city," Jocelyn answered, not caring that her remark sounded less than charitable.

Eleanor's smile twitched. "And so they will be. But gentlemen will always be gentlemen. And I'm glad Ananias is a bricklayer, for his skill will be sorely needed. Do you think the gentry can sit around all day and let the city build itself? Papa says the men of Raleigh must be men of ability, and my Ananias will be one of the best."

"I'm sorry to be so shrewish," Jocelyn answered, genuinely contrite. She patted Eleanor's hand. "My head hurts horribly, and I can't stop thinking about my father. At first I was angry to find myself here, but when I think of how sincerely Papa wanted me to leave, I am even more desperate to return to him."

Eleanor grimaced as a new wave of nausea hit her. "Are you

sure you won't stay with us?" she whimpered, clutching her stomach. "I need you, Coz."

Jocelyn gave Eleanor a sympathetic smile. "My father needs me more."

▼▲▼▲▼ John White stalked into his cabin and slammed the door behind him. Roger Bailie, his chief assistant, winced at the noise, then smoothed his face and returned his attention to the parchment on the small table that served as the governor's desk.

At sixty, Roger Bailie was one of the oldest colonists to make the journey, but he had been a devoted friend to John White for years. He stood five feet two inches tall, had sincere blue eyes, and was completely bald but for two hanks of blonde hair tied together at the nape of his neck. His chief attributes, White had discovered, were his loyalty and attention to detail.

"A plague on that Portuguese!" White shouted, flinging his hat against the wall of the cabin. "He argues with every decision I make. I am the governor of this colony, hence the commander of this expedition, but because he is master of this ship I am thwarted at every turn! I don't care how good a pilot he is; Raleigh was a fool to entrust the ship to him."

"What has Master Simon Fernandes done now?" Bailie asked, looking up from his parchment.

"Nothing that need concern you," White mumbled, sinking onto his narrow bed in frustration. He had tried to keep his suspicions to himself, but with every hour that passed he became more and more convinced that the Portuguese navigator was a traitor at best and a spy for the Spanish at worst.

"You don't know him like I do," White said, folding his hands across his chest. "I've sailed with the braggart before. The last time, Fernandes endangered our entire fleet and, through sheer carelessness, ran aground one of Her Majesty's largest ships at Roanoke Island. Fernandes cares nothing for the colony or the colonists. His ambitions are centered around privateering and whatever treasure and goods he can pluck from Spanish and French vessels that are unlucky enough to cross his path."

"Sir, I have the final count of colonists." Roger Bailie waved a sheet of parchment.

Confound the man, wasn't he even *listening?*

"Well?"

"Forty and eight seamen aboard the *Lion,* twenty and four each aboard Spicer's flyboat and the pinnace commanded by Captain Stafford. We have boarded upon our three ships ninety and seven colonists. Fifteen additional colonists, all men, are to join us at Plymouth."

"And the families?" John White threw an anxious glance over his shoulder. "How many families have we?"

Bailie scanned his register. "Fourteen. Four include a mother, father, and child. Two women, including your daughter, are due to deliver a baby soon. Six are married couples without children, four are fathers and sons whose wives have agreed to join them next year. I count nine children and seventeen women, eight of whom are serving women."

"My niece and her maid will be leaving the ship at Portsmouth," White murmured, absently scratching the two-day growth of beard on his chin. "'Twill leave fifteen women."

"Sir, there is one peculiar notation on this register," Bailie said, looking up. "There is a Reverend Thomas Colman listed among the men, and a 'Colman' listed among the women. But though the lady must be his wife, I can find no record of her Christian name. Nor have I seen a wife with the minister."

White stared at the ceiling for a moment, then smiled. He might solve one vexing problem, at least, before the ships departed England. "Thank you, Roger, I am glad you have reminded me, for the matter is of some importance." He sat up and nodded to his assistant. "Would you find this Reverend Colman and send him to me forthwith? I will settle the matter of his wife once and for all."

Roger Bailie stood from behind the desk and bowed politely, then turned to fulfill his employer's orders.

▼▲▼▲ "My niece—your intended bride—was most unhappy to find herself on the ship," John White explained to Thomas Colman in the privacy of his cabin. The young man stood as straight as before, the same hat in his hand, adorned in the same severe black doublet and hose. "She has made me promise to give her the opportunity to leave when we dock again at Portsmouth. But she must not do so, Reverend Colman. I have promised my dying brother that I would keep her with me."

"Surely the girl is reasonable," Colman answered, his voice dispassionate and almost uninterested. "If she wishes to go—"

"Unless you wish to give fifteen years of your life as my servant, you will not let her go," White said, pulling a rolled-up parchment from the desk beside his bed. He unrolled it before his dark-haired visitor, whose face emptied of expression when he recognized the signature on the page.

White dropped the parchment onto the desk. "We will be anchored here at Cowes for six more days before we return to Portsmouth," he said. "You have six days, Reverend Colman, to win yourself a bride. Her name is Jocelyn White, and you will find her either in the company of her maid, Audrey Tappan, or my daughter, Eleanor Dare."

He paused and studied the dark eyes of the young man before him. "Do we have an understanding, Reverend Colman?"

"Yes." The eyes that stared back at him were strangely veiled. "We do, indeed."

Audrey noticed the tall, dark-haired man first. For two days he had followed her and her mistress through the long, twice-a-day meal lines. He always stood at a respectful distance, allowing two or three other passengers to come between him and the girls, and after a while Audrey realized that his eyes did not follow her, but her mistress. His dark gaze flickered over Jocelyn's face and slender figure more than once, but he stared most often at her hands as if he judged her helpfulness or dexterity. Audrey's eyebrows lifted as a realization came to her. Could he be searching Jocelyn's left hand for a wedding band?

On the third day, Audrey smiled when she noticed that the man had pressed his way forward in the line until he stood directly behind her and Jocelyn. Audrey chatted freely about trivial things, mindful that the handsome stranger stood close enough to hear their conversation, but Jocelyn's thoughts seemed faraway. She gave only the meagerest of answers to Audrey's questions and did not look up to glance behind her. Would her mistress never see who followed her?

After taking her wooden plate from the ship's serving boy, Jocelyn led the way to a clearing on the crowded deck where she sank gracefully to her knees and tucked her skirts around her. Audrey sat next to her and bowed her head for Jocelyn's prayer of thanks, but kept her eyes open to cast furtive glances to find the man in black.

She stifled a squeal when the dark stranger took a seat on the floor near them. He continued his quiet surveillance as they ate, and Audrey nearly choked on her biscuit and dried beef, so nervous did his gaze make her. But Jocelyn ate silently, brooding about her father.

When they had finished, Audrey gathered their plates and returned them to the boy who had doled out the barely edible food. She lingered in the shadows to observe the man in black, curious about the obvious cat-and-mouse game of which her mistress seemed wholly unaware.

Still oblivious to the masculine interest that fairly sizzled from the man's eyes, Jocelyn shifted her position so that she leaned against a wall. Modestly tucking her skirts around her so that no part of her leg showed, she pulled a booklet from her pocket and began to read. While Audrey watched from behind a wooden beam, the man rose from his place and walked directly behind her mistress, doubtless to discover what Jocelyn read.

Audrey covered a smile with her hand. If this man expected to find that her young mistress read romantic adventures or tales of chivalry, he would be disappointed. Audrey knew Jocelyn was reading the only book she had thought to throw into her mistress's trunk: a compilation of the writings of Marcus Aurelius.

The man's dark brows lifted in surprise, and Audrey expected him to dart away like a man from an angry bee. No man, she had heard, wanted a bookish woman or one who understood more than he did, and Audrey was sure Jocelyn knew more than any man on the ship, with the possible exception of John White. What place did a scholar's daughter have among these uneducated ruffians? Indeed, what place could she have in Virginia?

But the man did not move away from her mistress. He sank gracefully to one knee at Jocelyn's side and gestured toward the book. Jocelyn, however, did not look up, and Audrey moved closer to hear what the young man had to say. It was her duty as chaperon, after all.

"'Either the world is a mere hotch-potch of random cohesions and dispersions,'" the man was saying, lowering his head near Jocelyn's as he read a passage from the book she held, "'or else it is a unity of order and providence. If the former, why care about anything, save the manner of the ultimate return to dust? But if the contrary be true—'" he paused as Jocelyn finally removed her eyes from the page to look at him—"'then I do reverence, I stand firmly, and I put my trust in the directing Power.'"

"I beg your pardon, sir." Jocelyn's voice was careful and reserved. "But I do not recall our meeting."

"We have not met, except through the pages of Marcus Aurelius," he said, motioning again toward the book she read. "But perchance our souls have met there hundreds of times, whilst we were unaware of the encounter."

"Perhaps we should remain unaware." Jocelyn looked away, her brows knitted in the stubborn frown Audrey knew well. "Despite my approachability in this unusual circumstance, sir, and the boredom that leads us to do things we would not ordinarily attempt, you should know that I am not available for discourse. Please be so kind as to discuss Aurelius with some other young lady."

Before he could protest, she stood and walked away, her chin lifted in a no-nonsense posture as she crossed the wooden floor. The man watched her departure solemnly, and Audrey thought she saw a flicker of something in his eyes. Was it defeat? The maid resisted the urge to clap her hands in victory. Sure, an' Jocelyn had certainly put him in his place! Despite the man's majestic figure and undeniably handsome features, he was as plainly dressed as a chimney sweep and had to be nearly twice Jocelyn's age! Audrey shuddered at the thought of his age and poverty intruding upon the gentle breeding and beauty of Jocelyn White; then with a swish of her skirts, she turned to follow her mistress.

▼▲▼▲▼ "Audrey, have you met everyone aboard this vessel?"

Jocelyn and Audrey lay in semidarkness on their straw mattresses in the women's section of the second deck. The bright colors of sunrise had been muted by a gentle rain falling outside, and a soft, humid mist had dampened everything aboard the ship, including Jocelyn's already depressed spirit. Everything on this cursed ship was pure and total drudgery! Except . . . the one intriguing man who had crossed her path. . . .

Audrey's face wore a mask of innocent surprise as she turned to face her mistress. "My heavens, Miss Jocelyn, think you I'm as forward as that? Of course not! I won't talk to the seamen, for they're too rough for me taste, or the married men, for obvious reasons, but of the unmarried men, surely 'tis not a bad thing to acquaint oneself with one's companions?"

"Don't become too . . . *acquainted* with anyone. We'll be leaving for London as soon as the ship returns to Portsmouth."

"Welladay, then, when will I ever have this chance again? Don't take offense, Miss Jocelyn, but if it's me fate to become an old spinster in London, why shouldn't I have some fun with the gents before me time to settle down?"

Ignoring her outrageous comment, Jocelyn went on. "I was wondering, in particular . . ." She hesitated, but there seemed to be no subtle way to phrase her question. "There's an older man— older than I, anyway—with dark hair and an . . . interesting face. He wears a black doublet and hose. He stood near us yesterday in the supper line and spoke to me after eating."

"Aye, I remember him." Audrey frowned, but leaned closer. "Though I don't think he's of your class, Miss Jocelyn, if ye have a yearnin' to know him better, I could put a word in among the men—"

"No!" Jocelyn whispered, horrified. She lowered her voice so the other women who still slept near them wouldn't hear. "I just wanted to know his name."

"Well—" Audrey snuggled closer and smiled brightly, eager to share her news—"naturally, I did see you talkin' to him the other night, and I've done some checking. They say he's called Thomas Colman, and I hear he's been made a gentleman with your uncle's other assistants." She paused. "On account of he's a minister."

A minister? So he had studied—which explained his familiarity with Marcus Aurelius—but why had her uncle elevated him to the level of his assistants?

"What else? What will be his role in the colony?"

Audrey shrugged. "Faith, Miss Jocelyn, I didna think you'd care anythin' about that. I believe he'll do what other ministers do." She giggled. "Probably means to convert the Indians, if you ask me."

Jocelyn leaned back on her mattress and folded her hands behind her head. From his expeditions to Virginia, her uncle had brought back fascinating portraits of the Indians he had met on ' Roanoke Island. Jocelyn's father had kept several of his brother's sketches in his chamber, where he could quietly envy John's role in the exploration of a new world. Jocelyn had known that her father, driven by the desire and need to show Christian love to the Indians in Virginia, had longed to go to Virginia himself. Did this same concern drive Thomas Colman?

Had her father not been ill, Jocelyn knew missionary zeal would have propelled him onto this ship. Like most in England, he believed God had reserved for England and Protestantism the area north of Florida and south of the French-owned Saint Lawrence. Tales of Spanish cruelty committed upon American Indians in the name of the Catholic church ran rampant in England. Like most of the English, Jocelyn and her father were convinced that the Spanish wanted nothing more than to crush England and bring English Protestants back under the iron rule of the Catholic church.

But the Spanish had not yet made inroads into Virginia, and the English were eager to pave the way for Protestantism. *The Indians are truly capable of Christian love,* her uncle had once written her father, *for they naturally share all things in common and know neither jealousy, selfishness, or ambition. They believe that one god created the world, and another restored it after the great flood. They have part of the truth and part of the nature of Christ, but they worship idols, fallen spirits, and can be most cruel to their enemies. We have a most urgent responsibility to bring them to the truth of the Gospel of Jesus Christ.*

Yes, had he not fallen ill, Robert White would have welcomed the chance to explore the New World. Like many others of his station, he believed that human beings had once known and understood all knowledge about the natural world through God's revelation to Adam. But as sin dulled the conscience and corrupted the intellect of mankind, this knowledge had been lost. Now it was up to godly men to recover the divine gift of knowledge, and all the world waited to be explored as God progressively revealed new fields to be researched. Cures for illness, precious goods for prosperity, freedom and hope for a fallen world—all this and more awaited godly men who sought the truth.

Jocelyn's forehead creased in thought. Which of these motivations drove Thomas Colman? She turned onto her side to hide from Audrey the emotions that surely flickered across her face. There was something admirable about a man who would leave his home and journey to America to convert the Indians. And his approach and words to her had not been unseemly. He had neither leered at her like most of the seamen nor patronized her like the older gentlemen. His tone had been most respectful, and the look in those amazingly dark eyes had been . . . interested.

Silly girl! Jocelyn admonished herself. *His interest was in Aurelius, not in you. And that is as it should be. I'faith, the man is a minister!*

Thus chastised, she closed her eyes. But sleep was elusive, and the face of Thomas Colman insisted on floating before her, his eyes sparkling, his mouth tilted in a slight smile. . . .

"Audrey," Jocelyn called softly over her shoulder. The maid grunted sleepily in reply.

"I pray you, find out more about this Thomas Colman," Jocelyn whispered. "Is he married? From what part of England did he come?"

"I'll do what I can," Audrey mumbled, and Jocelyn buried her face in the sour-smelling mattress and wondered why she cared at all about the purpose and background of such a strange man.

▼▲▼▲▼ Jocelyn's interest in Thomas Colman heightened when Audrey reported that Reverend Colman was a widower with a young son who had remained behind in England to be reared by the reverend's sister-in-law.

"How do you know this?" she asked, grasping Audrey's hand.

"William Clement told me," the girl answered proudly, lifting her delicate chin. "He's the servant to old Roger Bailie, your uncle's chief assistant. Got it straight from the records, we did."

"*We* did?"

"Well—" Audrey blushed—"William can't read, so he got me the records and I read them meself. But 'tis the truth. You know I'd as lief jump overboard as tell you a lie, Miss Jocelyn."

"All right." Jocelyn dropped Audrey's hand and sat back to think. How difficult it must have been for Thomas Colman to leave his son behind! How could he do such a thing? *Like me, he boarded this ship knowing he was needed elsewhere,* she thought. *Like me, he carries the weight of sorrow in his heart.*

From then on she watched him carefully, selecting places to sit and read or eat so she could watch him without being seen, but on more than one occasion he looked up and caught her eye. Embarrassed, she would lower her head, blushing furiously, determined that she would never, ever look his way again. But in the next hour she would invariably walk on one of the decks and spy him looking out to sea or talking to a group of men, and he would hold her rapt attention once more.

She couldn't help herself. Watching him was sheer pleasure. His dark hair grew upward and outward in great waves that begged detangling. His broad hands were generally clasped behind his back, but often reached down to help one of the young boys untangle a fishing line or tie a stubborn shoelace. The little ones would smile shyly at him, thanking him with the sincerity of the young.

One afternoon Jocelyn watched as Thomas comforted a small lad who had tripped and scraped his leg. The reverend's arms cradled the child gently, and though she could not hear the words, the tone of his low voice was sweetly comforting. When the boy's tears finally stilled and his leg was washed clean, he turned to slip his small arms around Thomas Colman's neck and pressed against the broad chest in a hug of gratitude. For a fleeting moment, Jocelyn caught an expression on Thomas's face, an odd mix of tenderness and pain, that pierced her heart. Indeed, the flash of emotion came and went so quickly she found herself wondering if she'd conjured it herself with wishful thinking.

Still, it was impossible to ignore him. Even seated, he seemed taller than anyone else aboard ship, and his deep eyes revealed the sensitivity and intelligence of a scholar. Jocelyn's father had eyes like Thomas Colman's, and she found herself yearning to surrender to the magnetic pull in those dark eyes. Especially when they would lock with hers, as they were wont to do more and more often . . .

He never laughed, though he usually wore a pleasant smile, and he seemed to generate awe among the other adults as he dispensed pleasantries, advice, and promises to pray for the passengers' various needs. With Jocelyn's uncle he was pleasant and attentive. He moved with disarming grace among the married women and upper-class gentlemen. To the outward eye he seemed polished and perfect, and yet at least once or twice a day Jocelyn caught his face in an unguarded moment. Once she caught him staring out to sea with an expression of infinite sorrow on his face, and she could not help but wonder if she had found a vein of softness in his granite strength. Did he think of the son he had left behind?

The tedious boredom of the ship dissipated as she watched the disturbingly attractive Thomas Colman, and almost she hoped he would speak to her again. But on their eighth day in port, Simon Fernandes gave the order to make sail, and the three ships left Cowes to cross The Solent for Portsmouth.

On the journey home, Jocelyn stood at the upper deck and felt the northward wind tug at her veil as resolutely as the image of Thomas Colman tugged at her heart. But her destiny could not lie in Virginia; she must return to London and her father. Thomas Colman would have to venture to the Indians alone, although she knew she would forever keep him in her thoughts and prayers.

The ocean breeze blew the ships back to Portsmouth in a matter of hours, and the seamen and passengers aboard all three ships crowded on the upper decks to catch a glimpse of the docks they had left only a week earlier. The seamen working on the docks recognized the ship's standards and greeted them with snide catcalls: "Some long journey, fellows! Did our lady the sea prove too much for you?"

As the *Lion* eased into her berth to take on fresh stores of food and water, Jocelyn jostled her way through the crowd on the deck, her hand firmly clasped around Audrey's wrist. Simon Fernandes stood near the gangplank, ready to command the seamen who waited on the docks, and John White stood behind him. Jocelyn wasn't about to let her uncle forget his promise.

"Faith, our trunks!" Audrey squealed as Jocelyn drew her through the press of people. "Can you be planning to leave without our things?"

"We'll have them taken off soon enough," Jocelyn promised. "But first *we're* going to get off. I'll not give my uncle an excuse to conveniently overlook us."

A sailor positioned the gangplank between the dock and the ship's rail; then a uniformed soldier strutted across and briefly saluted Simon Fernandes. "I have letters for Master John White," the soldier said, pulling sealed parchments from a leather pouch at his waist. "And I am to wait for a reply."

Jocelyn waited, impatiently, while her uncle received his letters, broke open the seal of the first, and read it. "It seems our Sir Walter Raleigh writes to assure us of his and the queen's prayers," he said, his mouth curving into a wry smile as he looked at the men crowded around him. They burst into cheers as White bowed to the courier. "You may tell Sir Walter and Her Gracious Majesty that we are most appreciative and grateful."

The second letter was smaller and not as heavily embossed, but Jocelyn saw her uncle's eyes mist as he read it. Instinctively, his eyes came to rest upon hers when he had finished the page, and she knew what news the letter had brought.

She closed her eyes and heard the crowd part as he made his way to her. "I'm sorry, Jocelyn," he said, his voice breaking as he placed the letter into her hand. "Your father—my brother—died three days ago." He embraced her briefly, and she opened her eyes to see that the other passengers stood in silent respect for their grief.

John White cleared his throat as he released her. "May God grant Robert the peace he deserves."

"Make way!" The impertinent cries of the *Lion*'s seamen disturbed the silent crowd at the gangplank. Through the heavy, sodden dullness that surrounded her, Jocelyn felt herself being pushed out of the way as barrels of water and supplies were brought on board. Audrey's hand held hers again, but this time it was Audrey who pulled Jocelyn through the crowd and down a companionway to the lower passenger deck. Jocelyn sat for some time without speaking, then lay down and watered the straw mattress beneath her with futile tears.

▼▲▼▲▼ "My father died alone, Uncle. You did wrong to bring me here." She had come to his small cabin for a private confrontation.

"No, child, you are wrong," John White whispered, correcting his niece even as he silently admired her courage in confronting him. Her eyes were red-rimmed from crying, and he envied her the freedom of tears. He had no time for grief and no privacy in which to vent it, though he had lost a dear brother and friend.

"Your father wanted you to come with me. He had been planning this for some time. If he had been well, he would have joined us on the journey himself, for he desired nothing more than to explore the New World. . . ."

His mind wandered off into a happy memory of a discussion he and his brother had once shared, and only when Jocelyn cleared her throat did his thoughts return to her. "But I would not have you unhappy, dear girl," he said, reaching out to clasp her hand in his. "If we can find you a position, perhaps as a governess for a noble family, you may remain in England. But we have not much time."

"No." Her response surprised him, and he lifted his brows in a questioning glance.

She took a step toward him as though being closer would help him understand. "I do not doubt my father's wisdom. I only regret that I was not with him at the end. He died alone, Uncle John, and I pray God will forgive me for allowing that to happen."

"You are not at fault, Jocelyn. Robert wanted you to go."

She shrugged gently. "Since he wanted me to be here with you, I will trust his judgment." She took a deep breath and gave him a wavering smile. "I will go with you and Eleanor to this City of Raleigh. England holds nothing for me, not anymore. You, Eleanor, and Audrey are my family now."

He patted her hand in pleased surprise and smiled as he recalled his first plan for his niece. Though Thomas Colman had apparently made no progress in the eight days since they first embarked, maybe he would fare better in the weeks ahead as they crossed the Western ocean.

Thomas Colman

*I said, I shall not see the Lord, even the Lord,
in the land of the living.*

Isaiah 38:11

Standing alone at the bulwark of the *Lion,* Jocelyn watched the docks and chimneys of Portsmouth retreat into the horizon as the ship turned its bow to follow the sun. The aquamarine water of the English Channel rippled gently toward the shoreline, and though sea shanties echoed behind her as the seamen worked the sails, Jocelyn clothed herself in silence as she said good-bye to her father, her childhood home, and memories too painful to recall.

"'By the rivers of Babylon, there we sat down, yea, we wept, when we remembered Zion,'" she quoted, recalling one of her father's favorite psalms. "'For there they that carried us away captive required of us a song; and they that wasted us required of us mirth, saying, Sing us one of the songs of Zion.'"

The wind caressed her face as she watched sparks of light reflect off the deep blue of the water, and a tear slipped from the corner of her eye as she remembered the touch of her father's hand on her cheek. "'How shall we sing the Lord's song in a strange land?'" she went on, choking on the words as if a hand lay at her throat. "'If I forget thee, *father,* let my right hand forget her cunning. If I do not remember thee, let my tongue cleave to the roof of my mouth.'"

A sudden breeze and dip of the ship sent a cool splash of spray into the air and across her face. She did not move, welcoming the tears of the sea as they joined her own as she lifted her heart in prayer.

To you, my Father God, I give these priceless memories. All I am, every dream I have ever known, came from the man who lies buried beyond these waters. I don't know why you compel me to leave all

behind, but Papa said you would give me grace to bear what lies ahead.
But mark me, my Lord, and know my heart: I would as lief die as con-
tinue without that grace. Cover me, Father, and hold me in the palm of
your protective hand.

▾▴▾▴▾ Behind the shadow of the mizzenmast,
Thomas Colman watched Jocelyn White stand with battleship
solidity at the stern, her eyes on the distant and receding horizon. The gravity that had filled her eyes in the past week had
bloomed fully into despair since the public news of her father's
death. This emotion Thomas understood. He knew something
about desperation. Once, as she raised her hand to wipe a tear
away, he thought about walking forward to comfort her, but common sense detained him.

If God ruled justly and honorably, this wonder of a girl could
not be meant for him. Why, then, did events conspire to push
them together?

On their first departure from Portsmouth, Thomas had been
shocked beyond words when John White pulled him aside and
pointed to the petite brunette who stormed about the ship
demanding to be taken off at the first opportunity. "That is your
niece?" he had gasped, amazed at the girl's beauty and temerity.
Any girl who had to be bartered in marriage should have been
less than beautiful or past the age of youth, but Jocelyn White
was rosy cheeked and full of energy, a vividly pretty young
woman whose hair blew in silky tangles around stormy blue
eyes. On that day her eyes had flashed with strength and anger,
making it clear she would bow before neither her uncle nor the
sallow-faced Captain Fernandes.

Thomas had known then that he could not marry her. Any
wife meant for him should have been mealy and plain, ill-tem-
pered or sickly. It wouldn't be fair to ask a stunning beauty to
serve as the wife of a minister, or to marry Thomas Colman,
indentured servant.

But White had held him fast and insisted: "Soft, good reverend, but watch her, talk to her, make her trust you."

He amazed himself when he began to shadow her movements. He had never intended to follow White's orders. But Jocelyn White fascinated him. *Fool! It's no more than the allure of forbidden fruit,* he scolded himself. And yet, he did not turn away from her. Could not, it seemed. In simple fact, she intrigued him greatly.

She was not like the other women aboard ship. The others collected themselves in small knots belowdecks and talked or giggled or wrung their hands in endless worry and boredom. But Jocelyn rarely spoke to anyone save her maid. She usually walked below or on deck with a book or parchment in her hands, and often he spied her writing at the table in her uncle's small cabin. What was she writing? Letters? To whom? Did she keep a journal? What in heaven could she find worthy of writing about on this horrid ship?

On one late afternoon Thomas stood outside the window of John White's cabin and peered inside. Miss White sat at the desk, her face like gold in the flickering light of sunset, her eyes concentrated upon the parchment under her small hands. Once or twice she sighed as she wrote, and Thomas longed to know what she was thinking. Then she put the pen down, and, fearful of being seen, Thomas jerked away from the window.

After a moment, he gathered the courage to look in again. She had rolled the parchment into a tube; then she leaned toward the small porthole in the cabin and thrust the rolled parchment through it. Startled, Thomas strode to the ship's railing in time to see the parchment unfurl in the wind and flatten itself upon the face of the billowing ocean.

What kind of woman wrote letters to the sea?

His fascination for her became a spying game; there was little else to do while aboard ship. It hadn't taken long for her young maid to catch him watching them and so alert her mistress. Then there was that humiliating afternoon when he had finally gathered courage enough to speak to her and had only succeeded in offending her. Bumptious fool! He should have known better than to approach her like one of the ill-mannered seamen.

Smarting under that humiliation, he renounced that day his fascination with Jocelyn White and consigned himself to fifteen years of celibate servitude. Apparently God had an even more severe plan in mind for Thomas Colman than the dedication required of a minister: God wanted him to subject his heart, his eyes, and his physical desires to the tyranny of slavery. So be it. He would do it, and gladly, for he deserved no better.

After the girl's scorching rebuke, a few days passed without event. Thomas stayed belowdecks in the men's section of the ship, never once allowing his eyes to lift in search of the girl.

All was well until God began to test his resolve. William Clement, an occasionally charming bloke who spent most of his time eying the serving women, whispered one afternoon that the fair niece of John White had asked in particular about the Reverend Thomas Colman.

Thomas found it difficult to remain aloof from Clement's taunting suggestion. Of the hundred or more men aboard ship, why would the girl notice him? Was his infatuation for her so obvious that the other men thought to bait him with rumors and false hope?

But often on sunny afternoons, when the sailors were willing to let passengers above deck, he roamed the ship and felt bright eyes upon him. When he turned suddenly, there she stood, caught in a nervous blush.

By themselves, these adolescent boy-girl games could not have turned him from his steadfast intention to forget Jocelyn White. But when John White read the letter announcing his brother's death, the girl exchanged maidenly blushing for the mantle of mourning. Watching from the crowd, Thomas read her grief in the line of her shoulders, the broken way her head lay on her uncle's chest, the helpless curl of her hands.

Still, surely God could not intend for Thomas to fulfill John White's secret contract of marriage. So why, then, did his heart

yearn to comfort the suffering girl who stood crying at the rail as
Portsmouth faded from view?

▼▲▼▲▼ Jocelyn did not know how long she stood at
the ship's rail, but Portsmouth had long disappeared when she
felt a warm hand cover her own. "I know it is not easy for you,"
Eleanor said, squeezing her cousin's hand gently. "I have my husband and father with me."

"It's not only my father I grieve for," Jocelyn stuttered, fresh
tears springing to her eyes, "but our way of life. My father's
books, my studies—they are all I have known. In truth, Eleanor, I
do not know what to expect in this Virginia of yours, and I fear I
am not equipped to face it. . . ."

Eleanor smiled and lightened her voice. "We will have everything English, dear Coz. We are not going to the wilderness to
live as savages, but to build an English colony. We are taking our
way of life with us. You will find that in time our City of Raleigh
will be as prosperous as London. My father will be the governor,
my husband an assistant, or at least a justice of the peace."

"But . . ." Jocelyn paused. The question would seem self-cen-
tered, but she had to know. "Eleanor, I am not married, nor am I
bound to a family as a servant. What will become of me?"

Eleanor gave her a bright look of eagerness. "You'll live with
us, of course, until you want to be married. Think you that you
should wither on the vine and misspend your youth? Shame on
you, Coz. I believe my father will find you a suitable husband,
and you will be very happy."

For this Jocelyn had no answer. Until her father's illness, she
had always believed he would arrange a marriage for her with a
man much like himself. Her chosen husband would have been a
teacher or a writer, and after their marriage she would have
lived with two men with whom she would share reading and
laughter, discussions and opinions. In the course of a fortnight,
however, that domestic vision had vanished and she had nothing
but fear with which to replace it.

Eleanor patted Jocelyn's hand again, then pressed her palms against her expanding stomach. "Only God knows what will become of all of us," she said, a breath of anxiety in her own voice. "But my father says we must trust in God's goodness, and in the strength of our English way of life."

Eleanor looked up, and the niggling thread of worry fled from her voice. "You will find a husband, dear Jocelyn, a gentleman who deserves you. You will establish a home and raise children and do all the things your sainted mother would have done had she lived. In time your grief for your father will ease, and you will find the happiness we all seek."

"A gentleman?" Jocelyn laughed and closed her eyes. "Forgive me, dear Eleanor, but where am I to find such a man?" For a fraction of a second, the image of Thomas Colman danced in her mind, but Jocelyn thrust it away impatiently. The man had made his disinterest in her more than clear. "This ship is filled with nothing but common passengers, crude seamen, and married gentlemen who do nothing but sit and dream of the riches they hope to reap from their export companies. So unless God can form a man of dust and breathe yet again—"

Eleanor leaned forward and pinched Jocelyn's cheek. "Trust in God, dear Cousin, and keep your eyes open. There are, I'm sure, gentle folk on board who do not dress in the satin doublets and silken hose of wealthy gentlemen, nor do they speak as you do, but they are gentle all the same."

"Would that such a one would find me," Jocelyn breathed, leaning forward on the ship's railing. "For I am well aware that I am the only woman on this ship without either a husband or a master. There are times, Cousin, especially when I must walk among the sailors, that I feel vulnerable—"

"You know my father will always act as your protector."

"Still . . ." Jocelyn hesitated, not wanting to sound critical of her uncle's efforts. She chose her words carefully. "He is very busy about the colony's affairs. He cannot be constantly by my side, nor do we talk every day."

"For conversation you have your maid and me," Eleanor

replied, her blue eyes dancing. "On any day when I am not way-laid with seasickness, feel free to talk about whatever you wish. And know this: Not a man aboard would dare insult or harm you, for they know you are John White's niece. So what could possibly worry you?"

The future. Loneliness. Death. The replies sprang easily to Jocelyn's lips, but she bit the words back. Her secure and lively cousin would not understand. So Jocelyn smiled as if she had been a mere child frantic over harmless shadows on the wall and returned Eleanor's reassuring embrace.

▼▲▼▲▼ On the sixth of May, the *Lion* and her two con-sorts arrived at Plymouth, where White welcomed fifteen colonists from the southwest of England on board. The newcomers, all men, included Manteo and Towaye, two American Indians who had crossed the ocean with Ralph Lane to present themselves to Sir Walter Raleigh and other investors in the colonial venture. The two natives had traveled throughout England at Raleigh's expense and were now welcomed to the fleet with great pomp and ceremony. John White himself ventured off the *Lion* to welcome them as they and the other newcomers were housed aboard the smaller flyboat.

Jocelyn watched the ceremony of welcome from the deck of the *Lion*, curiosity overcoming her grief. These were the first Indians she had ever seen, and she found them remarkably like the sketches her uncle had made in his journals. The taller of the two Indians, the one called Manteo, had a flat nose, coarse black hair, and dark brown eyes with the shining quickness of a robin's eyes. His companion looked much the same; indeed, they could have been brothers. Neither wore the doublet and hose of the English, but breeches of a supple leather, loosely fitting woven shirts, and cloaks. Dignified aloofness covered them like a mantle.

After John White's welcome, the Indians regally crossed the gangplank to Captain Edward Spicer's flyboat. The other arriving colonists, heavily laden with trunks, tools, and baskets of possessions, followed the newcomers on board. When the Indians disappeared into the hold of the ship, Jocelyn turned and nearly stumbled into a man standing close behind her.

"Pray excuse me," she murmured, without looking up.

"It was my fault." His voice was a wall of energy that lifted her eyes, and a trembling shiver raced through her when she saw that Thomas Colman stood only inches from her suddenly awkward feet. His presence was a physical force that unnerved her, yet something radiated from the dark depths of his eyes and held her to him. She was swept with the oddest sense of being lost in the gentle, probing expression on his face, which seemed to ask, *Is anything amiss?*

Yes, her eyes answered. *I'm desperately lonely, irrevocably alone.*

Audrey's Irish brogue cut through the spell: "Miss Jocelyn, think you that we should go belowdecks now?"

Embarrassed, Jocelyn tore her eyes away and stepped back. What had she revealed to this minister? What must he think of her? Surely he gave that compassionate look to everyone, for such was his calling, but not everyone lapped up his attention as eagerly as a starving cat lapped cream!

"Miss Jocelyn, think you that we should go below?" Audrey repeated, turning from the ship's rail. The maid stopped short, surveyed the situation between her mistress and the minister in one glance, then smiled coyly. "Och," she said, cooing. "Pardon me. Pray excuse the interruption, Miss Jocelyn. I'll just be waitin' for you on the lower deck—"

"I am coming now," Jocelyn said in a clear voice. She gathered her skirt and led the way to the companionway, determined not to look back.

▼▲▼▲▼ Later in the afternoon, William Clement grimaced and shifted his position on the narrow steps of the companionway as his best friend approached. "Well met, James," he muttered through clenched teeth. He turned his eyes from the sight of James's loaded plate. "How can you eat that swill they're passing off as dinner?" Compounded by the rocking of the ship, the sharp odors of the food made his stomach churn.

"If a man's hungry, 'e'll eat shoe leather," James Hynde answered, propping himself on a lower step as he gnawed on a bit of ship's biscuit. "You ought to get something to eat, for there won't be more until the morrow. And while this may be swill, 'tis only a bit below what we got in—"

William abruptly slapped his friend's leg and lowered his voice. "Aye, and let's keep our personal 'istory to ourselves, eh?" he said, pressing his face close to his friend's. "In truth," he continued, "you and I and our masters know we came from Colchester Castle, but there's no need for the entire ship's company to know, is there?"

James blinked nervously. "Do y' think I'd be telling anybody that the governor took us out of prison?" he whispered. "We served five years, William. I think five years is plenty to pay for stealing forty sheep."

"Still, some folks think that a thief remains a thief forever, and I won't be hung the first time a mistress mislays her silver plate," William answered. He clutched his queasy stomach and leaned back on the stairs. "'Tis bad enough that we're bound to serve our gentlemen 'till they die. But, as my sainted mother used to say, there's a bright linin' in every cloud. Being as I'm serving old man Roger Bailie, I expect to have my freedom in a few months."

"My man will live longer than that," James said, struggling to chew a bit of dried beef. "Master Cooper is not much older than the governor, and as full o' life as any man on this ship."

"One never knows what can happen in the wilderness," William answered, closing his eyes. "There's savages, and wild animals, and divers diseases. Say your prayers, friend James, and maybe you'll be free, like me, before you expect. I believe I'll be my own man, with my own woman, in a year's time."

James snickered. "A woman! And where would you be finding one? Are you thinking you'll take a savage to wife?"

"Not a savage, but a fair rose of England. A gentle lady, too, with breeding and such." He opened one eye and peered at James. "Do y' laugh? I've already espied such a girl. Jocelyn White, the governor's niece."

James pretended to choke on the hard biscuit. "That girl? Why, she'd never give you the time of day! Besides, hasn't her maid hinted that the girl has eyes for the minister?"

"Not to worry," William answered, shifting his position uneasily as he fought his rising nausea. "The maid's a pretty piece, and the best way to reach the lady."

A gust of wind cracked the sails, the ship pitched forward, and James moved his legs out of the way as William lunged forward.

"Great Neptune! I thought I'd given you every offering my poor belly could provide. Where's the bucket?"

John White would have liked to depart Plymouth the hour after they had received the last colonists, but Simon Fernandes seemed determined to take the devil's own sweet time. Fresh water and meat had to be put on board, Fernandes told White, for the colony had depleted a week's stores in the journey to Cowes and back. And since White had complained that many of the seamen were "coarse and unruly," Fernandes had released a dozen of them at Portsmouth and was scouring the docks of Plymouth for able-bodied replacements. As of May seventh, as White fretted over each hour they wasted in port, only four men had signed on for the voyage, and Fernandes refused to sail without a full complement.

It was bad enough that Fernandes recruited scoundrels, but the way he engaged them guaranteed that his ships were filled with the lowest sort of creature. White frowned in disapproval when he heard Fernandes enlisting sailors from a group of seamen lounging on the docks. No wages were given or guaranteed, but Fernandes made it clear that any booty plucked from Spanish ships was to be divided among the ships' crew upon their return to England. Such rewards could be great, Fernandes promised, and the privations of sea life were greatly worth the risk of treasure.

That evening White accosted Fernandes in his cabin. "We should be planting our crops now," White blustered, bringing his fist down on the captain's desk with as much anger as he dared display. "And yet, we sit here in the harbor! You will not go hungry this winter, Fernandes, but my daughter and the other women and children aboard this ship will. Make sail, I say, and do it tomorrow!"

Fernandes remained silent and smiled in his dark fashion, but the next day, May eighth, another ten seamen were persuaded to cast their lots with the voyage for Virginia. White gave the order to depart as soon as the ten were on board, but Fernandes ignored the command and set his men to checking and rechecking the ships' masts, sails, and caulking. Finally, as the heat of the sun bore fully upon them, Fernandes turned and casually shrugged toward White. "Now we will weigh anchor, bosun," he called to his mate, folding his arms. A smile crawled to his lips and underscored the silent message that his orders, not White's, were to be obeyed.

Fernandes's boatswain, the foreman of the deck crew, yelled, "Weigh anchor! Make sail!" and the energetic summons drew the passengers to the cannon ports of the lower decks. Men, women, and boys piled round the cannon or jostled for position on the quarterdecks of the three ships and watched with wide eyes as England slid away.

From the foredeck, White felt his heart pound with pride as he looked over the brave souls who had agreed to accompany him to Virginia. They were not enough to make a long-lived colony, but they were certainly enough to begin one. Fine, strong men and women they were, with hearts of steely courage, and fearless children who would grow up in a world unlike anything their parents had ever known. God had brought each of them to this place, White had no doubt, and God would honor their efforts and labors in the City of Raleigh.

▼▲▼▲▼ As the last pleats and tucks of the quilted English landscape faded into mist, Thomas Colman felt a weight lifting from his shoulders. Freedom! No more England to shadow his days, no congregation, questions, recriminations, protesting glances, secretive whispers, or public accusations. No bony fingers pointed in his direction, no need to prepare an ever-ready defense. No prophesyings where a man could be called out and accused openly of secret sin. No sermons to prepare. No nosy clergy members to question his role or duties.

He was alone, thank God, and out of the church. "A fish out of water," he muttered to himself. The sound of his voice startled a small red-haired boy at the railing who turned to stare, and Thomas felt himself smiling. "But a very happy fish," he added, and chuckled when the bewildered child tugged urgently on his mother's skirt.

Thomas left the stern with its view of the mists over England and climbed down from the quarterdeck to move toward the bow. Forward. It was the only place to be—even if moving forward meant serving John White for fifteen years. Surely serving White in Virginia would be better than living his old life in England.

Behind him, the sailors sang their shantey and glared at Thomas as he crossed the deck. Simon Fernandes had made it clear that passengers were to remain belowdecks as much as possible, and even though the sailors' song was lively, their glances were murderous.

> *"Oh, a-sailing on the ocean, every live-long day,*
> *'Tis a mariner's devotion for to go that way.*
> *Oh, the captain is a gentleman of finest rank and sway,*
> *The sea will prove his fortune should he go his way."*

Thomas pressed his hands on the ship's railing and obediently moved aside for a singing seaman who wrestled with a load of heavy rope. In time he might even be able to leave off these somber clothes and work half-naked like the seamen or fashion an outfit of animal skins like those the Indians wore. There would be no rigid dress code in Virginia, no social system to gauge a man by the starch in his ruff and the pounds in his purse, no superficial means of evaluating a soul and finding it lacking.

Ah, this Virginia would be a blessedly free Garden of Eden, where any man, if he had a mind to, could be Adam.

John White held the railing of the foredeck with both hands and boldly addressed the milling crowd below: "People of the City of Raleigh, in Her Majesty's Fair Province, Virginia!"

The crowd surged toward him. Children scampered up from the companionways; women shifted from the stern and tucked tearstained handkerchiefs into their sleeves. A score of men who had been gathered belowdecks moved, a little reluctantly, to the center of the ship to hear their governor's address. After the shuffling had subsided, no sound disturbed the stillness except an occasional crack of the square canvas sails as they tussled with the blessed ocean breeze.

"Dear people and fellow travelers—" White paused to smile down upon his colonists—"we embark today upon a journey that will test the character and courage of each man and woman among us. We go into a dark country with the light of the gospel; we will enter a primitive land with the spirit of civilization; we will make our homes in a rich country where trees still grow tall and the land is yet fertile and abundant. As we go, I would like to call upon the good Reverend Thomas Colman to ask God's blessing on our journey and voyage."

Thomas lifted a brow in wordless surprise but stepped forward as the crowd parted to let him through. Climbing slowly up to the foredeck, he surveyed the gathering from the lofty perspective, then bowed his head.

As the minister's voice rang out over the assembled passengers and seamen, John White nodded in silent satisfaction. Truly, this was a voice filled with the authority of one who knew God. It reached out as a jolt of energy, bending every head down and commanding every spirit to rise toward heaven. With such a man in control of the spiritual lives of his people, God could do great things.

White smiled. He had been wise to select Thomas Colman as a fellow traveler.

"Dear God, our sovereign Master," Colman prayed, gripping the rail of the foredeck so tightly that White could see the man's knuckles whiten, "we set forth today into the great unknown, where few have gone but many have dreamed of going. We follow not the sun nor the winds, but your divine will and your plan for our lives. We know that you are a severe and righteous judge, eternal God, who sees all and knows all and punishes those who trespass against you. So keep us pure in thought and deed, eternal Master, so we may bring an unblemished, pure light into the dark world before us. Keep before us the reality of hell and the certainty of death so that our lives and hearts may be refined and purified by your love. Keep us from sin, and keep sin from this ship. In the name of your righteous Son we pray, amen."

The solemnity of the moment passed as the minister left the raised platform. Caps and hats removed for prayer suddenly flew into the air as men were overcome with the joy of the journey. A great cheer rang across all three ships, and John White smiled indulgently at his people and lifted his arms high in celebration.

▼▲▼▲▼ Audrey stamped her small foot impatiently as she and Jocelyn waited in the afternoon line for their meal of biscuit and dried beef. "I'm thinkin' the minister's prayer was a wee bit severe, Miss!" Audrey whispered to her mistress. "All that talk about hell and sin? I'll be wantin' to leave this ship if 'tis loaded with sinners as bad as he said."

"We ought not to criticize him," Jocelyn answered, lowering her voice. "I think he's a Puritan. Such are naturally more severe than Anglicans."

"But all that talk about hell." Audrey shivered. "I thought 'twas creepy, that's all, with us about to undertake a journey to the end of the earth. Besides, me sainted father always said that anyone who prays much about the flames of hell has a genuine fear of goin' there."

Jocelyn did not laugh. Instead, she smiled politely at the pale face of the young belowdecks sailor who ladled murky brown water from a barrel. For her part, Audrey could not smile at the lad. The pale, pinched faces of the young "bilge rats" who were not allowed on the upper deck reminded her too much of herself. Just as living belowdecks was a sort of purgatory, so was living as a servant with no hope for the future. She supposed it was fated she be a servant, since she was an Irish orphan with no social standing or property to her name. Still, Audrey knew she was pretty, skilled, and tolerably bright. So apart from a person's conception, which Audrey allowed was accomplished the same way in poor families as in rich, what invisible quality did ladies possess that common women lacked?

Life didn't seem fair. She could read and write and dance and sing and had a smaller foot than Jocelyn, but she had been born common just as Jocelyn had been born gentle. No man but another commoner would marry her, and as he had to work for a living, so would she. It mattered little that Jocelyn was a kind mistress. Audrey knew that unless she miraculously found gold in the sands of Virginia or conjured up a gentleman willing to marry her, she'd be of the common serving class and doomed to the lower decks of life forever.

Audrey forced herself to look past the bilge boy's tired face, stained as it was with fatigue and despair. It was a mirror of what hers would look like in another year or two unless—

She caught sight of William Clement in the line behind her, and the brazen fool winked at her in front of his aging master, Roger Bailie. Audrey knew she ought to be offended, but the young man had a casual charm and fair good looks that made conversation with him easy. William was as common as an old shoe, but he stood on the tall side of six feet and moved with languid grace in his lanky frame. From under locks of shaggy blonde hair, his country-green eyes pinned her in an interested appraisal.

She pressed her lips together to hide a smile, and when she was sure Roger Bailie wasn't looking, she grinned and returned William's wink.

▼▲▼▲▼ The seamen aboard the *Lion* had their duties, leaving each passenger to devise his or her own way of combating boredom. John White divided his time between complaining about Simon Fernandes (certainly a Spanish spy, he confided to Jocelyn) and sketching pictures of the Indians he had met in his previous journeys to Virginia and the island of Roanoke. Eleanor spent her time sitting with Agnes or Ananias, but when the wind began to freshen and the ocean to roll, she went to her straw mattress, placed her hands on her belly, and begged God to calm the sea.

Margery Harvie, another heavily pregnant woman, laughed at Eleanor's constant nausea and went about her business. When Jocelyn mentioned that Margery had no trouble with seasickness, Eleanor retorted that Margery had no refinement and no manners. Gentlewomen were of a more delicate nature, she informed her cousin archly, and the delicate were meant to suffer.

Whenever she could, Jocelyn left Audrey to keep Eleanor company while she went to the upper deck to visit her uncle's small cabin. In rare moments when the cabin was empty, she sat at her uncle's desk and wrote long letters to her father. She had begun writing these letters while she waited to rejoin her father, and at first she had felt foolish putting her deepest thoughts into a letter that would never be read. But after hearing of her father's death, she wrote with renewed vigor since her father was in heaven with God. God knew her thoughts, so why couldn't the Master of the universe relay her thoughts and feelings to her beloved father?

For a while she wrote to her father and God as joint recipients.

By the time the *Lion* had headed out to sea, her letters were addressed to God alone. As she struggled to pen her hopes, fears, worries, and concerns, she felt a still, patient voice of encouragement speaking to her soul.

"I know, Father God, that you have not left me alone," she wrote, and heard the answer within the recesses of her heart: *Nor will I. I will not leave you nor forsake you.*

In her loneliness, through her letters, Jocelyn came to know God as one who listened and understood and healed. She had always known him as Creator, Savior, Master, and Teacher, but in the throes of grief, God revealed himself as a father.

She did not always find her uncle's office empty. Often John White sat at his desk, hunched over maps, journals, or sketches. When she entered, his wide eyes would blink as if he had never seen her before; then his easily distracted memory would return from wherever he had wandered. "Jocelyn!" he would cry, standing and extending his arms to embrace her. "How glad I am to see you! And how is my favorite niece today?"

After returning his embrace, she would take a seat on a stool and listen to him describe the progress of their journey. Captain Fernandes was amazingly tight-lipped and told his passengers little about the sea voyage, but John White had traveled the oceans enough to know that the ships would follow the coast of Portugal and North Africa to avoid the westerlies, which could blow the ships back to England. "At the Canaries we will catch the northeast tradewinds to blow us across the miles of the great Western ocean," her uncle told her, pointing at a rough map on his table. "With a good wind, we will reach land in twenty-eight days or less."

Jocelyn hoped for a speedy journey. She had already been aboard the ship for longer than she cared to be, and shipboard life was neither pleasurable nor luxurious.

Only Simon Fernandes and John White had private cabins aboard the *Lion*. Everyone else shared the decks equally. No one slept on the lowest deck, where barrels of water and supplies served as ballast; the bilge rats crowded themselves together among the passengers' trunks and supplies on the first deck. The second deck was divided into two halves: men slept aft, and the women bedded down on their straw mattresses at the fore. At night on the upper deck, the sailors of the *Lion* wrapped themselves in canvas and slept under the stars.

At its best, life on the ship was miserable. After sunset, every man and woman went to his or her assigned deck, rolled up in a blanket, and tried to sleep as best a person could on the damp and slimy floor. The straw mattresses used by the women were soaked by the first rain, and the stench of the resulting mildew forced the women to pitch the straw bundles overboard. It was better to sleep on a hardwood floor than to retch from yet another nauseating odor.

The lower decks were hellishly cramped and the air there was unbreathable, particularly in the hottest part of the day, but Simon Fernandes and his crew never allowed more than one or two passengers at a time on the upper deck. If by chance more than a few managed to slip up for a breath of air, Fernandes bellowed, "Clear the deck!" sending all passengers and idle crew back to the stifling lower levels. Jocelyn suspected that Fernandes considered the passengers no more than living cargo.

The stores of oatmeal, cheese, and butter remained fresh for four weeks only. Twice a week, on Sundays and Wednesdays, passengers were served a hot meal, but even this luxury afforded them little pleasure, for the food was cooked on a fire built on sand ballast in the forward section between decks. Before long smoke permeated the ship and sent the passengers scurrying to the upper decks to gasp in fresh air. The rest of the week the passengers ate salt beef, pork, and fish with biscuit, and hardtack so dense it had to be broken with a mallet. At every meal, Jocelyn had to force herself to offer thanks. She seldom managed more than "Father, for this food . . ." before the sight and smell of the fare on her crude plate set her stomach churning. Still, she knew the Lord, if not the food, would sustain her, and so finished the blessing with an obedient heart, ". . . may we be truly thankful. Amen."

One day Jocelyn saw Agnes hurrying Eleanor away from the dinner line. "What's wrong?" Jocelyn called, taking a step after her cousin.

"The barrel leaks; the biscuit is wet," Agnes answered, struggling to move Eleanor from the sights and smells of food. "How can they feed a lady such garbage?"

"Wet? It is softer, then?" Jocelyn asked.

"Aye," Agnes answered. She tossed a sour smile over her shoulder. "And turnin' blue with mildew before my eyes. Fair squirming with maggots, too. Even the beer is full o' life."

But crowded conditions and inedible food seemed like trivial concerns when the ships encountered bad weather. Eight days out to sea, a pillaring thunderhead in the west inexorably advanced toward their fleet. The sea rose up to snarl at them in the midst of gray-green gloom, and when flinty-eyed Fernandes bellowed, "Clear the decks!" in the face of the rising winds, the passengers hurried toward the companionways like frightened rats. Jocelyn joined the huddled stream of passengers flowing into the belly of the ship and covered her ears as women shrieked, children cried, and men shouted at one another as fear unleashed their tempers.

It was only noon, yet the sky darkened and churned around them. Scarce light came through the small openings in the sides of the ship. Jocelyn could hear the pounding of seamen's feet overhead as they rushed to take in the sails lest the ship be blown terribly off course by the approaching squall.

Suddenly the hold darkened entirely, and the cries of her fellow passengers quieted into piteous weeping and soft prayers: "Lord, have mercy upon us." From ninety throats the refrain echoed around her, and Jocelyn joined in, looking with dismay at the wooden timbers that stood as their only protection from a furious and fathomless ocean. For a dark moment she felt as if she were entombed in a large coffin soon to be buried in the depths of the sea.

Thunder roared overhead, cracking like a whip through the prayers around her. The ship shuddered as rain poured down on their heads through cracks in the wooden floor of the upper deck. The ship lifted and fell, rocked and listed, backward and forward, left and right. None stood on their feet. Even those who had been devoutly praying on their knees now lay prostrate on the floor, bodies piled upon one another like an odd assortment of rag dolls. The air was horribly thick and close, and Jocelyn threw herself on the floor next to Audrey and struggled to breathe a prayer: "Father God, are you there? Help us, I beg you!"

Someone tugged on her skirt, and Jocelyn looked up, expecting to find Eleanor in hysterics. But a boy crawled beside her, and in the white light of a lightning flash she recognized George Howe, the eleven-year-old son of one of her uncle's assistants.

"I cry you mercy, Miss," the boy whimpered, struggling manfully to hide his fear, "but I can't find my father."

Jocelyn looked about, but in the dim light of the hold she could see only huddled forms and the darkly wet forms of prostrate women. She turned back to the boy, about to tell him to wait until the storm had passed, but the sight of his quivering chin made her pause. *Father God, how am I to help this lad when I'm so frightened I can scarcely think straight?* her heart cried frantically.

Fear not. . . .

The assurance came softly, washing over her. Pressing her eyes closed, she drew a deep breath, then mustered a wan smile. "Come, we'll find him together," she said, reaching for his hand. She tried to rise to her feet, but the erratic rocking of the ship made balance impossible, so she crept forward, placing the boy's hand on her wet skirt.

"Don't lose me," she said, yelling to be heard above the din as she crawled forward on her hands and knees. "Your father's probably in the afterdeck. Isn't that where you sleep?"

She thought the boy nodded, but in the darkness she couldn't be sure. She continued through the black hold, stumbling over bodies, trunks, tools. Her progress was further hampered by the boy tugging at her skirt in the uneven rhythm of his crawling. Every five or ten feet she stopped, raised her voice, and cried,

"Master Howe? I have your son!" But no one called out above the voices clamoring in panic and prayer.

For half an hour she crawled over the wet floor and searched for the boy's father. Amid the crack and roll of thunder and cries of honest fear, rain thrummed on the upper deck and sloshed in the ship's belly as the vessel thrashed in the storm. Was George Howe even on this deck? *Dear God, let it be so, for I cannot bear the thought of going higher! Surely the waves would wash us away!* Nor could she fathom going lower, where rats and roaches darted uneasily among the trunks and barrels upset by the storm.

At one point Jocelyn slipped and fell, her head hitting a mast. She sat in dazed pain for a moment, rubbing the knot on her head, and felt again the insistent tug on her skirt. "Miss White—my father!" The pathos in George's voice drove her back to her hands and knees. Young George Howe needed his father, just as she needed hers, and in that frightened cry she recognized the same pain that had driven her to write letters to God. She had tried to tug on the heart of God just as George tugged now on her skirt.

Jocelyn turned her face to the boy in the darkness and hoped he could not hear the hopeless panic in her voice. "I don't know where your papa is, George." She bit her lip, fighting back tears of frustration, and suddenly a hand fell upon her shoulder.

"Seek you Master Howe?" Thomas Colman knelt beside her, his wet hair plastered to his face like dark silk ribbons. But his eyes, thank God, were capable and confident.

She nodded wordlessly, hoping he wouldn't see the fear in her eyes.

"Wait here. I'll take the boy to his father."

Jocelyn nodded again and pulled her raw and splintered hands into her lap. Thomas took young George's hand and led him across the deck. In less than a moment he had returned and knelt again by her side.

"Master Howe is against the far wall," Thomas said, yelling to be heard above the thrashing of the storm. "The boy is safe now, thanks to you."

"He went down too far, to the deck below this," she tried to explain, her voice ringing above the baritone prayers rising all around her. "But the lower hold is truly vile. There's no light, and the boy couldn't breathe."

"You were good to help him," Thomas Colman said, studying her in an oddly detached manner. He said nothing for a long moment, and she thought she saw something flicker in his eyes. Then he smiled and lifted a wet hand to indicate the storm. "This tempest is a fright, but we can bear this, and worse, if God be for us."

Jocelyn nodded and shivered, wrapping her arms about herself, too exhausted to move. In the dim gray light she saw Thomas Colman's eyes crinkle as he gave her a confident smile. "I may owe you an apology, Miss White, if I've made you uncomfortable in the last few days. It seems your uncle has been playing the matchmaker."

Jocelyn bit back a burst of hysterical laughter. How could he think of such things in the midst of this gale? But his calm attitude soothed her. For all the worry he showed, he might as well have said, *I apologize for stepping on your foot during the waltz.* Perhaps her fears were overblown. Surely seamen weathered storms like this every week.

She nodded a polite acknowledgement and waited for a moment of relative silence in which to make her reply. The sibilant whispers around her eased, and for a moment the hold seemed to grow brighter and the air still. Like the inhalation of breath, the storm quieted; the howling wind paused; the standing water on the deck floor shimmered in an unearthly gray light. She smiled at Thomas Colman, about to tell him that Audrey had played matchmaker, too, but suddenly lightning flashed, thunder cracked, and a fresh onslaught of rain slammed onto the deck above their heads.

It was the most horrific and powerful noise Jocelyn had ever heard in her life, and the ship shivered under the sound.

"God help us!" Jocelyn felt the cry escape her lips, and her arms reached out and clutched at empty air as the ship rolled in the sea. Tumbling across the deck, she caught a glimpse of young George and his father clinging tightly to each other as the ship twisted and fell against a wall of water that spewed forth from the openings above and broadside.

Her fellow passengers toppled from their places like toys caught in a gushing rain gutter. She would have slid helplessly, too, but suddenly she felt the strength of iron about her. In the brief flash of blinding white lightning she looked up, half expecting to see an angel sent to escort her to heaven. But it was not an angel's face above her, but that of Thomas Colman. He stood, solid and resolute, one of his arms tight about her waist, the other securely holding the pole of the mizzenmast.

And in the fury of the storm, when it appeared that at any minute the ship would be tossed from the hand of God to the ocean's murky floor, she didn't think to protest.

▼▲▼▲▼ John White brushed a pile of damp maps and sketches from the bench in his cabin and made a seat for Eleanor. Ananias, his countenance more troubled and worried than usual, nervously stroked his wife's hand. "We thought our lives were over," Ananias said, his wide forehead dotted with perspiration even in the cool aftermath of the gale. "I've never been through anything like that storm."

"Ah, I love a storm at sea," White answered, thankful that his passengers had not seen his own signs of panic. "It is the might of God turned loose afresh in an echo of the Creation. What, Eleanor, were you truly frightened? Think you that I should bring you up just to let you perish at sea? Never fear. This storm was but a thunderhead, though a nasty one, I'll warrant."

"Everyone was frightened," Ananias said, lifting his chin defensively. "'Twas horrible below."

"Soft, Ananias," White warned. "Speak not of fear or you'll breed dissension among our planters. Strengthen your resolve and keep your head high, Son, for you are a leader among these people. They must not see anything but strength in you."

"Papa, what if the baby comes during such a storm?" Eleanor asked, her eyes wide. Her dark hair hung wet about her face and magnified the pallor of her complexion. "I believe I cannot give birth on board this rollicking ship—why, there wasn't a woman aboard with any wits about her at all. 'Twas an absolute horror."

"Then pray we reach our destination soon." White smiled and winked at his daughter. "And pray that your child waits until his proper time. Do not fear, Eleanor; God holds us in his hand. If only—" A strident voice outside interrupted. John glanced out his window and saw Simon Fernandes directing his seamen to raise the sails.

John turned quickly to his son-in-law as a wave of anger surged within him. "A pox on that Portuguese tyrant! He thwarts us at every turn. Have you noticed, Ananias, that Spicer's flyboat is no longer with us?"

Ananias moved to the window and scanned the waters. "Cursed be this stormy ocean. Has the boat gone down?"

White shook his head. "Only God knows. The pinnace stayed with us during the storm, but Captain Spicer and his crew now are nowhere to be seen. Fernandes cares nothing for that ship, but we need those men. Manteo and Towaye are our best link to the Indians. We must pray that they will be able to pilot their way to Dominica."

"I'faith, Captain Spicer must do the impossible," Ananias muttered, turning away from the window. He lifted his wife's pale hand. "How many colonists were aboard?"

"Twenty," White answered. "Twenty strong men who would have made a vast difference in the success of our colony. If God does not bring them to us, we shall desperately rue their lack."

Eleanor stared out the window, one hand on her bulging stomach. "Surely nothing but evil came out of the storm," she said, her voice toneless and flat. "So much sorrow—"

"Where there is sorrow, one can find good," John interrupted, forcing a smile as he rose from his stool. It wouldn't do to have Eleanor spreading melancholy among the women. "God kept his hand on us, for we did not lose a single soul aboard the *Lion*.

One seaman broke his leg when a yard fell on him, but he will mend."

As he spoke, he surveyed the deck from his small window. Washed by the storm, the air shimmered with brilliant sunlight under a canopy of clean blue sky. It was difficult to believe that an hour ago the same sky had threatened their lives. . . .

White's attention was drawn by two forms coming out of the companionway. Jocelyn and Thomas Colman walked together, her dark head inclined toward his in deep conversation. White smiled.

"They say the ways of God are hard to comprehend," he said, turning back to Eleanor and Ananias. "Yonder walks your cousin with the minister. I have arranged that he should marry Jocelyn, but hesitated to force my will upon her. But look how God has brought them together—"

"Jocelyn marry the minister?" A horrified expression of disapproval flitted across Eleanor's face. "But he's a common man, and a strange one—"

"Let me remind you, Daughter, that you married a common bricklayer with more than one mark against him," White interrupted. Ananias squirmed uncomfortably, but White did not pause. "Your bricklayer is now a gentleman, due to his participation in this venture, and the same can be said of Thomas Colman. So say nothing of this, Eleanor, till all is come to pass. I have promised my departed brother to find a good husband for Jocelyn, and God has shown me how I must do it."

▼▲▼▲▼ It was strange, Jocelyn noticed, but despite its terrors, the storm melded the ship's passengers into a corporate body. Having experienced what they were sure was the worst nature could offer, the colonists thanked God for their survival, laughed at the memory of havoc in the lower decks, and fell into a gentle sort of camaraderie that pleased everyone but Simon Fernandes.

The general mood of relaxation especially pleased Jocelyn, for since the storm she had felt free to talk to Thomas Colman. He had sheltered and defended her, subjecting his own body to the battering of the storm in order to spare her. How could she refuse to speak to him? The crystal brightness of the cleansed and clear sky seemed to signal a new day, one in which the old restrictions of class and convention were relaxed.

Audrey eased herself away from Jocelyn's side and began to spend time with William Clement, the servant to Roger Bailie. Jocelyn didn't mind the girl's absence, for it gave her more time to spend in private conversation with Thomas.

She was so preoccupied with her newfound friend that she did not notice or care when the winds stopped blowing altogether. Though the tempers of the seamen and her uncle grew shorter with each day the sails hung limply from the masts, Jocelyn retreated with the minister to a quiet spot near the bow of the ship where she concentrated on understanding the enigma known as Thomas Colman.

Although he seemed to enjoy her company and often sought her out, at first he was reticent, preferring to watch the sea or walk about the deck by her side. They discussed the writings of Marcus Aurelius, and Jocelyn was impressed that Thomas did not always agree with the famous Roman's opinions. They also talked of the Indians, and Jocelyn was flattered when Thomas listened carefully to all she had learned from her uncle.

With each passing day, Jocelyn's thoughts were more taken with Thomas—as was her heart. Their conversations were lively and exhilarating, and brought to mind the precious discourses she and her father had shared. Like her father, Thomas seemed interested in every topic—and in what she had to say about it. Generally her ideas and opinions were in accordance with his, but on those occasions when she voiced a differing view, Thomas would listen thoughtfully, even respectfully—though his eyes often twinkled with an almost merry gleam. Once he even laughed out loud when she caught him—somewhat gleefully, she had to admit—in an error of interpretation.

"I concede to my wiser and more knowledgeable opponent," he had said, rising from his seat and bowing to her gracefully.

Jocelyn had glanced about nervously, worried lest anyone take note of the minister's outrageous display, and grasped his sleeve to pull him back down to his seat. The man was the most intriguing mixture of sobriety and gaiety she had ever met. But when his laughing eyes looked into hers for a moment, she could not suppress a smile—any more than she could stop the longing that pierced her heart: *Oh, for a lifetime of gazing into those eyes!*

And yet, in all their conversations, though she often mentioned her father and her life in London, Thomas Colman never unwrapped the details of his past or present life. Burning to know more about him, Jocelyn determined that she would simply ask all she wanted to know.

One afternoon they stood near the bowsprit on the upper deck. It was a glorious day, warmly washed by brilliant sunlight and canopied by a clean blue sky. Like a swimmer about to dive into cold water, Jocelyn took a breath and asked Thomas about his childhood.

He did not rebuke her gentle questions, and in time she learned that Thomas was the son of a reasonably prosperous Lincolnshire farmer. He had attended a village school until the age of fifteen, then had been apprenticed to a merchant with shipping interests at King's Lynn. His future had seemed assured until he ran away.

With this admission, Thomas fell silent and studied his hands. "What caused you to run away?" Jocelyn asked, wondering what thoughts lay behind his handsomely sculpted brow. "Was your master too severe?"

"You are young," he said, changing the subject. "How old are you, Miss White?"

"Seventeen," she answered, feeling herself blush. Though seventeen was a perfectly adult age, next to his maturity she felt as awkward as a five-year-old.

"I am nearly thirty," he said, looking past her at the gently roll-

ing waves. "I have lived a lifetime before this, and there is much
in my life that I cannot tell you."

"Is it so terrible?" she whispered, resisting the impulse to
place her hand on his. "I am known, Reverend Colman, as a
trustworthy and understanding confidante. My father told me
everything, and my cousin Eleanor trusts my ability to maintain
a confidence—"

"I do not doubt you, my—Miss White. There are things I have
buried, with God's help, and they must stay buried if I am to
serve God in the future."

His eyes brooded over the surface of the water, and Jocelyn
wondered if she should urge him to continue his story. After a
moment of hesitation she asked, "So you ran away from your
master. What then did you do?"

His cheek muscles stood out as he clenched his jaw. "I entered
the ministry. I studied. I devoted my life to the service of God
and his people. In due time, I married. We had a son. My wife
died. I relinquished my son to her sister's care. I surrendered my
church and chose to enlist as a colonist in the City of Raleigh."

His abrupt statement was laced with pain, and Jocelyn could
not look at him when he had finished speaking. She felt her
cheeks burning as her conscience smote her. The brittle reality of
his words made the romantic dreams she had harbored seem as
insubstantial as mists on water. This man was not interested in
love. He still grieved for his wife. He probably had sought Jocelyn out because he saw her as a lost child, a lonely girl who
stood in need of ministry and a scrap of Scripture.

Jocelyn's eyes smarted, and her heart felt as though it was suddenly leaden in her chest. It was now painfully obvious to her:
Thomas Colman had signed onto this voyage to escape the memory of his dead wife. He had been so in love that he could not
even bring himself to raise their son, so in love that he could not
remain in his village, even in England. . . .

"Pray pardon me," she said, biting her lip. "I didn't mean to
pry."

"I don't like to talk about it."

"I cry you mercy, I will never speak of it again."

He made no answer but continued looking out to sea. Embarrassed, Jocelyn slipped away. When she had reached the lower deck and knew for sure that he had not followed, she went to a private corner and wrapped herself in a blanket as her dashed dreams raked at her heart.

▼▲▼▲▼ The ship lay becalmed in the ocean for two days, and Jocelyn sat in her corner for the same length of time, rising only to eat and partake of the dark liquid that now sufficed for water. Eleanor, steady and at home on the becalmed ship, urged Jocelyn to join her and the other women in conversation, but Jocelyn turned a deaf ear to the entreaties of her cousin. Even Audrey tried to prod her mistress out of her depression by inviting her to play gleek, primero, or noddy with a group of gamers, but Jocelyn was not in the mood for cards.

She had read about lovesickness but had no idea it could be so physical. She had no appetite or desire to fill her empty stomach, no strength to pretend that all was well. She had lost her father and her first love within one month, and never in her life had she been so emotionally spent.

She did not want to talk to anyone. For the first time she understood the reason behind Thomas's guarded silence. Jocelyn knew Eleanor thought she was genuinely sick and would laugh if she knew the real cause of her cousin's sulkiness. She could not confide in Audrey, for the maid would only devise silly games to win Thomas Colman's attention or—even worse!— spread the story of Jocelyn's broken heart to every listening ear aboard the ship.

Jocelyn especially did not want to pray. If she opened her heart and feelings to God, how could she hide the anger that churned in her soul? She had found a man she could love—an intelligent, learned, and devout minister—but clearly he didn't love her. The slight beginnings of affection she thought she had seen seemed to have evaporated the moment she pried into the past he did not want to remember or discuss.

Indeed, what else could she have expected? Thomas Colman's great love had left him in eternal pain. Somehow he had found the strength to begin a new life, but in her selfish quest to know him completely she had torn open the scar and wounded him further.

She should have known better. She, more than most people on the ship, knew the face of grief intimately. Even now the thought of her father's voice or the memory of his hand on her head could reduce her to sobbing in the dead of night. On such nights, when she had exhausted her tears, she lay awake in the bowels of the ship and studied the creaking beams above her. How much time would have to pass before she could join her father in heaven?

Jocelyn's eyes teared yet again as she realized that, for all her pain, her grief was fresh and acute. Thomas Colman's was deeply rooted. She had lost a father; he, a wife and lover, the mother of his son.

Sitting in her corner, she drew her stiff blanket more closely about her and rested her head on her arms. She knew little of the physical love between a man and woman, but Eleanor glowed when she spoke of her husband and their soon-coming child. Her father's voice had always grown tender when recalling his wife. Surely it was a hundred times more tragic to lose a love than to lose a parent. God, after all, designed that parents give birth to children and precede them, when the children are grown, into heaven. Husbands shouldn't lose their wives, nor young children their mothers. It was not natural.

Her eyes filled up again. She had but faint memories of her own mother, yet her father had never recovered from that loss. To imagine Thomas Colman caught in a pain akin to her father's was sad indeed; to realize she had increased that pain was detestable.

How could she have done him such a great injustice?

▼▲▼▲▼ Eleanor followed Agnes carefully through the men's section of the passenger deck, remembering to keep her head well beneath the low roof while watching the floor lest she trip over a rope or a folded blanket. The child within her womb stirred, and for the first time in days she felt strong and active. It was a miracle she had survived the journey thus far! There had been times in the past few weeks when she wondered if she would survive the night.

A group of men sat huddled together, and snatches of ribald conversation caught her ear as she and Agnes approached. She continued forward, though, secure in her role as an assistant's wife and the governor's daughter. Every man in the group fell silent as the ladies drew near.

"Excuse me, sirs," she called, stepping out from behind Agnes's forbidding back, "but I am looking for the minister."

"Colman?" She recognized William Clement, the rakishly good-looking servant who often played cards with Audrey.

"Yes."

William jerked his thumb upward and gave her a slow smile. "Up there, Mistress Dare. The minister is too holy to join us."

The other men exploded in laughter at his remark, and Eleanor nodded her thanks without comment. Agnes frowned and pushed her mistress away from the men like a mother duck propelling her young from the jaws of crocodiles.

"And they call themselves Englishmen!" Agnes muttered under her breath as they climbed the narrow steps of the companionway. "The Englishmen I know don't spend their time idly repeating the vile tales of rank seamen."

"Soft, hold your tongue," Eleanor advised, recognizing the spare form of the Reverend Colman on the deck ahead. "Please, wait here. I would speak to this man in private."

Agnes obediently hung back while Eleanor advanced and tactfully cleared her throat. Turning from the rail, Thomas Colman seemed startled by the sight of the governor's daughter, but he bowed respectfully.

"I give you good day, Mistress Dare."

"Well met, Reverend." She gestured toward the calm sea. "A lovely day, is it not?"

He gave her a wry smile. "I doubt the seamen and the captain would agree with you, madam. A calm sea is not a sailor's delight. This mirrorlike ocean is the opposite of the stormy sea that caused the seamen to dump the rebellious Jonah, but if there is a sinner aboard—"

Eleanor waved his comments away. "'Tis not the sea, but my cousin I have come to discuss with you, Reverend Colman."

His smile vanished. "Your cousin?"

"Jocelyn White." When he did not answer, she stepped closer and placed her hands on the railing. "Surely you are aware that she has come to harbor tender feelings toward you. And my father has told my husband and me of your arrangement."

His dark brow shot up.

"Of course, we agree with Father's plan," she added quickly. "You would make a very suitable husband for Jocelyn. You are educated, as is she; you are both devoted to God; and Jocelyn has spent considerable time in your company. I trow she has found you agreeable."

"I believe you misunderstood her, madam. She has not spoken to me in several days."

"Indeed, she has not. But the problem isn't a lack of desire for your company, for I believe I never saw her so happy as when she was with you. Rather, I am of the impression that she fears she has insulted or offended you and that it is you who do not desire her companionship—"

"Truly?" For an instant the veil of reserve lifted from his eyes, but then the corner of his mouth fell and the wry smile curved again into place. "I almost believed you, madam, but surely you are mistaken. I have decided to forgo your uncle's offer and indenture myself to him in service. Your cousin is too beautiful and refined to be my wife. I fear I have neither the words nor the power to win her heart."

"But you are wrong!" In her eagerness she leaned toward him, and a disapproving snort from Agnes reminded Eleanor that she had nearly overstepped the bounds of propriety. A visibly pregnant woman did not speak to unmarried men unless her maid were present, and she certainly did not share secrets. . . .

"I am sure, sir, that if you approach Jocelyn today, you will find her of a willing, even eager, temperament," Eleanor said, collecting her dignity and reserve. She smiled. "Do not give up hope. If you believe in the God you serve, is it not within his power to grant this favor for you?"

"God does not grant favors," Colman answered, his dark eyes scanning the calm sea once again. "We do not deserve his grace. How then could we deserve favors?"

Eleanor shrugged lightly as she moved away. "Welladay, sir, what's the harm in asking?"

▼▲▼▲▼ What was the harm in asking? How dare the flippant wench suggest that God could be cajoled! He knew better, having tried long ago to bargain with the angry God who had taken his wife and demanded his son. God was a hard taskmaster, demanding all and giving nothing in this life but the promise of ease in the life to come.

And yet . . . Mistress Dare had come to him with words he had never hoped to hear. Jocelyn White favored him! She—how had the woman phrased it?—"harbored tender feelings for him"! Could God be softening toward his fallen minister? Was it possible that God had actually brought this young woman into his life? But if so, for what purpose? To bless or to test?

Thomas left the rail and gazed distractedly around the deck. There was no private place, no room for quiet musing unless one went to the very belly of the ship where rats and roaches and insects wormed their way into the barrels and casks of next week's victuals. Turning as if the hounds of hell nipped at his heels, he sprinted down the companionway through the lower decks until he crouched in the low-ceilinged orlop deck. Dark, dank, disgusting it might be, but here, at least, a man could be alone to think.

As vile bilge water soaked his shoes and crept up his hose to his knees, Thomas Colman considered his options.

One decision, two choices.

Two prizes, two liabilities.

If he refused to pursue Jocelyn White, he would be required to render fifteen years of indentured service to John White. But an indentured servant could not lead a church. The thought brought no pang of regret. Rather, Thomas felt an almost over-whelming solace at the notion. Never again would he have to subject himself to the rigors of spiritual leadership. In time, with the growth of the colony, even the knowledge of his ordination would fade, and he would become Thomas Colman, humble and ordinary servant, instead of Reverend Colman, stern judge and jury. In servitude, Thomas knew, lay the keys to personal free-dom.

And yet . . . the image of sparkling eyes and a gentle, eager smile came to him. Jocelyn! If he chose not to marry her, that lovely voice might never speak to him again. Already he had silenced her with his curt answers. And when she learned from her cousin or her uncle that he had been offered her hand and had refused, those blue eyes would flash at him in anger instead of affection. She would never again blush at his approach or smile and ask his thoughts or readily interpret the Latin verse he quoted from memory. Her small hand would never rest in his, the arms that had clung to him in the storm would never seek him again, and those petal-soft lips would be claimed by another man eager for a bride. . . .

Abruptly, he shifted in the murky water as a sag-bellied rat skittered across a row of barrels. His traitorous heart had soft-ened under the girl's influence! Either Jocelyn White had bewitched him, or God had devised the most enticing test ever imagined by the divine mind. But would God dangle this desir-able young woman before him merely to keep an errant and rebellious minister in his holy service?

"It isn't fair, God," Colman muttered, squatting in the filthy water. "Not to the girl, for you know what I am."

He didn't expect an answer so was not surprised when none came, though a pang of disappointment stabbed his heart briefly. Was God indeed so hardened toward him that he would ignore even his most sincere prayers?

Then came the echo of Eleanor Dare's words: *"She has come to harbor tender feelings toward you."* Thomas groaned. If he chose to ignore whatever tender feelings Jocelyn White had developed, was he not committing another wrong? As for his own emotions, he could repress his respect for her intellect, his joy in her company, the pleasure of hearing her speak his name. As a minister he was supposed to sacrifice his personal feelings on the altar of his jealous God, but his newly awakened heart would not let him hurt her. . . .

One decision, two choices, each leading to a form of slavery—one to a gentleman master; the other, to God himself. Service for John White would bring freedom and a life of solitude. Service for God would bring the lovely and charming Jocelyn and life at center stage in the rigorous leadership of a church.

He had been a minister. Well he knew it was little but grief and thankless work.

He had been married, too, and yet . . . he closed his eyes. His wife had never looked at him the way Jocelyn White did, and the way she breathed his name stirred his heart in a way it had never been stirred before. Ever.

Not even by the voice of God.

Sighing in resignation, Thomas turned and climbed upward.

John White reluctantly pulled his eyes from the silent sea as a knock sounded on his cabin door. He had lost himself again in frustration, unable to concentrate on his sketches, his journal, or his plans. The ship bobbed uselessly in the waters of the Western ocean as though some great hand held it in place. The vane outside his window hung limply; the sails sagged on the ship's masts like limp, sad flags, bleached by the relentless sun. Oh, the hours they had wasted! Every day adrift meant they spent much-needed supplies of water, food, and energy, all for nothing!

"Enter!" White barked, annoyed that someone had dared disturb his thoughts. Another fight had probably broken out among the impatient and short-tempered colonists. The camaraderie fostered by the storm had vanished during the days of sweltering stillness.

The door opened, and White grunted in surprise when he saw who had knocked. "Reverend Colman! Has the Lord God sent you to chastise us for some secret sin? Is it for some wrong that we sit on a becalmed sea, going nowhere?"

"I know of no sin," Colman answered, ducking as he entered through the low doorway. "Except the crime of hesitation. I verily would ask your niece to marry me, Governor White, in your presence. Since you are her guardian now, I assume you would want to have a hand in it."

White felt his jaw drop. "You'd ask to marry her now? When the entire ship is short-tempered and nasty? Are you a fool, man?"

"Perhaps." Colman's features were inscrutable, and White could not discern his thoughts.

After a moment the older man smiled. "So 'tis all or nothing, eh?" he asked, drumming his fingers on the desk. Either the man had courage, or he was the greatest of fools. It was impossible to tell which.

Colman's steady gaze never wavered. "If you would send for her, Governor, I'd like to ask her this very hour. I do not think it fair to prolong this situation further. I shall be her husband or your servant and would know my place now."

I'faith, he meant it! "So be it. I'll send for her," White answered, ringing the bell for his cabin boy. "Have a seat, Reverend Colman. By all means, let us settle this matter." He crinkled his nose as he looked at the minister's garb. Though all on board wore stiff and worn clothing, the minister positively reeked of filth, and his hose and shoes were wet with brownish-green slime.

"Is anything amiss?" Colman asked, noting White's expression.

White held a finger to the side of his nose. "I daresay, sir, if I were planning to ask for a maid's hand, I believe I'd clean up first."

"Mayhap you would," Colman answered, clapping his hands resolutely on his knees. "But the lady will have me as I am or she'll not have me at all."

"There is no gainsaying that," White said, shrugging as the cabin boy entered to take his message.

▼▲▼▲▼ Jocelyn smoothed her hair into place as she hurried toward her uncle's cabin. The boy had said that the governor had urgent business to discuss with her, and Jocelyn could not imagine how something so important could have come up in the middle of the ocean. She wondered if he had been reading and wanted to discuss a question of literature with her. Or he might want to share his stories of the savages of Virginia. Or, she thought, a twinge of guilt tweaking her conscience, perhaps he had heard that she was downhearted and sought to lift her spirits.

Whatever his reason for summoning her, she had to admit it was a pleasure to leave the choking heat of the lower deck and walk out into the sunshine. As the tropical sun beat down from the cloudless sky, the ship all but baked its occupants. The square openings in the lower deck were blocked by cannons, therefore no breeze was given ample entry to cool the air trapped between decks. The oak planks of the upper deck retained such heat that even seamen with toughened bare feet could not walk on them, and the resulting temperatures frayed the nerves of sailor and passenger alike. Everyone on board prayed for a wind, even the gentlest of breezes, to move and transform the living furnace in which they were trapped into something at least tolerable.

But the heat was only one foe with which the colonists had to contend. After four weeks at sea, the stench and fumes from filth on the ship had made nearly all the passengers ill, and Jocelyn felt truly sorry for the young boys who slept deep below on the lower decks. At any given time, nearly half the passengers lay on their stiff, mildewed blankets with headaches, fever, seasickness, or other diseases caused by the poor diet. Lice borne on the blankets infested nearly every passenger. In her melancholy time belowdecks, Jocelyn had spent hours nursing the sick, even to the point of scraping lice from their bodies with a strap of stiff leather.

The food provided no relief, either. It had gone from bad to worse in the last weeks, and now their rations were very poor and very little. The blackened water from the barrels squirmed with worms, and most meals consisted only of the ship's biscuit, which by now was little more than an insect-infested lump of flour.

Disgusting as they were, all these privations were bearable, Jocelyn reasoned, save the vermin. The mere thought of lice made her skin itch, but worse by far were the cockroaches and rats, which swarmed over the ship in search of a dry resting place during storms and rain. Just this morning she had tried to clean a rat bite on poor George Howe's leg, and the boy had buried his face in her skirt and wept for his mother who had remained behind in England.

Yes, whatever her uncle's news, it was good indeed to leave her fellow passengers on the lower deck and journey to the relative sanity of her uncle's small cabin.

▼▲▼▲▼ "Come in."

Jocelyn smiled at the faint note of triumph in her uncle's voice as she opened the door, but her smile froze at the sight of Thomas Colman in the room. Pained heat rose in her face as the terrible possibilities flew into her mind. Had he complained about her tactlessness? Had her uncle summoned her only to charge her to leave this man alone?

She suddenly grew aware of her appearance, and the blush in her face only burned the more. She had not had the opportunity to bathe in four weeks. Her hands were filthy, as were her clothes. She had dampened her skirt to wipe the Howe boy's infected leg because she had no other cloth available. Her hair hung in disheveled wisps about her face and clung to her perspiring neck.

It was little comfort that Thomas Colman looked worse than she did. His face was haggard and pale, his eyes dark and focused, his leggings wet and foul.

She felt the chasm between them like an open wound.

"Jocelyn, the Reverend Colman has come to me with an unusual request," her uncle said, slapping his hand upon his desk.

"I know what it is, Uncle," she whispered, lowering her head in shame. Oh, that the floor might give way and swallow her up!

"You do?" Pleased surprise rang in his voice; how could he be so cruel? Didn't he care that she was humiliated? "My dear minister, you have underestimated yourself." Jocelyn lifted her head in time to see her uncle step from behind the table and clap the minister on the shoulder. "'Twasn't so difficult, I'm certain."

Jocelyn felt the power of Thomas's gaze and turned her face to his for the flutter of a moment. The haunted expression in his eyes made her feel as though the small cabin whirled madly around her. "Why don't you say what you came to say?" she whispered, swallowing a hysterical surge of laughter. "Think you that I don't know why you are here? You want me to avoid your presence and never again speak with you. I have done you wrong. I am ill-bred and tactless, insensitive, cruel beyond belief—"

Her uncle's hand lifted, and she halted the flow of her words in mortified obedience.

"My dear Jocelyn," he said, his eyes squinting in secret amusement, "I'm sure we have no idea what you are talking about. The reverend minister here wishes to ask you to marry him."

Her head flew up in astonishment at his words, and she saw the triumphant gleam in her uncle's eyes as he continued.

"The good reverend needs a wife, and since you are an intelligent girl who is alone and well-suited to be the wife of a clergyman, I have given my blessing to this union. All that remains is your consent."

She felt a curious, tingling shock running through her and turned to look at Thomas in total incredulity. His dark eyes studied her with quiet intensity, not unlike a cat watching a bird. He voiced no disagreement with her uncle's words, but how could he possibly want *her*, a thoughtless girl, for his wife? Surely he didn't, unless—

Of course. The honorable Reverend Thomas Colman needed a wife. Her uncle had just said as much. Thomas would be the minister in the City of Raleigh and, as such, responsible for the spiritual life of each colonist. He would have to be well above reproach and slander. A married man would fare better in such a position, and since she was the only available gentlewoman on the ship, he had decided to do the prudent thing and marry her. Truly, it was simple enough. The idea made sense, even as it brought a sharp pain to her heart. Mayhap his interest in her of days past had been perfunctory, merely an experiment to see if he could bear her company.

O God, her disappointed heart cried out, *I thought he cared for me, at least a little.*

She felt both men watching her, and she turned reflexively to the small window to guard her all-too-open countenance. She struggled with the tears that threatened to overcome her.

Help me, Father. What should I do?

Could she marry a man who wanted a wife merely to share the burden of the ministry? A man who still mourned his one true love, a man whose imprisoned heart would never be opened to her?

"Father God," she murmured, her eyes on the silent sea, "can I marry a man who loves another?"

"When I found him whom my soul loves," the answer rang in her heart, *"I held on to him and would not let him go. . . . This is my beloved and this is my friend."*

She closed her eyes for a moment, an inexplicable joy surging through her. And she knew. Yes, she could marry Thomas Colman, for he was the one her soul loved. Why else would his grief so wound her, his broken heart so touch hers? Why else would the sight of his face so quicken her breathing, and the mere sound of his voice so stir her blood?

She loved him. Purely and truly. And if his love should remain removed from her, perchance she might yet have his friendship and his respect.

"I can love enough for both of us," she whispered to the sea.

"What say you, Jocelyn?" For the first time, Thomas spoke, and she thought she heard a trace of anxiety in his voice. She turned to meet his eyes and was surprised by the emotions she saw there—though only for a moment. Too quickly the veil was drawn, covering all. But she had seen something, she was sure of it. She held his gaze, wondering. Did she—could she—truly mean anything to him? If but a seed of affection for her resided in his heart, perhaps it could grow into something that resembled the love he had borne for his deceased wife. It could, God willing, become something even more.

"Yes," she answered, her gaze never wavering. "I will marry you, Reverend Colman." Hesitantly, she offered her hand, and, after bowing respectfully, he took it and dropped his eyes.

"Well, then," her uncle said, beaming in a self-satisfied smile. "Let's be done with it." As he searched among his books, Jocelyn felt the heavy strength of Thomas's hand around hers and knew she had chosen rightly. The same arms that had sheltered her during the storm would now hold her throughout life, whether in duty or love, it mattered not. For now.

"Ah, here 'tis." John White triumphantly flourished his copy of the *Book of Common Prayer.* "Who marries a minister when the minister's at sea? The governor, in truth, that's who," he said, chuckling as he opened the book. "Mark me, my friends, you'll be as married by these vows as by any ever uttered in a church."

He gave Jocelyn a loving kiss on the forehead before he began to read the marriage service, but she scarcely heard his words. Her eyes turned to the sea again, and her father's face seemed to appear in every gentle ruffle of the waves, his voice echoing in the ceremonial tones of her uncle as he read.

"Boldly, faithfully, successfully," her father's words rang in her memory. *"Boldly go, faithfully serve, successfully live. . . ."*

"Jocelyn White, will you be married to this man?"

Startled, she turned her face from the window. "I will."

"Thomas Colman, will you be married to this woman?"

"Yes, I will." Thomas did not look at her as he spoke.

"Then in the name of the Father, the Son, and the Holy Ghost, I pronounce that you are husband and wife this day." Her uncle snapped the prayer book shut and folded his hands behind his back. "I believe 'tis proper to have a ring, reverend sir. Have you anything that will suffice?"

Thomas gave her a quick, denying glance, and Jocelyn pulled her right hand from his grasp. "I have this," she said, removing the ring that had not left her finger since her father had placed it there. She pressed it into Thomas's palm.

"Place it on the fourth finger of her left hand, for there it will lie closest to her heart," White instructed.

Thomas fumbled with the ring for a moment, gave Jocelyn an embarrassed smile, then slipped it onto the proper finger of her hand. For an instant they stood awkward and still; then John White's rough voice boomed. "I'faith, are you waiting for my permission? Kiss your bride, son!"

Thomas stepped forward and lowered his dark head to hers, and Jocelyn's heart pounded as her husband's lips made whisper-light contact with her own. She wished for a moment that he would linger, hold her, speak her name, but a breeze blew through the small window and the vane outside creaked. John White broke between them as he rushed toward the deck.

"Praise God, the wind blows!" he cried, flinging the door open.

The freshening wind brought the ship to life. The sails cracked and flapped as the breeze tugged at the canvas, and seamen and colonists alike broke out of their lethargy and came toward the deck, crying out in gladness as, before their eyes, the sheets blew out and bellied taut, pulling the ship westward toward Virginia.

The sailors roared in ecstatic approval, and passengers from below crowded on the companionway to rejoice in the heaven-sent breeze. The whisper of wind brushed across Jocelyn's cheek as she looked at the man who was now her husband. Despite the tropical heat, she shivered.

Thomas saw Jocelyn's slight shiver, and his heart began to pound in the familiar rhythm of self-recrimination. *Now you've done it,* a nagging voice spoke from a dark chamber of his mind. *This girl is now your wife! What will you do with her?*

She was still watching the seamen on deck. Thomas let his eyes roam over her slender figure, the purity of her throat. Confused by the rampageous reactions that stirred his heart, he looked away and clenched his fists.

God, what are you doing?

▼▲▼▲▼ As Jocelyn watched the celebratory hubbub, she felt Thomas take her elbow. "I must thank you," he said politely, his voice strangely hoarse.

Jocelyn stared in surprise and her gaze met his. His dark eyes stirred, but whether with joy or dismay she could not tell.

If he feels the need to formally thank you, a dark voice whispered in her heart, *then beyond a doubt 'twas a marriage of partnership, a business arrangement and nothing more.* The good reverend had given an unattached and lonely girl a home and a place. She had given him the respectability of marriage and a partner in ministry in the years to come. In that instant Jocelyn felt she understood the situation clearly, but with her rueful acceptance came a stab of pain.

"Certainly you are welcome," she answered, moving toward the door. "I would stay, but Eleanor will wonder where I've gone."

"I understand." He stepped back to let her pass. "If you have any need, Miss White, as your husband I will provide for you."

"I believe I am Mistress Colman now," she corrected, and the name seemed to startle him.

"In truth, you are," he answered, picking up his cap from where it lay on her uncle's desk. He gave her an apologetic smile. "I cry you mercy, how could I forget?"

Because your first wife is yet your Mistress Colman, Jocelyn's traitorous heart answered, but she nodded and smiled politely. "If you need me, sir, I'll be below with my maid and my cousin."

"Aye." He nodded again and she left, feeling oddly detached from the celebration still taking place on deck. Indeed, she felt more affinity with the ship itself than with the people above her. Like the *Lion,* which now moved purposefully through the water, she had a new direction. In the last ten minutes, Jocelyn White had become Mistress Colman, the lady of a household and the wife of a minister. She had crossed a great social chasm.

Why, then, did it seem that nothing in her life had changed?

▼▲▼▲▼ "You've done *what?*" Audrey shrieked, but Eleanor smiled and patted her ever-increasing belly approvingly.

"I've married the minister," Jocelyn said again, sinking onto a soiled blanket near Eleanor. "Uncle John married us an hour ago."

"In truth, that's wonderful news, Cousin," Eleanor said, her voice oddly maternal.

"I'll be wantin' to hear all the details, since you didna see fit to call for me," Audrey said, pulling up her skirts to sit next to Jocelyn. "Well, then, tell us all about it. What did the minister say to win your heart? He's been so quiet and shylike; how'd he find the courage to ask for your hand?"

"He said nothing," Jocelyn answered, her head beginning to throb. Despite the ship's movement, the air belowdecks was still stagnant and sour. "Nor did he ask. My uncle told me the minister wished to marry me and asked if I was willing. I was and we

were married. 'Tis all that happened. And I suppose, Audrey,
that we both have a new master now."

She lay back upon the deck and closed her eyes while Audrey
sputtered in excitement. "Oh, and wouldn't your father be
proud, your marryin' a minister! He'd be right pleased, I know
he would, Miss Jocelyn. I saw right off that there was something
between you and the minister, I did—"

"Soft, Audrey, can't you see she's overcome?" Eleanor interrupted. "Let her rest. I think our Jocelyn needs some time to
adjust to the state of matrimony."

Jocelyn gave Eleanor a grateful smile as the older girl
stretched her swollen legs out on the slimy deck floor. Eleanor
leaned closer to Jocelyn and lowered her voice. "Nothing will
change until we reach land, Jocelyn, so don't fret about . . . you
know, living with a husband. Then you'll find 'tis natural and
perfectly lovely. You'll be glad you married him. Indeed, the minister is a handsome man, and respected, so you'll find nothing to
worry about. All will be well with you."

Jocelyn nodded and squeezed her eyes shut, trying to look
appropriately pleased, hoping against hope that Eleanor hadn't
seen the tears that threatened to overcome her.

▼▲▼▲▼ "And so me mistress has married the minis-
ter," Audrey finished, laying her cards down on the barrel with a
flourish of triumph. "And I've won, haven't I?"

"You have, indeed," William Clement answered, giving her
his brightest smile. Her hand was a far cry from the best on the
table, but it was best to let her think herself a winner. He felt
James Hynde staring at him and looked up to see the mocking
light in James's eyes. All right, so he hadn't been able to marry
the lady Jocelyn himself. Who'd have guessed she would fall for
that somber minister?

"Audrey," he said, purposefully turning to the flustered maid.
"I've been of a mind to tell you something for a while, but I'm
not sure how you'll be taking it."

"Why, whatever can you be meanin', William?"

He smiled as the girl blushed and lowered her blue eyes demurely. She was not gentry, that much was obvious by her rough Irish speech and her freckled complexion, but her manners were good, and she could rise above her birth, just as he planned to. If he couldn't win the mistress, it would be a shame to let his efforts in minding the maid go to waste.

He shuffled the cards into his hand and laid the stack on the table. Gently, carefully, he removed his cap with one hand and placed his other on the soft hands Audrey held in her lap.

"'Tis not my place, but I can't sleep another night without tellin' you this: You are a beautiful girl, Audrey Tappan, the most beautiful and bonny lass on the ship."

She blushed to the roots of her red hair, and he felt her hands clench under his. Ah, sure, and she had thought he'd been but playing a game till now. Well, hadn't he been? But it was time to state his intentions and make his claim before any of the other men on board realized how acute was the shortage of women bound for this colony.

"Why, William, I . . . ," she stammered in response.

He smiled at her confusion and pressed his finger across her pink lips. "Soft, dear, don't say a word. 'Tis enough that you know how I feel about you, and if the governor's up to performing one marriage, mayhap he'll perform another after we land at Chesapeake."

She paled then, and he smiled inwardly at his success. A gust of wind blew through the porthole and scattered the cards. William patted Audrey's hand, then released it. "You'd best be getting back to your mistress," he said, giving her a wink. "We'll talk later, love."

She moved away as if in a daze. When she was safely beyond hearing, James began to laugh. "How are you going to marry that girl?" James asked. "You can't marry until you are free, yet here you are making promises—"

"With any luck, old Roger Bailie will die from heatstroke before we reach land," William said, stacking the marked cards into a neat pile. "I could set foot on Virginian soil as a free man, with my five hundred acres and Audrey's five hundred acres . . ." He paused to figure in his head. "With one thousand acres to my name."

James gave his friend a doubtful look, and William neatly stuffed the cards into his doublet pocket. "Anything can happen at sea, my friend."

▼▲▼▲▼ From the small window on the passenger deck, Jocelyn studied the *Lion*'s shadow on the ruffled surface of the sea. The ship had spread her wings like a hawk eager to take advantage of the rising wind, and the miles streamed out behind her, a white path stretching straight and true into the east. Jocelyn felt that God had suddenly smiled on the ship. If only he would let her know whether he was as pleased with her quick marriage.

"I hear you've gone and married the minister."

The words broke Jocelyn's thoughts, and she looked down to see the petite form of Alice Chapman. She had only spoken with the lady a few times since boarding the ship, but she knew that Alice's husband had been the rector of a church in England.

"Yes." Jocelyn forced a smile. "I suppose I have."

The older woman noticed her hesitation. "Are you having second thoughts?" she asked, her hand coming to rest upon Jocelyn's. Her eyes scanned Jocelyn's face. "Why should you, my girl?"

Jocelyn looked out to sea, not sure she could be totally honest with this woman—or with any other. At last she spoke, quietly and hesitantly. "How can you know if a marriage is right?" She twisted a handkerchief in her hands. "I asked God to show me what was right, but he didn't write my answer on the wall. I thought I knew what he wanted of me, but what if I have made a mistake?"

The lady clucked in quiet sympathy. "My child, we don't know anything until we take a step of faith. God has promised to direct our paths, but paths are made for walking, you know. The moment you accepted the minister as your husband, he became God's choice for you."

"Really?" A bud of hope sprouted in Jocelyn's heart.

"Do you love him, dear?"

Jocelyn pressed her lips together. "Yes."

"Why?"

Jocelyn felt herself dimpling in embarrassment. "Well . . . you wouldn't know it to look upon him, but he has a wonderful sense of humor. Often as we talked on the deck, he told me funny stories about growing up in the country. And he's kind—haven't you seen the gentle way he works with the young boys? And of course he's honorable and wants to serve God. I don't think he fears the Indians or any danger we might meet in Virginia." Her spirits lifted as she talked, and she ended by giving Mistress Chapman a shy smile. "I think I can trust him to be a good husband, even if he never loves me in the way I love him."

The freckled hand over hers moved in a gentle patting motion. "Love is a decision, my dear, and today you have both made it. Trust God to do the rest."

The older woman moved away, but the echo of her words rang in Jocelyn's heart as she stared out to sea. *Trust God. . . .*

Indeed, God would have to work a miracle to make Thomas love her. Could she trust him for that?

▼▲▼▲▼ The welcome wind of the afternoon blew into a thundering gale, and once again the passengers and seamen on the *Lion* were soaked, rattled, and rolled about on the ship. Jocelyn wanted to go to the afterdeck and find Thomas, but Eleanor panicked, afraid she would be knocked about and injure her baby. Agnes could not calm her, nor Audrey. Only Jocelyn would do.

The ship rocked for two full hours in the night; then finally the ocean calmed itself, and Eleanor and the other women slept. Through the cannon ports Jocelyn could see the pinking of dawn in the east, and she climbed the narrow companionway to the upper deck to enjoy the morning breezes.

The sailor atop the crow's nest whistled appreciatively as she walked below, but Jocelyn ignored him and climbed to the quarterdeck at the stern of the ship. The deck gleamed in the early morning sun, fresh and clean from the storm. A gentle rain still fell, but Jocelyn welcomed it, for it washed the grime of sea salt from her hair and skin. Reaching out her hands to catch a few drops of the blessedly clean water, she stood silently with her eyes closed.

Footsteps sounded and stopped beside her, and Jocelyn shook herself from her reverie and opened her eyes. Thomas stood at the ship's rail, his eyes focused on the sunrise, his lean back angled toward her. He must have seen her, though he did not speak, and she wondered if he prayed or meditated. She was about to go below, unwilling to disturb his thoughts, but as she turned, he spoke.

"Good morrow, Miss—Mistress Colman. Did you fare well in the storm?" His eyes did not move from the eastern horizon.

"Yes." She hurriedly wiped her wet hands on her skirt. "My cousin would not let me leave her. I would have, but she was frantic. Otherwise I would have—" She stopped. Did she dare mention that she wanted to find him?

"You are quite a help to your cousin." He gave her a quick glance over his shoulder. "You are to be commended. Self-sacrifice is a virtue and seems to be part of your nature."

Jocelyn bit her lip. Were his words a genuine compliment, or was he simply measuring her for her role as a minister's wife?

"I serve Eleanor because I love her."

"As I serve God." His knuckles tightened on the railing. "Last night I thought God would surely sink us all, for, like Jonah, I fear I have sinned against him."

"You have sinned?" He was not making idle conversation; she could hear honest pain in his voice. She moved closer to his side. "What could you have possibly done?"

"I married you."

The words struck at Jocelyn's heart and she gasped as if he had thrown a dagger into her bosom. He continued, his words cutting her more deeply.

"In the midst of the storm last night I thought I should come here, to this very deck, and throw myself overboard to appease our angry God. Then I remembered that God prepared a great fish for Jonah, and I believe he surely would have prepared a great fish to wait for me."

"In truth, you are speaking in riddles," Jocelyn whispered, searching anxiously for the meaning behind his words. She dared to place her hand over his. "Why should our marriage be such a sin?"

"I have wronged you." He turned to face her, and his dark eyes glinted with the power and passion for which she had searched in vain as they were married. "Verily, I made a mistake in marrying you, Jocelyn White. I pray you will forgive me. It might be best if you see your uncle about having the marriage annulled."

"Annulled?" She clung to the rail for support as he pulled away. "How can you decree that you have made a mistake when I, too, have a voice in this matter? I would not have married you, sir, unless I was certain our marriage was according to God's will and favor." She gripped his arm and forced him to look at her. "I thought you saw, sir, that our marriage is the best solution for both of us. I have no one, now that my father is dead, except my uncle. And he judged it right that I marry you. I love the same God you have pledged your life to serve! I can be your helper, your friend, your companion as you undertake your work in Virginia, so why would you turn me away?"

Her breath came quickly; his eyes seemed to focus on her lips. He spoke as though dazed. "I had hoped you would refuse me. The work of the ministry demands all of a man—"

Jocelyn pulled herself up to her full height and lifted her chin. "I am strong, sir, and not easily bowed. You have reasons for regretting this marriage, but I swear I will not require much of you. You have given your word, and to cast me aside—"

He leaned closer, and she felt the powerful draw of his gaze. "Would you stay with a man thirteen years your senior?"

"Yes."

"A man of the common folk, and you being a lady?"

"In Virginia all men are equal."

"You, young and virtuous, would be wife to a man who has left his son? A man who already has buried a wife?"

"My own mother died before her time. I never faulted my father for it. And you have done what is best for your son, I have no doubt."

"You would marry an imperfect man, a man who has committed the vilest sins recorded in the Holy Scriptures?"

"Who among us has not sinned? And do not the Scriptures say that one sin is as another in the eyes of God? I am as vile a sinner as you, Thomas Colman, and as dedicated to God's service."

She felt her cheeks burning and her heart racing. She had not felt so alive in weeks! Thomas's eyes darkened with some indescribable emotion as she blazed up at him. "I understand your reluctance, for I know your character better than you think, Thomas Colman. You may believe you were wrong to marry me, but you would commit a far greater wrong if you turn me away."

He said nothing for a moment, but his look traveled up and down her. "Yes," he whispered finally, smiling as his eyes watered in the damp breeze that blew in their faces. "That would be a sin, indeed."

She caught her breath at the unexpected warmth in his words. He lifted his hand to her hair and caressed her with his eyes for a brief moment, then abruptly turned and left the quarterdeck.

Jocelyn sighed in exasperation. He saw her all too clearly, read her face like an open book, and still he kept himself carefully guarded. Did grief hold him prisoner? Very well. If he still grieved for his wife, she would be patient. But God had called her to serve with this man, and serve she would until he finally found freedom in her love.

Whatever uncertainties she had felt regarding the wisdom of

their marriage fell away, and she knew that after this moment she would never look back.

▼▲▼▲▼ "My father crossed the Western ocean in only twenty-eight days two years ago," Eleanor whispered one hot afternoon. She lay on her back upon the hard wooden floor, and her skin glistened with perspiration even though Agnes had not ceased to fan her for the last hour. "We have been at sea how long now, Jocelyn?"

"Forty and two days," Jocelyn murmured, drawing her knees to her chest under her long skirt. She rested her head on her arms. "Surely we are nearly done with this endless ocean."

"Ananias assures me so every day, but every night I find myself lying here on this floor." The ghost of a smile crossed Eleanor's face. A small twinge of discomfort fluttered across her brow, but she dismissed it with another smile. "In truth, my baby is impatient, too. He kicks in protest."

"What does the reverend your husband say, Mistress Jocelyn?" Agnes asked, a new tone of respect in her voice.

Jocelyn shrugged. "He knows no more than we do. I doubt if even Simon Fernandes knows when we will reach land."

"I heard the lookout say he spotted birds yesterday," Audrey volunteered, opening her eyes from where she lay on the floor. Jocelyn had thought her asleep, for the girl had been unusually quiet and thoughtful in the last few days. "The seamen say if birds are about, land is no more than two days away."

"I wouldn't know, bein' as I don't talk to the seamen," Agnes retorted loftily, lifting her chin. "A lady's maid shouldn't mix with the likes of them. . . ."

Jocelyn sighed and rose to her feet. She could not bear the stifling atmosphere of the confining hold for one moment more, and though she knew Fernandes had been short-tempered with any passenger who dared ascend to the upper deck, she would gladly risk a confrontation with the captain for ten minutes of the breeze in her hair.

She climbed the narrow companionway to the deck and nodded to a seaman who grinned at her. "Please, I won't get in the way, but I must have a breath of air," she whispered.

"Aye, missy, and would I be denying you breath for your pretty self? Stand over there behind the capstan, and the captain won't be seein' you for a good time. But 'twill do me eyes good just to look at you."

Jocelyn smiled her thanks and moved to the rail beside the capstan, a large, revolving drum used to raise and lower the anchor. She stood at the rail for a long time, her eyes closed. The rhythmic thump of waves against the ship, the sailors' sea songs, and the mellow creaks and groans of the ship's timbers—all were nothing but background noise now, and she thought she could hear the breathing of sea creatures, a whale, maybe, or a porpoise. Several times she had seen dolphins racing the ship, but today all was quiet on the broad expanse of the deep.

Keeping a careful eye out for Captain Fernandes, she moved toward the bow. As the bowsprit rose and fell, flecks of sea spray fell upon her cheek, and the moist Caribbean air blew through her hair. She inhaled deeply.

Ah, Audrey's sailor was right, she could smell land, a rich, earthy, humid, living scent of trees and grass and animals. . . .

She leaned dangerously forward, scanning the horizon. Clouds hung lazily between the sea and sky, but something brown did seem to rise in the distance. She turned and looked up toward the crow's nest, a question on her face.

"Yes, Mistress Colman." Simon Fernandes's voice came from directly behind her, and she jumped. "That is Dominica on the horizon. We have arrived."

"Does my uncle know?" Despite her displeasure at seeing the captain, she felt like screaming with joy.

Fernandes nodded. "I have told him myself. He wants us to land immediately, of course, but that is impossible."

Jocelyn's heart sank. "We cannot land?"

"Of course not. These are the waters of the Caribbean. The Spaniards race their treasure ships through these waters and would escape us if we were anchored in the harbor. Part of our mission, Mistress Colman, is to recapture the value of goods that have been pirated from our English ships."

"But we need water!" Jocelyn's hands gripped her skirt in rage. Could he not look at her and the others and see how badly they needed fresh food, fruit, and water for bathing? "Please, captain, let us anchor wherever we can. My cousin and Mistress Harvie are pregnant, Mistress Viccars has an infant, the young boys have grown so pale. Why, George Howe's leg is infected, and there is no fresh water to cleanse his wound—"

"We will land when I give the order," Fernandes answered, stepping back. "You are too much like your uncle, Mistress Colman. You forget who commands this ship. Now I'd like you to rejoin the others belowdecks."

Jocelyn squared her shoulders and moved past him to the companionway. It wouldn't be fair to tell the others what she'd seen. The sight and smell of land, with no hope of landing, would be too great a frustration.

The *Lion* spent the next three weeks cruising through the islands of the Caribbean. John White grew angrier with each day that he and his people were held prisoner aboard ship, but Simon Fernandes, intent upon finding and capturing the cargoes of Spanish treasure ships, cared only for piracy. After three weeks with no sign of Spanish ships, neither man was satisfied.

Finally Fernandes anchored off St. Croix and allowed his passengers three days and nights on the island. Despite her joy at being released from the filthy ship, Jocelyn looked forward to going ashore with mixed feelings. As a married woman, would she spend her nights with her husband, or would Thomas expect her to remain with the women?

Once the shallop deposited them on shore, Jocelyn no longer had time to worry. While she and several other women gathered fruits that resembled green apples, Thomas went off with a group of men to scout the seashore for food.

The green fruit proved to be poisonous, and the women who ate of it felt their mouths burning within minutes. Several of the women's tongues swelled to the point that they could not speak, and Elizabeth Viccars's nursing infant was even affected through his mother's milk.

Hours later, the group of meat hunters returned, exhausted from struggling to carry a giant sea turtle back to camp. While searching for water, another group made the mistake of bathing in a stagnant pond. The water proved to be a miasma, poisoning those who drank from or bathed in it, and caused such swelling that those who splashed their faces in it could not see for five or six days.

By nightfall, fully half the colonists lay atop palmetto fronds, moaning or retching in the sand, while the others nursed them with healthy slices of tortoise and handfuls of fresh water, finally found on the far side of the island.

Jocelyn's youth and strength had borne the poor food and conditions on the ship easily enough, but the ravages of the bitter fruit left her weak and wanting to die. Audrey lay stricken, too, and was of no help, so Jocelyn curled into a tight knot and lay quietly in the sand, her arms wrapped around her aching stomach.

"Please, Father God," she mumbled over her swollen tongue, not caring who heard her, "let this be the end. If this is what you have in store for us, show mercy and end it now."

"Such a little suffering, and yet you are ready to die?"

She opened one eye. Thomas stood above her, taller than ever, with reproach clearly written on his face.

"Go away," she muttered into the sand. "You can't know how this feels. There's nothing like it in England, and I wouldn't wish this even on you, though you probably deserve it."

He knelt beside her and lowered his voice. "Why would I deserve it?" he asked, an odd mingling of wariness and amusement in his eyes. "Have you at last come to regret our marriage?"

"I will if you don't leave me alone!"

He surprised her by laughing. She had seldom heard him laugh, and the honest and free sound made her feel better even as it made her angry.

"I'll get you some water," he said, casually brushing wayward tendrils of hair from her forehead so he could see her face. "And they're serving sea turtle soup, so I'll bring you some. If your stomach rebels from the fruit, perchance some meat will help you regain your strength."

"No. I can't eat—"

"You don't have to take it. But I'm your husband and responsible for you, so let me do my duty and bring what you require."

She groaned and clenched her hands as another spasm gripped her stomach. Thomas left, but returned a few moments later with food and a shell filled with water. He insisted she drink the water and held the scalloped shell to her lips; then he put his hand behind her head and held her upright as he offered the tortoise.

The sight and smell of the food assailed her nostrils, and Jocelyn refused it. The pressure of his hand on her head lingered a moment; then Thomas gently lowered her to the ground and sat in the sand next to her. They stared at the stars in the Caribbean sky overhead, and she retched and shuddered and sweated the poison from her system as he talked of the adventure of finding the giant sea turtle and how it had required sixteen men just to carry it back to camp. He talked of the sea, of the vastness of the ocean reaches, and of "the glory of circling God's wondrous globe with the wake of a ship, like a ribbon about a pomander orange."

Before he had finished, Jocelyn drifted into merciful slumber.

▼▲▼▲▼ After their three disastrous days on St. Croix, Simon Fernandes sent Captain Stafford and the pinnace to Vieques Island to find sheep, while the *Lion* guardedly put into port near the Spanish fort at Puerto Rico to take on fresh water. Jocelyn's uncle complained that Fernandes had made yet another poor decision, for the seamen consumed more beer during their Puerto Rico stop than the colonists gained in water.

White personally believed the sea captain's excessive drinking was born of his vexation that the flyboat, which he had maliciously abandoned during the storm off the coast of Portugal, had arrived at Dominica only two days behind the *Lion*. Apparently Captain Edward Spicer was as good a pilot as Fernandes— a fact that greatly cheered White. If not for Fernandes's indisputable expertise and the authority granted him by the colony's charter, White would gladly have had the man imprisoned for endangering the colony with his foolish quest for treasure.

As the *Lion* weighed anchor to leave Puerto Rico, John White discovered another insult—two colonists, Darby Glavin and Dennis Carrol, had crept off the ship with Fernandes's sailors and had not returned. Both were Irishmen and Catholics. White suspected immediately that the two were spies for the Spanish and considered briefly that perhaps even Fernandes was somehow in league with the deserters.

Governor White called a meeting of his assistants on the lower deck, inviting John Jones, a doctor, Simon Fernandes, and the Reverend Thomas Colman to sit in at the council meeting. Jocelyn slipped into a quiet spot behind the circle of men to satisfy her curiosity about the colony's future and to further observe her husband.

Thomas conducted himself with dignity in the meeting, giving clear, concise answers when called upon to speak, and the other assistants listened respectfully to his opinions. "Surely these two deserters pose no real danger to us," Thomas said, nodding to John White. "They are but two men—what harm could they do?"

"You don't know the Spanish," Simon Fernandes interrupted, squinting in amused condescension. "The poxy Spanish dogs have been searching for our outpost at Roanoke for years. Why should they allow a base for English privateering ships which plunder Spanish treasure? If these men tell the Spanish of our plans for a colony at Chesapeake, you can be sure the Spanish will feel well of a mind to destroy it."

Jocelyn felt her blood run cold at his words. Was it not enough that the colonists might face the fury of nature and fierce natives? Would they have to face the poleaxes of Spanish soldiers as well?

"God will protect us from the Spanish." Her husband's iron voice rang in the stillness of the circle, and no man dared refute him.

John White glared at Fernandes, then capably changed the subject. "I worry about the loss of Glavin's experience. He was with me at Roanoke in the last venture and knows much about the land, the Indians, and soldiering."

"We have the benefit of your experience," Ananias Dare spoke up. "And we have your journals from the first expedition. And we are yeomen and families, not soldiers interested in exploration. We want only to make our homes and plant our crops in fertile land, and we can do that as well in Chesapeake as we could in England."

"Aye," several voices agreed.

"We will do *better* in Virginia than in England," White answered. "We are planning to pick up orange, pineapple, banana, and mamey apple plants on another of these islands. I saw them on my previous journey and know where they can be found. Cattle and salt we will find at Rojo Bay, if—" he glared again at Fernandes—"our captain chooses to stop so we may fill our stores."

Fernandes bowed his head before the assembled company. "The safety of my ship comes first, always," he said, his dark eyes glinting with malevolence. "But surely these things can be arranged."

"After our stores are filled, then what?" the elder George Howe asked. "Are we free to sail to the Chesapeake? Already 'tis July, and I have heard that fierce storms sweep across these waters in late summer."

"We have but one other stop," White said. "After our departure from Roanoke, Grenville left a holding party of fifteen soldiers on the island to hold the land for England. I believe those lads are eager for home, so we'll stop at Roanoke and transfer them with us to Chesapeake."

"Will they join us in the colony?" John Jones asked.

"'Twill be their decision to join us or return to England," White answered.

"If it please you, sir, I have a question." John Sampson, a young assistant, spoke up. Jocelyn knew he had left his wife and small daughter waiting in London, though his twelve-year-old son accompanied him on the journey.

"Ask it, John."

Sampson looked uneasily at the floor. "I have heard, from the seamen, that the Chesapeake Bay Indians are more highly organized and warlike than those of the Roanoke area. One sailor told me of a company of Jesuits who were exterminated over ten years ago. And it is common knowledge that the Chesapeake savages attacked Amadas and his men in eighty-four. It's even rumored that the savages ate those they killed."

John White snorted in contempt. "Ridiculous. Impossible. Whether they live on Roanoke or in the Chesapeake region, savages can be cruel, but they are not cannibals. We go in God's hands, John Sampson, and we will trust his providence and our own good sense. If we treat the savages with kindness, with such will we be treated."

"Let us go forward, then!" George Howe said, raising a fist into the air.

"Aye!" several of the men shouted.

John White smiled and held up his hand. "God has not only seen fit to supply us with yeomen, coopers, a doctor, a lawyer, and a sempstress, but he has sent one of his ministers." He turned to Thomas. "Will you lead us in prayer, Reverend? Invoke the blessings of God upon us, Thomas, for we will need them in the days to come."

Jocelyn felt her heart stir with pride as Thomas stood, tall and confident, and bowed his head. Even the sailors above stopped singing as his resonant voice filled the ship, beseeching God to show mercy and grant grace to those who traveled in his name.

▼▲▼▲▼ John White's pretense of friendliness with Simon Fernandes vanished immediately after the meeting. On deck the next day White pointed out the island where they should stop for the tropical fruit trees he wanted to gather. Fernandes said such a stop was impossible but that he could procure plants and cattle for them on the island of Hispaniola, where a Frenchman called Alençon would give them supplies.

On July fourth, Fernandes sailed past the island of Hispaniola without stopping, and when White thundered onto the bridge and demanded to know why the ship had not anchored,

Fernandes said he had suddenly remembered that Sir Walter Raleigh had told him that the King of Spain had captured Alençon. Without an ally, a stop at Hispaniola would be useless.

White demanded another stop. Fernandes had promised that salt, essential for food preservation, would be found near Cape Rojo, but there was none. White persisted in voicing his grievances, and Fernandes finally agreed to stop in the Caicos Islands. After anchoring, the landing party filled the shallop and went ashore. Once on land, Fernandes withdrew with a pretty maid while the men desperately sought salt pans and hunted for fresh meat. No salt was found, but several men did catch swans, which were roasted on the beach for the meat-hungry colonists.

The only consolation for the tired and frustrated colonists lay in the knowledge that the next land they would see would be the shores of Virginia.

On July sixteenth the *Lion* and the pinnace came to an anchorage off what Fernandes believed to be Croatoan Island, but White insisted the captain had made a mistake. After three days, Fernandes agreed and led the way farther up the coast. The ships were almost wrecked on the breakfront off Cape Lookout, but due to the great vigilance of Captain Stafford in the pinnace, the ships pulled out to sea in time and finally anchored outside the narrow barrier islands on July twenty-second.

Looking at the narrow strip of brown land that bordered the ocean, John White knew he could never mistake this coastline for any other. He had last seen it one year before, on the day when Ralph Lane's expedition had fled from their guilt and certain destruction. The beach looked today just as it had on the morning of their ill-fated journey to the Indian camp, on the first day of June, 1586. As he thought of that abhorrent day, sharp regret washed over him, and images came, unbidden, to once again flood his mind: the attack on the natives, the cries of terror, the carnage, Pemisapan's severed head. . . .

A forceful slap on the back jolted White back into the present. "Begging your pardon, Governor." Roger Bailie stood beside him, his wispy blonde hair blowing in the breeze.

White blinked, remembering when and where he was, and managed a weak smile. "What is it, Roger?"

"I'd like to be in the landing party," Roger said, pointing to the revolver tucked into his belt. "I'm ready for anything that might come against us."

After his recent thoughts, the sight of a gun in mild Bailie's belt was too much to bear. "I need you to remain behind, my friend," White said, placing his hand upon the man's shoulder. "I trust no one else to look after my niece and my daughter. You'll do it, won't you?"

Frowning slightly, Roger Bailie agreed.

Jocelyn thought the coastline of Virginia largely disappointing. The long, sandy coast of the barrier islands stretched uneventfully until it disappeared into the horizon. Much of the land had been cleared by fire or washed clean by tides, and she saw little of the wild forest she had expected. Inwardly, she rejoiced that this was not the place where they would settle permanently.

Determination lay in the jut of her uncle's chin as he marched across the deck and commanded forty of the planters to go ashore. They would seek out the holding party left by Grenville, he explained to the men assembled on the deck, and learn from them the state of the country. He was curious to hear about relations with the Indians, particularly since Ralph Lane's men had left so soon after the English attack on the high chief Pemisapan.

"After that, gentlemen, we will return to the ship and sail on to the intended site of our City of Raleigh. I have written orders from Sir Walter to accomplish our goals in haste."

The men cheered, and a few women wiped the corners of their eyes with handkerchiefs, but Jocelyn kept her eyes glued upon the tall figure of her husband. Thomas had volunteered to go ashore with the other men, and for a moment an irrational fear seized her. What if savages waited even now on Roanoke Island? What if this day should prove her to be a widow without ever knowing what it was to be a wife?

Roanoke Island lay behind the strip of barrier islands, safely tucked away from the eyes of Spanish invaders, but the shallow waters surrounding it were no more than six feet deep. The *Lion* could not venture through the narrow inlet Fernandes pompously referred to as Port Ferdinando, so the smaller, more maneuverable pinnace moved into position abreast of the *Lion* to make the journey. Once the ships were joined by a gangplank, White's valiant men marched resolutely aboard the pinnace, a musket on each shoulder. Thomas Colman alone carried no weapon, and Jocelyn was not sure if she found his conviction against weapons admirable or foolish. Her uncle admired and respected the savages, but even he carried a revolver in his belt and a musket in his hand.

Once the landing party was aboard the pinnace, the women and remaining passengers crowded the leeward side of the ship and waved farewell as the sheets of the pinnace bellied taut and pulled the ship through the narrow inlet toward Roanoke. Suddenly the *Lion*'s bosun called to the seamen aboard the pinnace, "Captain Fernandes orders that these men not be brought back aboard ship. All are to be left on the island of Roanoke."

From his place on the bridge, Fernandes's dark, hawkish face broke into a confirming smile while Jocelyn's head spun. Left there! What could Fernandes be thinking? Forgetting her place, Jocelyn whirled and ran toward the captain's bridge as the men on the pinnace jerked angry fists toward the captain of the *Lion*.

"Master Fernandes, you are sorely mistaken!" she yelled up at the captain. She gathered her skirts to ascend to the bridge, and by the time she reached him, the pinnace was nearly out of sight.

"Do not worry, Mistress Colman," Fernandes said, his eyes toward the pinnace in the west. "I will allow your uncle and possibly your husband back aboard to supervise the collection of the other passengers. I assure you I am not interested in pirating your supplies and trunks of woolens."

"But Sir Walter's charter specifically commands that our colony be established at Chesapeake!"

His reply seemed rehearsed: "'Tis late in the year, and the storm season approaches. 'Tis risky for us to sail further north."

"'Tis risky for us to remain here!" Jocelyn forced herself to lower her voice, for she knew things the other passengers did not. "My uncle has told me that Ralph Lane massacred an Indian chief before he left. The savages in this area were violated and may not be friendly to us—"

Fernandes cut her off with a shrug. "Do you doubt the power of English sovereignty?" A stream of bitterness ran through his words. "Surely a handful of English could stand against a forest full of ignorant savages. Grenville's fifteen will no doubt be full of boasts."

She lowered her voice further. "Sir, I will be surprised if Grenville's fifteen men still live. You must take us to Chesapeake."

He looked at her then, and the derision and hatred in his eyes startled her. "Your uncle and people like you," he said, his voice warped with malice, "have ordered me around long enough. I am the captain of this ship, and I refuse to carry you vainglorious English any further. You will disembark here, you will build here, and the devil take any of you who would rather drown in the sea."

"You only want more time to chase Spanish treasure!"

He did not deny her accusation, but smiled, his neat row of teeth startlingly white against his dark moustache and beard. "You are too much like your uncle," he said, moving toward the sanctity of his cabin. "Troublesome and stubborn."

Jocelyn sputtered in helpless fury as the door to his cabin slammed shut; then she sank onto the wooden deck and raked her fingers through her hair. There was nothing she could do. Now she would have to find the courage to tell Eleanor and the others to gather their things. They would soon be moving to Roanoke Island, the spot her uncle expected to find littered with the bones of fifteen Englishmen.

George Howe

But I was like a lamb or an ox that
is brought to the slaughter;
and I knew not that they had
devised devices against me, saying,
Let us destroy the tree with the fruit thereof,
and let us cut him off from the land of the living.

Jeremiah 11:19

A whirlwind of emotions stirred John White's soul as the pinnace drew near Roanoke Island. Except for the horrible days following Lane's attack on the Indians, Roanoke had been a happy
place for him. He knew well the surrounding country. Many of
the neighboring savages were his friends. His eyes caressed the
familiar strip of beach and thick stand of trees, and he
wordlessly raised his arm and pointed the sailors toward the
best beach for anchoring the boat.

Silence lay upon the island as the small ship approached; the
absence of sound had almost a physical density. The quiet lap of
waves against the shore and the quickened breaths of his fellow
travelers were muffled by the strangely thickened air. Nothing
stirred on land or upon the ship until the bow of the pinnace
struck hard in the sand and heavily booted feet jostled against
the wooden deck.

Standing at the bow, White hesitated before turning to face the
men behind him. What would he tell them? Fernandes had
openly defied his authority as governor by declaring that the colonists should remain on Roanoke Island, and White's pride
urged him to demand the planters be carried on to Chesapeake.
But another voice in his head reminded him that Roanoke was
familiar, it was near Manteo's home, and much of the work
involved in building houses and a fort had already been done.

His daughter's face, swollen and tired, flitted across his mind.
Eleanor's time was near. Would it not be better to have the first
Virginian child born in a proper house, rather than aboard ship
or in a hastily constructed Chesapeake hut?

Whatever happened, he must not let his people think he had

been cowed by that cursed Portuguese. He composed his face
into stern lines and turned to face his men. "Grenville left fifteen
men here. We are to find them," he announced, placing his hand
on the revolver in his belt. "But search no farther than this island.
If you come upon any savage, stand with your weapon drawn,
but do not fire unless his intentions are clearly hostile."

The men, sallow faced and serious, nodded as one.

▼▲▼▲▼ Summoning his courage, White led the men
up the beach and down the trail that took them to the remains of
"the New Fort in Virginia," built and named by Lane's party. The
earthworks had been partially razed by the elements, but the
star-shaped wooden fort and the wattle-and-daub houses outside the walls still stood. Two buildings within the fort formerly
used for storage had been burned, but the blackened hulls
remained.

White gazed at the sight without speaking. Melon vines had
overtaken the lower floors of all the buildings, and a small herd
of deer stopped grazing among them and lifted velvet brown
eyes to stare at the interlopers. Unafraid, they lowered their
heads for a last bite before turning to amble away.

Behind him, the flintlock of a musket clicked, and White held
up a restraining hand. "Do not fire," he said, not even glancing
over his shoulder. "The noise will travel to the ears of the savages. Our advantage persists as long as they are ignorant of our
presence."

"Is there anything to fear?" George Howe asked, his pale
round face streaked with perspiration. His hands trembled upon
his musket.

"Not yet," White answered, his eyes expertly scanning the interior of the fort and the standing trees beyond the clearing.
When he was convinced they were alone, he motioned for the
men to fan out, and they walked carefully through the area surrounding the fort. Grenville's fifteen apparently had not been
here in some time, for all the fire pits had been washed clean by

rain and not a single house had been kept clear of the encroaching vines and weeds.

The sea breeze blew a cloud in front of the burning sun, and White sighed in gratitude. The heat could bake a man inside his doublet. . . .

"Governor! Here lies a man!"

The line broke, and all hurried toward Ambrose Viccars, whose trembling hand pointed to a bleached skeleton in the sand. The crushed skull lay above the tattered uniform and rusted breastplate of an English soldier, but between the elements and the area's wildlife, most of the unfortunate soldier's bones had been spirited away.

"One of the fifteen," White murmured, watching in fascination as a spider peered out at them from one of the clean sockets of the skull. "We must see if others lie nearby."

"First we must bury this man," Thomas Colman interrupted, his voice booming like thunder over the group. "'Tis our Christian duty. I must insist that we see to it immediately."

"It can wait," interjected Ananias Dare, "for if we find others, 'twould be more convenient to hold a common burial."

White glanced uneasily between the two men, both of whom were now related to him. "Reverend, do what you must with these bones," he directed, gesturing toward the skeleton. "Ananias, direct these men to fan out and search for others. Be wary. And Thomas—" White turned to Colman again—"when you are done with the burial, bestow a blessing on each of these houses. Unless Simon Fernandes proves willing to carry us forward to Chesapeake, I expect we will occupy them before nightfall."

▼▲▼▲▼ Later that afternoon, as the men continued to scour the island for signs of the living or dead, John White called his son-in-law and Thomas Colman to his side. "Would that my brother were here," he fumed, squatting in the shade of the large house that had once belonged to Governor Lane. "He would guide the decision I must make regarding Simon Fernandes. Robert was never a man of action, but he always knew his mind."

"Your decision should be simple," Ananias spoke up. "You are the governor appointed by Sir Walter Raleigh. Mutiny, if need be. With Fernandes in chains, the crew will have to sail us to Chesapeake."

"It is not that simple," Thomas interrupted, his dark eyes flashing. "You have not mingled with the seamen, Ananias, and I have walked often among them. They respect their captain and would not support us in a mutiny. 'Tis more likely they'd pitch us and our goods into the sea, for their hearts are set on capturing the treasure Fernandes has promised. We should be grateful the captain brought us this far."

"Chesapeake is a better land, with a better harbor," White said, thinking aloud. "But there's no gainsaying that the savages there are more hostile. Here we are among Manteo's people and have an ally—"

"You told us Lane mistreated the Indians here," Ananias retorted. "And if we stay, we will surely reap the consequences of Ralph Lane's folly!"

"Would you have your wife give birth aboard the ship in view of a hundred eyes?" White flamed into anger. "At least here my daughter would have a roof over her head!"

"What of the others, sir?" Thomas said, the deep baritone of his voice cooling the fevered tempers of both men. "All would be subjected to hardship if forced to remain aboard ship much longer. Perchance there is a compromise, gentlemen. Why not winter here on Roanoke and move northward in the spring? Then we will have a better idea of our situation, our women would be settled, and the savages befriended."

White rocked back on his heels, mollified. The minister spoke the truth. And as long as it was known that John White had agreed to stay at Roanoke for the good of the colony and not because of the wiles of Simon Fernandes, all would be well.

"That shall be our plan, then," White said, rising to his feet. He nodded toward the others and brushed his hands. "We will settle here immediately, put in a quick corn crop, secure peace with our savage neighbors, and move toward the Chesapeake before planting time in the spring."

He strode confidently away from the house, only dimly aware of the uncomfortable silence that had fallen between the two men he left behind.

▼▲▼▲▼ At White's command, Ananias lit a smoky signal fire on the beach, and the remaining passengers aboard the *Lion* knew it was safe to join the others. Fernandes ordered the *Lion*'s shallop to be lowered to the water so supplies and passengers could be ferried ashore. The men went first; then the shallop returned for the women. Jocelyn held Eleanor's hand as they negotiated the narrow plankway between the ship and the small boat.

"Faith, and wouldn't you know the baby's kicking," Eleanor said, laughing nervously, with one hand on Agnes's broad shoulder and the other extended backward to Jocelyn. Behind Jocelyn, Audrey squealed fearfully with each step and steadfastly refused to look down at the water beneath her feet. Jocelyn tugged at the dead weight of Audrey's hand and idly considered slapping the silliness out of the girl. Servants were supposed to be a help, not a hindrance.

Once all seventeen women were safely aboard the shallop, the small boat pulled away from the side of the *Lion* and passed through the narrow inlet between the barrier islands. To the left and right of the boat were stretches of sandy, grass-strewn shore dotted with the tallest trees Jocelyn had ever seen. Such trees were rare in England except on wealthy estates, for daily fires had consumed many of England's forests.

The island of Roanoke was a mountain of tall trees rising from the gray-brown water, and Jocelyn gasped at her first sight of it. Gnarled oaks bent low to the ground behind the shoreline, limbs growing askew as if cowering before the force of ocean winds. As the boat neared the point of landing, a group of men waved in greeting and hurried forward to lend a hand to the women, who would have to wade through the water to reach shore.

While her cousin and the servants twittered nervously and lifted their skirts to avoid the water, Jocelyn stepped confidently to the side of the boat and spurned a grinning sailor who offered to carry her. She turned and stepped instead into the cool salt water and felt the sea cover her boots and tug on her suddenly heavy skirt.

As Audrey squealed that she did not want to get wet, Jocelyn awkwardly trudged forward, her face set. The discomfort of wet clothing was of no importance. Being home was all that mattered.

▼▲▼▲▼ Ignoring the other women, who waited in an anxious knot on the beach, Jocelyn followed the wide trail of footprints in the sand and came to the fort. Inside the wooden walls she found her uncle poring over a sheaf of papers with Ananias Dare.

"Uncle," she said, pausing by his side. He glanced up at her, distracted. "I would like to know what I should do. I'm here to work."

His tired face rearranged itself into a grin. "Ah, Jocelyn, my practical niece. Well, we are fortunate, dear, that the houses still stand. There." He put his arm on her shoulder, turning her toward the opening of the many-sided fort. "The houses are grouped outside the fort, do y' see? I'll share that largest house with Ananias and Eleanor and the servants. Thirteen houses will be provided for our families; one house for the two Indians; one house for Roger Bailie, Christopher Cooper, and Thomas Stevens and their servants; and seven houses will shelter ten unmarried men each. The remaining four buildings will be storehouses for our corn, arms, and tools."

His arm fell from her shoulders, and he turned back to his notes. "You can help, dear girl, by going 'round the circle and making sure the women have found their way into their proper houses. Take this list—" he thrust a freshly marked parchment toward her—"and make your rounds as soon as possible. For today, we must leave it to you women to make the houses habitable. I need every man to prepare the fort in case of an attack."

"Yes, sir," she said, glancing over the list in her hand. With the chilling shock of recognition she saw her own name, listed as "Reverend Thomas, Mistress Jocelyn Colman, and Audrey Tappan, servant," among the family groups.

A family! She had yet to spend an hour, a single night totally alone with her husband. How could they be considered a family?

▼▲▼▲▼ Elizabeth Viccars grumbled good-naturedly about the tangle of vines carpeting her new house, but she deposited her sleeping son into the arms of Emme Merrimoth, her maid, and dismissed Jocelyn with a smile.

"'Tis better to sleep amongst vines than on that rank ship," she said, placing her hands on her ample hips as she looked around. "Don't you worry. We'll tend to our own house and not be a bother."

Next to the Viccarses' house, young Wenefrid Powell directed her four-year-old nephew, William Wythers, to run outside and help Thomas Smart, the family servant. Wenefrid was Jocelyn's age and her husband only eighteen, and for a moment Jocelyn was tempted to ask her thoughts about marriage and husbands. But Wenefrid had work to do and a youngster to watch, so Jocelyn wished her a good day and moved on to the next house.

Joyce Archard stood in the rubble of her new home with her ten-year-old son, Thomas, clinging to her skirt. The boy had been sick with a cough for the entire journey and coughed even now as he stared miserably at the house. The Archards' servant, eighteen-year-old Margaret Lawrence, stood with her hands on her hips and declared, "I'faith, I can't believe it! I would as lief sleep in the woods as in this weed patch!"

Next to the Archards, the heavily pregnant Margery Harvie tried to pluck melon vines from the mud between the logs of her house while Jane Pierce, her servant, struggled to push their trunk into the interior of the shelter. The small house next door stood in remarkably good condition, and Jocelyn saw on her list that it had been assigned to John and Jane Jones, the doctor and his wife who had no children and only one servant, Joan Warren.

Next door to the doctor, Jane Mannering had energetically set about clearing the Chapmans' house, while in the next dwelling Rose Payne of Suffolk immediately set her servant, Beth Glane, to work while she sat on a trunk to stare out a window. "Why is Eleanor Dare's house much bigger than mine?" she asked, her voice an annoying whine in the hot afternoon.

"Thou shalt do all things without murmuring or disputing," Beth answered, moving like a dark shadow through the house in her somber black kirtle and bodice. Despite the heat, the servant wore a black bonnet devoid of any decoration, and Jocelyn wondered how the spoiled Rose and devout Beth had learned to coexist. *Perhaps they balance each other,* Jocelyn thought as she moved on to the next residence.

White-haired Alice Chapman stood in the center of the clearing with a lost look on her face, and Jocelyn pointed out the house where her servant Jane was already at work. Alice's husband, John, had given up his Anglican church in Suffolk and journeyed to America with hopes of becoming a planter. If Rose Payne continued to whine, Jocelyn thought guiltily, perhaps the saintly influence of the elderly John Chapman would sweeten her spirit. In any case, the devoutly religious Beth Glane would doubtless find comfort in living so near a former cleric.

Roger Prat and his son, John, had been assigned the next house, and George Howe and his son, young George, were to be housed next to the Prats. On the door of the next deserted building Jocelyn scrawled the name of John Sampson and his son, young John.

Her uncle had assigned the next house, which was larger than most, to the unmarried assistants: Roger Bailie, Christopher Cooper, and Thomas Stevens. Bailie and Cooper each had a manservant, William Clement and James Hynde, respectively, so Jocelyn scratched the entire list of surnames onto the dried clay wall.

Manteo and Towaye would share a house, four houses were designated for storage, and seven houses would serve as barracks for the seventy unmarried men who completed the colony.

Only one building in the circle remained unaccounted for, a small house next to the governor's. It was a sad structure of clay and timber, with two drooping shuttered windows and a door that hung askew on rusty iron hinges. But like the others it had two stories and two rooms, one up and one down, though the upper room was exposed to the elements because of gaping holes in the straw-thatched roof.

Jocelyn picked up a piece of charcoal from a cold fire pit and scratched three names upon the rough-hewn doorpost: "Thomas Colman, Jocelyn Colman, and Audrey Tappan." With her work done, Jocelyn knotted her hair at the back of her neck, wiped her damp hands on her skirt, and strode inside her house to rid it of whatever evils lurked inside.

▼▲▼▲▼ Thomas paused in his work, arrested by the sight of Jocelyn's determined knotting of her hair. She marched into the house with the courage of a military general heading into battle, and the expression of her youthful enthusiasm made him smile.

Perhaps, God willing, this girl can mark a new beginning in my life, he thought, his eyes yearning for another glimpse of her. Since their marriage they had scarcely spoken, but sometimes he had the feeling he could feel her thoughts. She was watching and waiting for him to take command, with no idea of the power she held in her own hands. She did not know that he had been immediately and totally attracted to her, that a single disapproving glance from her blue eyes had the ability to send a wave of dismay along his pulses—

With a jerk of his head, Thomas chastised himself yet again. Curse his faithless heart! Would he always be so easily drawn to the girl and her charms? He breathed a sigh of thanks that she knew nothing of her effect on him and determined that that was how things should remain. Despite the feeling of streaming hope that poured from his heart, Jocelyn could not become emotionally involved with him, for he would only hurt her—as he had hurt everything and everyone in his life. Even himself . . .

And yet the sound of her voice as she raised it in song stirred a response in him as age-old as the sea.

▼▲▼▲▼ When Audrey finally arrived at the house, Jocelyn sent her maid back to the beach to fetch the trunks that contained all their worldly goods. Thomas stopped by once in the afternoon, remarked upon the good progress she had made, and promised to bring his trunk himself. "You could not carry it," he said, his eyes smiling as he seemed to measure the strength of her slender frame. "I'm afraid 'tis full of books. Not very useful here, but I couldn't imagine leaving them behind."

He left before she could think of a reply, and so she continued working. She pulled weeds from the walls, brushed dead leaves from the floor, and swept spiderwebs from the ceiling with a limber tree branch. In one corner of the house she found a gigantic nest of ants in the earthen floor. As she shoveled the nest from the house, the aggressive insects swarmed over her hands, and Jocelyn yelped in pain. She slapped them away, crying in frustration, and when welts rose on her fingers she ran to the beach to immerse her hands in the cool sea water.

All of the houses around the fort were built with two floors, but after stacking her trunk atop Audrey's and cautiously climbing high enough to peer into the attic space, Jocelyn knew the upper floor would not be habitable for a long time. The thatched roof had long been blown away, and rain had rotted the timber flooring in several places. The unmistakable odor of animal droppings assaulted her nostrils as soon as she lifted the trapdoor leading into the attic room, and Jocelyn was relieved to drop the door and concentrate instead on the lower floor of the house.

They could live in the lower room for months if they had to. She, Audrey, and Thomas. And since her husband had married her only to safeguard his respectability, he was certainly in no rush for a private bedchamber.

As the sun began its slow glide into the west, a horn blew from the direction of the sea. Jocelyn wiped her dirty, blistered hands on her skirt and straightened her back. She felt brittle, as if any sudden movement would snap her in two like a twig. Audrey had disappeared hours before, and as Jocelyn stepped out into the gathering gloom, she started in surprise when Thomas appeared at her side.

"Your uncle says we must sleep on the ship until the fort is ready," he said, peering past her into the house. "Are you ready to go?"

"Yes," she snapped, irritated at his apparent appraisal of her work. "I'm tired. I don't know what you did all day, but I worked hard."

"I know you did," he answered, stepping away from the door. He extended his hand. "Shall we walk to the boat together?"

She nodded, then blushed in pleased surprise when he took her filthy hand in his. "You have worked harder than the others," he said as they began to walk, his deep voice lifting the hairs on her arm. "I went to each house to ask for God's blessing, and I am amazed at what you have accomplished. Rose Payne has done nothing but sit and look out her window. Even with her servant's help, her house will have melons growing from its seams well into the fall."

Jocelyn laughed, and something seemed to glow in Thomas's eyes. "And what else did you do today, besides exhausting yourself in prayer?" she asked, taking care to keep her voice light.

"I buried a man long dead," Thomas said, pulling her arm through his while he held her hand. "And even I, who am no surgeon, could see that the man's skull had been cleft by a war ax."

His thoughts seemed to drift away as they joined the stream of others headed back to the shallop and the nighttime safety of the ship at anchor. But it wasn't the thought of the ship that Jocelyn found most comforting—it was the warmth of Thomas's hand around her own.

The next morning Eleanor Dare sat helplessly on the lid of her trunk and listened to Agnes scold ten-year-old Thomas Humfrey, her father's young servant. The boy was slow, was easily distracted, and did not work to Agnes's satisfaction, but was that reason enough to fill the air with a never-ending stream of reproach?

"Agnes, I shall leave you alone," Eleanor said, pushing her ponderous weight from the trunk. "I am of no help. The upper room must be readied for my father, the back room for Ananias—"

"Never fear, mistress," Agnes said, abruptly turning from the boy to her lady. "A walk will do you good."

"I doubt it," Eleanor muttered under her breath, but she did feel better once she had left the somber darkness of the house and stepped into the clearing outside. The late morning air was bathed in honey-thick sunshine, and the bustle of a hundred busy colonists stood in delightful contrast to the claustrophobic captivity of the ship.

Next door, Audrey Tappan slapped a rug into submission, and dust particles floated lazily in the sunshine. Jocelyn and Thomas stood in front of the house, sorting a pile of freshly chopped branches.

"Watch, Jocelyn, and see how this tool strips the bark from the branch." Thomas's rich baritone carried through the noise of the colony, and Eleanor put aside all thoughts of a walk and settled into the shade of an oak tree to watch her cousin. Jocelyn's expression was concentrated on the tool and the branch in her hand, yet tenderness lay in the curve of Thomas's arm as he guided her, and his voice gentled as he spoke to his wife.

Why, the minister behaves as if he really loves her! The idea struck Eleanor with a tingle of delight. *And Papa thought the man would marry only to avoid indentured service!*

The idea that her headstrong cousin might indeed find love brought a smile to Eleanor's lips, but the smile faded when Audrey's strident brogue broke the concentration of the newlywed pair. How could a couple who were practically strangers learn to love each other with their maid always around? Jocelyn and Thomas had had no time alone on the ship and would have no time alone together as long as Audrey slept an arm's distance away.

The baby kicked, hard, and Eleanor pressed her hand to her lower back and sighed. She would have to do something about Jocelyn and the minister. As soon as her father gave permission for the colonists to remain ashore at night, she would.

▼▲▼▲ Later that afternoon Eleanor slipped away from her house and went in search of Reverend Colman. The sun glared hotter than it ever had in England, or was it carrying the baby that took her breath away? She leaned against a tree and took a handkerchief from her bosom to wipe her forehead. If she did not find the minister soon, she was likely to melt in the heat. . . .

But then he strode out of the fort on the path toward the houses, his long stride erasing the distance between them. "Reverend Colman, I would have a word with you," Eleanor called, waving feebly at the minister as he walked by.

"Mistress Dare? How can I help you?" he asked, stopping. His manner was aloof and properly formal, but Eleanor had no patience for propriety.

"I want to ask you about my cousin." She had to make an effort to breathe slowly to avoid panting in the heat.

"Jocelyn? Surely it would be more appropriate for you to speak to her—"

"I want to know why you married her."

His face darkened, and for a moment Eleanor regretted her forthrightness.

"Surely you know the story, else you would not ask."

"My father has told me," she said, pausing to wipe her forehead again, "about the arrangement of the marriage. What he has not told me—" she made an effort to smile—"is that love has begun to bloom in your arid heart. Surely 'tis so, Reverend Colman, for I see things—"

"Things, madam, that you ought not to see. A man's relationship with his wife is entirely private." He thrust his hands behind his back as a mask of indifference covered his face.

"But how can these things be . . . private . . . when a lady's maid will sleep in the same room?"

He flushed and looked away, and Eleanor wondered that a man could have reached thirty years of age with such delicate sensibilities. She pulled herself upright. "What I want to do, Reverend, is help you win your own wife. Jocelyn is uncertain of men; she has no experience. But she holds you in the greatest respect and admiration, and I believe she might be won to your heart as well as to your side if you will but put forth an effort."

He did not laugh or grow angry, but stood silent, his hands still behind his back. After a moment, he looked down at the ground and gently nudged a mound of earth with his boot. "How do you intend to help?"

Ah, she had him. "I intend to beg for Audrey's help on the first night we remain ashore here in the fort," Eleanor explained, lowering her voice. "You will be alone, Reverend, with your wife. Whatever else you do is entirely up to you."

For a moment, a hopeful gleam shone in his eye; then his face emptied of expression. "Have you anything else to say?" he asked, bowing formally.

"No."

"Then I give you good day, Mistress Dare."

▼▲▼▲▼ As he joined in the work of building a new colony, Thomas could not forget Eleanor Dare's words. They rattled in his brain as he hauled supplies from the beach; they pricked

his heart as he dug new trenches behind the earthworks surrounding the fort. Governor White had decreed that mornings
were to be spent in unloading the ships and afternoons in
rebuilding the homes and structures of the fort. All the men
seemed eager for both phases of the work, for at last they had
found a home, and the sandy soil, now claimed as English land,
felt good under their feet.

Thomas was even surprised to discover how pleasing the
aches and pains of hard work could be. He had never really
known menial labor, preferring in the past to expend his energy
in studies and reading. But on Roanoke he doffed his cloak and
doublet and worked like a common laborer with the other men.
It was rough work, but satisfying, and after a few days Thomas
knew he could stand with the others and take pride in the
English city that would rise from the sweat of their brows and
the strain of their muscles. Elizabeth's proud men, they were, out
to tame the Virginian wilderness.

The afternoon following his encounter with Eleanor, Thomas
joined a crew of men pounding timber posts into the ground. *I
could have fared well as an indentured servant,* he told himself as
sweat trickled down his back. *It would have suited me. So why,
God, did you lead me to marry Jocelyn and retain a place in your service?*

He had to admit his young wife was beautiful and virtuous.
All spoke of her with respect, and he well knew how her startlingly blue eyes could flash with passion and keen intellect. His
heart had been smitten on that first day when he saw her storming across the decks calling for her uncle, but his head would not
allow him to love her. Love was but the foil of popinjays, a foolish expenditure of emotion. A man ought to love God, and God
only. *He that loves father or mother more than me . . .*

But Jocelyn held tender feelings for him. He could see it in her
glance, in the gentle way she inclined toward him when they
spoke together. He had never dreamed she would agree to marry
him. In truth, on the day when he had emerged from the stinking
orlop deck caked in filth, he had hoped she would run from his

proposal as if the hounds of hell were giving chase. But she hadn't. Somehow, through some miracle, she had agreed to give herself to him.

Did he feel so grateful that he had begun to act the part of husband? Eleanor Dare said she saw signs of love. Thomas did not know how that could be so, for after his wife's death he had vowed never to love a woman again. But Jocelyn did move him . . . he could not help but admire her gentleness and wit, and despite his chaste intentions he found himself enticed by her eyes and the tangled ringlets of her hair. What man would not want to ensnare his fingers in that golden brown mesh?

Of all the women aboard ship, only she had a glance with the power to make his heart pound like a drum. Was it only a fleshly response to her beauty or a God-given impulse? Thomas could not tell, but the carefree days of sun and wind and seashore had relaxed him. He had no real ministerial duties yet, no reason to position himself as an example or rein in his thoughts.

Why not woo the woman who had become his wife?

▼▲▼▲▼ On July twenty-fifth, the fourth day of work, a horn blew unexpectedly from the *Lion* at midday. Nervous flutterings pricked Jocelyn's chest as her uncle and a group of his assistants raced toward the beach. With oars askew in panic, the men in the shallop set out immediately for the ship while Eleanor and Agnes clutched each other in fear. Had Spaniards attacked? Had the two deserters sealed the colonists' doom in their eagerness to be free?

The men and women remaining on Roanoke rushed to secure the fort in case of attack. Jocelyn and Audrey left the field where they had been planting and raced to the fort with the others. Edward Powell appointed armed men to stand atop the earthworks to scout for enemies, and Jocelyn found her eyes wandering throughout the milling crowd. Thomas was nowhere in sight. Had he gone with the shallop back to the ship?

The shallop returned within the hour, however, and John

White and his assistants wore triumphant smiles as they stepped ashore. "Captain Spicer's flyboat has finally arrived, with Manteo and Towaye safely aboard," White reported to the anxious colonists who streamed from the safety of the fort. "There is no need to fear this day. Our colony is complete."

The arrival of the flyboat brought great cause for rejoicing, for the boat contained not only the Indians and additional men for the colony, but badly needed stores of wheat, tools, and goods for eventual bartering with the Indians.

That night White welcomed the new men with a great feast inside the fort. As the colonists gathered around the large fire pit where two deer roasted over the flames, the governor proudly reported that the City of Raleigh at Roanoke, now complete, would sleep this night under its own protection and upon English soil.

From her place near her uncle, Jocelyn's eyes searched round the circle of celebrants until she spied Thomas. He wore a white cotton shirt that was open at the neck and smudged with dirt. Bronzed from four days in the blistering sun, his hair unkempt and touching his shoulders, he looked taller, darker, and less like a minister than ever. She had not seen him all day, and the sight of his easy, relaxed smile above the fire made her catch her breath.

She watched him in fascination. The past days of hard work had calmed him somehow, and Jocelyn had never seen him in this light. Kneeling by the fire, one arm carelessly resting on his knee, Thomas joked with the men at his side, drank freely from the mug of ale passed round the circle, and even joined in one of the sea shanties the men began to sing:

Oh, the gov'nor is a gentleman of rank and sway,
The sea will prove his fortune should he go her way.

Jocelyn felt someone nudge her shoulder. "Don't be thinkin' I don't see you peerin' at your husband," Audrey said, sinking to

Jocelyn's side in the sand. "He looks right handsome at this moment, I'd have to agree."

"Yes, he does," Jocelyn whispered, turning from the sight of the men with reluctance. She gave Audrey a teasing smile. "And who would you be watching amongst yonder men?"

"Ah, 'tis no secret, that," Audrey answered, swiveling her blue eyes toward another group of men across the circle. "It's a bit strange, mind you, but William's gone and said he wants to marry me as soon as he's able."

"You'd leave me?" Jocelyn pretended to be shocked, though she had been aware of Audrey's infatuation with William Clement for over a month. "Faith, Audrey, what would I do without you?"

Audrey pushed her bottom lip forward in a pout. "You'd do fine, and you know it, miss. Anyway, we're supposed to be free to choose our own course here in Virginia and—"

"You are free," Jocelyn answered, leaning against Audrey's shoulder affectionately. "If you want to marry William Clement, I'll not stop you. But I hear he's bound to Roger Bailie for life, so he'll have to gain Master Bailie's permission."

"Aye, but 'e won't be bound long. Master Bailie is sixty years if he's a day," Audrey pointed out. "And mayhap he's a kind-hearted soul who wouldn't be against a servant marrying. I'd serve Master Bailie, too, if I could be married to William. He'd be gettin' two pairs of hands, he would, and at his age, he's likely to be needing them."

The flames of the fire before them danced in the wind, and Jocelyn let her eyes follow a stream of sparks that whirled off into the darkness. "I'll miss you, Audrey," Jocelyn said, nudging her maid.

The younger girl's lip quivered, and she threw her arms around Jocelyn. "In truth, I'll miss you, too, miss. But 'tisn't like we'll never see each other again."

"Not in this place," Jocelyn answered, laughing.

Audrey released Jocelyn and looked at the ground. "Besides, it would be well done, me marryin' or movin' out," she whis-

pered. "I know you are anxious to be alone with your new husband—"

"Cry you mercy," Jocelyn answered, jerking away in sudden
annoyance. Hadn't the girl seen anything? Thomas had scarcely
spoken to her since their marriage, and surely he was in no
hurry to spend a night alone with his wife.

"Audrey," she said, smiling at the girl, "you may stay with me
as long as you like. Mark me, I'm in no hurry to have you away."

John White stood and removed his cap. "I believe it is time to
ask God's blessing on our settlement here," he said, looking
around the circle until his eyes stopped on Thomas Colman.
"Will you, Reverend, lead us in a prayer?"

An almost imperceptible change seemed to come over
Thomas as he stood. The casual smile disappeared; his face
lengthened; his eyes instantly became more somber. It was
almost as if he had donned his black doublet and cloak, Jocelyn
thought, though he still wore the rough work shirt of the day.

The minister thrust his hands behind his back, deepened his
voice, and frowned as he bowed his head. But despite the seriousness of his demeanor, his voice surrounded the company like
a warm embrace in the chill air of early evening: "Our Master
and God, we stand before thee as unworthy creatures who dare
to beg for thy guidance, wisdom, and protection in the days
ahead. We thank thee for bringing our brothers to us safely. We
thank thee for these houses and supplies we found waiting here.
We thank thee for this food, these fellow workers, these leaders
who labor under thy divine grace. Protect us, O God, and keep
us from sin. In the most holy name of Christ, our Lord, amen."

Jocelyn lifted her eyes, stirred by the beauty of his words. No
memorized petitions from the *Book of Common Prayer* or oft-
quoted psalms for Thomas. His words came easily, as if he spoke
to God often.

Suddenly she felt the admiring and faintly jealous eyes of
other women upon her, and she blushed and looked at the
ground. She had spent all day planting wheat with the other
women, and not once had any of them remarked upon her mar-

riage. But now that they had seen him in the firelight and heard his voice of authority, well . . .

She lifted her head and gave all who watched her a tight, defiant smile. *He does not love me,* she wanted to tell them. *Though I sleep in his house and share his name, his heart will never be mine. Envy me not.*

The other women, seeing her smile, turned away without a word, save for the devout and most pious Beth Glane, whose eyes burned with disapproval.

▼▲▼▲▼ After the festive dinner of venison, dried peas, and dandelion greens, the women stood to put the utensils away while the men banked the fire for the night. Eleanor came near and tugged gently on Jocelyn's sleeve. "I pray you, dear Coz," she whispered, "lend me your maid tonight. Agnes is frightened to sleep alone in her room, and you will have your husband for company."

Jocelyn's smile froze on her face. Send Audrey away? She couldn't face Thomas alone, but if Eleanor's request was sincere—

"Is anything amiss, Mistress Colman?" Thomas's voice cut through her thoughts like a hot knife through butter. He had come to stand behind her as the company broke up, and Jocelyn was so distracted by his presence that she could not answer.

"I need your Audrey tonight," Eleanor said, nodding formally out of respect to the minister. "Agnes fears an Indian attack and will not sleep alone till we have passed a night safely in this place. Indeed," she laughed and smiled, "I don't know if Agnes will ever be willing to sleep alone."

"I don't think I can spare—," Jocelyn began, sputtering helplessly, but Thomas raised a hand and smiled at Eleanor.

"If you have need of anything, Cousin, you have but to ask. We will send Audrey to you immediately."

"My thanks to you," Eleanor said, dimpling, and Jocelyn

stared at her husband through a lace of confused thoughts. Why
would he send Audrey away? Could he possibly want—

Nay. The voice of common sense interrupted her flight of fan-
tasy. *He has agreed to send Audrey because ministers naturally want
to serve others.* Eleanor had a need; he was happy to meet it. And
as a minister's wife, she would have to be among the first to vol-
unteer her servant, her time, her energy. She felt her cheeks burn
with shame. He must think her terribly selfish for trying to keep
Audrey at her side.

"Have I done anything to displease you?" Thomas's voice
was low in her ear.

"No," she said, tipping her mouth in a faint smile. "You have
done nothing amiss."

▼▲▼▲▼ Night had spread its dark mantle fully over
the island by the time guards were posted and the families sent
to their homes. Raucous laughter echoed from the barracks of
the unmarried men, and Jocelyn wished for a moment that the
houses were lined in rows rather than in a circle—it felt strangely
indecent to slip through the doorway of her house with her husband while ten single men across the way watched with indolent
eyes as she closed the low door and barred it shut.

The interior of the house was as black as pitch, and Jocelyn
laughed nervously as Thomas stumbled among their few furnishings to find the lantern.

"I'm sorry, but I haven't been here since this morning," she
said, rubbing her hands briskly over her arms to fight off a sudden chill. The sleeves she wore were fresh from her trunk, as was
the bodice and kirtle. The dress was of common fabric and
undecorated, but the color was deep blue, the same shade as her
eyes—had he noticed? Despite the rough, workday fabric of the
dress, she had felt like a queen in a ball gown when she put it on.
It was a glorious difference after over ten weeks of rough shipboard life in her old dress.

She heard Thomas's footstep on the small hearth she had dug

and laid with stones; then the metallic sound of the box that held a glowing lump of charcoal. His face leapt from the darkness as he held a long wick to the coal, but there was no look of the minister about him now. In the loose, open-collared work shirt, with his dark hair askew and windblown, he seemed a pirate worthy of battle even with Simon Fernandes.

In a moment the wick was ablaze; in another the lamp was lit.

Jocelyn gasped as light filled the room. When she had left the house earlier, the only furnishings inside were three trunks, a small table, and a wooden stool, but now a bed dominated the corner of the room. It was a proper bed, too, with four rough-hewn posts, curtains of white cambric, and a stuffed mattress. She could not speak, but shifted her gaze from the bed to the amazing stranger who stood beside her.

His eyes, dark as the night, swept her face for a response. "Do you like it?" he asked, his voice low and searching. "I wanted you to be surprised."

"I am," she whispered, barely able to find her voice. She put her hand on the bedpost and felt the raised grain of the newly stripped wood. He had carved the posts, hammered the frame, stuffed the mattress . . . all for her? No other man in the colony had done as much for his wife; not even Eleanor would sleep tonight in a bed as fine as this one. But then again, Eleanor slept not with her husband for the first time.

Jocelyn felt her cheeks flood with color. She turned to the wall and studied the distance between their shadows, pretending to fumble with the sleeves on her dress. "But you shouldn't have troubled yourself so," she said, uncomfortably aware that her voice trembled. "I believe I don't deserve such a—such an effort. I would as lief sleep on the floor like the others, in a blanket like on the ship. . . ."

As her voice trailed off, she heard him place the lamp on the table; then his shadow loomed closer until it swallowed hers completely. "You deserve this and more, Jocelyn Colman," he said, his voice low and tense—the voice of conviction, finality, faith. "If you are set upon being my wife, as God is my judge and witness, I will treat you with the respect and honor you deserve."

She felt his hands on her shoulders, and the pressure of his touch ran down through her arms and prickled her skin. "You are kind, and I appreciate your efforts on my behalf," she said, abandoning the useless pretense of fussing with her clothing. She turned to face him, and his hands fell to her elbows, but still he held her.

"You are kind," she began again, but she made the mistake of looking up. His dark eyes moved into hers, and then she could feel nothing but his hands on her arms, hear nothing but the rush of his breath that came quickly now and more raggedly than when he had been laboring in the hot sun.

"Jocelyn, I must know," he said, drawing her so near that she could hear the pounding of his heart. "Are you willingly my wife? Does it truly please you to remain with me?"

"Yes," she answered, her common sense skittering into the shadows of the room as she lifted her head to look at him again. "*You* please me, Thomas Colman."

She felt her heart skip as his lips met hers, and she could feel the telling heat in her face as an unexpected tremor of pleasure shook her. He kissed her, again and again, and Jocelyn let herself go where he led her, lost somewhere between disbelief and enchantment.

A howling wind outside brushed the last webs of sleep from Jocelyn's mind, and she awoke to see dawn brightening through the bed curtains. Beside her, Thomas's place was empty, and she shivered, unaccustomed to the thought of a man sharing her bed.

She sat up and hugged her knees. The night she had dreaded had come and gone, and never would she think of marriage in the same light. No wonder Eleanor twittered with delight when talking about her husband! But, she sternly reminded herself, Thomas had done all out of gratitude, not love. Even last night as she lay in his arms near sleep, he had turned to her and whispered, "I give you thanks, Jocelyn Colman."

The gift of the bed, the surprise, and his gentle attention had been a demonstration of gratitude, payment for the work she would do and the role she would play as the minister's wife.

But, a sly inner voice mocked her, *such gifts could make life vastly rewarding. . . .*

Last night, after Thomas had fallen asleep, she had relit the lamp and sat up, hugging her knees, to ponder her thoughts. Her husband stirred in sleep, and when his arm moved in her direction Jocelyn had to fight her modest impulse to pull away lest he touch her. She was his wife, he was her husband, and they had a right to each other.

What did the Word of God say? Words she had often read but never before fully understood had come to her mind: "The wife hath not power of her own body, but the husband: and likewise also the husband hath not power of his own body, but the wife."

A smile tugged at the corner of her mouth. Her father, God rest his soul, would probably be momentarily shocked to see her in this man's bed, but she knew he would approve of Thomas Colman. And though she had few memories of her father and mother together, she knew their love contained the elements she and Thomas had just shared.

She had been about to put out the light when a word from her husband stopped her.

"Jocelyn." She froze, arm outstretched, and waited.

"Did you call?" She whispered the words.

He had grunted as if only half hearing, and with a sigh of relief, she realized he still slept. Yet he had called her name. Perchance he dreamed of her.

Intrigued with the idea, she held the lamp high and studied his face for a sign of what he might be dreaming. Seen in the dim lamplight, his dark good looks captivated her totally. He was so unlike her father's young students, who had flirted outrageously with her. His was the face of a serious and dedicated man. Even in sleep, intelligence and hard-bitten strength were etched into every feature. She had always thought him lean, but his shoulders were broad, the skin around his neck faintly reddened where his collar had lain open in the summer sun.

She had put out a finger and gingerly lifted a lock of his glossy dark hair from his forehead, then smiled when it fell back into place. "I love you, Thomas Colman," she whispered, watching his face for a response. He did not move, and after tenderly placing a kiss on his ear, she had blown out the light.

The sudden sound of footsteps outside the house brought her out of her reverie, and Jocelyn sprang up and closed the bed curtains behind her. After a discreet knock at the door, Audrey came into the house. "Good morrow to you, Miss," the maid said, lifting an eloquent eyebrow at the sight of the new bed in the room. "I hope you'll not be tellin' me I've come too early."

"No," Jocelyn said, slipping into the blue skirt and bodice she'd worn the day before. "Thomas—I mean, Reverend Colman has already gone. I'll be out of your way in a moment, Audrey."

She ignored the sly grin on her maid's face as she fastened the buttons on her bodice. "Have you seen my husband this morning?"

"No, Miss," Audrey answered, taking a seat on the stool by the cold hearth. What a silly grin the girl wore!

"Well, I'll be right to work, should anyone ask where I am," Jocelyn said, searching for her bonnet. "I just want to have a word with Thomas—"

Still smiling, Audrey retrieved Jocelyn's bonnet from the floor and held it up with a flourish. "It's a bit strange, don't you think, that the bride should be askin' about the bridegroom?" Audrey asked as Jocelyn took the bonnet and tied it under her chin. "Lost him so soon, have you?"

"He was up and out early this morning," Jocelyn answered, stepping into her slippers. She paused at the door and turned to her maid. "I'll be working in the maize field again today, Audrey, so I'd be pleased if you'd join me there later."

"Aye, Miss." Audrey looked as though she would burst out laughing at any moment, and Jocelyn hurried out of the house and slammed the door behind her. Oh! It was bad enough she had to face her maid after her first night alone with her husband, but how could she modestly explain Thomas's handcrafted bed?

"Would that this island were not so small," Jocelyn muttered, heading toward the beach where Thomas was likely to be working. "A man and his wife must have their privacy."

▼▲▼▲▼ She found her husband in a brigade line moving casks of supplies from the shallop to the fort. He wore dark work breeches and the same white shirt, open in the heat, and moved with masculine power and ease as he worked. Jocelyn thought him more handsome and appealing than ever, and she felt like a silly schoolgirl as she hid behind a tree and whispered, "Thomas!"

One of the seamen heard her, spied her hiding place, and came forward gallantly to take Thomas's place in line. "There's a pretty wench that wants to speak with you, Reverend," the seaman said, winking as the other men roared in laughter. "Hiding in the trees, she is."

Thomas's smile faded slightly as he came toward her, but she took his hand and led him deeper into the woods, out of sight and away from the others. He moved stiffly now, reluctantly, and for a moment she wondered if she had made a mistake.

She stopped in a clearing and whirled to face him. "You left this morning without saying good-bye," she said, struggling to contain her emotions. Was he not glad to see her? With all they had shared in the past hours . . .

"I am your husband. I will return tonight," he answered, his dark eyes sweeping her face. "Is it necessary for me to bid you farewell every time I leave my house?"

"No," she whispered, turning away, her heart dropping. *Dear God, will I never stop making mistakes? The man does not love me, not in the least. But how is it possible that he could be one man by night and another by day?*

"Do you have something else to say?" he asked, his eyes searching her face like a lantern. His voice was cool, distant.

"Nothing of importance," she answered, her heart sinking.

She forced herself to meet his gaze, and for a moment she caught tiny twin reflections of herself in his dark eyes: a wide-eyed girl in work dress and bonnet with silvery tears upon her cheeks.

"Yes," he said, nodding grimly at the sight of her tears. "Now you are sorry that you married me."

Bewildered at the change in his attitude, she could not answer. Last night he had been strong and sure—he *had* felt something for her, she knew it—but now he stood locked away from her, his heart imprisoned in some glacial palace where she was not allowed.

"I am sorry for yesternight, Jocelyn," he whispered gruffly, his hand lifting her face to his. The veil behind his eyes lifted long enough for her to see his compassion, and she suddenly understood. He believed he had failed her somehow, had done her a great injustice. . . .

He had not.

"I am not sorry," she said, mustering all her pride. She lifted her chin and clenched her fists at her side. "I regret nothing but the sins that I have done, and marrying you was no sin, Thomas Colman."

His lips parted in a reluctant smile, and before she knew what had happened, he slipped his arm about her waist. Her heart fluttered as his breath whispered on her cheek. "You are a delightful girl," he said, crushing her to him as she trembled in his arms. "That God should see fit to bring you to me—"

She interrupted him with a bold kiss, and he returned it, knocking her bonnet from her head in his ardor. Laughing, she pulled away and bent to retrieve her bonnet, and he knelt beside her in the grass, pulling her into his arms again. Smiling against her mouth, he kissed her slowly as insects buzzed in the trees and birds twittered in the bush, and Jocelyn's mind idly drifted to thoughts of the first man and woman who celebrated their life and love in a similar garden. . . .

"Reverend Colman!"

The horrified trumpeting of disapproval poured like ice water over Jocelyn's soul. Thomas must have felt the same sensation, for he tensed and stared toward the interloper with fire in his eyes.

Not knowing whether to blush or giggle, Jocelyn turned around. Beth Glane stood behind a screen of leafy shrubbery, a pillar of black from her boots to the bonnet tied securely under her condemning chin. Behind Beth stood Ananias Dare and the doctor, John Jones.

Thomas stood to his feet without a word while the trio of visitors came forward. Beth Glane shook her head in shock and dismay.

Jocelyn quickly replaced her bonnet.

"I wouldn't fault a man for sporting with his own wife, Reverend," Ananias said quietly, "but we have need of you. The boy William Wythers has stolen an apple from the storeroom, and

Governor White has called for you. The council must convene and decide what must be done."

"An apple?" Jocelyn felt the words slip from her tongue before she could stop them. The council found it necessary to convene over a stolen apple?

"There is more," Beth Glane said, pressing her lips together in a thin line. "Joyce Archard's son, Thomas, is ill, and prayers must be said. But you, Reverend Colman—" Her words sputtered away, but it was clear from her tone that Beth Glane didn't believe the prayers of a man who kissed in public would avail much.

"I'll come at once," Thomas said, moving away from Jocelyn. The mask had again settled over his dark features, and Jocelyn felt her hope slip away as her husband moved toward the invading trio.

"Sirrah, I must have a word with you before we go," John Jones spoke up. The doctor pulled back his shoulders and lifted his heavy jaw. "Know you not the Scriptures that command the clergy to remain sober, temperate, and to exercise self-control at all times? You have forgotten that Scripture today, sir. And this young girl here—" the finger he pointed at Jocelyn shook with anger—"this girl is of an age to be your daughter, and she's the second wife you've taken."

Beth Glane's homely face rearranged itself into a grim smile. "I've had my doubts about you all along, Reverend," she said, folding her hands primly, "and will talk to the governor and our council about removing you at once. What I've seen here today leads me to believe that you are not fit to lead the flock of God in this colony, and I'll stand with Doctor Jones to give witness to the questionable character of this girl and you, reverend sir!"

Thomas's face darkened. "The character of my wife is not at issue here," he snapped, all goodwill gone from his voice. "If you have anything against me, you may speak your mind before the council. Until then, I trust you will keep your peace and hold your tongues, lest your lives be as rigorously examined as mine."

Without a further word, Thomas passed through the group of

inquisitors, leaving Jocelyn to stand helpless before them until Beth Glane dismissed her with a contemptuous glance.

▼▲▼▲▼ Jocelyn learned the results of the council meeting later that afternoon. William Wythers, the freckle-faced, red-haired four-year-old nephew of Edward and Wenefrid Powell, was pronounced guilty of thievery and sentenced to ten lashes with a switch. And since the boy had no father, Thomas Colman, as spiritual leader of the colony, was directed to administer the whipping.

Audrey brought the news as Jocelyn worked in the fields, and Jocelyn dropped her basket of corn kernels and ran toward the fort where the whipping was to take place. Colony discipline wasted no time and invited no mercy, for by the time Jocelyn reached the village, the assistants stood as a dark circle inside the fort, ready to administer and observe the enforcement of justice.

Jocelyn felt her heart pound as she slipped through the circle of curious colonists. The child's sobbing reached her ears long before she saw his tear-streaked face. His guardians, Edward and Wenefrid Powell, stood to the side, sober-faced, as John White handed a limber green branch to the minister.

Thomas nodded to two assistants, who picked the child up and laid him upon a rough table. The boy's breeches were pulled down, exposing the fair skin, and Jocelyn felt herself shudder at the sight of the boy's terrified face.

"'Obey them that have the rule over you, and submit yourselves: for they watch for your souls, as they that must give account, that they may do it with joy, and not with grief: for that is unprofitable for you,'" Thomas quoted, his stentorian voice echoing in the stillness of the fort. The news of this first public chastisement had traveled rapidly. Mothers and fathers widened the circle and pushed their children to the fore to witness the example another child would set. "You, William Wythers, have stolen from the common storehouse, a grievous offense. We will discipline you today and spare your soul for tomorrow."

Thomas paused and seem to search through the crowd until his eyes met Jocelyn's. *Spare him; be gentle,* she begged silently, knowing that her countenance revealed the revulsion she felt toward this harsh act. Surely he could voice his opinion that ten lashes were too much for a small, hungry boy. . . .

"'Chasten thy son while there is hope, and let not thy soul spare for his crying,'" Thomas said abruptly, denying her unspoken plea. His arm rose and fell sharply, William Wythers screamed, and the crowd emitted a collective gasp. Jocelyn clenched her fists and hurried away from the unbearable sight and sound.

▼▲▼▲ The elder George Howe grimaced with each blow, thankful that, thus far, his son had brought him no reason for shame. When the whipping was done, the gathering dispersed and the Powells took their nephew home. "A bad business, this," Howe said, nodding politely to the minister. "But it set a fine example to the other young ones, don't you think?"

"Certainly," the minister replied, his dark eyes squinting toward the cloudless sky in the east. "It will be an example to all of us. Now, if you'll excuse me, Master Howe, I must meditate on some matters. I thought I'd walk down by the tidal pools." He nodded and moved away, but Howe kept pace with the younger man.

"Then I'll be good company, for that's where I'm headed," Howe answered, hurrying to catch up. He fell easily into Thomas Colman's long stride. "I'm set for crabbing. The governor told me of an old Indian trick—if you check the rocks along the beaches after low tide, you'll find snails, limpets, and crabs. In the tidal pools you can find mollusks just under the sand. You only need a long stick to stir things up a bit."

"Mayhap we'll have a feast tonight with your catch," Colman answered, glancing absently toward the ring of houses as they walked along the trail that led to the beach.

"Aye." Howe studied his younger companion. The minister

was preoccupied, but with what? Since their landing, George Howe had never felt freer. Indeed, there was that disagreeable business with the Wythers boy and that reprimand given the minister in the council meeting, but no one but John Jones and Beth Glane was truly offended that the minister had been seen kissing his wife. Surely the man had not let their narrow-minded accusations upset him! Such trivial annoyances had no place in this island paradise. On Roanoke there were no orphans in the streets, no tax collectors to contend with, and no cursed ruffs around their necks, by heaven—

He remembered the minister's absent glance toward the houses and laughed. Of course, the man worried about his pretty new wife. Perhaps they'd had a spat, and the minister sought time alone to think things through.

"Excuse my lack of manners, Reverend," Howe said, feeling a surge of fatherly affection for the minister, "but I should have inquired after your lovely wife. My son thinks the world of her, you know. How is Mistress Colman enjoying our new island home?"

"She enjoys it well enough," the minister answered, seeming to study the sand as they walked.

"And her house? What did she think of her first night on the island?"

The minister stopped abruptly and placed his hands behind his back. "My wife is well, Master Howe," he said, an oddly distant tone in his voice.

Howe ignored the man's aloofness and continued walking. "I'm only asking because my son has taken quite a liking to her, his own mother being yet in England, you know. If there is ever anything I or my boy can do for you and Mistress Colman, you won't hesitate to let me know, will you, Reverend?"

Colman had not moved. Surprised, Howe turned and lifted a questioning brow toward the sober minister. "If you please, Master Howe," the minister said, nodding sharply, "I am not inclined to talk with my fellowman while God calls me to converse with him."

Howe grinned and turned away, his eyes on the tidal pools that shimmered in the distance. Surely he had once been as transparent as the minister, worried about his new wife but hiding his concern under a cloak of proud indifference. "Go ahead, my young friend, and tell God everything you must," he answered, not caring if the minister heard or not. "But whatever it is you are running from will be waiting when you come back."

▼▲▼▲▼ Two miles away from the fort, George Howe knelt on the rock-rimmed bank and scanned the sand below the clear water. Recalling John White's instructions, he prodded the shallows with a forked stick. How, exactly, did a mollusk react when disturbed? The governor had not been explicit in his directions.

The rocks that rimmed the shallow pools bit into the soft flesh of his knees, and the shy shellfish hid in crevices accessible only from the water. "It must be done, then," Howe said, surveying the pool. He dropped his stick onto the ground and peeled off his dark leggings, his pleated trunks, and his doublet. At least he was alone and far away from the prying eyes of any who might take offense at his state of undress.

Standing nearly naked on the bank, the elder George Howe, assistant to the governor, and esteemed graduate of Jesus College, Cambridge, dipped his toes into the shallow water. The warm morning sun shone bright on his pale skin, and George caught sight of his reflection in the still pool. Well, then, he had shed his dignity as well as his clothes. He felt himself laughing, and in a breathless instant of release he kicked the warm water into a towering flume. Small fish scattered at the approach of the strange pale interloper, and George forgot his mission and his propriety and splashed in the water with reckless abandon.

The water trickled gloriously down his head and arms and over his back, cooling his legs and feet. His rough skin, tormented by lice and other vermin while aboard ship, tingled beneath the cleansing droplets of water. Howe danced himself breathless, then sank in the pool and reclined upon his elbows as the water surrounded and invigorated him.

Too late, he heard the rustle of leaves. Too late, he saw shadows fall over the pool. He turned, expecting to meet the accusing eyes of Beth Glane or John Jones, but what he saw made his blood run cold with terror. A half-circle of natives stood on the bank, their faces painted red, their bows held high. The sharpened stone tips of their arrows glinted in the late afternoon sun.

George tried his best to smile. "I am a friend," he said, his voice quivering despite his intention to remain steadfast. He rose to his feet, trembling, and held out his empty hands.

The most heavily painted Indian gave a war cry, and George heard himself screaming as the arrows flew; then he fell facefirst into the cleansing waters of Roanoke.

"Miss Jocelyn?"

Jocelyn put aside the dark thoughts that had occupied her mind since the public whipping and listened again for the soft call as someone knocked. She smiled as she answered the door. Outside her family, only young George Howe called her by her Christian name.

"Yes, George?"

"I wondered if you've seen my papa. He left to go crabbing hours ago and promised he'd be back by supper."

"No, George, I haven't seen him." Jocelyn looked out into the clearing, where many of the colonists bustled around in preparation for the late afternoon meal. "Have you asked everyone?"

George nodded. "I checked the fields, the armory, the place where they're setting up the brick-making house. The governor, ma'am, told me he saw your husband and my father walking together this afternoon."

"Well, then," Jocelyn said, putting down her mending and taking the boy's hand. "Let us find my husband and see if he has hidden your father."

Jocelyn had reasons of her own for wanting to find Thomas, for she had not seen him since that awful scene in the fort. She wanted to know what the council had said to him and if he had truly thought it necessary to punish a four-year-old boy so severely. She wanted desperately to talk to him, to plumb the meaning of his odd behavior, to open her heart and honestly reveal all she felt for him. But she had the feeling he would not seek her out, so young George had provided the perfect opportunity. She'd find Thomas, send George to his father, and, if God was willing, she'd have another chance to speak alone with her husband before nightfall.

She saw Thomas before George did, and her heart leapt at the sight of him. He stood alone on a sandy stretch of beach, a shovel in his hand, with the sea behind him and the wind ruffling his dark hair. He had put his dark doublet over his work shirt but left it unbuttoned, and that, Jocelyn thought, made him look less like a minister and more like a gentleman pirate.

"Reverend Colman!" George sprinted away from her and raced ahead as Jocelyn smoothed her expression and her untidy hair.

Thomas was standing above one of the barrels the colonists buried in the sand to collect water. Underneath the barrier islands lay pockets of fresh water, the accumulation of many years of rainfall. By digging in the sandy hills, casks of fresh water were easily filled.

Thomas rested upon his shovel while he answered George's questions, then paused to wipe perspiration from his face and neck as Jocelyn approached.

George whirled and grabbed Jocelyn's hand. "The minister says Papa went to the tidal basins to catch crabs. Come with me, Miss Jocelyn."

"You are a big boy, George; you can go alone," Jocelyn said, her eyes locked on Thomas's face. George hesitated for a moment, then took off running toward the shallow tidal pools that lay south of the fort.

Thomas watched the boy go with a measure of sadness in his eyes, and Jocelyn felt her heart sink. Did George remind him of the son he had left behind in England? Or perhaps the boy reminded him of this morning's terrible scene with William Wythers.

"Is there anything that you need?" she asked, twisting her hands even as her heart twisted before the sorrow in his eyes. He looked at her then, and his expression adjusted as his emotions hid themselves from her gaze.

"No," he said, his voice oddly gentle. "I thank you for asking."

"You don't have to thank me, Thomas. I'm your wife. 'Tis my duty to help you, to serve you—" She wanted to add *to love you,* but the cold aloofness in his eyes blocked the words. "I'faith, Thomas, I wanted to talk to you about this morning. I would rather hurt myself than bring you trouble in the council, but then there was that horrible whipping—"

He thrust the shovel into the sand and brushed a layer of grit from his hands. "Do you know how beautiful you are?" he asked, his smile twisting as he leaned his weight upon the shovel's handle. "I've spent the afternoon asking God why he would bring you into my life, for unless his plan is to torture me—"

A terrible wailing interrupted his words. Thomas flashed into movement, sprinting toward the sound, and Jocelyn's heart went into sudden shock as she recognized the frenzied cries of young George Howe.

▼▲▼▲▼ Young George stood as if he were frozen, his head thrown back in numb terror, his fists clenched in frustrated horror. The elder Howe lay in a pool of reddened water, his body pierced by more than a dozen arrows, his head battered to an unrecognizable pulp. His clothes lay strewn on the sand; his forked stick floated innocently in the water near his body.

Jocelyn ran to young George and turned his head away from the carnage, muffling his cries with her body.

"Savages!" Thomas spat the word, raising a fist to heaven. "God help us, are these the people we came to redeem?"

Jocelyn squinted to block out the sight. Both the living and the dead man frightened her. And if the primitives were still in the area—

"Soft, Thomas, we must warn the others!" she said, pulling the boy away from the water. "You can't stay here!"

"God help any savage who strikes me!" Thomas said, his stern expression set as though in stone as he climbed over the rocks and splashed into the pool. He lifted the dead man's body from the water, and Jocelyn cried out again at the sight of what had been the face of gentle George Howe.

At the sound of her cry, Thomas looked up. "Go bring a company of men," he directed. "I'll stay here. I'll not leave my brother's body undefended."

"But what if—," Jocelyn stammered, her heart pounding at the thought of Indians in the woods.

"Go!" Thomas's voice rang over the beach. "Get out of here!"

Closing her ears to the sound of the boy's cries, Jocelyn took his hand and ran to the safety of the fort.

▼▲▼▲▼ Back aboard the *Lion,* Jocelyn listened to the steady creaking of the ship's timbers and shuddered. How quickly life could change! Last night she had been the happy and contented new bride of a minister; tonight she was fevered and frantic with fear. Of all the men in the colony, George Howe had been the most pleasant and easygoing. Why, then, had the savages set upon him? In his almighty wisdom, why had God allowed such a terrible thing to happen?

Even more worrisome was Thomas's attitude. The other men of the colony had been quick to praise Thomas's devotion to duty and his steely courage in the face of certain danger, but they hadn't seen the glint of defiance in his eyes when he had commanded Jocelyn to leave him on the beach. It was as if he dared the natives to appear and strike him down. In that instant, Jocelyn had thought him suicidal.

But harboring such thoughts would do her no good. What minister would commit suicide? Her doubts only proved how little she knew and understood him. Certainly he was brave and courageous. Everyone told her so. And it was far better to think on that than to wonder if her husband would actually defy the savages to kill him.

Next to Jocelyn, young George lay sleeping on a pile of mildewed canvas, for all the blankets had been left ashore in the colonists' haste to leave the island. Only a handful of men were ashore this night, and they walked the ramparts of the fort with loaded muskets and anxious eyes, looking for the gleam of a torch, the movement of a single leaf.

John White had warned his people that the Indians might be bent on revenge, but the ferocious and unnecessary attack upon George Howe had unnerved even Manteo and Towaye. They, too, were aboard the *Lion*, awaiting daylight and a decision from the governor as to what action should be taken in retaliation for Howe's death.

Most of the women slept now belowdecks while the council assembled up on the quarterdeck to discuss the day's events. Too shaken to sleep, Jocelyn left George in the room of sleeping women and went above, huddling in the shadows behind the capstan to listen to the men.

John White's face was pale and strained before his fellow settlers. "I thought Roanoke would be safer, for all have heard of the barbaric savages of the Chesapeake," he said, his shoulders bowed. "I shall never forgive myself for this! George Howe was an esteemed friend and a valuable part of our community."

"Blame not yourself. This could have happened anywhere," Thomas Stevens spoke up, nodding soberly toward his fellows. "No matter where we plant our city, the savages will fear us because they do not know our intentions. We should do more to convince them that we are peaceful."

"And how do we do that?" Ananias Dare asked. He looked toward Manteo, who sat silently in the circle. "What, my friend, do you say? Think you that we should stay here?"

Manteo nodded slowly, weighing his words. "My English brothers were too free," he said, looking around the circle for signs of disagreement. "Not one of my race would live as you did. We do not travel alone. We do not fish without regard for the avenger who waits in the reeds. You, my friends, are fortunate that Roanoac did not vent their wrath on an earlier day. Only because they feared your anger for the killing of the white bones did they not come sooner."

"What does he mean?" Ananias asked, looking at his father-in-law as the circle of men buzzed.

John White held up his hand. "As always, there is wisdom in Manteo's words. We assumed that because we saw no natives there were none, and we can never make that assumption. Manteo believes the arrows came from a tribe of Roanoac, whose friendship with the English ended years ago."

"Why did their friendship end?" Thomas Colman's deep voice broke through the buzzing of the men, and Jocelyn lifted her head as every man in the circle gave attention to her husband's question. If any in the colony had ever doubted Thomas Colman was worthy of leadership, none did so after this afternoon.

John White gave the minister a rueful smile. "The Roanoac were pleasant and friendly people when I landed here with Ralph Lane's party two years ago. Wingina was their chief, and their camp lay on the mainland due east of our island, a place called Dasemunkepeuc. Wingina's brother, Granganimeo, invited Lane to settle here on Roanoke Island so the English would be near Dasemunkepeuc."

"Why would the savages want the English near?" Thomas asked. "If they do not want us to interfere—"

White lifted an eyebrow. "For power, my dear minister. The Indians dwelling near us gained status, because they were in close contact with our iron and copper and pots and beads. But they did not realize that English soldiers are not farmers, and the English needed food to remain alive through the winter. As they incessantly bartered with us, they soon depleted their own winter stores."

White's eyes strafed the gathering, then trained in on the minister. "But when Granganimeo died, Wingina announced that his name had changed to Pemisapan, a word meaning 'watchful' or 'wary' in their tongue. From that day he became an enemy of the English, undermining Lane's efforts until finally Pemisapan was killed. Within a month Lane and all with him left for England, but the rift between the English and Roanoac has never been healed."

"The skeleton we buried—," Thomas Stevens interrupted.

"The white bones." White nodded knowingly. "Probably one of Grenville's fifteen, and most likely killed by the Roanoac." White stood to his feet. "We will see shortly. Sleep, my friends, for tomorrow we will scout the island thoroughly and make sure no other savages lie in wait to attack us."

"And if we find none?" This from Ananias Dare.

"We will sail to Croatoan Island, home of Manteo's people, and greet our friends at the village of Chacandepeco. They are our eyes and ears, and after talking to them, we will decide what to do."

Jocelyn watched as the group dispersed. Most of the men broke up into groups of two or three and threw their heads together as they buzzed with speculation. Only two men held themselves aloof from the fray: Manteo, the Indian, and her husband, the minister.

▼▲▼▲▼ The armed search parties found no signs of natives on the island, and on the second day after George Howe's death, John White sent Edward Stafford, Manteo, Ananias Dare, the Reverend Thomas Colman, and twenty other armed men southward to Croatoan Island. They sailed in the small pinnace, piloted by Captain Stafford, and every man but the minister carried a dagger or revolver in his belt as well as a musket in his hand.

Edward Stafford stared grimly at the familiar shoreline of Croatoan Island as the pinnace neared the shore. The men, angry and ready for vengeance, leapt overboard as soon as the bow hit sand, and he reined in their impatient spirits with some difficulty.

"Remember that the Croatoan are as different from the Roanoac as we are from the Spanish," Stafford said, raising a hand to silence the men. "Peace is our motive, and knowledge our goal." He paused and looked at the group. "But arm yourselves and line up five abreast as if for battle. We have been gone from this place for a very long time."

The men behind him nodded their assent, all but the unarmed minister and the two Indians. Stafford motioned to them and indicated that they should take their places at the rear of the guard. With four lines of men in battle formation, he led the way up the beach.

They had not journeyed twenty feet into the tangled brush when a vicious battle cry lifted the hair on the back of his neck. He heard the intake of a dozen breaths and raised his musket as limbs and leaves thrashed frantically around him.

Pushing his way through the breaking battle lines, Manteo hastily called a greeting in the Indian tongue. The faceless activity in the woods stilled. Manteo called out again. After a moment, browned and painted faces appeared like disembodied ghosts in the brush; then one warrior stepped forward, a long arrow notched in his bowstring.

Manteo spoke rapidly to the warrior, who answered in the Indian tongue and jerked his head toward the English.

"In God's name, Captain, tell the men to lower their guns!" Thomas Colman shouted from the rear of the company.

With a careful eye on the woods around him, Stafford gave the order to lower their weapons, and the men did so, reluctantly. The warrior's face widened in a grin. He dropped his bow and leapt forward to embrace Manteo, and the woods came alive with the high-pitched calls of a score of other Indians who leapt from tree limbs and from behind shrubs to surround the English in happy bedlam.

Edward Stafford felt the arms of a dozen warriors encircle him in joy, and the hard knot of fear in his stomach began to relax. As part of Lane's expedition, he had spent many weeks with the Croatoan in peace. Perchance those memories and that friendship would save his landing party yet.

After the joyful reunion in the forest, the Indians of Croatoan Island led the landing party to their village at Chacandepeco. With Manteo and Towaye acting as interpreters, the Croatoan invited Stafford and Ananias Dare to sit with them in a council meeting. Stafford asked that Thomas Colman be allowed to sit with them, too, as a representative of the Englishmen's God, and the village chief, the werowance, nodded in agreement.

Stafford gave his warmest greetings and regards to the chief, then asked the chief to spread the word of the colonists' arrival to the other friendly tribes on the mainland: the Secotan, Aquascogoc, and Pomeioc. After listening to Stafford's description of George Howe's mutilated body, the village chief agreed that a band of murderous Roanoac were guilty of the murder on Roanoke Island.

"They may have been hunting deer, or they may have come to draw blood," Manteo said, translating for the gray-haired werowance. "The Croatoan do not know. But they will speak to you of another matter."

The werowance gestured to a fiercely painted warrior who stood at his side. The man left the circle and returned a moment later carrying a slender young man in his arms. Stafford judged the invalid to be about nineteen, but it was difficult to tell whether he was man or child because he kept his face down as if ashamed, and long, unkempt hair hid his features. The elder warrior gently deposited the young man on a grass mat at the chief's side, then moved away from the circle with a darkly accusing look on his face.

Ananias Dare leaned toward Stafford. "Do you know this man?"

"I do not recognize him," Stafford murmured in reply. "But surely the chief will explain."

The dark eyes of the werowance did a long, slow slide over the younger man, who sat with his atrophied legs straight out in front of him and kept his head down. Gesturing broadly, the chief spoke in a loud voice; then he lowered his hands and waited for the English reaction.

Manteo listened without expression, then turned to the Englishmen. "This young man, a nephew of the chief's, was injured by an English musket and has not been able to move his legs since that day. The chief knows that the English mistook this man for one of Wingina's Indians and are therefore not to blame, but he wants your promise that such evil will never befall the Croatoan again."

Thomas Colman leaned forward into Stafford's view. "What happened here, Captain? Surely one of your people—"

"They were Lane's people, not mine," Stafford snapped, forgetting for a moment that the chief watched him closely. "They were all soldiers."

He lowered his voice and took pains to guard his expression. "To an Englishman, one savage looks very much like another. Wingina's Indians were out for our blood and killed more than one of our men. Do you not remember the skeleton in the sand? It is likely this lad stumbled into a landing party of Lane's men and was injured. I do not know why he does not walk. Sometimes these things happen."

"What will you tell the chief?" Ananias asked, his eyes carefully searching Stafford's face.

Stafford stared without expression at the chief for a moment. To apologize would admit wrongdoing; an expression of sorrow might be interpreted as weakness. One had to be firm with the savages; one had to keep the upper hand. The Indians' fear and uncertainty were powerful weapons for the English.

Stafford raised a gently wagging finger.

"Tell the chief," he said, shifting his weight in the sand, "that this will not happen again if the other villages of his tribe make contact with us within a week. After seven days our governor will severely punish the Roanoac, and the Croatoan must stay away from our swords and long guns."

Manteo relayed the message. The werowance nodded gravely and stared at Stafford with deadly concentration. After a moment, he settled his elbows on his knees and steepled his fingers as he made another short statement.

"There is more," Manteo said, nodding to Stafford. "The werowance and his village welcome you with joy, but ask that the English not gather or spill any of their corn, for they have but little to get through the winter."

From the corner of his eye, Stafford saw the minister squint in embarrassment. The chief's request was really a warning: The tribe was not prepared to feed an ill-equipped English colony through the winter. *This is another legacy of Ralph Lane,* Stafford thought wryly, remembering the former English governor's brash assumption that the Indians should and would feed them when Lane's soldiers proved themselves to be poor farmers. *These people, who once thought we could do no wrong, have learned how little prepared we are to face the wilderness.*

Stafford nodded respectfully toward the chief. "Tell the chief we have no intention of asking anything but friendship from the Croatoan," he told Manteo. "We want only to live alongside them as brethren and friends."

Manteo translated. The werowance nodded and gave the Englishmen a wide smile. He clapped his hands, and women came from timbered huts to lay wooden bowls of steaming stewed venison at the men's feet. Stafford smothered a smile as the minister lowered his eyes before the bare-breasted women.

"Now we feast," Manteo said simply, looking at his English friends.

"God be thanked," Thomas Colman answered, keeping his eyes steadfastly fixed upon the bowl in front of him.

▼▲▼▲▼ Along with promises of peace, the Croatoan landing party brought back an accounting of what had happened to Grenville's fifteen caretakers. After Lane's colony departed in such haste, Edward Stafford reported, the fifteen men left to guard the island as England's possession lived in peace for a time. The Croatoan marveled that the men took few precautions and lived as though the only threat they might face was Spanish ships from the sea.

The real danger, however, came from the mainland. The gruesome story had filtered through the Indian villages and tribes for months, and Stafford did not spare details when he related it to John White and an assembled company of colonists aboard the *Lion*.

Sitting next to her father on the deck, Eleanor held his hand tightly as Stafford related the terrible tale. "The men were living carelessly," he explained, "and the savages attacked by treachery and stealth. Thirty Roanoac approached the village—"

"Where we are living now?" Eleanor burst out, unable to contain her fear.

Stafford ignored her. "The thirty approached," he went on, "most of them hiding behind trees. The Indians could see only eleven of the fifteen men, so they sent two emissaries to ask for a parley. The two savages appeared to be unarmed, so the English sent out two unarmed men to talk with them. As they were embracing in friendship, one of the Roanoac took a wooden sword from under his mantle and killed one of the English with a blow to the head. Then his tribesmen attacked. The unharmed English delegate ran back to the storehouse where the food and ammunition were kept, but the Indians set it ablaze. The soldiers ran out in complete disorder with whatever weapons they could find."

Eleanor felt the blood in her veins grow cold as she thought of savages appearing outside her house; then Stafford took a breath and continued, "They fought for an hour. Another Englishman and an Indian were killed before the remainder of Grenville's men, many of whom were wounded, escaped to their shallop.

They managed to pick up four men who had been gathering oysters at the tidal pool, then rowed to a small island between Port Lane and Port Ferdinando. After a while, the Croatoan saw them leave. They have not been back."

"The sea took them," Fernandes offered, looking around at the group. "A shallop could never survive the sea."

The company buzzed with speculation until the governor held up a hand. "It was their own fault," John White announced solemnly. "And I believe there is a lesson for us in the story. We cannot live as carelessly as they did. We cannot let acts of murder go unavenged. Trust me, gentle ladies and men, the fate of the fifteen will not befall us."

▼▲▼▲▼ Despite the good news of peace from the Croatoan landing party, the colonists did not sleep on the island for several days after the return of Captain Stafford and his men. Every morning they rose and filled the shallops as the small boats journeyed again and again to the island fort. After a full day's work they returned to the *Lion* and the flyboat to fall asleep, exhausted, on the bare wooden floors of the ships' decks.

Eleanor watched Jocelyn bear the endless days of fearful waiting without complaint, but she was terrified each time she stepped onto the sand of Roanoke Island. Had her fellow colonists forgotten so soon that George Howe died in daylight? Had they not heard the horror stories of cannibals and treachery? And she, pregnant and practically immobile, how was she to escape if a savage presented himself in her house or accosted her on the beach?

She would not let Agnes leave her side and demanded Audrey's presence as well. Most of all she found Jocelyn's company soothing, and despite her cousin's pale, thoughtful expression, she called for Jocelyn often. Eleanor knew her demands grew more and more unreasonable as her belly grew tighter and her temper more explosive, but she could not help herself. Ananias had long since deserted her, first with the landing party, and now he drilled daily with the squad of militia her father had organized. And for what? So that they might feel safe enough to sleep again on the island and be killed in their beds?

▼▲▼▲▼ The ship's deck rocked beneath Jocelyn as she vainly tried to sleep. It wasn't the ship's rocking that kept her awake, nor the hardness of the planks against her bones, but her thoughts about Thomas. In the seven days since George Howe's death her husband had spoken little more than ten words to her and had barely looked in her direction. Something seemed to press heavily on his mind, but she could not guess what it might be. He had listened to Edward Stafford's report of the landing party without disagreement and had ventured onto the mainland every day to observe the select militia drilling under John White's direction and Edward Stafford's firm hand. Aboard the ship in the evenings, he consoled the sick, prayed with the weary, and nodded absently at her if she happened to cross his path.

It's as if he is trying to distance himself from me, she had thought earlier that evening as Thomas lingered in her uncle's cabin, where a group of assistants huddled in secrecy. *But why? And what did he mean that day on the beach when he said God had sent me to torture him?*

Lying next to Jocelyn on the grimy deck, Eleanor groaned and mumbled in discomfort as the weight of her pregnancy pressed upon her. Snapping at each other like ill-bred cats, Agnes and Audrey jostled one another on the crowded floor. Jocelyn drew her light cloak around her and stood up. She'd find more rest walking the decks than trying to sleep in these conditions.

Despite the late hour, footsteps sounded on the deck above. Jocelyn's curiosity led her to the companionway, for usually even the seamen had bedded down by the darkest hour of night. Intrigued, she crept upwards and felt the warm August wind brush her hair from her face as she climbed out onto the upper deck.

The pinnace had been brought alongside the *Lion;* the gang-plank lay in place, and several of the colony's men were filing silently onto the smaller ship. In the gleaming moonlight she recognized the white hair of her uncle and the glint of a musket in his hand. The wind flapped her cloak as she edged toward them; then she gasped as a hand fell upon her shoulder.

"Well met, Jocelyn." Thomas stood behind her, his face hidden in a shadow cast by the ship's mast.

"Thomas! How you frightened me! What are you doing up here? Where are they going?"

His voice was dark, restrained. "They are going where they need to go, and you should be below. Your uncle will be upset if he sees you here."

"But why are they going ashore in the dead of night?" She raised her voice as the wind began to blow in earnest, a fierce, steady bluster that shrilled toward the island and threatened to blow the pinnace out from under the waiting gangplank.

"I have to pray for them, Jocelyn, so go below and wait. You'll understand everything later."

He stepped away from her, but fury flamed in Jocelyn's soul and her hand flew out to catch his arm. "You can't just walk away from me, Thomas Colman! What will I understand later?"

His dark eyes were inscrutable in the dim shadow, but she heard a trace of gentleness in his voice, the tenderness a father displays toward a foolish child. "Go below, Jocelyn. Say a prayer for these men. You will have to wait until morning."

And firmly, gently, he removed her hand from his arm, brought it to his lips, then left her standing in the wind-whipped shadows.

▼▲▼▲▼ Under the command of Edward Stafford, the guidance of Manteo, and the blessing of Thomas Colman, the twenty-four men aboard the pinnace slipped westward through the dark waters. The high arc of the bow dipped and rose through the waters, sending a cool splash of spray over Stafford's face. It was well that this was over and done. The morrow would bring either victory or death to the fledgling settlement. But if it was the latter, the remaining colonists upon the *Lion* could still sail for England.

A strong wind pushed the boat silently across the waters, and Stafford saw Roanoke Island slip by to his left; then the mainland rose ahead of him through a ghostly fog. Too quickly, Stafford thought, the small ship silently beached itself less than a mile from the Roanoac village of Dasemunkepeuc.

The flintlock of his musket glinted in the moonlight, and the full significance of their action suddenly struck Stafford. This was to be the first occasion in which John White had approved violence against the natives, and he had done so only at the urging of Stafford and a few other assistants. English law demanded revenge, but was this action truly wise?

After scanning the dark forest at the edge of the shore, Manteo nodded gravely to Stafford, who barked a single command. The men shouldered their guns in unison and stepped from the boat. The attack to avenge George Howe and Grenville's fifteen had begun.

▼▲▼▲▼ Edward Stafford realized later that he would remember the horror of that night until his dying day. The fires of the Indian town had burned bright through the forest, lighting the way like signal beacons. Like the Indians, Stafford's men approached with stealth and silence. From their hiding places in the trees outside the village, Stafford and the others could see no movement near the grass huts, only a small circle of savages huddled around a predawn fire.

As leader of the war party and chief avenger for George Howe, Edward Stafford raised his musket to his shoulder, aimed, and fired at one of the men. His ears roared with the deafening explosion of the gun, and families staggered from the huts as the Indians around the fire fled in bewilderment. The English line moved forward into the circle of the camp, firing at will as women and children ran screaming into the dark woods.

Stafford moved confidently into the camp as the sounds of gunfire drowned out screams of panic. The Indian he had shot lay by the fire where a red pool bloomed from his head. A woman with a child on her back sat by the fire with her hands folded as if begging for mercy. From a distance, someone screamed, "Stafford! Stafford!" and Stafford automatically turned to help the man in trouble.

His eyes widened in atavistic horror. The man who knelt now before him was not English; he wore the familiar painted designs of the Croatoan.

Stafford winced as a whisper of horror ran through him. Surely God would not allow such an egregious error! He whirled around as the woman with the babe on her back spoke English words. "Stafford, Manteo, Manteo, our friend!" The dead man on the ground wore a necklace of iron beads, a recent gift from the English.

"Stop firing!" Stafford shouted, thrusting his hand into the smoke-filled air. Manteo caught his eye and echoed the cry. "Stop firing! These people are Croatoan!"

The jubilant cries of the English faded, but the sobbing of the women did not cease so quickly. Before the sun rose, Edward Stafford realized that the Roanoac they had come to punish had fled days before. The Croatoan in this camp had come to gather the Roanoac's abandoned stores. One Indian lay dead, and one woman, the wife of one of the werowances of the Croatoan tribe, was badly injured.

As he surveyed the confusion of carnage, Stafford felt the blood lust drain from his heart. English and Indians alike looked to him for direction, and he gestured abruptly to Manteo, the unenviable man who had inadvertently led the English to attack his own people. But Manteo's face was locked, void of expression. He was undoubtedly more horrified than Stafford.

"Gather these people, with whatever food you can find," Stafford commanded, his voice hoarse as he shouldered his musket. "Bring them to the boat. We'll take them with us to the fort."

Simon Fernandes, who had come along to pilot the shallop, read the anguish on Stafford's face. "You should be pleased," he said, his smile gleaming from beneath his clipped moustache. "The enemy have fled, have they not?"

Stafford knew he would never be able to find joy in this victory. He had fired upon and killed innocent people. His blunder had been worse than Ralph Lane's.

But he could not show his remorse. He forced a smile worthy of a triumphant victor. "As of this day—" he bowed to his men— "we live on Roanoke Island." Without looking back, Edward Stafford left the camp.

▼▲▼▲▼ On August thirteenth, in front of more than one hundred colonists and thirty of the Croatoan tribe, the Reverend Thomas Colman baptized Manteo into the Christian faith while John White declared him Lord of Roanoke and Dasemunkepeuc. "This I do in reward of his faithful service and according to the wishes of our lord Sir Walter Raleigh," White announced to the assembly.

Watching from the crowd, Jocelyn thought she understood the reason for Manteo's honor. Raleigh had instructed her uncle to so honor Manteo in the hope that the native would remain behind on the island when the colony left for Chesapeake. With Manteo in place as lord and overseer, the island of Roanoke and the coast of Virginia would then be held in Raleigh's name until Sir Walter was ready to promote another Virginia expedition.

But Manteo's unprecedented honor could have waited until the colony was ready to depart for the Chesapeake. It had been advanced because Manteo had worn a haunted look ever since the morning when the English war party had returned with threescore Indians and no clear answers to the other colonists' questions. Afraid to face either his English friends or his Croatoan brothers, Manteo had appeared unstable, and Jocelyn knew her uncle and the assistants worried about his influence on the other Indians. In order to ensure that Manteo would not betray the English as did Wingina, Manteo was officially forgiven, baptized, and declared lord of the land.

Jocelyn wondered privately if the Croatoan bore Manteo any ill feeling. From Towaye she had learned that Manteo's mother had been chief of the Croatoan at the time he had been captured by the English. Apparently the Croatoan had a time-honored practice of placing members of the chief's family in other villages to control relationships, so before the massacre at Dasemunkepeuc, Manteo's "adoption" by the English had seemed to work to the Croatoan's advantage.

Only God and Manteo now knew what his people thought of him, but Manteo's formalized position meant that the colonists' days on Roanoke were numbered. He would naturally want to set up a dynasty of his own on the island, so the colonists would have no choice but to move on to Chesapeake in the spring.

And though the colonists had returned to their homes after the raid on Dasemunkepeuc, Jocelyn had yet to spend time with Thomas alone, for Eleanor demanded her constant presence. As her baby's birth drew near, Eleanor grew more and more worried about attacks by the savages, and Jocelyn and Agnes spent most of their time trying to assure Eleanor that they were safe.

Audrey, Jocelyn came to realize, could not be counted on to help Eleanor. Whenever possible, the girl slipped away to loiter with William Clement, whose intentions remained hazy but whose interest in the girl apparently had not waned.

Jocelyn began to look forward to the arrival of this first Virginian baby. After the child came, she would be able to return to life with her husband in her own home, a life she had barely begun. And once she was sure of her own husband, she would marry Audrey to William, and life would be all it could be in the barbaric wilderness of Virginia.

The eighteenth of August dawned hot and sticky, and water poured from Eleanor's loins at the first morning light. Audrey, foolish and immature, fell to pieces when she realized Eleanor would soon have the baby, and Jocelyn sent the girl away. "I believe I don't know what good I'll be to you, Coz," she whispered as Eleanor settled back upon her freshly stuffed mattress to await the travail of birth. "I'faith, I don't know anything about babies."

"You don't—oh, heaven help me!" Eleanor sputtered, gripping Jocelyn's hand as a painful spasm distorted her face. She panted for a moment until the pain subsided, then took one look at Jocelyn's face and laughed. "Did no woman ever tell you anything about babies?"

Jocelyn looked down at her hands and blushed. "No. There was no woman to tell me."

Eleanor paused. "Your father—"

Jocelyn shook her head rapidly. "No. He would never speak of such things. He gave me books to read, though."

"Books." Eleanor let her head fall onto the mattress. "What books?"

"Well," Jocelyn began hesitantly, "I have read Ovid. *Amores.*"

"What?" Eleanor lifted her head and crossed her eyes. "My dear Coz, whatever was your father thinking? What can a girl learn from reading a dead Greek?"

"A dead Roman," Jocelyn answered. "My father wished me to know the thoughts of the world. He said that in order to appreciate light, one needed to recognize darkness."

"Your father was always . . . impractical," Eleanor grunted, squeezing Jocelyn's hand as another pain gripped her. She waited until the spasm had passed, then raised herself up onto her elbows. "My father says the savage women merely squat over a hole when giving birth." She grinned at Jocelyn. "Would you dig me a hole, Cousin?"

"Never!" Jocelyn was horrified at her cousin's playful attitude. Had pain driven Eleanor from her senses?

As the day wore on, Eleanor grunted and groaned and screamed. By noon, Elizabeth Viccars had been sent for. By dusk, Eleanor's child had arrived. Perfectly healthy and robust, the first English child born in Her Majesty's Virginia was a dark-haired, blue-eyed girl.

Jocelyn carried the swaddled child to her uncle. John White gingerly took his new granddaughter into his arms as a circle of English and Indian women watched with something akin to reverence in their eyes. "Eleanor has said she is to be christened Virginia Elizabeth Dare," he said, his eyes misting as he beheld the miracle of life in his wide hands. "Her Majesty will be pleased."

▼▲▼▲▼ As Eleanor privately nursed her newborn the next day, the remaining colonists gathered in the center of the fort for a community meeting. All supplies had been unloaded from the flyboat and the *Lion,* and Simon Fernandes was readying the fleet for its departure for England. The ballast had been removed from the lower decks, the holds rummaged, the ships newly caulked. The seamen had spent the last few days loading fresh water and a cargo of precious wood, one commodity that was plentiful in America and scarce in England. Most of the settlers had been busy writing letters and preparing souvenir tokens for friends and family who waited in England.

But John White knew the mood of the colonists at this meeting would be anything but tranquil. John Sampson had begun a petition to demand that at least two of the assistants return to England. "The assistants in England cannot be trusted to know what we really need," Sampson explained, standing in the clearing as the other colonists listened. "And while our sea captain would dispute my words, not one of us truly trusts Simon Fernandes to give a true and fair report of our needs."

John White nodded. "You have a point, John," he said, rubbing his beard. "I thought Christopher Cooper had agreed to go. But now that Cooper has changed his opinion . . ."

The governor paused, and the colonists respectfully fell silent to give him time to think. White knew they were right to be concerned. Food supplies were short and would grow shorter in the months ahead. Thanks to Fernandes, they had arrived too late to put in a decent crop, and winter loomed ahead. Even the friendly Croatoan had stated flatly that they would not feed the English at Roanoke as they had fed the Lane colony.

White took a deep breath and sighed. He knew the colonists wanted him to return to England. Of all the men, he could most easily gain the ear of Raleigh, maybe even the queen. These men and women needed him to be their voice in England, but how could he leave his daughter and days-old granddaughter?

"You, Governor, know what we face here," Edward Powell spoke up. "The assistants in England have no idea."

"But 'twould appear I have deserted you," White argued, beating the air with his fist. "And I, who have convinced you to stake your lives and fortunes upon this journey, cannot desert the expedition."

"You can make Sir Walter Raleigh understand our precarious position," Arnold Archard argued. "The others are concerned with their own affairs."

"Raleigh understands already. He is a man of action."

"I hate to say it, sir, but Eleanor and I would feel more secure if you were filling a ship to meet our needs," Ananias said, his eyes lifting to meet those of his father-in-law. The young father's mouth curved in a proud smile. "And for the sake of your granddaughter, will you not consider going?"

White felt his resolve slipping. "What about my papers?" he stammered. "My books. All my earthly belongings are here, on Roanoke."

"We'll guard your belongings and your trunks." Thomas Colman stepped forward and nodded resolutely. "You have my word as a man of God that no harm shall come to anything that belongs to John White."

John felt his heart stir with respect for the man who stood before him. The somber minister had proved to be a man of loyalty and courage. If anyone could be trusted to help oversee the colony in White's absence, surely it was Thomas Colman.

"All right," John said, waving his hands in surrender. "I am not certain, but I will consider your request. But it must be in writing, lest any in England say I have deserted you. The document must make it fully clear that I go to meet your needs and that I leave only because of your great insistence that I go."

"We will write whatever you like," John Sampson said, "if you will only go and return with the supplies we need. After all, Governor, we know you will return." The man turned to smile at the assembly. "We have your daughter and granddaughter."

Nodding mutely, John White turned on his heel and went home to consider his options.

▼▲▼▲▼ On the twenty-first of August, John White set a single sea trunk in front of his house to be loaded upon the flyboat. His other trunks, filled with his sketches, books, manuscripts, maps, and armor, were locked and placed in a separate room off the governor's large house.

Jocelyn and Thomas waited in the lower room of the house while her uncle said his good-byes to Ananias, Eleanor, and the baby. When her uncle finally came out of their chamber, Jocelyn embraced him gently. "Must you go today?" she said, pulling away. "The wind is strong outside."

"Fernandes gives the orders at sea; have you forgotten?" White answered wryly, raising a bushy brow. He extended a hand to the minister. "God sent you to us, my friend; of that I am more certain each day. Take good care of my niece. I think of her as a daughter."

"You have no need to worry," Thomas answered, grasping White's hand. "God himself holds me responsible for her."

After an awkward farewell, Thomas excused himself and left the house. Jocelyn took pains to smooth her face so that her uncle would not see her unhappiness at her husband's departure. She had returned to their house a week ago, and Thomas had gallantly offered to let her and Audrey have the downstairs room while he slept on a cot in the attic above. His behavior with her was polite, ever aloof, and held no more affection than he might have shown a distant cousin. Worst of all, he refused to be alone with her, so she had not had a single opportunity to ask why he kept her at arm's length.

Wild wind hooted outside the house, and lightning cracked the skies apart as a sudden rain fell. Caught in the storm, surprised men and women called to each other outside, and Jocelyn heard the pounding of footsteps as colonists scurried for shelter.

"Perchance it is God's will that I remain here," her uncle said, peering out a wooden shutter as the wind came sliding through cracks in the house. He frowned. "A storm from the northeast. I hope Fernandes has enough sense to keep the ships from being battered onto the lee shore."

He turned from the window and smiled at Jocelyn's strained face. "There is nothing to worry about, my dear. Why don't you settle in here until the storm stops blowing? These storms spring up and pass in a matter of hours."

He walked again toward Eleanor's chamber to steal a few more moments with his grandchild, and Jocelyn sank onto a low stool at the table. There was nothing to do but wait.

▾▴▾▴ For nearly a week the storm battered the barrier islands. During one lull John White ventured down to the beach to discover that Simon Fernandes had cut his cables to protect the ships from the wind. The *Lion* and the flyboat had run for the open sea without even a full complement of seamen aboard, and White secretly suspected that Fernandes would have happily sailed for England and left the colonists forever had he not been missing most of his crew. Finally, six days after the storm's onslaught, the *Lion* and the flyboat were spotted off the coast. Word came from Captain Fernandes shortly after mid-day on August twenty-seventh: If John White still planned to go to England, he had half a day to get himself and his supplies on board. Simon Fernandes was sailing at midnight, and he would wait no longer.

▼▲▼▲▼ After supper that evening, Ananias Dare and Thomas Colman presented John White with a single document:

> May it please you, Her Majesty's subjects of England, we your friends and countrymen, the planters in Virginia, do by these presents let you and every of you to under-stand that, for the present and speedy supply of our known and apparent lacks and needs, most requisite and necessary, for the good and happy planting of us or any other in this land of Virginia, we all, of one mind and consent, have most earnestly entreated and inces-santly requested John White, Governor of the Planters in Virginia, to pass into England for the better and most assured help and setting forward of the foresaid sup-plies. And knowing, assuredly, that he both can best and will labor and take pains in that behalf for us all, and he not once, but often, refusing it, for our sakes and for the honor and maintenance of the action, has at last, though much against his will, through our importunacy, yielded to leave his government and all his goods among us and, himself, pass into England, of whose knowledge and fidelity in handling this matter, as all others, we do assure ourselves by these presents and will you to give all credit thereunto.

The document was signed by all adult men and women in the colony.

▼▲▼▲▼ Standing on the storm-littered beach in the darkness of early evening, Jocelyn tried to swallow the lump that rose in her throat each time she looked at her weary uncle. In his worn doublet and patched leggings, he looked less like an important governor than a beggar, but he carried himself with the dignity of a prince.

Lit only by the glow of torchlight, Thomas led the gathering in a benedictory prayer. The entire colony watched as John White kissed his daughter, embraced his son-in-law, and then paused with his aged hand on the dewy head of nine-day-old Virginia. "I'll be back before she knows I've gone," he said, smiling at Eleanor. "I promise you, my daughter, I'll be back very soon."

He turned, waved his hat at the crowd, and splashed through the dark waters where the shallop waited to convey him to the fleet, which rode at anchor offshore. Eleanor sobbed openly, her head buried in Ananias's shoulder, and Jocelyn felt suddenly chilled in the warm evening wind.

Ananias Dare

But where shall wisdom be found?
And where is the place of understanding?
Man knoweth not the price thereof;
Neither is it found in the land of the living.

Job 28:12-13

The dark waters chopped against the flyboat in the darkness, and John White paced the deck uneasily, his hands clasped behind his back. Was he wrong to leave the colony? A thousand voices called him back: his daughter, her baby, his niece, his belongings, the role of leadership that could not be freely abdicated. He had planned to give a lifetime to the colony, and his own people had sent him away after only a month and two days. A dark inner voice nagged at him: *Did they send you away because you are no leader?*

He turned swiftly and regarded the darkened shores of the barrier islands. If he had not been continually thrust against Simon Fernandes or if the swarthy Portuguese had not been so intent on capturing cursed Spanish treasure, the colony would have fared better. At least for this return voyage he would sail on Edward Spicer's flyboat, not on Fernandes's *Lion*. He could eat, sleep, and drink without seeing the face of that loathsome sea captain.

A bell rang across the black waters; the *Lion* was raising her anchor. On the flyboat, Captain Spicer gave the same order, and a crew of seamen sprang to turn the capstan, the large revolving drum around which the anchor cable was wound. Fifteen men—eight on the upper deck and seven on the lower—each grabbed one of the wooden bars protruding from the capstan. As the bosun chimed on the ship's bell, they rhythmically pushed the circular drum, slowly raising the anchor as the ship stirred on the murky waters.

"And so begins the next chapter," White told the darkness, bitterness in his voice. The journey home. The revelation of his failure to all who waited in England. Fernandes would tell horror stories about George Howe's murder, the primitive conditions, the attack on the fifteen caretakers, and the ill-fated assault at Dasemunkepeuc. Edward Stafford, also on board the *Lion,* might be counted upon to give a more truthful retelling of events, but White knew it would not be easy to convince Raleigh to continue what he might be persuaded to consider a hopeless venture.

A sudden crack ripped through the silence of the night, and men screamed as a hollow, thudding sound echoed along the deck. White turned in horror toward the capstan: one of the rods had broken, and the cylinder spun like a whirling dervish on the deck, its wooden bars thudding against the ribs of sailors who scrambled to move out of the way. The anchor cable hissed and thrummed as it ran back out to sea, and White watched in stunned amazement until the cable finally lay still.

Spicer thrust his head over the bridge and shouted orders. The dazed and wounded men rose, placed their hands on the remaining bars of the capstan, and tried again to raise the anchor. Several cried out in pain, one stumbled and fell, and White grimaced when another bar broke and the capstan again spun free and battered seamen as it sent the anchor back to its watery bed.

Spicer looked over the deck and caught White's eye. The torchlit *Lion* had already made her way into the east. With his shoulders drooping in resignation, Spicer gave the order to cut the cable and leave the anchor behind.

White knew the dangers of traveling without an anchor. If a storm should arise, the flyboat would be at the mercy of the winds, possibly to be wrecked on rocky northern shores. But with such a treacherous capstan, there seemed little else they could do.

The boatswain appeared below the captain's bridge. "If it please you, sir, twelve of the crew are badly injured," he called to Spicer, squinting in his reluctance to speak. "Something's broken inside 'em, Captain, and I don't know what to do."

"Twelve?" Spicer spoke with a voice of iron, but White heard a thread of uncertainty in it. The flyboat was a ship of one hundred tons, but her crew numbered only fifteen seamen, the captain, and the boatswain. Could such a skeleton crew bring the ship safely back to England?

"Aye, sir. Twelve," the boatswain called, folding his arms.

Spicer gripped the rail and stared out over the bow. "Then the remaining five of us will sail her home, won't we?"

The boatswain's graveled face broke into an admiring grin. "Aye, sir, by God's grace we will try."

Spicer nodded his dismissal, and as the boatswain hurried to move the injured men belowdecks, the captain turned to White. "How handy are you with a sail and cable?" he asked, raising one eyebrow quizzically.

White took a deep breath. "If it will get us back to England, I'll do anything I can to aid you."

"Good. We will need you," Spicer replied, moving confidently away.

The Sunday after John White's departure, Jocelyn sat outdoors with the other colonists and listened to her husband congratulate Dennis and Margery Harvie on the birth of their new daughter, Sylvie, the second child to be born in Her Majesty's Virginia.

After the murmurs of approval had faded, Thomas proceeded to detail a long list of rules recently approved by the council: thievery, bearing false witness, and slothfulness would be punished by public whipping. No Indian woman would be allowed to enter the village without proper and modest clothing. And given the great number of unmarried men in the colony, all English women were to journey in pairs, for modesty and safety's sake. No lady should ever walk abroad without her maidservant, and no maid should ever talk to a man after dark unless her mistress were also present.

Thomas stretched his long arm toward Ananias Dare, who stood and nodded solemnly toward the assembly. "This man will act as governor until John White's return," he said. "The council—Roger Prat, Roger Bailie, Christopher Cooper, and Thomas Stevens—will assist him when necessary. Civil affairs will be tried by Ananias and the council. Spiritual affairs are to be brought to me."

The assembly nodded in agreement; then Thomas stepped aside while Ananias listed the council's specific rules about English-Indian relations. He spoke bluntly: "Any Englishman who forces labor from an unwilling savage will be imprisoned for three months. Any Englishman who strikes an Indian will receive twenty blows with a cudgel in the Indian's presence. Any Englishman who enters an Indian's house without permission will be punished with six months' imprisonment. And any Englishman who forces his attention upon an Indian woman will be put to death."

The colonists received the list of rules without complaint, and Jocelyn lifted her chin proudly when she thought of the work done by Thomas and Ananias. In theory, the leaders of the colony had adhered to Raleigh's policies of equality for all and gentleness for the Indian savages. But as she stood with the others to sing a closing hymn, Jocelyn found herself thinking of little William Wythers. She had not found the time nor the courage to confront Thomas about the harshness of his judgment, but she was sure the whipping had done more than punish the child: It had changed him from a happy, bubbly boy into a shy, withdrawn shadow of what he once had been. And though no one spoke any more of the colony's attack on Dasemunkepeuc, that forgotten episode had been anything but gentle.

Could Raleigh's benevolent theories and ideals be put into practice?

▼▲▼▲▼ The merciless sun of early September smote the green fields where the colonists had planted corn and beans, and Jocelyn felt her stomach churn as she moved slowly among the tall plants. She had not breakfasted, for Thomas had proclaimed a day of fasting and prayer for John White's safe return to England, and she felt weak and dizzy in the blinding sunlight.

Speaking for the righteous good of the colony, Thomas had proclaimed many things since John White's departure. In an ever-lengthening series of pronouncements from his pulpit, he declared that women ought to always have their heads covered out of doors, since bonnets were necessary to shield a lady's fair skin from the harsh Virginia sun. "Furthermore," he admitted, "the sight of free-flying hair distracts men from their labors." Thomas later declared that Sunday morning sermon attendance would be compulsory, so that all colonists would have a weekly reminder that God's eye hovered over the colony and sin would not be tolerated. Recreation must be reserved for the Sabbath, he went on, swimming on the beach was strictly prohibited, and dancing should not be practiced in the colony lest the Indians see it and think the colonists bewitched.

The longer they remained on the island, the harder Thomas seemed to grow. Now that life had settled into a routine of sorts, Thomas seemed to wear an armor forged of duty and the expectations of pious people like Beth Glane. With every passing day, Jocelyn saw less and less of the man she loved and more of a man who was cold and demanding.

"Hurry, Miss Jocelyn, the sun will be wantin' to fry us soon." Audrey's sharp voice brought Jocelyn back from her musings, and she shifted the nearly empty basket on her hip and moved toward shade in the planted field.

The other women moved easily among the small planted hills, pulling ears of corn from the tall stalks as they gossiped about their men and their duties. Governor White had directed the colonists to plant corn as soon as possible in July, and that meager crop was now ready for harvesting and likely to produce their major store of food for the winter. Jocelyn tried not to think about the reality of possible starvation. She knew the Indians planted three different corn crops, one in May, one in June, and one in July, and even their villages found it difficult to feed themselves through the winter. How then were the English to survive?

The thought of starvation seemed not to have occurred to anyone else. Every day she joined the women harvesting the ripening food, but the other women seemed more interested in small talk and gossip than the crop. The governor had told them to assign one of the children to guard the corn from marauding animals, and this they had done, but only until John White left on the flyboat. He had also told them to water the plants daily and to plant beans in the shadow of the corn until the first frost, but lately those directives had been ignored as well. The corn withered in the heat. The straggly bean plants sprouted and died without ever bearing fruit.

White's instructions had been overlooked because Ananias

Dare insisted that the colonists concentrate on preparing for the
northward voyage to establish the City of Raleigh. Since White's
departure, Ananias brandished his strong opinion as fearlessly
as the remaining assistants murmured against him privately. But
in view of the knowledge that John White would soon return,
none dared speak out against the governor's son-in-law in council meetings. Only one dared speak out against Ananias at all,
and Jocelyn blushed whenever she heard reports that her own
husband was Ananias's chief adversary.

She reached for an ear of corn on a fresh green stalk, then
jerked her hand back when something stung her. A caterpillar
lay upon the husk of the corn, a horrid orange creature with
black spurs protruding from its head and tail.

Instantly, Jocelyn's arm tingled, then slowly grew numb. She
cried out in dismay, then childishly bit the reddening spot on her
hand. She heard Audrey's worried questions through a daze of
pain, then felt the earth shift beneath her feet as she fell into
blackness.

▼▲▼▲▼ She awoke on her own bed and felt the cool
dampness of cloths on her hand and head. Audrey stood between a crack of the bed curtains at the foot of the bed, her eyes
wide with fear. Jocelyn licked her parched lips before speaking.
"What happened?" she asked, trying to lift her head.

"An insect," Audrey began, glancing fearfully at someone else
in the room. "It must have been poisonous, Miss Jocelyn."

"You are quite all right, then." Thomas's deep voice startled
her, and his broad hand parted the curtains at the side of her
bed. He stood there, proper and unruffled in his dark leggings
and doublet, but in his hand lay another wet cloth for her hand.
He glanced at Audrey. "You may go back to the fields, Audrey.
I'll stay with Mistress Colman until she's well enough to join
you."

Jocelyn closed her eyes as Audrey left, and when she opened
them, Thomas leaned toward her, a polite smile on his face. "I

didn't know you were unused to fasting, my dear. If missing one meal makes you faint, how will you ever manage to fast for a week?"

"It wasn't the fast," she said, pressing her hands to the mattress beneath her to sit up. "It was a caterpillar. A horridly fearsome thing, all black and green and orange—"

"Such a little thing should not cause such a great reaction. Is anything else amiss?"

She felt her face go crimson. She had not been entirely surprised to find herself in bed, for she had felt ill for several days. But she knew the colony could not afford to spare a single pair of hands for nursing, and she had not even discussed her condition with Eleanor or Audrey. But she awoke every morning with queasiness in her stomach, and her monthly flow of blood had not come for weeks. She waited every day for her cycle to begin, remembering with shame that years ago she had thought herself dying when she first began to bleed. But Eleanor had laughed at her fears and told her that it was the curse of women to bleed every month, and as long as she did, all was well. But now that it had stopped . . .

"I am sick." The words slipped from her traitorous tongue, and Thomas's dark eyes narrowed in concentration.

"You are ill? Why didn't you say something sooner?"

Jocelyn shook her head. He had loved a woman and lost her. What right had she to make him go through the experience again? Better that she live as though nothing were wrong for as long as possible; then she could leave the village to die in peace and privacy as her father had.

"Tell me, Jocelyn! What is wrong?" Thomas's tone was urgent, and his hand closed around her upper arm so tightly that she wanted to cry out.

"Nothing of importance, I'm sure, and I didn't want to bother you. But I am sick in the morning and evening, and I no longer bleed like other women—"

With a swift intake of breath, he released her arm and stepped back, clearly stunned. His eyes widened. "Impossible!" he murmured, a crazily twisted smile upon his face.

"I'm sorry, Thomas," she said, alarmed at his expression. She must be dying. Why else would he react so strangely? How had he known she would bring him so much pain? He had resisted her from the beginning, but she had insisted upon staying with him. Why? To wound him yet again?

"Let me go live with Eleanor," she said, lowering her eyes from his distorted face. "She is my family. You won't have to nurse me. I do not want to be a burden to you as I grow ill—"

"Hush, girl!" He pressed his hand to his forehead, then raked his fingers through his hair. His eyes, when he looked at her again, glowed with an inner fire. "Is it possible that you do not know?"

"Know what?" she asked, scarcely daring to breathe.

He sank onto the mattress and stared at his tented hands. "Did no woman explain these things to you?"

"What things?" Suddenly she felt very childish, and he turned to her, his eyes gentling. Tenderly, he laid his hand upon her stomach. "When a man and a woman are married, when they share private moments as we did—"

She blushed and looked away. His palm seemed to burn her flesh through her clothing.

He paused, then lowered his voice as he removed his hand. "I'm sorry. I did not mean for this to happen, Jocelyn. I never wanted to—but I am flesh, and you were mine, and we were alone, and in those first days I thought perhaps things would be different here."

"What we did—was wrong?" she whispered, not daring to look up.

"No." He lowered his head to look into her eyes. "Our act of love was designed by God for the procreation of children. You are with child, my wife. In seven or eight months, if God is willing, you will bear me a son or a daughter."

The chill of shock left her silent. A child! Like Eleanor, she would swell with a baby within her, and on a given day that child would come forth from within her womb and wake the village with its cries. She wanted to laugh; she wanted to cry. She had a husband; she would have a baby. Why, then, did she not feel like a mother or even a proper wife?

She lifted her eyes and saw a mingling of pity and regret on her husband's face. "Why are you sorry?" she demanded, strengthened by sudden fury. "You created this—situation, and yet you say you regret it. Why, Thomas?"

His face emptied of expression, and he turned away to face the blank wall. She shivered, suddenly cold.

"I have a son already," he said tonelessly. "I never wanted another. I should not have—I do not want other children."

"But if what we did was not wrong, then it was right. This is God's doing."

He nodded soberly and stood, adjusting his doublet with a sharp downward pull. "God is forever punishing me," he said, stepping toward the door. He paused and glanced at her again. "Tell no one of this until the truth cannot be avoided. But you should not work in the field until you feel strong enough. Break your fast, Mistress Colman, and I will send Audrey to you with some soup. If God has seen fit to do this thing, I will accept his hand of judgment."

"Judgment?" Jocelyn's mouth went dry.

"Aye. But you need not fear, my wife." His mouth tipped in a faint smile. "I have promised to take care of you, and I will."

▼▲▼▲▼ After leaving his wife, Thomas Colman purposely broke one of the council's rules and walked alone in the woods outside the village. Let the savages find and kill him. It would only be another proof of God's hand of judgment upon his soul.

How could he have allowed passion to escape the bonds of self-control? In a moment of weakness he had allowed his heart and soul to be overcome by the vain notion that the girl loved him. He had dared to dream that this was an island paradise where the conventions of a righteous civilization might easily be left behind, and he had taken his wife into his arms. He had been totally entranced by her love and the joy of being with her—until God had sent Beth Glane and John Jones to remind him of his place in the colony. And the council, speaking harshly that afternoon, had reminded him that he was to be the embodiment of righteous living, the example to whom they could all turn in times of temptation.

On that afternoon, the chains and dark habits of his past life fell upon him again, and he accepted them all as meet punishment from the hand of God. *Fool!* he cried in his heart. *How could you think you had left your shackles far beyond the sea?* For a brief time, he had been a free man, and in that time he had fallen in love with the young woman who now carried his child . . . a woman whose presence was intoxicating . . . a woman he must put out of sight and out of mind lest he fall again.

He slammed his hand on a tree trunk in fury. It should not be! He had already sacrificed one child on the altar of submission; how could he surrender another? And how could he tell his fellow colonists, so many of them unmarried men, that they must subjugate their fleshly desires when it would now be obvious that he had not been able to master his own? For a brief, shining moment when he realized that Jocelyn carried his child, joy had risen in his heart like a summer morn. But then he had remembered the others and their wagging tongues, and darkness blotted out his joy like blackest night.

"God in heaven," he roared, scattering a flock of birds as he lifted a fist into the bright afternoon sun, "why do you torment me so? What must I do to appease your anger? And why—" his voice broke—"why do you punish sweet Jocelyn so? She does not deserve to bear my punishment!"

But through the mouths of Beth Glane and John Jones, God had spoken. He had allowed his erring sheep a season of sinful pleasure and then relentlessly goaded him back into the fold.

Out at sea, Captain Edward Spicer's flyboat kept pace with Simon Fernandes's flagship until the ships arrived at Terceira in the Azores. Here Fernandes and his crew were eager to linger, hoping to snare a treasure ship bound for Spain and share its riches, but White convinced Spicer that the more prudent action lay in continuing to England.

With a shipload of injured seamen, Spicer had little choice. Privately, White reminded his friend and captain that the colony's survival depended in part upon their reaching England before Fernandes, who would surely spread stories to discourage further colonial investors.

The crew of the flyboat left the *Lion* in a safe harbor and headed east to England, but for twenty days they drifted aimlessly under scarce and variable winds. White was concerned for the injured seamen, for they spat blood and lay pale and lifeless belowdecks. He became truly alarmed when he discovered that leaks in the water barrels had almost completely depleted their supply of fresh water.

On September twenty-eighth, after twenty days of purposeless drifting, a storm arose from the northeast and blew the ship so far off course that Spicer had no idea where they were. Pilots had no way of determining a ship's longitude, and by using the astrolabe to measure the elevation of the sun above the horizon at noon, Spicer could only determine that they were more than two weeks away from their position before the storm.

Belowdecks, conditions worsened. The sailors, already weak from internal injuries suffered by the buffeting of the capstan, began to fall sick and die. Their food supply, even the insect-infested and petrified sea biscuit, had long been gone. Only one barrel did not leak, and into this the boatswain poured the remains of the blackened water, the dregs of beer, and a few inches of wet sediment from emptied casks of wine. Altogether, less than three gallons of liquid remained, and White fully expected the entire company to perish at sea from dehydration. The stinking liquid, precious nonetheless, was carefully rationed each day as the weak seamen set the sails and contemplated death.

After a blur of days in such dreary speculation, a sailor in the crow's nest called out, "Land ho!" and White stirred from the tattered blanket on which he had been lying. Was it possible that he should be saved? He had thought the trials of this trip God's just punishment for deserting the colony, but perhaps salvation loomed ahead.

The uninjured seamen used their remaining strength to survey the harbor into which they sailed. An English pinnace lay at anchor there, and after an hour, her shallop approached. After answering the visitors' greeting, the men of the flyboat learned that they were in the port of Smerwick, on the west coast of Ireland.

The men of the pinnace provided Spicer's crew with desperately needed fresh water, wine, and meat, but three of the injured men died within a day of reaching Ireland, and three more were taken off the ship, too sick to continue.

With regret, White knocked on Spicer's door.

"Come in."

White pushed the cabin door open and found Edward Spicer writing in his log. "Excuse me, Captain, but another ship, the *Monkey*, leaves on the morrow for England. I plan to book passage on her."

Spicer looked up, his face clear and untroubled. "Do not bother yourself with me, John. I know you are eager to return to England."

"I am sorry, Edward, but everything depends on me. If Fernandes reaches England before I do—"

Spicer waved a hand. "I'm only sorry that we can't be ready to sail so soon. But I can't risk my ship."

"Your ship is done, Edward. Leave it to a salvage crew, and let your men stay here in Ireland until they are well. I must return to England, but I'll need a witness to combat Fernandes's lies when I get there." He lowered his voice and took a seat on a stool across from the sea captain. "You know the condition of those we left behind in Virginia. They'll not last until spring unless we get help to them. I am begging you, friend. Come to England with me on the morrow."

Spicer put down his pen and folded his hands. "Aye, sir, there's truth in your words. As long as Raleigh understands that I'm not deserting his ship here in Ireland—"

"Have you forgotten how Fernandes deserted you in the Bay of Portugal?" White felt his anger rising, but for Eleanor's sake, and the baby's, he had to calm himself. "Come with me, Edward. I'faith, there are one hundred sixteen people on Roanoke who are depending on us. Can we forget them?"

Spicer's eyes darkened in pity. "No," he answered, closing his journal. "I cannot."

The next morning John White and Edward Spicer took passage on the *Monkey*, which landed them at Marazion in Cornwall. From there they rode to Southampton, arriving on November eighth.

▼▲▼▲▼ When John White arrived at Southampton in November 1587, he discovered that Simon Fernandes had been in England for three weeks. But the Portuguese captain had reported little about the misfortunes of the Roanoke colony, so terrible had been his own fate since leaving the Azores. One of Fernandes's seamen confided to White that not only had the ship not captured any Spanish treasure but the *Lion*'s crew, too, had been overcome by sickness and many had died. The remaining crew had been too weak to even bring the ship into the harbor and had been forced to drop anchor in the open sea. Had a small bark not happened to spot the desolate ship, they might all have died while on board.

As eager as he was to see his enemy confounded, White was not cheered by news of the *Lion*'s troubles. Though the misfortunes of Spicer's and Fernandes's ships had nothing to do with the Virginian colony, the investors in England would frown on news about the difficulty in seafaring. To them, the colony at Roanoke was still little more than a possible base for privateering, and if English ships did not perform profitably at sea, of what use was a colony?

With the colony's new prohibition on unmarried men and women meeting together privately, Jocelyn found herself much in demand as a chaperon whenever William Clement summoned Audrey. Often Jocelyn forgot who was the mistress and who the servant as she walked discreetly ahead of the pair, for Audrey seemed to be deliriously in love with the man whom Jocelyn privately considered to be a scoundrel. She could not fault William Clement's words or manners, for both were suitably polished in the presence of ladies, nor his appearance, for he cleaned up considerably well. But a shadowy sneer hovered about his heavy mouth, and once or twice she felt his cool blue eyes studying her in a way that made her blush. Pure masculine interest radiated in his glance when any pretty woman crossed his path, and Jocelyn marveled that Audrey did not see it.

But he played the role of suitor to Audrey wonderfully, often exclaiming that if Fate had only dealt the cards differently, he would have married Audrey in England and installed her as his lady on the prosperous family estate.

Jocelyn knew there was no family estate, for it was common knowledge that William Clement and James Hynde had been released from prison to serve as indentured servants in Virginia. She wondered that Audrey did not doubt her suitor's tale, for he spoke with the unmistakable accent of an eastern herdsman, and a genuine noble would never have ended up on Roanoke as an indentured servant, no matter how fallen the family fortunes. But Audrey was obviously smitten with the charming young man, and Jocelyn determined to keep silent despite her reservations.

Perchance, she asked herself one afternoon as the lovers walked along the beach behind her, *if someone had told you that you would encounter heartbreak and sorrow if you married Thomas Colman, would you have listened?*

And because her heart answered no, she kept quiet and said nothing.

▼▲▼▲▼ Walking to Eleanor's house one afternoon, Jocelyn wrapped her wool cloak around her and lowered her head as the biting wind threatened to chill her to the bone. November in Roanoke blew alternately warm and cool, depending upon whether the wind came from the chilly north or the more temperate south, but this morning's winds were the coldest the colony had yet experienced. For the first time Jocelyn felt that winter had arrived.

The colonists were prepared. The small bounty of the field had long been interned inside the storehouse, and the houses and fort reinforced with fresh mud and timber for the wrath of the coming weather.

Jocelyn noticed that her own body had thickened as if to fortify itself for the winter, but she knew it struggled to shelter and preserve the small life that grew within. It had been four months since the time the child had been conceived, and she yearned to share her secret with Audrey or Eleanor. But each time she looked to Thomas to see if she ought to tell, his stony glance stilled the question on her lips.

She had thought him distant after his confrontation with Beth Glane and John Jones, but since the hot September day when he had explained that she would bear a child, he had been even more so. Every afternoon he came home late from his work, ate his supper silently by the hearth, then climbed the ladder to the upper floor, where he slept and studied. He had not touched her—indeed, he had scarcely even *looked* at her during the past weeks. If Audrey thought the situation strange, she said nothing.

Jocelyn's teeth chattered as she pressed through the whirling air to Eleanor's house. It was possible that Audrey said nothing because she profited from the couple's odd arrangement. By all rights, she should have been sleeping upstairs in the drafty attic, so she did not complain that Jocelyn allowed Audrey to share the pleasant and comfortable mattress downstairs. "Just like sisters, we are," Audrey often said as she slipped on her nightgown and climbed into the tall bed.

Jocelyn knew little of proper behavior between husbands and their wives, but she knew it was unusual for her husband to choose to sleep in the attic. Even if he did not love her, why would he not do the simple things other married couples took for granted?

Did he feel guilty for betraying the first love of his life or the child he had left behind in England? *Surely, Father God, there is a way to convince him to begin life anew!* Jocelyn prayed, standing still in the bawling winds. *We have all begun new lives here, so why can't Thomas leave the past behind? I love him, Lord, and have love enough for both of us, but if my presence only serves to remind him of the wife he lost, how am I to show my love? How can he love our child if our baby reminds him of the son he can no longer see? Help me to understand him, Lord. Love him through me.*

"Is that you, Miss Jocelyn?"

Agnes Wood's voice cut through Jocelyn's concentration, and she opened her eyes and gave the maid a smile. Agnes had apparently just returned from the community woodpile, for she carried a bundle of logs in a leather sling.

"I've come for a little visit," Jocelyn said, rubbing her hands together to keep warm.

"Why, come on in, dear. Miss Eleanor will be glad to see you." Agnes led the way to the house and opened the door, and Eleanor looked up from her stool with a smile. Three-month-old Virginia nursed greedily at her mother's breast.

"What brings you here, Cousin?" Eleanor asked pleasantly as Jocelyn came in and Agnes latched the door behind her. "Surely your husband would rather you spent the Sabbath with him."

Abruptly, Jocelyn told Eleanor she was going to have a baby.

▼▲▼▲▼ Eleanor read the worry and fear in her young cousin's eyes and told Agnes to tend the mending and leave them alone. When the servant had left the room and Jocelyn had removed her cloak and taken a seat on a low stool, Eleanor leaned forward and lightly ran her finger down Jocelyn's cheek. "I know what you must be feeling, Coz. Myself, I was frightened to death when I first realized I would have a baby. But God will keep you in his care. How proud Thomas must be!"

A flood of tears sprang to Jocelyn's eyes, and Eleanor was wholly taken aback when the younger girl covered her face with her hands and began to weep. Surely this news alone could not be so upsetting! Every married woman expected a child sooner or later. It was God's plan and only natural.

"Softly now," Eleanor said, smoothing Jocelyn's windblown hair. "I understand how frightened you must feel. 'Tis a daunting prospect, giving birth in the wilderness, but I'll be here for you, Cousin. You will have a lovely baby. Thomas will be thrilled, no doubt, and baptize the babe in front of the entire village—"

"Thomas does not want a baby," Jocelyn said, choking on her tears. "He told me he was sorry for it, that God was tormenting him. He said the baby was—"

"Ofttimes men don't know what they say," Eleanor interrupted, placing her own infant in a rough-hewn cradle near the fire. She turned and knelt at Jocelyn's feet. "Dear Coz, all men feel differently when they hold their babes in their arms. I believe even Ananias was discomfited when he learned we would have a baby in America, but see how he dotes on Virginia now!"

Jocelyn sniffed. "Thomas says the baby is God's way of punishing him," she said, wiping her tears on her sleeve.

"Faith, the man's lost his mind!" Eleanor cried, then struggled to control her anger as she took Jocelyn's hands. "Perhaps he thinks a baby would make him feel old or some such thing; that is all. You mark my words, Coz, he will change." She lowered her voice and gave Jocelyn a secret smile. "When the babe is old enough to kick, place your hand over his and guide it to your belly. The babe will kick him, and then, dear Cousin, he will change his way of thinking!"

She flashed Jocelyn a triumphant smile, but the younger girl blushed deeply and shook her head. She shuddered, as if parting with a secret too terrible to be borne, then confessed, "Eleanor, he sleeps in the attic."

Stung, Eleanor sat back, then realized with numb astonishment that her cousin spoke the truth. "What?" she whispered, taking care that Agnes shouldn't overhear. "Indeed, it's not natural, Jocelyn. Why does he sleep in the attic?"

Jocelyn only shook her head while Eleanor's mind reeled through realms of bizarre possibilities. "Is it possible he's a Catholic?" she whispered, leaning forward. "I hear the Catholic priests have sworn not to touch women. Could he be a Spaniard? A spy? He is dark enough, there's no gainsaying that. Think, Jocelyn, if he has ever said anything to you or done anything to impede our cause here . . ."

Jocelyn wept anew, burying her face in her hands, and Eleanor bit her lip. Should she report this to her husband? Ananias had reported that the minister was frequently at odds with him, arguing over foolish ideas. Was it possible Eleanor's own father had been duped by a Catholic Spaniard in disguise?

"I must warn Ananias," Eleanor said, standing. She moved toward the wall where her cloak hung. "Stay here, dear, and do not go home. You and Audrey can have my father's room, while Ananias and I—"

"No, Eleanor!" Jocelyn flew from the stool and wrapped her arms around her cousin's shoulders. "He is not a spy. He has taken no vow. He sleeps in the attic because he loves his first wife still, a woman who died after giving him a son. He weeps for his lost love, Eleanor, and will not let me replace her in his heart."

Shaken, Eleanor pulled herself from Jocelyn's embrace. "How do you know this?" she whispered.

Jocelyn shrugged unhappily. "He told me the story while we

were on the ship. I married him knowing full well that he still grieved for his wife, but I thought I could be his helper, a fellow worker for the cause of the gospel. I did not—I have not dared hope he would love me, but thought he might, in time, come to have affection for me."

"Apparently he has some liking, for you carry his baby," Eleanor pointed out.

Jocelyn's chin quivered. "One night we were alone. He asked me if I truly wanted to be his wife, and I said yes. . . ."

"I see." Eleanor studied her cousin's unhappy face. Twin reflections of the fire danced in her liquid blue eyes, but behind the reflections lay bottomless pools of grief. "Perchance," Eleanor whispered, slipping her arm around Jocelyn's shoulders, "in time, your Thomas will come to love his child. You must trust God, Jocelyn, for this thing to come to pass. You are young, and your marriage is new. Give God time."

A flurry of chilled autumn wind blew into the room as Ananias opened the door and came into the house. He raised an eyebrow at the sight of Jocelyn's tear-streaked face, but said nothing as he removed his cloak and hung it on a peg in the wall.

Eleanor ran her eyes over him carefully. "Are you well, my husband?" she asked.

"Very well," he said, smiling politely at Jocelyn. He walked over to the fire, held his hands over the crackling blaze, then brushed his hands together and looked up the stairs toward the attic room. "Where's Agnes? Is our supper almost ready?"

"It will be soon enough," Eleanor answered, giving Jocelyn an encouraging smile. The younger girl wiped her eyes and nodded her thanks, then moved to the door. "So will you be going, Cousin?"

"Yes," Jocelyn answered, taking her cloak from the wall. "Thank you for your counsel, Eleanor. I will trust all to our Lord's hands."

"Marry, you have spoken well," Eleanor answered, opening the door for her cousin. After Jocelyn had slipped out of the house, Eleanor latched the door and turned to stare at her husband.

"What?" he demanded, turning to her in exasperation. "What have I done now, woman?"

"Mayhap you should tell me," Eleanor answered, moving smoothly to stir the hanging iron pot in the hearth fire. "Where have you been, Ananias?"

In the elaborately paneled drawing room of Sir Walter Raleigh's royal apartments, John White used every glowing adjective he could remember as he described the progress of the Roanoke colony. He explained that the colony had disembarked at Roanoke only because of the treachery of Simon Fernandes, and the group had made plans to move northward in the spring to found the City of Raleigh in the Chesapeake region.

Sir Walter, as handsome and debonair as ever, stroked his manicured beard thoughtfully. "If the settlers are not on Roanoke Island when you arrive, how will you know where they have gone?" he asked, leaning forward in his chair.

"We have agreed upon a sign," White answered, folding his hands in what he hoped was a casual gesture. "They will inscribe the location of their destination in a tree trunk, plainly visible. If they have left in distress or under attack, they will also inscribe a Maltese cross upon the tree. When we return with the supplies, we will be able to reach the colonists in a matter of days."

Raleigh sank back in his chair and rested his head on his hand. For a moment he neither spoke nor moved, a handsome statue resplendent in a doublet and hose of straw-colored satin and a cloak of gilded Spanish leather. Perfumed gloves lay across his knee. The perfect picture of refinement. But John White hoped that under Raleigh's polished exterior still beat the heart of an adventurer, someone who would take a risk for the planters on Roanoke.

"So what do you suggest we do, John White?" Raleigh finally said, his brown eyes shining with interest.

John tried to curb his eagerness. He was virtually bursting with information and news he wanted to impart, but one never, ever wanted Sir Walter to feel ordered about. "I propose to equip a pinnace with supplies and a group of new settlers, particularly those wives who wait in England to join their husbands," White said, leaning gently forward. "The colony does need some provisions to ensure a safe passage through the winter, so the pinnace should depart immediately. While the pinnace sails, we will outfit a major supply fleet of seven or eight ships to sail in the spring. If Sir Richard Grenville would lead the fleet—"

"Why not Simon Fernandes?" Raleigh interrupted.

White made a face. "If you will read my journal, sir, you will see why I cannot sail again with Simon Fernandes. I have suspicions that he is at worst a spy, at best an opportunist concerned only with privateering for his personal gain."

Raleigh leaned back in his chair and stroked his beard again. "Your former colleague, Thomas Hariot, has a manuscript ready for publication," he said. "If this work were published to increase interest, investors would more readily sign on to support our venture."

"Exactly!" White pummeled the air with his fist and saw Raleigh smile at his enthusiasm.

"Enough," Raleigh said, standing to his feet. "We will do what must be done, Governor White. You did right by coming here personally, and we will do right by sending you back to your daughter and granddaughter with all due haste."

White stood, too, and bowed, silently thanking God that Raleigh's visions of a sprawling and prosperous Virginian estate outrivaled his doubts about the benefits and profits of privateering.

▼▲▼▲▼ During the English winter of 1587, draughts whistled among the tapestries of London's fine houses. The constant damp made fires balk and turned the gentry's fine clothing slick and musty. Biting winds churned the unruly waves of the

English Channel so violently that John White's pinnace could not sail.

Bravely shouldering his disappointment, John White said innumerable prayers for the safety of the colony and his family, then concentrated his efforts upon equipping the large fleet that was to sail in the late spring. The wives of Roger Bailie, Thomas Stevens, Roger Prat, and John Sampson were contacted and began making arrangements to sail to Virginia, and White had the sad responsibility of visiting the widow of George Howe to inform her of her husband's death. The widow Howe elected to remain in England rather than join her son, consigning him to the care of God and John White. White could not pass judgment upon the grieving woman. Those who did not have the courage to cross the Western ocean should not set out on such a journey.

His disappointment over the pinnace's failure to sail was tempered by the discussion of Thomas Hariot's manuscript, *A Brief and True Report of the New Found Land of Virginia*. Interest in the colony and in Virginia soared, and White found himself in demand as a dinner guest of gentlefolk who peered over their silver plate to inquire about rumors of savages, wild animals, and the possibility of gold in the sandy shores of Virginia.

"God will not bless us if we neglect his worship any longer!"
Thomas Colman's angry voice echoed over the assembly, and
Ananias Dare noticed several of the colonists nodding in agreement. This minister was dangerous and, in Ananias's opinion, an
unwelcome addition to the colony.

"Would you prefer to starve or pray this winter?" Ananias
asked, opening his hands to the men and women who had gathered on benches in the circular clearing to hear the minister's sermon. "The Reverend wants us to take precious time and energy
to build a church, but I say it's more important to hunt. Winter is
upon us, but with salted meat in the storehouse—"

"Hunting will take us into the forests of the Indians," Arnold
Archard spoke up, his hand on his young son's head. "And I
dare not venture from this island nor from my house without the
blessing and protection of God."

"Aye," Edward Powell stood. "Does not the Word of God
instruct us to bring our firstfruits into the storehouse? We have
made no storehouse for God, and we need a place fit for worship. This open space—" he spread his hands to indicate the
clearing where they had gathered—"is not sufficient. Our
women and children will not want to meet here in the cold of
January. But we can build a church for worship, and a place for
assembly."

"Mark me, why should we build?" John Sampson interrupted, standing. "I would as lief build a castle as a church. We
are leaving this place in the spring, so we don't need a permanent building."

"The building can be disassembled, as can our homes."

Thomas Colman stepped forward again, and Ananias noticed with disapproval that nearly every eye turned respectfully toward the minister. "We can build a sound structure of wattle-and-daub panels. When it comes time to leave, the house of God can easily be carried with us."

"The house of God." Ananias stepped forward, his upper lip curling in distaste. "We worship God in our hearts and in our homes. We do not need to invest our labor in this man's idea. He merely seeks an outlet for his calling, for he is no farmer. If you let him build this church, he will demand a tithe of your crops next, a tithe of your venison, your squirrel, your gold. If we give in to his demands for God at this juncture, I believe we will be supporting the minister and his wife for years to come." He slammed his fist onto his open palm. "'Tis not to be borne! Would you serve the state church of England even here? We were promised self-government, and we ought to worship in the sanctity of our own homes. Each man must see to his own to prepare for the winter. We do not have time to build a church!"

Ananias smiled inwardly when many faces nodded in agreement and voices buzzed in private discussion. But then the minister stepped forward and held up his strong hands. The crowd stilled.

"God demands nothing from a heathen man," he said, his dark eyes sweeping over the assembled group. "But of those who call themselves his people, he demands everything. The tithe is the Lord's, but more than that, everything we are and own is his. I beseech you, my brothers and sisters, to make of yourselves a living sacrifice, holy, acceptable unto God, which is your reasonable service."

Ananias felt the pull of the minister's dark eyes, and he looked steadfastly away.

"I will not command you to build a church," the minister went on. "I will ask you to commit yourselves to this duty. Whatever man will come to build, let him come. Whatever man will ignore the blessings and commands of God, let him stay away and tend to his own affairs. But if you would ask God to provide safety, security, and provision for the winter, 'tis only fair that you provide the same for God's people who want to worship. If you care not for the things of God, consider this: There are savage arrows in the forest. Will the one flying toward you be swayed by the hand of God or find its place in your breast?"

The minister sat down, but the air trembled with his thinly veiled threat. Wives whispered into the ears of their husbands; men nodded in reply. Ananias knew in that moment the minister had won. How could he compete against a man who, seemingly backed by the Almighty, promised certain death if they did not obey his wishes?

Nudged by his wife, Henry Payne stood. "I will meet you tomorrow, Reverend, to begin building," he said.

"So will I!" This from Roger Bailie.

Cries of agreement echoed through the camp until nearly all the men stood. The minister nodded soberly in agreement, and Ananias wiped all signs of defeat from his face. The minister had won this time. But he would not win again.

▾▲▾▲▾ Thomas paused in his labor to wipe the sweat from his brow. Nearly all the colonists had turned out to build the church, even Ananias's followers. Though they had complained loud and long in the town meeting, not one of them wanted to be thought less Christian than the next man.

The sound of laughter interrupted his thoughts, and Thomas turned to see old Roger Bailie sharing a laugh with Jocelyn and Audrey. The women were gathering the slender twigs that would be woven into thatching for the roof, and the elder gentleman had taken time out to do a bit of harmless flirting. An irrational spirit of jealousy rose in Thomas's soul. Why did the man think it proper to smile at his wife?

He was about to open his mouth and say something, but at that moment Jocelyn caught Thomas's eye. The smile disappeared from her face as completely as if she'd wiped it away with her hand, and Thomas's jealousy was instantly displaced by guilt. Jocelyn was always hiding her smiles in his presence. He knew she felt the need to bridle her natural high spirits when he was near, and the steely strength he had first noticed in her had long been buried under a cloak of submission and forbearance. She worked hard to be a good minister's wife, and truly he had no complaints—but regret was sharp as he wondered where she had secreted away the spirited girl he loved.

▼▲▼▲▼ Eleanor threw her cousin a sparkling smile and shifted baby Virginia in her arms as she embraced Jocelyn. "There, Cousin, I am glad you have come! Agnes is of no help to me with Virginia, for she spends all day cooking or gossiping with the other servants. How are you feeling?"

Jocelyn shrugged as she untied her cloak, then sank onto a stool near the warm hearth fire. "I am well. The baby has begun to move and kick."

"Ah," Eleanor smiled, struggling with the active child in her arms. "And has Thomas—"

Jocelyn shook her head. "Thomas still sleeps above in the attic. It's all right. We are both busy. He works all day to build the church, and I am helping Beth Glane gather limbs for the walls. Thomas and I never speak, even while I am helping with the building."

"You shouldn't be working so!" Eleanor said, alarm crossing her face. "I'm surprised he would let you."

Jocelyn stared into the dancing flames. "I'm only helping to weave the twigs into the walls. Tomorrow we begin to cover the twigs with clay, then the men will put the walls into position. The church should be finished very soon."

"So Thomas is happy?" Eleanor asked gently.

"Thomas is never happy. He is . . . satisfied."

Jocelyn's lovely face was strained by exhaustion, her brows a brooding knot over her eyes. Eleanor studied her young cousin's countenance for a moment, then clucked in quiet sympathy. "Why don't you carry Virginia to the upstairs room for me?" she suggested, hoping that time alone with the playful baby might lift Jocelyn's spirits. What woman did not love a baby, particularly when her own womb brimmed with new life? "She has nursed, and she may want to play for a bit before falling asleep."

Jocelyn nodded in quiet agreement, then lifted Virginia from Eleanor's arms and carefully climbed the narrow staircase to the attic room. Eleanor watched them go, then bit her lip. The minister had seemed a decent sort of man in the beginning, but of late he had made her cousin miserable and turned Ananias into a raging tyrant. Ever since the colony chose to follow the minister instead of bowing before Ananias's recommendation—

The door opened, and Ananias entered in a whirl of bitter cold. Of all the colonists and council members, only he had absolutely refused to work on the church in any way, preferring to spend his time hunting. His face was red with cold as he entered, his eyes steely glints of anger.

Eleanor pressed her lips together. There was nothing she could say to him when he was in such a mood.

"Well," he snapped, tossing his cloak to her. "Aren't you going to inquire where I've been?"

"It's obvious you've been hunting," she answered, hanging his cloak on a peg.

"Are you certain?" he taunted, standing his musket near the door. "How do you know I wasn't with one of the servant girls? Aren't you going to send your spies among the villagers to establish how I spent my afternoon?"

Eleanor turned and lowered her voice, mindful of Jocelyn in the attic. "Soft, Ananias, I have forgiven you, have I not said so? You gave me your word that it would not happen again, and I have chosen to trust you."

"Then why do you look at me like that every time I come in late?"

"How do I look at you?" She found herself hissing.

"Like I'm an adulterer! If you are still upset about the child in England—"

"I'm not upset. I just wish you'd told me before we married."

She lowered her voice and sat on her stool near the fire. "'Tis an awful surprise to hear that your husband's got a child hidden out in the country. What was I supposed to think? I couldn't help wondering how many others can call you papa."

His jaw clenched. "I've done nothing since we married, Eleanor. I've not been unfaithful to you."

"A husband can be unfaithful in more than one way." She bit her lip, instantly regretting her words. "Please, Ananias, I trust you. The past is past, so pray let the matter lie."

"Yet you look at me with hate in your eyes."

She sighed and leaned her head on her hand. "I look at you with less than love because I am tired. Your guilt drives you to believe otherwise."

"My *guilt?*" Ananias thrust his hands on his hips. "First you, and then the minister. Every eye in the colony turns on me with suspicion."

Eleanor felt her heart beat faster. "They don't know—"

"No." Ananias waved away her concerns. "They think I am a heathen, an apostate, an ungodly leader because I would have led them to neglect their duties to God. If not for that cursed Thomas Colman—"

"Pray hold your tongue!" Eleanor lifted her eyes to the ceiling and pointed upward. "My cousin is in the attic with the baby."

"Think you that I care?" Ananias snorted, falling onto a stool by the fire. "He is a cursed minister, and 'tis time Jocelyn learned the truth. He would not have married her—"

Eleanor reached out and grabbed his arm. "Ananias, please!"

He thrust her off with a powerful push and stood beneath the opening to the attic. "He would not have married Jocelyn at all if not for our governor's arrangement," he called up the stairs. "A poor man, Thomas Colman was, without the money for passage. Rather than sell himself into indentured service, the honorable John White arranged for the minister to marry his niece."

"Ananias!" Eleanor screamed in fury, her patience gone.

The muscles in Ananias's face tightened into a mask of rage, but he continued. "That cursed minister bought his way into this family! The governor himself would wash his hands of the entire affair if he were here!"

Eleanor trembled, resisting the urge to fly at him; then he yanked his cloak from the wall and slammed the door as he stormed into the night.

Eleanor fell onto her bed, shaking beyond control. What he had done was monstrously cruel with Jocelyn so vulnerable. She did not have to look up to know that Jocelyn's pale face peered down from the attic. "A pox upon him!" Eleanor whispered, clenching her fists. "He didn't mean it, Coz. He was angry." *Please believe me.*

She heard the swish of Jocelyn's garments upon the stairs, then, stone-faced, Jocelyn slipped her cloak over her shoulders. "The baby is asleep," she whispered, tying the ribbon of her cloak. "She will sleep till the morrow, I think.

Jocelyn turned toward the door, and Eleanor rose up and caught her hand. The younger girl's eyes shone like a wounded animal's.

Eleanor tried to inject confidence into her voice. "In truth, Ananias does not know of what he speaks. Whatever you have heard here today, 'tis best forgotten."

Jocelyn stared blankly past her, then turned again for the door. "I give you good day, Coz. Sleep well."

▼▲▼▲▼ Jocelyn did not say a word to Thomas during supper, and he seemed too preoccupied with his own thoughts to notice her silence. Audrey shot Jocelyn a questioning glance once, but after Thomas had climbed up to his attic and the women had settled downstairs, Audrey fell asleep without any discussion of the chilly supper.

But Jocelyn could not sleep. The initial shock of the afternoon's revelation had worn off, and Jocelyn slumped into morose musings as she lay in the darkness. The heaviness in her chest felt like a millstone, the thickness of her belly a terrible burden. No wonder the baby seemed a horror to him. He had not

married her out of affection or even friendship—Thomas Colman had proposed marriage to avoid servitude!

The truth stung like salt upon an open wound. She had
believed, given the advance of their friendship upon the ship,
that he at least considered her an equal, someone with whom he
might build a passable marriage. She had known he did not love
her, but she had thought he enjoyed her company.

But it had all been a pretense, an act. The most holy and reverend Thomas Colman had married her only to keep his own life
free from the bonds of her uncle's service.

She had thought her husband a great and selfless man.

In truth he was a selfish opportunist. In truth—she shuddered—he had taken her into his arms not out of love, but for the
basest reasons imaginable. No wonder he had been reviled by
her pregnancy. The entire world would know that the minister
who proclaimed holiness was anything but holy and pure.

How could she live with this knowledge? What, if anything,
should she tell the community? The colonists were giving their
time to build the church at his insistence when they should have
been gathering food and skins for the winter. He might even
intend to move into the church himself. The colony might have
been better served had they listened to Ananias.

The life within her stirred, and Jocelyn's hand automatically
sheltered her unborn child. Exposing her husband would bring
the greatest humiliation she had ever known. To admit she had
been duped, bought, bartered like a cheap necklace—it would be
too much to bear. And the child . . . what would the others think
of the child she carried?

No wonder he had been repulsed by the news of her pregnancy. An honest marriage, complete with children, was the last
thing he wanted.

Why, God, have you led me to this man? her heart cried silently
as she gazed up at the ceiling. *How much more pain and sacrifice
will you demand of me? I was certain I followed your will by marrying
Thomas, and yet he does not love me; he does not love the baby I carry. I
married him because my father wanted me to go to Virginia. I married*

him because I believed you were speaking through my uncle John. I thought I could love enough for both of us, for I have your own love in my heart. But why is it so difficult? I want to trust you, I want to believe that Thomas will change, but the darkness in him is great and my candle is so small. . . .

Huddling in the darkness, Jocelyn bit her clenched fist. Sobs threatened to erupt from within her as she grappled with her thoughts. For the sake of the child, she could not publicly denounce him. The others would have to decide for themselves whether to follow the minister or Ananias, but she could not ruin the life of her baby before the child had even seen the light of day. After all, marriages were arranged every day, and there was no shame in the truth that her uncle had apparently chosen Thomas Colman as her husband. The terms of the matrimonial agreement were no one else's concern. Surely the colonists had more pressing needs to consider.

No one else need know what she had learned in Eleanor's house, but she knew she had to confront Thomas with the truth. And after that, she would trust God to show her what to do.

▼▲▼▲▼ Jocelyn waited until Audrey had left to fetch water the next morning before lifting her eyes to look at her husband. He sat at the board, his eyes on his bowl of breakfast pottage, and actually jumped when she said his name.

"Pray do not frighten me," he said, giving her an abashed smile. "I was thinking about my sermon."

"I know." She regarded him impassively, having spent all her tears during the night. Knowing full well that her words had the power to drive all thoughts of a sermon from his mind, she spoke up: "Did you think you could forever hide the truth, Thomas? Ananias told me yesterday about the terms of our marriage. You had no money for the voyage and agreed to marry me rather than become my uncle's servant."

Thomas stopped chewing for a moment, then put down his

biscuit and cleared his throat. "Ananias was wrong to tell you that, Jocelyn."

"Do you deny it?"

"No. It is true." She felt her last hope slip away. Some resilient part of her had clung to the thought that perhaps Ananias had lied in a fit of anger and jealousy, but Thomas confirmed the story without flinching.

"So, in truth, you married me to free yourself."

"There's no gainsaying that, but it is not the entire story." He leaned forward, and for a moment she thought he would take her hand, but he made a fist and blinked nervously. "I struck the bargain with your uncle, but decided not to marry you after we were on board."

Her temper flared. "Was I so horrible?"

"No," he shook his head. "Far from it! You were—" He halted his words, paused as though to regain control, then went on. "I didn't want to hurt you. But I knew your uncle wanted us to marry, so I—"

"You had him ask me to marry you. And I agreed, and we were married, and you've regretted it ever since."

A wall seemed to come up behind his eyes. "I have had my regrets."

Jocelyn felt a rock fall through her heart. Silently she slipped from her stool and tied her cloak around her shoulders. Despite his repeated pleas, she left the house and walked through the village.

Nothing mattered except her escape. In a day, perhaps two, she would think clearly, but nothing seemed clear now. She was beyond all pain except a harrowing headache that pounded her temples, and she ignored the shouted greetings from other women and walked straight toward the beach.

She would leave Roanoke. She would leave Virginia if she could. Perhaps a Spanish vessel would sail by. She would climb aboard with no qualms whatsoever and sail wherever it chose to take her. She would wander into an Indian camp, sit by the fire, and never rise again, not even if they cut her throat.

She was eighteen and filled with such pain that not even death could frighten her.

▾▴▾▴▾ She walked for three hours down the beach. When the southern shore curved into the west, she paused. There was no place to go. Nothing lay before her but sand, surf, and December's bitter howling wind. No boat to take her south to Croatoan or west to the mainland. No worried husband searching for her. No father to take her home.

She wrung her hands, not knowing where to go, and felt the cold hardness of her father's ring around her finger. Boldly, faithfully, successfully. Bah! It was all a monstrous joke. She had tried to live for God, to be a good wife, to work hard in the colony, and for what? Despite her efforts, she was cowardly, faithless, and a miserable failure. She wasn't pretty enough to hold her husband's interest. She wasn't even godly enough to earn his respect.

A thick stand of forest stood a distance behind the beach, and Jocelyn turned toward the woods, wanting to lose herself. When at last the trees surrounded her in a sanctuary of silence, she walked until she was exhausted, then lay down upon a wide, flat rock and slid into a restless sleep.

She dreamed easily of home, of England and her father, of books and a crackling fire and her father's merry voice as he sang and they danced in the small hall of their cozy house. The fire crackled louder and louder, but gave no heat, and suddenly she woke and remembered where she was.

Her eyes flew open in time to see a nearby crow flap into flight. The crackling sounds had certainly come from him. She closed her eyes in relief, then felt a tiny tremor of fear that had nothing to do with the darkness of the forest. The wind hooted around her, a breeze lifted her hair from her brow. When she opened her eyes again, a savage boy stood in front of her.

All lingering wisps of sleep vanished as she pushed herself up to look at him. The boy wore a stenciled breechcloth, and his face and chest were painted in bright designs of red and black. A deerskin hung around his shoulders, and his glossy ebony hair had been pulled back and braided with many feathers. He held a bow into which an arrow had been mounted, but he made no move to raise the bow or disturb her. His bright eyes were wide with youthful curiosity. Jocelyn judged him to be about nine years old.

After her initial alarm had passed, she made an effort to smile. "Hello," she whispered, and the boy took a step backward. So he was wary of her, a helpless pregnant woman! She tempered her smile and struggled to remember the few Indian words her uncle had taught her. *"Hau,"* she said, slowly nodding.

The greeting seemed to please the boy, for he tilted his head and regarded her again. His dark brown eyes were inscrutable. She could not tell if he found her loathsome or beautiful. "I am Jocelyn," she said, slowly raising her hand to point to herself. "Jocelyn."

The boy cocked his head again, and for a moment his eyes narrowed. Then he nodded gravely and thumped his own chest. "Kitchi," he said.

"Kitchi," she repeated, nodding in pleasure.

The boy's eyes twinkled responsively, and she thought he would speak again, but a sudden snap in the brush caught his attention, and he darted toward the sound, disappearing as suddenly as he had appeared.

Jocelyn felt her heart beat faster. Had he gone to bring others? The designs on his skin and clothing were very different from those of the Croatoan. What if he was from an unfriendly tribe, even the Roanoac? Images of the battered body of George Howe flooded her mind. Like her, he had been foolish enough to wander off alone, and he had been murdered. What chance would she have if discovered?

In a single movement she threw herself off the rock and crouched behind it, peering anxiously toward the west. After what felt like an eternity of silence, Jocelyn turned and fled through the woods to the familiar southern beach. As she ran, a new thought struck her: What if the boy had purposely led the others away from her? They might even be here, on the southern end of the island, and she would run headlong into their hunting party, a crazed, pregnant English woman . . .

She skirted the open areas of beach and crept home through the woods, heading steadily north until she at last caught sight of tendrils of smoke from the village's supper fires. It was dusk when she entered the circle of houses, and a group of angry colonists awaited her.

"The minister had us organize search parties for you," John Sampson told her, his voice rough and accusing. "We've wasted half a day in the woods when we ought to have been working."

"We thought you had been kidnapped by savages," Beth Glane added, her thin voice even more sour in the twilight. "And yet you amble home as if you have been out for a walk, never minding our trouble on your behalf."

"I thank you for your trouble," Jocelyn answered, well aware of the hostility in the faces before her. "I—was upset, but I am fine now. I beg your forgiveness for my folly."

"We were afraid the savages had returned," Arnold Archard offered, a worried look in his eyes.

"Pray do not worry," Jocelyn answered, pushing past the assembled group. "I must go home."

"I'll take you home," John Chapman volunteered, stepping forward and gallantly offering Jocelyn his arm. Relieved and touched, she took his arm, and he escorted her to her house while the knot of colonists dispersed.

They walked without speaking through the darkness, the air of the clearing vibrating softly with the insect hum of the wood. After a moment, the old minister's step slowed.

"Are things so hard, my daughter?" he asked, his eyes shining in compassion through the gloom. "Was it so bad that you had to run away?"

Surprised by his insight, Jocelyn pressed her hand to her mouth, stopping the sound of tears.

"Our blessed Lord understands what you're feeling," the minister went on, his rough hand patting hers in a paternal gesture. "The Christian life often seems hard, and the life of a Christian servant even harder."

"Thomas bears it well enough," Jocelyn stammered, her voice breaking. "I am the weak one—"

"I wasn't speaking about the minister," Chapman answered, stopping on the path. "We are all Christ's servants, but remember this, my child: His yoke is easy, and his burden is light. Anything you find hard to bear is not from God. Cast that burden off, and walk in his grace. In grace you will find the strength to be free."

Overcome with feelings too deep to express, Jocelyn pressed her lips together and nodded.

Thomas opened the door just as she and John Chapman reached the house. "Here is your wife," the elder minister said, transferring Jocelyn's hand to Thomas's. Jocelyn looked into the dark, unreadable eyes of her husband; there was no sign that he had worried, no sign that he was glad for her return.

"Let us thank God she is safe," Thomas said, gracing John with a slight smile. So saying, he bade the retired minister goodnight, latched the door, and left Jocelyn with Audrey in the lower room while he climbed to his solitary attic.

Audrey welcomed Jocelyn with frantic questions, but Jocelyn abruptly told the girl to go spend the night with Eleanor. The maid obeyed, taking her cloak from the wall with only a single questioning glance at her mistress, but Jocelyn ignored her and stood motionless before the fire.

Her feet ached from her frantic race through the forest, her slippers were worn from the sharp shells of the beach, and the skin of her hands and face had been stung and scratched by brambles. Ravenous, her body demanded to be fed, but she could not summon the strength to ladle pottage from the stew pot that sat in the glowing embers of the hearth fire.

She sank onto the bed and struggled to slip her shoes from her feet. A sharp pain in her ribs made her gasp. For a moment she feared that she had somehow harmed the baby, but after a moment the spasm passed. In relief, she fell back onto the bed as hot, silent tears sprang from the corners of her eyes.

She might have fallen asleep, but the ladder creaked and Thomas thrust his lantern into the darkening room. "Is anything amiss?" he asked, his eyes searching her face. "You need someone to care for you. Why did you send Audrey away?"

She limply waved her hand in answer.

"Are you bewitched, girl?" He made his way down the ladder, and if not for the lantern in his hand, Jocelyn was sure he would have wagged his finger at her like a scolding schoolmaster. "I don't know what evil possessed you this morning, but you have broken every rule of the colony. It was a terrible example to set, and only your condition made it excusable."

"I have done much thinking today," she said, struggling to sit up so she might look him in the eye. "About us, Thomas."

A dark cloud seemed to pass before his face, and Jocelyn quickened her words. "I have known all along that you do not love me, so I suppose I am not surprised that you made an arrangement with my uncle."

"Jocelyn, that is past." He set the lantern on their small table and folded his arms. "We must get on with our work."

"Yes." She held up a restraining hand. "But our work now involves a new life, Thomas, and I will not harm this child—our child. God would not want us to neglect our baby."

"I have no intention of neglecting my son, if he survives this place. He will be trained to do the work of the ministry."

"If he survives?" She caught her breath. "Marry, why would he not survive? Eleanor's child is faring well—"

"Are you familiar with the story of David and Bathsheba? God took the life of their son in payment for David's sin."

"David's *sin?*" Thoroughly confused, Jocelyn shook her head and struggled to understand. "But we have not sinned, Thomas. You told me yourself—"

"You may not have sinned, girl, but God holds me to a—" Bitterness flooded his voice. "God holds his ministers to a higher standard. I did wrong to marry you, and a greater wrong still to beget this child."

"I don't understand!" Her voice was a plaintive wail. Would he never stop speaking in religious riddles?

"Jocelyn—" for a moment he smiled at her in the old way, reminding her of their days upon the ship when his eyes had seemed to regard her with affection—"how can I make you understand? You know so little of men."

"You forget, I lived with my father for most of my life."

"But still you were sheltered. I don't want to bring pain into your heart or to sully your ears with things you ought not to hear, but remember always that we live on an island with seventeen women and ninety unmarried men."

"So? What have they to do with us?"

Thomas lifted his hand in an emphatic gesture. "They have everything to do with us! I am their shepherd. I must model a life of holiness, and they must curb their natural appetites. How can I preach to them about righteous, self-controlled living when it has become obvious that I cannot control myself?"

His face reddened in his confession. Honest shame colored his countenance. Jocelyn bit her lip, amazed at the change in him.

"Thomas," she began, "no one will expect you to live as a Catholic monk. Indeed, all would rejoice at the birth of your son, just as they rejoice at any birth."

"No, Jocelyn. It should be enough that I am a spiritual father to all in the colony. And you should know—I do not want to have children."

Powerful emotions struggled in his face, and she felt she knew what he was trying to tell her. "Am I truly so horrible, Thomas?" she asked, lowering her eyes.

He squinted in embarrassment. "No, Jocelyn, do not think so," he whispered, his voice ragged.

"I see." She looked at her rough hands, swollen from her pregnancy and the stress of the day. She was not the fragile girl he had met on board the *Lion;* did the sight of her thickening body repel him? Still, he had married her. He was her husband and the father of her child, and he must fulfill his responsibilities.

"Our child will survive, Thomas," she whispered, struggling to keep her emotions under control. "And he must have more than training. Our child must be loved."

He turned away from her, and she thought his shoulders trembled. "You will have to love him, Jocelyn. Such things are not meant for me."

"Think you that you cannot love your own child? I'faith, Thomas—"

"Don't swear, Jocelyn." His voice was filled with pain she couldn't understand.

"I'm not swearing." She sighed in exasperation. "A plague upon your self-righteousness! Thomas, you *must* allow yourself to love—"

"No." He kept his back to her, and she rose from the bed and placed a tentative hand on his back. He pulled away, stung, his face etched with fear as he faced her.

"Thomas—" she grasped his unwilling hand and held it with all her strength—"feel the life within me."

He resisted, pulling away like a frightened child, but she would not let go. Finally he relented, and she drew his hand to her stomach.

She took a deep breath, willing the child within her to move. There! Thomas felt it, too, for his face paled and his eyes glittered strangely. "I do not know what you feel today or what you felt when you and my uncle arranged our marriage," she whispered, searching his face even as she kept his hand upon her belly. "But I do know that on at least one night, you felt affection for me. And mark this, Husband: If the people of this place believe the child is yours, yet know that you live in the attic, they will laugh at you, Thomas, and mock your words about self-control. Do you want that?"

"No." He spoke through clenched teeth as though she held his hand to a red-hot iron.

"Then, I pray you, Thomas, you must behave as a proper husband." She lifted her chin, allowing her tears to plead for the child. "Audrey must sleep in the attic, and you must share my chamber. 'Tis a wonder Audrey has not already spread tales throughout the colony."

"I cannot—"

"Yes, you can," she answered. "I will not expect what you cannot give, Thomas, but you can do this simple thing. Beginning tonight, and from this night forward. I will not have our child called a mistake."

His eyes met hers, and for a moment she thought he was honestly afraid of her. Slowly, he nodded in assent, and she released his hand.

He moved again toward the ladder. "I must get my books. My Bible, my papers . . . everything is upstairs."

"Bring them down. You can move Audrey's trunk to the attic on the morrow."

He placed a foot on the ladder, then turned to her again. "By the by, where did you go today? I worried about you."

The corner of her mouth drooped in a wry smile. "You don't have to pretend when we're alone, Thomas."

He nodded without much conviction. "In truth, I did worry. It's dangerous for a woman to wander alone. If savages had come onto the island—"

"There were Indians on the island." She felt a twinge of satisfaction when his eyes widened in surprise. "I slept on a rock and awoke to find an Indian boy standing over me." She smiled. "His name was Kitchi, I think."

"Did he harm you?"

"No, Thomas, he was only a boy. I think he was more frightened of me than I of him. But he was not alone, and when I heard a noise in the bush, he leapt away. I think he meant to draw the others away from me."

"Why didn't you tell Ananias?" He took his foot from the ladder as if he would move to the door. "The savages may be scouting the island, testing our strength. Did you think you could keep this news to yourself?"

"We will say nothing, Thomas." She filled her voice with all the authority she could muster and turned to face him directly. "Would you send our men out on another raid like the one that nearly killed the Croatoan in George Howe's name? I was not harmed today, and we will say nothing."

He clamped his mouth shut abruptly, then placed his hand again on the ladder. "I bid you good night, Mistress Colman," he answered. "I will spend the night in prayer, but there is one thing I must require of you."

"What?" she turned, ready to promise him anything.

He turned to climb the ladder and tossed the words over his shoulder: "Stop singing as you work."

▼▲▼▲ Safe in the attic, Thomas turned the lamp down to a steady glow and opened his Bible upon his knees. Flipping with trembling fingers through the pages, he found the verse he sought: *Lust not after her beauty in thine heart. . . .*

The verse had become a mantra for him in the past few days. Ever since John White had dismissed the first charges brought months ago by John Jones and Beth Glane, those two devout colonists had consistently approached the council with complaints about the Reverend Thomas Colman. The last attack had come but a week ago.

In the latest charge, Beth Glane had recited a portion of Scripture from Paul's letter to Timothy: "And let these church authorities also first be proved; then let them use the office of a deacon, being found blameless. Even so must their wives be grave, not slanderers, sober, faithful in all things. Let the deacons be the husbands of one wife, ruling their children and their own houses well."

When she finished reading, John Jones took up the attack. "It is well known that you, sir, had a wife in England." As he spoke, the vein in his forehead swelled indignantly like a thick, black snake. "If we were in England, a charivari would have denounced your marriage to this young girl. 'Tis not right that you should have two wives while many men here will have none."

"Nor is it right that your wife is a mere girl, certainly not a grave and sober woman," Beth Glane added, her face a battlefield of scornful wrinkles. "I've heard her singing at her work. Who, sir, has time for singing? She is not a fit wife for a minister, and the marriage should be dissolved."

Roger Bailie, as the eldest council member, turned to Thomas with a genial and forgiving smile on his face. "If, Reverend, there is reason why we should not dissolve this marriage, we would be happy to hear of it."

Thomas heard the unspoken plea: *Tell us you love the girl. Speak nobly of love, defend your wife, and all will be forgiven.*

But as he thought of what he should say, Thomas caught the

clear, cool gaze of Ananias Dare. Ananias knew the circumstances of his arranged marriage. He probably knew that Jocelyn was desperately unhappy. If Thomas gave anything other than the absolute truth, Ananias would be sure to prove him a liar.

He could not paint his marriage as a happy one.

He could not have the marriage annulled.

And so, feeling the scourge of the Almighty upon his back, Thomas folded his hands behind his back and uttered the single most humiliating confession of his life: "I have had two wives. Mayhap I did wrong to marry a young girl. And I am sorry if it proves to be an impediment, but the marriage should not be annulled. My wife, you see, is with child."

Beth Glane gasped in horror, John Jones harumphed in disapproval, and the heads of the council members rushed together for a hurried consultation. After a moment, Ananias Dare had spoken for the council: "We cannot undo what has been done under the direction of our governor. Mistress Glane and Master Jones, we beg you to keep the peace in the colony. Reverend Colman, we ask you to do the same. Keep the news of your former wife to yourself, and live as circumspectly as possible."

But, Thomas wondered now as he closed his eyes in preparation for prayer, how would it be possible to live circumspectly now that Jocelyn insisted that he actually live with her? Thus far he had been able to busy himself in the work of the colony, keeping her image and voice in the back of his mind and subjugating his own desires to the demands of the work. But to have her so close, to know that she would be breathing, laughing, sleeping only inches away—

He bowed his head and prayed for strength.

▼▲▼▲▼ No matter how new or treacherous, life has a way of falling into a routine. At the first sign of a brightening sky, Jocelyn would awaken to sounds of Thomas rising. He dressed and left for the church without breakfast. Invariably Audrey would descend from the attic to help Jocelyn dress after

Thomas's departure, and Jocelyn wasn't sure whether Audrey waited because she feared Thomas or merely wanted to stay out of his way. It was an unusual existence, Jocelyn knew, but Audrey seemed pleased to be sleeping in her rightful place, and the people of the colony seemed to know intuitively that the minister belonged to them.

The church building was the one place he seemed to feel truly at home. During the week, his parishioners visited him there, often bringing him food or other tokens of appreciation for his prayers, and Jocelyn felt that in an odd way the entire village was more wedded to him than she was. Very few of the Christmas gifts Thomas brought home were designed for Jocelyn's enjoyment as well as his, and the friendly nods of appreciation after his Sunday sermon were directed toward him alone. Men and women alike shared with him their confidences as they asked for prayer, children ran to him for his blessing, and his resonant voice could cut through any argument and settle it with a well-placed quote from Holy Scriptures. Only Beth Glane and John and Jane Jones kept a careful distance from him, lifting their Bibles before their eyes as he spoke his Sunday sermon, seeming to prefer their own communion with God to the village's communal worship.

When his day was done, Thomas came home to sit at the board and eat the supper Jocelyn and Audrey had prepared. During the meal he inquired about what each woman had accomplished. His tone was always agreeable and respectful, but his pleasantness vanished each night as Audrey climbed the ladder to the loft where her mattress now lay. After Thomas dimmed the lamp, he would kneel by the hearth and pray in a rough whisper for an hour or more, and after saying her brief prayers, Jocelyn rarely remained awake long enough to feel the mattress shift as he climbed into bed beside her. He never spoke to her, never touched her, never reached for her as he had on their first night together.

Often, when she awoke in the middle of the night and heard his deep, labored breathing, Jocelyn pressed her hands onto her belly and told herself that it was enough having him at her side. She had never expected joy or happiness in marriage, and she had known from the beginning that his heart belonged to another. It was natural that he wanted no more children to replace the boy he had had to leave behind, but he had promised to take care of her and her child. It was enough, wasn't it?

But then she would close her eyes and see her father, his eyes filled with pity and compassion as he gazed at her. And she would cry, lifting her heart to the God in whom she and her father had trusted. Why had God taken her from her secure world and thrust her into this cold, alien wilderness? In the new world Jocelyn Colman had relatives, a servant, and a husband . . . but she had never felt more alone.

▼▲▼▲▼ "Are you sure you won't come with us, Reverend?" Henry Payne called, his musket over his shoulder. "I would love to see you bring a deer home to your missus."

"No, Henry, I will not carry a gun," Thomas called as the hunting party of a dozen men made its way toward the thick stand of forest behind the village. "But I will pray that God will bless your efforts."

A wicked winter wind howled from the east and a heaven full of gray scud seemed to press down upon the earth, but the bearded men shouldered their guns and waved farewell to the women watching from the circle of houses. Jocelyn whispered a prayer for them as they left the village. Though they wore careless smiles and treated the excursion as a grand adventure, she knew desperation drove them into the woods, because the food supplies in the storehouse were dangerously low. Their meager corn crop had been devoured before the end of December, and the few dried foodstuffs that remained had been aboard the *Lion* and were barely edible.

Ananias, last in the line of hunters, turned and saluted those who remained behind, and Jocelyn saw his eyes light on Thomas and grow cold. He would never forgive Thomas for winning the

battle over the church, Jocelyn knew, and since the church's com-
pletion, Ananias had not once stepped inside. He held council
meetings in his own crowded house and had not yet called one
of the promised assemblies for self-government.

The men disappeared into the yawning mouth of the forest,
and the villagers went back to their work. Thomas gave Jocelyn
a brief glance in farewell, studied his hands absently for a
moment, then clasped them behind his back and made his way
toward the church.

▼▲▼▲▼ Hours later, a strange series of shouts passed
through the colony, and Jocelyn paused from sewing, her needle
in the air. Goosebumps lifted on her arm; something had happened. She tossed her mending aside and rushed to the door of
her house as other women ran to the center of the village.

Five men of the hunting party had returned, and two of them
carried a sixth man between them. Jocelyn gasped as she recognized the blood-streaked form of Ananias Dare. While Roger
Prat ran for Doctor Jones, two hunters carefully lowered Ananias
to the ground. A bloody gash had parted his scalp and an arrow
protruded from his belly.

Eleanor screamed and ran from her house, her apron flapping
in the wind. Henry Payne caught her by the shoulders and held
her still while Doctor Jones ran up from the beach and shouted
for the men to carry Ananias to his own house. From the church,
Thomas strode forward with urgent steps. "Keep away, good
women, and pray for our brother," he told the pressing crowd as
he hurried toward the Dares' house.

Jocelyn turned to Audrey for reassurance, but the younger
girl's mouth hung open in a whine of mounting dread. There
had been no trouble with the Indians for many months. What
had brought on this attack? Jocelyn felt a sudden stab of guilt
that made her knees go weak. What if Thomas had been right?
She should have told Ananias of the Indian she had seen on the

island the afternoon she ran away. The boy Kitchi might have been a spy, sent to prepare for this attack.

Jocelyn put her arms around Audrey to guide her back into the house. "What happened, Miss Jocelyn?" Audrey whispered, her wide eyes irresistibly drawn to the forest. "Where are the other six men?"

Weary and rumpled, Thomas Colman sat silently on his stool as Audrey propped the board upon its supports, and Jocelyn ladled a bowl of pottage for his supper. Night had fallen and the village lay in a shroud of silence, its citizens stunned by the ferociousness of the day's misadventure.

Thomas raised his head and regarded his wife with tired eyes. "Our brother Ananias will live," he said simply. "But six others have been killed. Five of the men were unmarried, thank God, but Elizabeth Viccars has been made a widow today."

"Not Ambrose!" Jocelyn whispered, sinking down to her stool. "And Elizabeth with a baby!"

"Ambrose was a righteous man and had no fear of death," Thomas said dully. "Surely he is in heaven today, with the others."

"What happened?" Jocelyn asked, still haunted by the suspicion that she had somehow brought on this attack. "Was it the Roanoac?"

Thomas stirred his pottage with his wooden spoon. "John Chapman says they were tracking a herd of deer when they were ambushed by a war party. The Indians sent a rainstorm of arrows before our men could even load their guns."

"What kind of war party?" Jocelyn pressed. "Roanoac? Surely they weren't Croatoan."

"That is what we must discover," Thomas answered. "Until Ananias is well, one of the other assistants must form our answer to this attack."

"Perchance it wasn't an attack at all," Jocelyn said, thinking again of the boy in the woods. "What if the Indians were following the deer as well, and the two hunting parties happened to meet? If we are taking their food, Thomas, surely we must understand—"

"Roanoke Island belongs to Her Majesty Queen Elizabeth of England," Thomas interrupted, "not to the savages. Indeed, the entire land of Virginia and everything on it belongs to our queen. The savages have no rights unless they become English subjects."

Jocelyn sat back and stared at him, amazed beyond words.

▼▲▼▲▼ Ananias Dare recovered enough from his wounds to attend church on Sunday, and every eye in the building turned to stare as he and Eleanor entered and seated themselves on the last row. Jocelyn saw the corner of Thomas's mouth droop in a wry smile as he stood to face his congregation. She knew Thomas understood that Ananias had only condescended to present himself in the church because he wanted to prove himself capable of leadership. His appearance reinforced his worthiness to lead, and he wore his wound as a badge of honor.

After leading the congregation in a hymn, Thomas spoke for an hour on the importance of holy living. "'This I say then,'" he quoted, reading from the heavy Bible that lay upon the lectern, "'walk in the Spirit, and ye shall not fulfill the lust of the flesh. For the flesh lusteth against the Spirit, and the Spirit against the flesh: and these are contrary the one to the other: so that ye cannot do the things that ye would. But if ye be led of the Spirit, ye are not under the law. Now the works of the flesh are manifest, which are these: adultery, fornication, uncleanness, lasciviousness, idolatry, witchcraft, hatred, variance, emulations, wrath, strife, seditions, heresies, envyings, murders, drunkenness, revellings, and such like: of the which I tell you before, as I have also told you in time past, that they which do such things shall not inherit the kingdom of God.'

"We intend," Thomas said, his voice rumbling with authority over the gathering, "to build such a colony as would mirror the kingdom of God. In order to do so, we must put away all uncleanness and evil from our midst. If, therefore, a fellow colonist tells you of sin in your life, be grateful, thank them for their knowledge, and thank God for revealing the flaw in your character. We will inherit the kingdom of God, my friends, by living righteously and purely before the eyes of God."

He led the congregation in a benediction, but before they could depart, Ananias stood and held up his hand. "I would like to address the colony," he said, moving gingerly down the aisle. He stood beside the lectern until Thomas grudgingly moved out of the way; then Ananias gripped the wooden pulpit with both hands and leaned his weight upon it.

"It is obvious from the attack of the savages last week," he said, his brown eyes circling the entire room, "that this island is no longer safe for us. I therefore have planned, with the counsel of the assistants, that we should move the colony in March."

A collective gasp rose from the crowd. So soon, and in the heart of winter? The assistants' original plan, drafted by John White, had called for the colony to move during the milder month of April or May.

"The sooner we move," Ananias persisted, his knuckles whitening as he gripped the lectern, "the sooner we can plant crops and settle our houses."

"What of our supplies?" a man in the crowd called out. "The governor will return any day with our provisions."

"We will send thirty unmarried men south to Croatoan, where the supply ship can be spotted," Ananias said. "The rest of us will journey north to the Chesapeake."

"Chesapeake!" The widow Viccars stood, as pale as a frail china doll, but her voice carried the iron of anger. "I have heard the savages are even more fierce in that place. I have lost a husband, sir, and I do not want to lose a son."

"The Spanish know of Chesapeake harbor," Edward Powell shouted, standing to his feet. "It's likely they have not discovered our fort here because we are protected by the barrier islands. But if we move to a natural deep water harbor, the poxy Spaniards are certain to discover us—"

"We will send a scouting party ahead," Ananias promised, holding his hands aloft to restore order. "We will find a place where the natives are hospitable, the harbor isolated, and the situation ideal. You must trust me, my friends. God has protected us thus far, but we are not safe here. We must move on to establish our permanent settlement."

The meeting broke up in a storm of speculative and angry voices. Jocelyn remained behind in the silence of the church as the others moved outside to argue in the open air. Sitting motionless on her bench, she considered Ananias's words. Her baby would be born in April or May, and she had always visualized the birth occurring in her small house. But apparently she would not give birth on Roanoke. She would bring her child into the world somewhere farther away from the sea that bound her, however remotely, to England and her past.

She yearned suddenly for Audrey or Eleanor. She would need a friend in the days ahead.

▼▲▼▲▼ The January wind blew from the Western ocean with sleet in its breath, and none of the colonists ventured outside their homes except the hardiest—among them Thomas Colman. Though the temperature was never cold enough to completely freeze the water in the storage barrels, the biting wind made outdoor work miserable, and the colonists made only brief trips to the storehouse or the communal woodpile.

Each colonist seemed to be content to remain in his home—except the minister. Jocelyn watched him rise each morning as usual and doggedly resist the wind until he was safe within the wood-and-clay walls of the house of God. Only on unusually bitter days of freezing rain did he remain at home, and Jocelyn knew he stayed with her only because the church had no hearth and, therefore, no fire. But even on days of frightful weather, he spent little time with his wife, waiting until Audrey had come down the ladder, then climbing to the attic to pray and study in preparation for his next sermon.

"Y' know, 'tis almost as if he's afraid of you," Audrey whispered one morning as she laid the day's fire.

"Mind your tongue," Jocelyn warned. The girl had forgotten her place; servants did not remark upon the private habits of their masters. But after a moment, Jocelyn's curiosity got the better of her. "In truth, do you really think so?" she whispered back.

Audrey lifted her pretty little nose into the air. "I'm sure I couldn't say. I'm mindin' me tongue," she replied tartly.

In mid-January Ananias announced that any willing man could join the expedition to seek a new location for the colony. Jocelyn felt her jaw drop in astonishment when Thomas found her at the hearth and told her he had signed on for the journey.

"Why?" she asked, her spoon clattering from her hands to the floor. "You won't even carry a gun. Why would you want to venture into the wilderness?"

Thomas slid his eyes toward Audrey, and Jocelyn understood that he would not discuss his reasons until after Audrey had gone to bed. So Jocelyn finished her meager bowl of pottage, helped Audrey clean the bowls and cooking pot, and dismissed her maid with a curt nod.

When at last the overhead noises had stilled and Jocelyn lay in her own bed, she sat up and interrupted Thomas as he knelt in prayer. "God hears you all the time," she said, taking pains to keep her voice low. "Now it's time for you to talk to me. Pray tell me why you must journey with Ananias. You know he dislikes you. If perchance you are killed with a bullet to the back, how am I to know he did not strike you down himself?"

"God will protect me as he pleases," Thomas answered, rising from his knees. He unbuttoned his doublet in the semidarkness and slipped it from his shoulders. "I came as a colonist to your uncle's office, Jocelyn, because I thought God might have me spend my life in service to the American Indians. I had heard much of them and their need for the true gospel, but since we have arrived here I have ministered only to the type of folk I would have met in England."

"Would it not be better to wait until we have established the

City of Raleigh?" Jocelyn asked. "Then you can journey into the lands of Indians who regard us with affection. You would know they are receptive to your message, and you would not risk your life—"

"My life is not my own. I belong to God." He sat on the edge of the bed, raised the quilt, and lifted his legs beneath it. Jocelyn felt a strange stirring of her heart. Though he had been sharing her bed for weeks, this was the first conversation they had ever had beneath its blanket.

"My life belongs to God, too," Jocelyn said, reclining upon her pillow. "But God would have me safeguard his possessions and not squander them uselessly. We have a child to think of, Thomas. Or think you that I would like to be a widow like poor Elizabeth Viccars?"

He turned his head to look at her. "So you say," he whispered, his voice strangely tense. "Would widowhood not suit you better? You are not happy with me, and if I were gone—"

"You are not fair!" she cried, pushing the words across to him. "I do not want you to die! I want you to be—"

The words stopped at her lips. What was the use in uttering them? She wanted him to be her husband—to love her, cherish her, rejoice in their coming child—but he would not. He had made his position abundantly clear, and he reinforced it every day as he held her at arm's length.

"I don't want you to die," she repeated, folding her arms across her chest. The mountain of her belly rose beneath her arms, and she resisted the impulse to stroke the unborn babe.

She thought she heard him sigh; then he turned his back to her. "Pray, then, that God preserves me," he said, tossing the words over his shoulder, "for I have agreed to join the expedition, and I am a man of my word."

▼▲▼▲▼ William Clement decided it was his manly duty to join the expedition, and Jocelyn was surprised when his master, Roger Bailie, agreed that the young man should go. Privately, Jocelyn wondered if perhaps the old man had grown tired of William Clement's artificial deference, but her thoughts were soon diverted by Audrey's breathless news that William had asked to marry her after the colony had moved to its new location.

"Did Roger Bailie give his permission?" Jocelyn asked as the two women walked home from church. While it was possible Bailie wanted to be rid of his servant for a few weeks, it was overly generous to assume that Roger Bailie would give an indentured servant his freedom.

"William says he'll be wantin' to ask his master for permission when he returns from the voyage," Audrey explained, her green eyes dancing with delight. She clapped her hands together. "And sure, don't I know that the old man will agree? I'm only sorry that I'll be leavin' you, Miss Jocelyn."

"Marry, you'll only be a stone's throw away," Jocelyn answered, smiling. She turned in at the door of their house as Audrey followed. "But it would be nice if William asked Thomas's permission to marry you."

"Haven't I told William so?" Audrey answered, pouting prettily. "But I'm thinkin' there's plenty of time for that since they will be together on the ship."

"Yes, plenty of time," Jocelyn echoed, looking out the window for some sight of the man who seemed determined to leave her.

▼▲▼▲▼ One week later Jocelyn joined Eleanor and Audrey on the beach as the search party set sail in the pinnace. Ananias stood by Thomas as the minister led the party in a benediction; then the sail lifted, bellied taut, and carried the ship away from shore and out of sight. William Clement made a great show of waving to Audrey, and for a moment Jocelyn thought Audrey would swim out to the ship for one last embrace. Jocelyn herself waved until she thought her arm would break, but no response came from the dark figure she knew to be her husband.

Over the next four weeks, thirteen people in the colony died from sickness and the privations of winter: eleven of the unmarried men; Jane Mannering, maidservant to John and Alice Chapman; and Elizabeth Viccars's eighteen-month-old son, Ambrose. In Thomas's place, John Chapman directed the burial of the dead. When the baby was laid to rest, Jocelyn sat and prayed with Elizabeth Viccars, who clutched her son's blanket in her arms and wept for hours.

At the end of February, a bitterly cold rainstorm assaulted the village. As rain soaked the thatched roof of her house and sheets of water streamed over the shuttered windows, Jocelyn waited anxiously for Thomas's return. Gusts of freezing wind blew through chinks in the walls, rippling puddles on the floor, and shook dead tree limbs down upon the house as easily as a dog shakes itself dry.

How could the men survive in such terrible weather without shelter? Eleanor steadfastly refused to consider the possibility that Ananias would not return, but Jocelyn understood the danger and prayed hourly for Thomas's safe journey. Publicly, the colonists assured each other that the scouting party had undoubtedly met with great success; privately, they wondered if the entire group had been slaughtered or imprisoned by the Indians.

Little food remained in the village. The best hunters were away on the expedition, and several of the remaining men were tempted to raid a Croatoan village for food. The suggestion was proffered one Sunday afternoon after John Chapman had led the colony in a worship service, and Jocelyn could not believe that others were willing to seriously consider the idea.

"We must not do such a thing!" she cried, leaping to her feet. She felt huge and awkward and embarrassed as scores of eyes turned to her, but no one seemed surprised that she had spoken. She was, after all, the minister's wife and allowed to speak in her husband's absence.

She ignored the burning of her cheeks and plunged ahead to speak her thoughts. "What would Ananias and Thomas say if they were here? What would Governor White and Sir Walter Raleigh think of such an idea? Our colony is to be a place of peace, a means of spreading the gospel to the savages. We cannot consider entering their camps and taking what does not belong to us!"

"None of those people are here now," a man called from a front row. "White and Raleigh have full bellies and are safe and warm in England. And for all we know, Ananias and the minister are even now in a cannibal's dinner pot—"

Eleanor cried out, her eyes wide with horror, and Jocelyn trained a furious glare on the man who had spoken. "The Croatoan have told us from the beginning that they have barely enough to last through the winter," she said, turning to survey the entire room. "We have let fear control our reason, and we have turned our profession of faith to a lie. If we believe in God as we say we do, we must trust him for the future. The winter is nearly over, we have stores yet—"

"If you call cracked peas a decent meal," another of the men shouted. "I don't."

"Have we not venison in the woods? Crab in the sea? Fowl and birds? God will provide for us if we seek him. He did not let the children of Israel starve in the wilderness, so why would he let us starve now? We have but to trust him, my friends, and put away these thoughts of war."

John Chapman held up his hand for silence. "Mistress Colman speaks the truth," he said, nodding sagely. "God would not want us to raid the homes of our friends, no more than we would want the Indians to steal from us. Let us remember, dear brothers and sisters, that no one can live in doubt when he has prayed in faith. If we say we trust God, we must allow our faith to destroy our fear."

A universal grumbling filled the room, but after a moment the group filed out. A hunting party braved the weather the next day and returned with two deer and a fox, and talk of raiding the Indian camps abated, if only for the moment.

But still the winds blew and the foodstuffs failed and the fresh water that seeped up from beneath the sandy hills iced over in the collection barrels. The women worked hard to chip ice into their buckets, often cutting their hands until they ran red with blood. And often Jocelyn found Eleanor on the eastern beach, her face toward England, her bundled baby in her arms.

While Jocelyn waited for her husband and the others, Eleanor waited for John White.

As his daughter waited for the men in her life to return, John White sat in his new dockside office and checked the list of supplies and passengers for his next voyage. A great fleet it would be, with supplies enough to last the colony two years, and fresh colonists to fortify the weary souls left behind on Roanoke. Eight ships had been prepared, fine crafts with capable and healthy crews. They would sail under Sir Richard Grenville, a true Englishman if ever such a man existed. Hariot's *Brief and True Report* had done its work, and a flurry of speculation and investment had accompanied the loading of this fleet. All stood in readiness, and White could not wait to sail.

A knock upon his door disturbed his reverie, and White jumped to attention. "Enter!"

A uniformed messenger came through the doorway. From an inner pocket he produced a sealed letter. "To John White, sir, with respect, from the Queen's Captain of the Privy Council," he announced, bowing as he presented the letter.

White accepted the parchment and allowed the messenger to leave before he broke the seal. A keening wind rattled the windows of his office as he read:

Greetings, Honorable John White:
By the order of Elizabeth I, Queen of England and Ireland, Defender of the Faith, etc., any ships capable of service in war are forbidden to leave English harbors unless

under command of Lord Admiral Charles Howard of the Queen's Navy.

White sank upon the stool behind his desk, crumpled the parchment, and slammed his fist upon the desk. Had the devil himself set his face against Roanoke?

A shout from a lookout at the beach brought the colonists running from their homes on a gray afternoon in March. Their apprehension turned to rejoicing as the pinnace, the British flag flying high upon her mast, passed through the narrow inlet of the barrier islands and swung into view. A crew of men hastily turned the shallop into the bay, and the scouting party spilled from it in their eagerness to come ashore.

Laden with deerskins and furs, husbands ran to the arms of their wives, and the unmarried men stole kisses from the maids and promised their fellows to tell exciting tales in the quiet of the barracks.

Jocelyn waited on the beach with Audrey. After a moment Audrey squealed and ran into the shallows to throw her arms about the golden-haired and bearded William Clement, but Jocelyn saw no sign of Thomas's dark and somber figure until a voice spoke from behind her: "Good morrow, Mistress Colman."

She felt herself blushing as she turned to look at Thomas. He had slipped ashore in the shallop and wore a dark beard with a touch of gray that she found strangely appealing. He smelled of earth, leaves, and fish, and his expressive hands were stained and dirty.

But as surprised as she was by his appearance, his greeting startled her even more. Dropping the leather pouches he carried, he wrapped his arms about her and lifted her from her feet in an enthusiastic embrace while she sputtered in confusion and embarrassment.

As Audrey ran off with William Clement, Thomas took Jocelyn's arm and walked her home, telling her of their journey and how he had wondered if he'd ever see Roanoke Island again. He spoke freely, without regard for the others who walked around him, and sought her eyes often as Jocelyn listened in wonder and bewilderment.

At supper that night he spoke of their journey up a dark river where Indians had approached with bows and arrows aimed at their pinnace. But he had stood in the front of the boat and prayed, and the savages did not attack. They welcomed the strangers into their camps with joy, freely sharing all they had and exchanging what few trinkets the colonists had to barter for bags of corn and furs.

"And so we have found land for our city," Thomas said, his dark eyes twinkling in the lamplight. "The Indians call the river the 'Chowan,' and our town is quite near a village of friendly savages. The land is accessible through a deep body of water north of here, so the fleet can anchor there with our supplies."

"The land isn't too close to the shore, is it?" Jocelyn asked. "The Spaniards—"

"The place is far enough inland so the Spaniards will tire of looking before they find us."

After supper, Thomas asked about the colony, expressed his sorrow at the news of so many deaths, and finally asked about Jocelyn's health. "I am well," she answered, not knowing whether to be grateful or alarmed at his personal questions. It was almost as though she had sent one husband away, and a new one had returned in his stead.

The fire was dying when Audrey slipped into the house and climbed into her attic. After latching the door, Jocelyn slipped into her nightgown and climbed into bed. She felt huge and was a bit ashamed of her distorted appearance, but Thomas crept in beside her and gazed at her in open delight. "I had forgotten how beautiful you are," he whispered, nuzzling his beard close to her ear. "Living with such a motley crew of men forced me to appreciate the wonder you are. What a wife God has given me."

And before the hearth had grown cold, he slept, his breath tickling her ear and his words warming her heart.

▼▲▼▲▼ Within the next week, the colonists dismantled the walls of their houses, gathered their trunks and belongings, and deposited everything on the beach. Ananias Dare and Roger Bailie surveyed the growing mound of supplies to decide what should be transported and what should remain behind.

Remembering her father's concern over his books, armor, and maps, Eleanor made certain that John White's trunks were buried in a trench outside his house. Henry Payne was set to work carving "CROATOAN" on a post near the gate of the fort, while Roger Prat and his son loaded the smaller guns and cannons from the armory onto a cart.

"Why doesn't Henry carve 'Chowan' on the post?" Jocelyn asked Thomas as he supervised the dismantling of the church.

He gave her a fondly indulgent smile that left her knees weak. "The Governor will have no idea where we are," he said, his voice warm. "The Chowan is a long river. But the men who will be installed on Croatoan will be able to direct him to us."

Manteo and Towaye, who had been living in Dasemunkepeuc village with a band of the Croatoan, canoed to the island in time to bid farewell to the remaining colonists. As the group prepared to pull out, Jocelyn stood alone for a moment and considered the deserted fort. All that remained of the walls of their houses were timber posts sunk at regular intervals in the sand. Three huge cannons deemed too heavy to transport loomed upward from behind an earthen rampart of the fort, and three rows of freshly mounded graves lay in the far corner of the clearing. Though only yesterday the place had brimmed with life, an air of desolation now surrounded the village.

"Are you coming, Mistress Colman?" Thomas called, eager to join the others on the beach. Jocelyn nodded and hurried to his side, wondering again what had come over her husband.

Regina

I had fainted, unless I had believed to see the goodness of the Lord in the land of the living.

Psalm 27:13

The colonists gathered anxiously around Ananias for one final bit of government. All family units were to be transported to the new site on the Chowan River, but the sixty-three unmarried men had to draw lots, for thirty of them were to remain on Roanoke until all the goods had been transported, then move to Croatoan Island to wait for John White's arrival.

"A delegation will visit Croatoan in three months and offer whatever assistance you may need," Ananias promised the group of unmarried men before the drawing began. "But I am certain our governor will return before the end of three months' time."

From the corner of her eye, Jocelyn could see Audrey chewing on her thumbnail as the drawing began. If Roger Bailie drew a marked slip of parchment, William Clement would be required to live on Croatoan with his master until White returned, and Audrey desperately wanted to be married. As an assistant and council member, Bailie was among the first to draw, and Audrey breathed an audible sigh of relief when he held his clean slip of parchment aloft.

The long line of men silently advanced and drew their lots. When all had drawn, the thirty men with marked parchments stood apart and looked toward Ananias with resignation in their eyes.

"We will leave you behind with what we cannot transport today," Ananias announced. He stepped forward and clapped his hand on the back of Richard Taverner, a broad-shouldered, dependable man who had proved himself a capable seaman and hunter. The parchment in Taverner's hand was marked with a large X. Ananias's voice rang out as he said, "I hereby appoint this able man as your captain until you join us at the City of Raleigh."

Taverner was respected and well liked, so the men nodded in agreement, though Jocelyn couldn't help but notice that a few faces appeared crestfallen at the prospect of remaining behind.

Audrey squeezed her hand. "'Pon my soul, Miss Jocelyn, I'd have thrown meself in the sea and swum to Croatoan if William had been sent there."

Jocelyn said nothing but patted her maid's hand affectionately while she wondered if she would have felt so desperate had Thomas chosen to remain behind.

▼▲▼▲▼ Jocelyn was amazed at how much the colony had managed to accumulate in such a short time. It would take three complete voyages in the pinnace to transport everything, but Ananias declared the food supplies and munitions a priority. Among the items put aboard the pinnace was a collection of light artillery, including a mortar and two falcons. Each of the colonists had at least one one-hundred-pound trunk, and many of the assistants and married women had two. Added to this bulk were seed and food supplies, farming tools, and the timber-and-clay walls of their houses, ready for reassembly in their new city.

After saying their farewells to the men who would wait on Roanoke, the women boarded the pinnace and helped settle the cargo into the ship's hold. Many of the women complained about the close and crowded quarters, but the familiar rolling of the sea only reminded Jocelyn of the days when she had first met and fallen in love with Thomas Colman. Had similar memories influenced him while he was away on the expedition? Were they the cause of his newly affectionate behavior?

In late afternoon, the colonists aboard the heavily loaded pinnace called farewells to the men left on shore. The men raised the ship's anchor, and the vessel left the eastern beach of Roanoke Island and headed west into a large sound. Though they were traveling into unfamiliar waterways, Jocelyn had to admit that from where she stood on the deck, the passage did appear safe. The narrow strip of barrier islands off the coast, passable only through two narrow slipways, effectively disguised the wide body of water through which they traveled.

The land to the north and south stretched as far as Jocelyn could see in a vast swampy marsh, with tall pines periodically poking through the gray-brown reeds. Wildlife peered at the ship from beneath the inky surface of the water, then dove for cover as the pinnace approached. Jocelyn shivered and drew her cloak more closely about her. Were human eyes watching their progress as well?

Though she could hear sounds of laughter and relaxed conversation in the hold beneath her feet, the mood on the upper deck was tense and quiet. Ananias and Thomas stood together at the bow, one man watching the north bank and the other the south, and old Roger Bailie leaned against the mainmast and hummed a comfortingly familiar English tune. It was as if they were trying to appear relaxed for the sake of the women, Jocelyn thought, for though the scouting party had traveled this waterway recently, no one could be sure of what lay ahead.

The pinnace sailed westward until the land locked before her; then she turned northward and followed a narrow river. "The Chowan," Thomas said, coming to stand beside Jocelyn. His dark eyes scanned the riverbank ahead. "The river narrows and turns ahead of us, and a friendly tribe of Chawanoac Indians have established a town called Ohanoak on the river. They have bade us welcome at a place nearby, and there we will establish our City of Raleigh."

"Is it truly safe?" Jocelyn asked, disturbed by movements in the dense undergrowth that lined the riverbanks.

"We are as safe as God would have us be," Thomas answered, the grooves beside his mouth deepening into a smile. He put his hands on her shoulders and squeezed gently. "And if we are in the center of God's will, we are invincible."

▼▲▼▲ The ship dropped her anchor at a small clearing west of the river, and Jocelyn could see that the scouting party had already done substantial work. A sturdy wall of felled logs created a rounded palisade, and the area inside had already been burned and cleared of brush. "We were busy while we were gone," Thomas said, grinning as he offered his hand and helped her down the gangplank from the ship to the shallop. "But now the real work begins."

For the rest of the day the men unloaded the pinnace while the women prepared cooking fires inside the palisade. Mindful that the area was occupied by savages, Jocelyn walked with Audrey outside the enclosure to collect kindling for the fires. Audrey babbled happily about her upcoming marriage and the virtues of William Clement, and Jocelyn listened halfheartedly, her mind on other things.

As she struggled to bend over her thickened belly and pick up a twig, a pensive face in the nearby greenery startled her. She stifled her scream, remembering the innocent curiosity of the Indian boy she had met earlier, and the ebony eyes of the savage blinked rapidly at her. *"Hau,"* she whispered, lifting her empty hand, but at the sound of her voice the savage fled through the brush.

Audrey whirled around at the sound, ready to scream in earnest, and Jocelyn shushed her. "There is nothing to worry about," she said, forcing a lighthearted smile. "But perhaps we should go back."

Little Virginia Dare lay dozing on a blanket under a tree while Agnes and Eleanor worked at a fire pit, and Jocelyn dumped her bundle of wood next to Eleanor's fire. "They're watching us," Jocelyn whispered, feeling inquisitive eyes burn her skin. She glanced upward at the trees that loomed over the high fence of the palisade.

"Where?" Eleanor looked up, alarmed.

"I don't know," Jocelyn answered, searching the leafy branches beyond them. "But I saw someone in the brush. I couldn't tell if it was a man or woman. But when I spoke, the Indian ran away."

"Good." Eleanor hoisted her heavy iron pot onto the fire. "Let them stay away. When Papa comes back, then we'll entertain them."

The colony feasted that night on a thick soup of fish and pine nuggets; then the men barricaded the gate of the palisade while the women spread their blankets inside the only structure that had been erected. Jocelyn spread her sleeping quilt between Audrey and Eleanor, and after lying down between them, she fell instantly asleep.

At sunrise the next morning, a crew of men took the pinnace for its second trip to fetch the remaining supplies while the colonists set to work in earnest. Tall poles were sunk into the sandy ground; then the prefabricated walls of timber and clay were lashed to the supporting poles. The simple, one-story storehouses rose quickly; the two-story houses were more difficult to raise.

A scouting party of children found a wild shrub with leaves nearly two feet across. Jocelyn recalled seeing a similar plant used to roof native huts in the Caribbean islands, so she sent the children out to gather more of the broad leaves while the women tied them onto branches.

The pinnace returned just before sunset, and the men aboard hurried into the palisade before night fell. Too tired to eat the supper several women had prepared, Jocelyn went straight to the newly erected house she and Thomas would share and spread her blanket on the earthen floor. Though the wind whistled through the green roof and the house still smelled of soil and crawling things, she closed her eyes and slept, too exhausted to care.

As invading daylight streamed through the open doorway the next morning, Jocelyn groaned and pulled her blanket over her eyes. Eight months of pregnancy and several days of difficult physical exertion had left her sore and tired. The night brought her but little rest, for she could not sleep on her stomach, and the hard earth beneath her brought no ease to her tired muscles.

"Good morrow, Mistress Colman."

She lowered the blanket and peered out. Thomas sat on the ground next to her, his hands casually resting on his knees. He still wore the white work shirt he had worn the previous day, and his tired face made him look older than his years.

"Good morrow." Her voice cracked.

"William Clement has asked to marry our Audrey," he said, smiling more from habitual civility than honest pleasure. "I told him the girl was your maid and that I must speak with you."

She lifted her head, and Thomas thoughtfully extended his hand to help her sit up. "I have already given Audrey my permission," she said, pushing her disheveled hair from her eyes. "She is in love with the man."

"So I hear," Thomas answered, his voice flat. Was that sarcasm in his voice? Jocelyn could not tell.

"Of course, the happy couple will have to ask the council's permission to wed," Thomas added.

"Why should they? We did not ask anyone's permission to marry."

"We had your uncle's blessing," Thomas answered, wearily studying his blistered hands. "We were both—free. We had no masters to object." He dropped his hands suddenly into his lap. "Except God."

A sudden shaft of morning light from the doorway focused itself upon Thomas, haloing him in an unearthly light. Layers of dark wrinkles lined his coal-black eyes, etched by the travail of suffering. But though the death of his wife and the separation from his son were a part of his past, why couldn't he rejoice in this new city, in their new life?

"Thomas," she began, hoping that this rare privacy might enable him to speak freely, "why should God object to our marriage? Surely if a man and woman wish to join together and there is no impediment between them—"

"They say I was wrong to take a second wife. The Scripture

itself says a spiritual leader should be the husband of one wife, and I cannot argue against God's Word."

"But perhaps the Scripture means you should be the husband of one wife at a time! Does not the Word of God allow widows to remarry? You are a widower—"

"You do not understand."

"In truth, I do not." Her anger of weeks past had dissipated. When she looked at him now she felt only love and an overwhelming sense of despair. Inside her the baby woke and kicked vigorously at the sound of Thomas's voice.

They sat for a moment in silence; then Thomas raised his eyes to her face in an oddly keen, swift look. "I never meant to hurt you. Upon my soul, I never did."

She shook her head. "I do not blame you for our loveless marriage, for I know you cannot give what you do not have. I only hoped that you would—"

He continued as if he hadn't heard her. "I know I have hurt you, Jocelyn, and I would as lief cut off my arm as bring you pain. During the weeks I was away, I realized how hard you have worked to make a home for us." His voice softened. "It's nice to wake up next to you. And to come home from a busy day and see you stirring supper by the fire. A cozy house, mended clothes, an honest and frank discussion—"

He looked up at her. "I found that I have come to depend upon those things. And God has shown me, very clearly, that I have wronged you."

Tears sprang to her eyes, but Jocelyn blinked them away. Thomas stared again at his hands. "I never meant to hurt you. I never meant to have a child. You are my sister in Christ, and as such I will hold you in great esteem."

Jocelyn ran her hand over her belly to soothe the active child. So his increased affection resulted from missing the comforts of home! And while affection was better than indifference, it was not what she had been hoping for. Still . . . it was a start. And if God proved willing, perchance love would come later.

"Thank you, Reverend Colman," she whispered. She leaned

over to kiss his cheek, and though he pulled away, she persisted until he relented, and she felt the smoothness of his skin under her lips.

She gave him a slow smile. "Thank you very much."

"I *must* speak to the queen, I tell you. It is a matter of life and death!"

The sour-faced courtier who stood entrance to the queen's private chambers only shook his head and glared at John White. "I am sorry, but Her Majesty the queen cannot see you. She has expressly requested that you go away until she calls for you, Master White."

White closed his eyes and took a deep breath, torn between ranting like a madman and leaving to try another diplomatic route. During his time in England, none of his attempts at political posturing had been successful, and few would even listen to his concerns about the deserted colonists. The queen flatly refused to grant him an audience. He even found himself banned from mingling at the royal court. Obviously Elizabeth considered John White a noisome and pesky fly. She would give audience to none but a preferred handful of advisers, chief among whom was Sir Walter Raleigh.

In any other time Raleigh would have been White's savior and swiftest route to the queen, but a more pressing problem than Virginian colonization loomed before England in the person of Philip II of Spain. For years Philip had borne the occasional piracy of his treasure ships, but now that his empire had come to depend heavily upon the gold and silver from Spanish conquests in America, England's persistent meddling propelled the Spanish king toward war. As a rigid and devout Catholic, Philip found it particularly galling that Elizabeth's England, the leader of the Protestant nations, could cause him such difficulties.

Philip decided that the path to victory lay in the open sea. He would assemble the mightiest fleet of warships ever seen on the surface of the earth: one hundred thirty ships manned with eight thousand sailors and nineteen thousand soldiers. With high wooden castles fore and aft and powerful cannons belowdecks, the Spanish vessels were designed for battle. His growing Armada had only one purpose: to thrust his soldiers alongside enemy galleons so the men could board and take the blood of battlefields to the open sea.

Elizabeth's spies had been reporting news of this great and terrible armada for months. The Spanish fleet had been poised and ready to sail in 1587 but was prevented by a stroke of God, and Elizabeth and her councilors waited uneasily to see what Philip might do next.

As a defensive measure, Elizabeth appointed Ralph Lane, Sir Walter Raleigh, and Sir Richard Grenville to a committee to plan the overall protection of England. Raleigh and Grenville were given the job of organizing the defense of England's western shore should the Spanish attempt an attack there, therefore neither man had much time to devote to John White when he made his precarious way back to England in November 1587.

White was particularly horrified to learn that one reason for Raleigh's reluctance to aid the colonists was the tremendous profit he and Grenville had earned from their recent service to queen and country. As part of the government's strategy for controlling Ireland, Raleigh and Grenville were given large tracts of Irish land that had been confiscated from rebels. They were chartered to colonize these lands and create happy English citizens in Ireland, so both Raleigh and Grenville had diverted their attention from distant Virginia toward the more visible and profitable shores of the Emerald Isle.

As months passed and the political truth gradually revealed itself, John White felt fear rising like the quick, hot touch of the devil in his veins. To all appearances, the colonists' worst fears had come to pass: the people of Roanoke had slipped to the bottom of a long list of English priorities. By the spring of 1588, his was the sole voice speaking on their behalf.

▼▲▼▲▼ For the sake of his daughter and infant grand-daughter, White did not give up after the queen's Privy Council forbade him to sail. He wrote countless letters and spent endless days pacing the drawing room of Raleigh's house until he was finally granted permission to detach two of the smaller ships from Sir Richard Grenville's fleet for a journey back to Roanoke.

He had lost an appreciable number of prospective settlers when Grenville's Virginia expedition was canceled by royal decree, but seven men and the four wives of men waiting in the colony—Mistress Sampson, Mistress Prat, Mistress Cooper, and Mistress Stevens—were still determined to make the journey.

From his tiny office on the docks of Bideford Bar, White oversaw the rapid provisioning of the *Brave,* a ship of thirty tons, and the *Row,* a clumsy-looking pinnace of twenty-five tons. Seeds, tools, munitions, livestock, and the baggage of eleven passengers were loaded onto the ships as quickly as possible, for White feared that Raleigh or the queen might yet postpone his journey.

On April twenty-second John White boarded the *Brave* with hope in his heart and a very important letter in his satchel. Sir Walter Raleigh had sent a dispatch at the last moment, a letter to cheer the colonists, in which he promised that with all convenient speed he would prepare "a good supply of shipping and men with sufficience of all things needful" which, God willing, should be with them the summer following.

The cool April breeze ruffled John White's white hair as Arthur Facy, commander of the *Brave,* gave the command to raise the anchor. As the ship raised her sails and slipped from her moorings at the docks, John White prayed that his colonists would be able to survive until he reached them. Springtime in the wilderness, when stores of winter were depleted and the new crops not yet sprung, oft proved to be a starving time.

▼▲▼▲▼ They had barely been under sail for one full day when John White sensed the familiar stirring of trouble. Like Simon Fernandes of the *Lion,* Arthur Facy considered piracy his first priority. And his seamen, who were but castoffs since Grenville had been instructed to reserve his best men to confront the Armada, were little more than cutthroats and thieves.

As the two English ships emerged from the Bristol Channel, they chased and then boarded four vessels, taking three sailors prisoner to fulfill the necessary complement of seamen. On the second morning, without conscience or character, Facy lobbed a cannonball at a small pinnace from Scotland and robbed her of everything of value. That afternoon he brazenly attacked and looted a Breton vessel.

In White's pleas for restraint Arthur Facy seemed to find only further excuse for foolhardiness. It seemed the men and women who waited below were nothing but incidental cargo, and thoughts of the colony were the last thing on Facy's mind. When he gave the order to chase and attack a two-hundred-ton ship, a move that made as much sense as a minnow attacking a whale, White launched a verbal assault that only broadened the swarthy sailor's impenitent grin. In the end, White went belowdecks to await disaster and pray. Mercifully, the larger ship escaped. Separated now from the *Row*, the *Brave* sailed on toward Madeira.

The new Virginian village, or the City of Raleigh, as Ananias declared it, rose from within the palisade more quickly than Jocelyn thought possible. The prefabricated walls, which had served them so well in Roanoke, made home building easy, and Thomas was pleased when the settlers did not hesitate to lend a hand in reassembling the church. Wells were dug, outhouses built, and the young boys set to building enclosures for breeding rabbits and wild turkeys. Jocelyn had to smother a grin when young George Howe brought her a turkey for dinner and expected that she'd cook it with the feathers still attached.

Young George, as he was still called, had taken up residence with the unmarried men and seemed to have aged two years in the eight months since his father's death. Because she knew how bereft a fatherless child could feel, Jocelyn worried about young George and often invited him to have dinner with her and Thomas. But George usually declined, preferring to eat with the other men. All the children of the colony, Jocelyn noticed, grew up too quickly, with chores and lessons and the danger of death looming constantly in the distance.

But Ananias and the council followed Raleigh's instructions, and the colony was well prepared for the future. To prepare for planting, additional fields were burned outside the palisade to clear the land of brush, and the trees that remained in the fields were girdled.

Jocelyn thought the act of girdling strange at first, but she understood why the procedure was necessary. With no horses or mules available, girdling was quicker and easier than felling or uprooting trees and achieved the desired effect. After a continuous ring of bark was chipped or torn from trees, the trees slowly died where they stood. Leaves fell from the dead limbs to provide a rich compost for the soil beneath, and sunlight poured through the leafless branches to warm the ground. But Jocelyn could not shake an eerie murderous feeling as she helped the other women strip the bark from trees in the burnt field. Many of the trees were giants that had stood for scores of years before the colonists' arrival. In time, the blackened, dead trees would stand as ghostly sentinels over the fields.

By the end of April the village had been fully erected. True to his word, William Clement took Audrey Tappan to the church to approach the council. Ananias Dare, Roger Bailie, Christopher Cooper, Thomas Stevens, Roger Prat, and John Sampson sat at their places around the long council table at the front of the building, and, as interested parties, Jocelyn and Thomas sat in the back of the church and listened intently.

William Clement lifted his golden head confidently. "I'd like to request permission from my master, Roger Bailie, and the council to marry Audrey Tappan," he said, smiling.

Jocelyn wryly noted that the smile that drew women like moths to a lamp did little to impress the council. "How can an indentured servant marry?" Christopher Cooper asked, doubtless worried that his servant, James Hynde, might be unduly influenced by William's brashness.

John Sampson shook his head in stern disapproval. "May I remind you, sir, that you were a convict? Sentenced to prison for the rest of your life? And that you came here willingly to serve your lifetime—"

"Beggin' your pardon, Master Sampson, but my crime was stealin' forty sheep. Are forty sheep worth a man's life?"

"Could be," Roger Prat answered slowly. "Marry, it all depends. If forty sheep are all a man has, and they're stolen by a couple of blackguards, then yes, I'd have to say the knaves should pay with their lives."

"I cry you mercy, sir!" William answered, offended. "Have I

not worked as willingly as any man in this colony? Have I not given good service to my master?"

The members of the council turned to look at Roger Bailie, who scratched his white beard and said nothing.

William turned in exasperation to Thomas and Jocelyn. "There!" he said, pointing to them. "My lady's master and mistress have consented to let her be free to marry. In Virginia, a man is supposed to be free to make what he likes of his life—"

Thomas Stevens held up a gnarled finger. "Miss Tappan's life was not claimed by the courts of England before coming to Virginia," he pointed out, practically snarling at William. "She is a free and moral woman, sir, and you paid for your passage and your freedom with indentured service to Roger Bailie for the rest of his natural life. I am inclined to believe that you should render this service without the distraction of a wife until you are released from your bond."

William thrust his hands on his hips, pouting, and Jocelyn turned her gaze toward Roger Bailie. The old man's eyes flickered from William Clement to Audrey, who sat silently on a bench, her face flushed, her hands clasped as if for prayer. Her red hair glowed in the lamplight, and something akin to pity flitted across Roger Bailie's gentle face.

'Pon my soul, he would let them be married, Jocelyn thought, inwardly rejoicing. The council members continued in noisy debate; then Ananias raised his hand for silence. "This debate belongs to Master Bailie," he said, nodding gravely to the elder council member. "William's his servant, and there's no doubt he'll be the most affected. Roger, what say you?"

Roger Bailie stood to his feet and nodded pleasantly to Audrey, then to William. The long strands of wispy blonde hair straggled over his shoulders while his bald head gleamed in the dim light. "I would agree to this request," he said simply, his fingers nervously tapping the top of the table before him, "but I am an old man and likely to need help in the years to come. Still, I'll not stand in the way of young love, nor would I forbid this union and drive them to immorality or some such thing."

Audrey bowed her head and blushed, and the effect was not lost on Roger Bailie. His eyes gentled as he spoke: "'Tis this I propose, then: When I die and William Clement is released from his bond to me, then he may marry Audrey Tappan if he so chooses."

William expelled a loud breath of frustration, and Roger held up a restraining hand. "Be not so impatient, my friend. If your love is as strong and eternal as you say it is and if the young lady desires a new home, then I pray she will consider another proposal."

Roger looked toward Audrey and squinted in embarrassment. She raised a questioning brow. "Another proposal, sir?"

"Yes, Miss Tappan. You may wed William at my death, but you may come to live at my house if you will marry me now."

A collective gasp shattered the stillness of the room, and Jocelyn sat immobile in the chill shock of surprise. The old man wanted Audrey for himself! Who would have ever imagined such a thing?

Red-faced, William lunged toward the council table, and for an instant Jocelyn thought he would hit his master. But Thomas sprang forward to hold William back, and Ananias stepped in front of Roger Bailie.

"'Tis an interesting proposal, certainly," Ananias said, looking at the other council members with a smile in his eyes. "I'm sure Miss Tappan would like time to think about it. What say you, Roger, shall she have time?"

"Two days," Roger Bailie answered, taking his seat behind the table. "I will hear her answer in two days."

▼▲▼▲▼ Audrey's weeping could be heard from the attic throughout the night, and Thomas rolled out of bed the next morning muttering. "Talk to her, Jocelyn, and help her decide yes or no," he said, his eyes red from lack of sleep. "But beg her to stop crying!"

When he had left the house, Jocelyn greeted the bleary-eyed

Audrey, who apologized for not rising sooner. "I just can't stop
seein' the old man's face," she said, blowing her nose into a
square of linen. "I would liefer die than marry old Roger Bailie!"

"So you would wait until William is freed?" Jocelyn asked,
raising an eyebrow as she placed a fresh log on the fire. "That
might take years, Audrey. You might be twenty, twenty-and-five,
even thirty years old before you married."

Audrey burst forth into fresh wailing, and Jocelyn rolled her
eyes. *Some comfort I am,* she thought. *It's a good thing Thomas is not
here to see how well I encourage the downtrodden.*

"Soft, Audrey," she said, leaving the fire. She reached for
Audrey's hand. "I can tell you this: Marry neither Roger Bailie
nor William Clement; in truth, marry no man unless God has
given you a deep love for him. For 'twill take every ounce of
love in your heart to survive the things that will come."

Audrey stopped crying. Sniffling, she asked, "But what of me
husband's love for me? I know William loves me, but Master Bailie—"

"Who can know what thoughts guide a man's heart?" Jocelyn
asked, smiling through tears of her own. "But as God has called
me to love Thomas, I trust that God will someday bring Thomas
to return my love." Audrey's eyes widened. "Yes, I know you
have seen the state of my marriage," Jocelyn said, releasing
Audrey's hand. She caressed her mounded belly, round with her
unborn child. "And yet God gives me the grace to wait, to hope
and pray for the day that will come. Thomas is God's child, and
the Father will bring him home."

"Faith, what a way to talk about the minister!" Audrey
blurted out, then clapped her hand over her disobedient mouth.

Jocelyn said nothing, but banked the morning fire. After breakfast William Clement himself knocked at the door to see Audrey,
and Jocelyn watched them walk away, certain that William
would advise Audrey to wait for marriage or else run away with
him. But where, in this wilderness, could they run?

▼▲▼▲▼ William wrapped his hand around Audrey's long fingers and pulled her behind a tree for a forbidden kiss. "William!" she fussed through her tears, turning her head from his. "What if somebody's watchin'?"

"Forget it," he said, pulling her toward the gate of the palisade and away from curious eyes. "I've been thinking and I've made our plans. You will marry the old man, Audrey, and then we'll be together always."

"Marry him? Have you lost your mind?"

"No, lass," he said, slipping an arm about her slender waist. He drew her closer as they walked, and she liked the masculine smell about him. "Just think of this: We'll be livin' in the same house. He's an old man and bound to meet his Maker in a few months, just wait and see. And if, perchance, we can hasten him on to heaven—"

Audrey stopped in her tracks, truly horrified. "William!" she gasped, searching his face. "Are you sayin' we should kill him?"

"No, my love," he said, his smile broad and reassuring. "We won't lift a finger to harm him, I promise. But we won't do anything to keep him around longer than his due time, neither."

"I don't know," Audrey answered, her flesh crawling with the idea of loving one man while sleeping with another. She shivered, and William tightened his arm around her.

"Do y' love me?"

"Aye, I suppose I do." One part of her mind held back, unable to forget William's callous suggestion that they hasten the old man to his grave.

"Then marry him, Audrey. Trust me, lass. All will be well, and you'll still be able to stand before God with a clear conscience. On my word as a gentleman, I promise you that."

▼▲▼▲▼ Audrey seemed troubled and thoughtful when she returned from her walk with William, but Jocelyn noticed that the girl's tears had stopped. Thomas would be grateful.

"Is all well?" she asked, as Audrey climbed the ladder into her loft.

"Aye," Audrey answered distractedly. "I'm goin' to pack my things."

"You are going somewhere?" Jocelyn called up, perplexed.

"Aye," Audrey called down. "On the morrow I'm to marry Master Bailie."

▼▲▼▲▼ The absurd wedding took place in the church before a handful of witnesses. Thomas read the marriage service from the *Book of Common Prayer* while William Clement stood behind his master's back and watched his intended bride blush and stammer as she married another man.

At the conclusion of the ceremony, Roger Bailie took Audrey's hands and held them as he bowed to her. "My life, my respect, and my love are yours to do with as you will," he said simply. "With my home and all that I possess I do thee endow."

Audrey forced a pitiful, small smile, curtsied slightly, then turned and ran from the church.

▼▲▼▲▼ It was a bright blue morning in early May when Jocelyn next met Audrey. The girl had been married for two days, and Jocelyn was desperately curious to know how her friend had fared.

"Master Bailie has banished William from the house," Audrey said, giving Jocelyn a troubled smile when they met in the clearing at the center of the village. "'Tis better, after all. William now sleeps with the unmarried men in the house across the way, but I still see him as we work together."

"Is Master Bailie kind to you?" Jocelyn asked as they gathered water buckets to fill at the well.

"Very kind," Audrey admitted, falling into step beside Jocelyn as they began to walk. She lowered her voice lest anyone be hiding in the bushes that surrounded them. "On me wedding night,

I could not stop crying. Master Bailie let me cry for a bit, then at length he climbed into bed and put his arm around me. He stroked me hair until I fell asleep."

Jocelyn sighed. Although hers wasn't the only loveless marriage in the village, at least Master Bailie dared to be kindly affectionate with his wife.

"He is—good," Audrey said, her eyes welling with tears. "I can say nothin' against him, Miss Jocelyn, and it bothers me to think William is watchin' like a hawk lest Master Bailie touch me hand or whisper in me ear. . . ."

"Then stay clear of William Clement," Jocelyn advised her. They reached the well, and Jocelyn tied her bucket onto the rope, then lowered it carefully into the depths. "If your love for William is true, it will last until God's time for you to be together. But in the meantime, 'twill do you no good to feast your eyes on something you cannot have."

"Aye," Audrey agreed, helping Jocelyn haul her bucket back up. She colored slightly and twirled a strand of hair around her finger. "I asked Master Bailie why he married me."

"In truth! What did he say?"

Audrey shrugged. "He said he did it to save me from meself. Isn't that odd, now? What do you suppose he meant?"

Jocelyn rolled her eyes. "What woman can know what's in a man's mind? He might be teasing, but—" A sudden twinge made Jocelyn catch her breath. She moaned, carefully lowering her bucket at her side, and a sudden wetness on her kirtle made her wonder if she had somehow spilled the water from her bucket. As a full-fledged birth pang struck, Jocelyn gasped and clutched her belly.

Audrey dropped her water bucket and shrieked. "Och, Miss Jocelyn, 'tis your time!" She left Jocelyn and raced for help in the village.

The pain passed after a moment, but Jocelyn knew it wouldn't do to waste water, so she picked up the heavy buckets and attempted to walk toward the shade of her house. She knew that some babies took hours in coming, and she wanted to be home when the baby arrived. Home with Thomas, for in the last few weeks, she had formulated a plan and a prayer. If Thomas could not find room in his heart for another wife or even another son, she prayed he could find love for a daughter. And if God in heaven was just and kind, Jocelyn would give birth to a girl.

▼▲▼▲▼ After nearly two days of sweaty, teeth-grinding labor, the baby had not come. Eleanor stood back from her cousin's bedside and wiped a strand of sticky hair from her brow. Babies ought not take so long! Virginia had not been this difficult to birth. And Margery Harvie had given birth in five hours. Eleanor bit her lip fretfully. If only her father were here— he would know what to do.

Audrey sat quaking on a stool in a dark corner of the room, and Eleanor tugged on the girl's sleeve, then led her outside the house. The village lay quiet and still at this hour of the night. The only visible lamplight came from Jocelyn's house and the window of the church, where Thomas held a solitary prayer vigil.

"We must have help," Eleanor whispered fiercely while Audrey trembled with fear and exhaustion. "Miss Jocelyn is not strong enough to continue like this. The baby will die if not released soon."

"I don't know how long she'll be takin'," Audrey wailed, wringing her hands in her apron. "And I spoke to Doctor Jones earlier, mind you, and he said 'tis improper for him to be treatin' women." Her eyes glistened with tears of fear. "He says babies come naturally."

"What about the other women? Surely one of them must have some idea how to help."

"Mistress Viccars helped with your child, Miss, but she's too torn up, she is, with grief over losin' her own baby to come help Miss Jocelyn. And Agnes—"

"Agnes is with Virginia. And she is less experienced than I."

Eleanor silently twisted the edge of her apron, fretting, when a low voice spoke from the darkness. "Mistress Dare, how is my wife faring?"

She lifted her eyes and recognized the dim outline of the minister. "I believe not well, Reverend, and I'm at a loss as to what we should do. Doctor Jones won't come, and I've done all I can think of to help—"

A pain-filled scream ripped through the silence of the night, and Audrey darted back into the house to comfort Jocelyn. Eleanor turned to go, too, but the minister's hand caught her arm. A nighttime cloud shifted overhead, and for the first time Eleanor could see his face in the moonlight. His dark eyes were swollen; she thought even his lips trembled. But his voice was as calm and sure as when he gave the sermon on Sunday mornings. "Can you think of nothing else? I have heard of an Indian woman in the next village who is skilled in midwifery."

"I'faith, God has given you that answer!" Eleanor said, impulsively grabbing the sleeve of his doublet. "Go to her. If you hurry, there may be time."

"I . . . cannot go." His voice had dropped.

Eleanor could not believe she heard him correctly. "You cannot go? Faith, what do you mean? You alone *can* go, for who else ought to? She is *your wife!*"

"I am—" He raised his eyes to the dark sky overhead, and for a brief instant his face bore evidence of the struggle in his soul. "I am a minister of the holy gospel, and I cannot, I must not, go to a devil-worshiping heathen for help."

Fury rendered Eleanor momentarily speechless. Then she found her tongue: "You, sirrah, can go to the devil!"

"You could fetch your husband," the minister said, his voice quietly flat.

Eleanor stared at him with the wide, unthinking eyes of a trapped animal; then she turned and sprinted toward her own house, where Ananias lay sleeping. She was so intent upon rousing her husband that she did not stop to consider that the minister had virtually arranged for her to send Ananias to the savages.

▼▲▼▲▼ Dawn had just begun to pink the skies when the waking colony saw Ananias Dare emerge from the woods with two savages, a man and an older woman. The man walked proudly, his eyes planted firmly on the back of Ananias's head, and the woman followed the man, seemingly oblivious to the curious eyes of the colonists. The strange party walked to the minister's home; then the Indian man stood outside with Ananias while Eleanor Dare allowed the woman into the house.

A moment later Audrey Bailie emerged. Exhaustion lined the young girl's face, and Roger Bailie stepped forward to escort his wife home. Ananias took a seat outside on the ground next to the Indian and glanced resentfully toward the church, where through the open windows all could see the spare form of the minister kneeling in prayer.

No sound came from the small house for more than an hour, and many feared the minister's young wife had died. Still, the curious colonists went about their work with frequent sidelong glances toward the house. Did Thomas Colman, who had often preached against adopting heathen practices, know that his wife's life lay in the hands of a savage woman?

Not one of the villagers felt inclined to tell him.

▼▲▼▲▼ Jocelyn drifted uneasily through a pain-filled mist, her body swollen and racked with agony. Pain had heightened her senses until she lay senseless. She felt nothing and sensed nothing but a dull presence that begged to be released.

"Jocelyn!" From far away, she thought she heard Thomas's voice. "Jocelyn! God in heaven, do not take her, too!" Was he next to her or in the attic room? She tried to lift her head but could not do more than turn it.

A dark-haired Indian woman in a split skirt of deerskins determinedly dug a hole in the earthen floor next to her bed.

"Dear God," Thomas called again, "I love her. Spare her for me." Jocelyn closed her eyes to hold back tears. "Jocelyn!" More sounds of sobbing broke the stillness.

She turned her head slowly toward the sound of brokenness and saw Thomas on his knees, his hands uplifted, his cheeks wet with tears. "God, don't let her leave me, please! Halt your heavy hand. I am not worthy, but show mercy this once, I pray you. Don't take her from me."

Jocelyn blinked. Exhaustion pulled her down like a drowning soul, but she was not ready to surrender. There was a time to be born, a time to die, and a time to live boldly, faithfully, successfully. . . .

Anguish. Suffering. She felt her leaden arms and legs and the weight of the child within her body. A cutting pain between her legs. Someone, no, two people, pulled at her arms, urging her into an upright position. A voice commanded her in an abrupt foreign tongue, and Jocelyn cried out as her legs crumpled beneath her and she squatted over the hole in the floor.

Skilled, deft hands pressed upon her belly. A final effort, a release, an expulsion of air and weight, and then the sound of furious crying as the dark-haired woman lifted a child from the cavity in the floor. *Her* child—caked with earth and blood, head pointed, eyes closed, and mouth open in a scream. Jocelyn drank in the sight of the babe. She saw the woman hand the child to Eleanor, who briskly set about cleaning the tiny body. Then the native woman pressed Jocelyn back onto a blanket and began to rub a foul-smelling ointment over her torn and ragged flesh.

Jocelyn stirred and limply lifted a hand toward her cousin. Had she imagined Thomas's presence? She tried to ask for him, but her tongue was heavy and would not work. Eleanor saw the wave and nodded briskly. "The baby's fine, and so are you, dear Coz. Lay back and sleep, Jocelyn. The good Lord knows you deserve a rest."

So she must have imagined it all. Thomas was not there. Pain could do strange things to a woman's mind. Even so, she was at peace. Her baby was here and safe. She closed her eyes and smiled through the embracing folds of sleep.

▼▲▼▲▼ Eleanor finished swaddling the baby girl and breathed a sigh of relief when the child responded to her breast and began to nurse. At least the babe had been born. If Jocelyn died, some part of her would continue. "John White will be glad to see you when he comes," she whispered to the infant. The child blinked wide blue eyes, and Eleanor smiled. "He'll be here soon, and the governor will be mighty proud of you."

She waited a few moments, letting the infant suckle, then crossed the room to the bed where her cousin lay. At first glance, Jocelyn appeared to be asleep—her arms were crossed over her chest, her lips still a rosy pink—but surely no woman could endure the pain and loss of blood Jocelyn had and live.

An ammoniac smell of sweat and urine rose from a salve the savage woman was rubbing into Jocelyn's skin, and Eleanor wanted to tell the woman to stop, but she did not know how. The child wriggled with surprising strength in Eleanor's arms. She gazed at the tiny form and smiled. Without a doubt, Jocelyn's strong will would live on.

The sound of the baby's crying had carried through the village, and a crowd had assembled outside the door. Eleanor closed her bodice and stepped outside with the baby, squinting in the bright sunlight.

"The baby is born?"

"Boy or girl?"

"How's the mother?"

"Has anyone told the minister?"

"'Tis a beautiful child—just like her mother."

She answered their questions as best she could and held the baby patiently as a stream of villagers came by to take a look. After a moment, the crowd parted like the Red Sea as the minister came forward, his eyes weary and bloodshot. Defeat covered him like a mantle.

"My wife is dead, then."

Eleanor shook her head slightly. "I know not. Perchance she has a little life left. Why don't you go to her?"

He paused, and Eleanor remembered his reluctance to associate with the Indian woman he had called a heathen. But then the woman came out of the house, murmured something to Ananias, and left with her husband in the same dignified manner in which she had come.

The minister stepped back and surveyed the crowd as if he would say something; then he seemed to change his mind. He stooped through the low door of the house and closed it, leaving the villagers to their speculations.

And outside, Eleanor Dare wondered why he had not even looked at his new daughter.

▼▲▼▲▼ Thomas marveled that anyone could go through such agony and look so peaceful. Jocelyn lay under her blanket as if sleeping, her hair brushed away from her forehead, a gentle smile curving upon her lips. He stepped forward and took her hand in his and was surprised to find the skin still warm.

"Thomas?" The sleepy murmur jolted him.

"Yes?"

She opened sleepy-cat eyes and smiled. "I saw the baby. A girl."

"Yes." He could not trust himself to say more, so full was his heart. Had God heard his prayer, then? He didn't deserve an answer, for he had played the fool and the coward, but God was sovereign and sent his mercy to the just and the unjust. . . .

Jocelyn said nothing more but seemed to sleep, and he pulled up a stool and sat silently, holding her hand, until Eleanor came into the house and placed the baby into an empty trunk Jocelyn had prepared as a cradle.

Thomas released his wife's hand. "Mistress Dare, I must know. What evil did the savage woman commit in this house?"

Eleanor turned, a spark of fire in her eyes. "Evil? Why none, sirrah! Though I've never seen anything like it, she cut Jocelyn with a sharpened shell and dug a hole. Together we propped her upright, and the baby came swiftly after that."

"And that smell?" Thomas crinkled his nose.

Eleanor shrugged. "A paste to stop the bleeding. Nothing of importance, Reverend, and nothing of evil." She stood by the door a moment. "Shall I send Audrey?"

"Yes," the minister answered, wishing her gone. "Send her later." When he heard the door close and latch behind him, he picked up his wife's hand once again.

▼▲▼▲▼ As Audrey nursed Jocelyn back to health, Eleanor nursed Jocelyn's baby. One lovely afternoon Eleanor sat outside with the baby under the sun-shot leaves of an oak tree. A medley of spring flowers bobbed in the gentle breeze, and the turquoise sky beyond the rim of the palisade seemed filled with gold radiance and the promise of prosperity. Covering herself modestly while the baby suckled, she spied the minister walking through the clearing.

"Reverend, this baby must be named," she called, glancing up at the preoccupied minister. "And we already have a Virginia, in honor of our Virgin Queen."

Thomas came toward her and thrust his hands behind his back for a moment, then gave Eleanor a polite smile. "Then this child shall be called Regina," he said, "for she is a queen in her own right and in a new country."

Eleanor felt a twist of unreasonable jealousy. It was bad enough that Margery Harvie had given birth to a daughter only days after Eleanor, but now her own cousin's baby had a name to rival Virginia's. Still, her daughter, at least, was the governor's granddaughter. . . .

"I have heard criticism that you allowed a savage to tend your wife," Eleanor said, shifting the baby in her arms and adjusting the cloth covering that preserved her modesty. "They say you should have lain down before the door to keep the heathen out. They say your faith in God is small."

Thomas gave her a smile that did not reach his eyes. "And what do you say, Mistress Dare?"

She tilted her head to look at him. "I say you are ofttimes a fool for God," she answered slowly, wondering if he would threaten her with hellfire for what surely amounted to blasphemy in his eyes. "But I recall that you sent me to fetch Ananias to save your wife. Therefore you are not as foolish as I first thought. Howbeit, I cannot judge your faith."

His jaw tightened. "I have faith aplenty," he said, the words fairly hissing from between his clenched teeth. "Faith that God will punish evildoers. Faith that God will hold men accountable for their dark deeds. This faith, Mistress Dare, convinced me that Jocelyn would die if left to me. For I am guilty, you see, and do not deserve a wife or a child and would not have them had your uncle and God himself not forced them upon me!"

Eleanor felt her blood run cold. "Why?" she stammered, suddenly wishing she could escape him, but his strong gaze held her fast.

"You would know why?" he asked, a confused and crazily furious light in his eyes. He took a deep breath as if he would continue, but suddenly stopped and closed his eyes. Thirty seconds elapsed with neither sound nor movement from him; then he opened his eyes again and his mouth tipped in a faint smile.

"You must excuse me, Mistress Dare. I am not myself these days."

Eleanor said nothing, but studied him carefully.

"I cry you mercy," he said, clearing his throat. "I have accepted my situation. I will be a good husband to your cousin, a father to the child—"

"A good husband? In truth, do you think you can call yourself that?" Eleanor said, watching his smile stiffen. "Jocelyn gives continually, sir, and receives very little from you. Yet she is devoted to you; she works harder than any woman in this village so that none may criticize her husband—"

Abruptly, he thrust his hand up, cutting her off. "I cannot allow myself to kindle fires of love in her heart, for she would only be hurt."

Eleanor gave him a brittle, one-sided smile. "Think you she is not hurt already, sir? Then you are indeed a fool. But don't worry," she finished, rising to take the baby inside, "she is devoted, as I said. But she loves you not at all."

The disaster John White expected finally arrived on the fifth of May. Thirty leagues out of Madeira, the *Brave* was overtaken by a sixty-ton French ship from La Rochelle. From the bridge, Arthur Facy made friendly overtures to the passing vessel, even inviting the captain aboard to share a bottle of wine. When White protested against wasting time in such a frivolous encounter, Facy rudely adjured him to go below and keep quiet.

White ignored the sounds of drinking and rioting above deck as the seamen cavorted. His colonists huddled below in quiet groups, many of the men praying for God's mercy for themselves and divine judgment upon the drunken crew. The women, who had seen more uncouth behavior in the past week than they had in their entire lives, sat with their eyes glued to their prayer books as Mistress Sampson read aloud.

As the passengers below watched the dark come on, the sounds of riotous partying finally ceased, and the French ship pulled away at nightfall. But on the morrow, as the *Brave* prepared to raise anchor and make sail, Facy was surprised by a round of cannon fire from the ship, which had returned with its consort, a one-hundred-ton warship.

"What the devil?" Facy stammered, and White, who had come up the companionway, nodded in grim satisfaction.

"They have taken your measure," he said, throwing a dark glance of dislike toward the rheumy-eyed captain. "And they mean to have you for dinner, my friend."

The French ships wasted no time as they closed in for the kill. The English guns boomed in the *Brave*'s defense until the seamen ran out of powder. Then the French sailors spilled like rats over their boarding nets and roamed the upper deck of the *Brave* at will. For more than an hour the sounds of hand-to-hand combat raged over the heads of the frightened colonists belowdecks; then several of the enemy streamed down the companionway and roared in delight at the sight of the quaking passengers cornered like animals in a slaughterhouse.

White directed the women to a hidden area behind a group of barrels and pulled his sword from its scabbard. The fighting was fierce and not of his doing, but it was time to fight or die.

▼▲▼▲▼ Within an hour and a half after the enemy's boarding, the ship, crew, and passengers of the *Brave* lay firmly in the hands of the French. Twenty-three lay dead on the upper deck, among them the *Brave*'s first mate and master gunner. Three of the colonists were injured; one man had been pierced by a French sword nearly a dozen times.

White himself had been cut in the head twice, once by a sword and again by a pike. He wiped blood from his head and tore a strip of cloth from the lining of his doublet to bandage his upper thigh, where he had been shot. Limping badly, he stood with the surviving seamen and Arthur Facy on the upper deck to formally surrender.

In a group around the mainmast, the four women wept silently into their handkerchiefs as the French captain walked over the decks of the captive ship with an imperial air. The English sailors in line with John White stood with their heads down, bloody and bowed. White glared at the conquering captain. The Frenchman would certainly order the execution of all English survivors since so many French lay dead and injured.

The captain's second in command walked behind him and caught White's eye. Returning White's glare, the man gave a furious speech to his commanding officer. The captain, White noted with relief, seemed not to care for the man's words but gave a simple order and gestured toward the line of English survivors. Another French sailor pointed to the afterdeck, and the English survivors were herded to the back of the vessel while the French seamen swarmed over the ship and began to carry away everything of value.

For the rest of the night and through the morning of the following day the French hauled away everything of value, including the passengers' personal belongings and the supplies intended for Virginia: food, barrels of wine and water, tools, copper utensils, maps, charts, even the sketches White had drawn in his idle hours at sea. Most disturbing was the abduction of Pedro Diaz, the ship's pilot. Without Diaz, White knew the ship would never reach America.

In their haste to strip the *Brave,* the French sailors overloaded their shallops, sinking one and severely damaging another. White breathed a sigh of relief when the French were forced to cease their plunder while the *Brave* still had her sails, cables, anchors, and ordnance. If they had taken any more, the *Brave* would have been only a helpless floating hulk.

While the French ship sailed victoriously away, the remaining crew and passengers of the English vessel bound their wounds, then began to repair the rigging. The women mended the sails while the men recaulked splintered beams, and after three days the English ship gingerly edged her way back to Bideford. They arrived on the twenty-second of May, exactly one month after leaving. To White's sharp disappointment, the *Row* arrived back in port a few weeks later.

'Twas a cruel fight at sea, he wrote in his journal, *but just punishment by God for the thievery of our evil disposed mariners. Both vessels returned to England without performing our intended voyage for the relief of the planters in Virginia, which, thereby, we were not a little distressed.*

But the ones who would suffer the most were the colonists who waited in Virginia.

At the City of Raleigh, Ananias Dare waited for the last of his twenty men to board the pinnace, then gave the order to raise the anchor. As the ship slipped past the beachhead near the village, the men aboard waved jaunty farewells to the women who had gathered on the shore. Eleanor waved tentatively, unhappy to see Ananias leaving again, and ten-month-old Virginia managed a childish wave from her mother's arms.

Ananias saw Jocelyn Colman waving weakly at the minister, her baby held close in a maternal embrace. He had not wanted to take the minister on this trip, but Thomas Colman had insisted upon journeying back to Roanoke and Croatoan.

Ananias frowned. The minister insisted on entirely too much these days, and usually got his way.

The pinnace sailed easily through the waters of the Chowan River, and Ananias turned from his thoughts of the minister and looked over the bow of the ship. John White and his relief supplies were long overdue, and Ananias knew it was time to check on the welfare of the men holding the lookout on Croatoan Island. An unsettling thought haunted him: Had the thirty men on Croatoan come to the same bloody end as the fifteen caretaker colonists Grenville had left on Roanoke?

The crew aboard the pinnace spotted Roanoke Island after two hours, and as they sailed round to the fort, Ananias heard frantic whispers from the men behind him. Even from this distance they could see that the fort had been razed, but whether by an act of nature or hostile savages they could not tell. The once tall timbers of the palisade stood as blackened stumps behind the sandy beach.

They lowered the shallop and disembarked. As soon as the shallop hit soft sand, Ananias jumped out and waded toward the beach. The structure of the palisade still stood, though it was burned, and the timbers that had supported the houses stood as well, though blackened by the same fire that had ravaged the palisade. But through an act of God's mercy, the timber carved with the word "Croatoan" stood unmarred, and Ananias breathed a sigh of relief. If John White had come here, he would have gone to Croatoan. And if God was faithful, his men still waited there. Perhaps they entertained Governor White even now.

Wasting no further time on Roanoke, Ananias called for the others to rejoin the ship.

▼▲▼▲▼ Jocelyn placed her baby to sleep in the trunk and stretched out on her bed, her strength utterly gone. Childbirth had left her weaker than she had imagined it could, and the demands of working for survival and nursing an infant dwindled her feeble strength to nothingness by the end of the day. If not for Audrey's and Eleanor's help, Jocelyn knew she would never have been able to keep her home and family together.

And as much as she wanted Thomas to feel a part of the family, she was relieved that he had gone with Ananias to Croatoan. She could not tell if he resented the baby or thought that overt affection was frivolous, but he watched her disapprovingly when she cooed at Regina, and his critical attitude made her uneasy. On several occasions after the infant's birth, she had asked him to hold the baby, but he refused with a somber look that broke her heart every time she saw it.

His brooding, sober presence made her feel self-conscious as she tended the baby, and the way he averted his eyes when she nursed the child at first made her feel guilty, then angry. By heaven, she was doing nothing wrong! Why did he refuse to enjoy his own child?

But he explained nothing and treated her little better than he would a casual friend. Ofttimes when the baby was asleep he would read something or tell Jocelyn a story, and on those nights she felt that his heart might thaw in time. But then the baby would cry or stir in sleep, and Jocelyn would rush to Regina's side. When she returned, the walls would once again stand behind Thomas's eyes.

God had answered her prayer and given her a daughter, but since the baby's birth, all signs of her husband's affection had vanished. She used to think his heart distant; now she wondered if he had a heart at all.

She sighed and closed her eyes as she stretched out in weariness on the bed. He had left home once and come home a changed man. Mayhap God would work a miracle again.

▼▲▼▲▼ Thomas stood at the side of the pinnace and stared at the mighty Western ocean. Its vastness never ceased to awe him, and as he gazed at the distant horizon, he felt a sudden urge to flee. It was the same urge that had propelled him into John White's dockside office.

I'faith, it felt good to get away from the town! Everything he had left behind in England had surrounded him again in the City of Raleigh: the snooping Pharisees, the rigid standards of behavior, the tendency for lawlessness that corrupted peaceful living. In England, he had run from a dead wife and a son. Here, he longed to escape a living wife and a daughter.

He chuckled bitterly. *Who can say, God, that you do not laugh at your servants?* Jonah, running from his calling, fled the great fish only to find himself parched by a desert sun. From the water to a desert, from a son to a daughter, from a dead wife to a living one. Thomas's heart constricted with pain and regret. Truly, there was no escaping God's justice.

▼▲▼▲▼ The men on Croatoan embraced their fellow colonists eagerly, then led them to their small circle of huts inside a high palisade. "These men," explained Richard Taverner, secure in his role as leader, "live simply, with fish for food and water from the rain barrels. We have a watch posted on the beach during every daylight hour."

"Do you light signal fires at night?" Ananias asked.

Taverner shook his head. "No. The danger—"

Ananias pounded his fist upon his palm in frustration. "What danger? Our danger of starvation is greater than any you might face, man! If John White does not see your fires here, he'll go round to Roanoke and waste precious time."

Taverner pressed his lips together firmly. "With respect, sir, you don't know what you are talking about. Two days ago we spotted a sail off the coast and ran down to the beach. We laid a fire and were about to light it, when one of our men with an eagle eye saw that the ship bore, not the flag of England, but of Spain. Spanish marauders, they were, looking for our colony, no doubt. We doused our fires and lay low for the day, hoping they had not caught sight of us. Fortunately, God was on our side, and the ship never came back."

Ananias caught his breath. Spaniards! Truly, he had been so eager to welcome an English supply ship that he had nearly forgotten about the war on the high seas. If the war had escalated, it was possible that White would not be able to get ships through. . . .

"Thank you." Ananias clasped Taverner on the shoulder. "You've done a good work. We pray God will keep you in good health as you serve him and our interests here."

"Aye," Taverner answered. "And ask the good reverend to say a prayer for us, will you? John White promised to bring us wives, you know."

Ananias raised an eyebrow until he caught the gleam in Taverner's eye and realized the man was joking.

▼▲▼▲▼ As the pinnace threaded her way home up the Chowan, Thomas stood at the railing with Christopher Cooper. "Taverner was pretty funny, eh, Reverend?" Cooper asked, his eyes squinting in the sunlight that reflected off the river. "Bring 'em wives? Where's John White supposed to get wives for that scruffy lot?"

"Yes, he was funny," Thomas agreed, nodding politely.

"Of course, you didn't have any trouble landing yourself a pretty wife, eh, Reverend?" Cooper persisted, elbowing Thomas roughly. "'Twasn't fair, though; you didn't give the rest of us a decent shot at the prize. If you'd waited until we landed, things might have turned out differently."

Thomas sighed and moved away, hoping the man would take the hint. If Cooper didn't leave him alone, he just might tell the entire story, and then what would they think?

They would think you crazy, the answer came, *because you live with a beautiful woman who makes you weak with longing every time she glances your way, and yet you ignore her, turn from her, snuff out every affectionate moment that springs up between you.*

Thomas bit his lip until he tasted blood. The thought of Jocelyn at home, his baby at her breast, sent a wave of warmth along his pulses and made his knees weak. Home had been bearable, at least, when she was swollen and heavy with child, and he had not been afraid to stay by her side when she was near death.

But now it seemed that God, in his harsh wisdom, had brought her from the brink of heaven and kept her in Thomas's house. *Why, God? Why?* Thomas cried out wordlessly. *Why did you not set her free from this cursed life with one who must bear your punishment?*

He hung his head in defeat. How could he endure living with her now, when she had never looked more beautiful?

▼▲▼▲▼ Life settled again into a normal routine after Ananias and the men returned from Croatoan. John White had not come as yet, Ananias told the village, but surely each day that passed brought him closer.

As Jocelyn gradually convalesced from the exhaustion and travail of childbirth, she learned that by inviting the Indians to help

her, Ananias had opened a door to the Indian village of
Ohanoak. The Chawanoac Indians who dwelt nearby, while
friendly, had hitherto avoided daily contact with the English. But
since the werowance, Abooksigun, and his wife had entered the
City of Raleigh at Ananias's invitation, a steady stream of Indian
visitors arrived at the gates of the English palisade every morning.

They brought furs, fish, and seed corn to trade. After spreading their wares on the ground, the savages stood back and
waited for offers to be made. The townspeople learned quickly
that the Indian manner of trading involved equal reciprocation.
Nothing was given without the expectation of something in
return, and nothing could be accepted without giving a gift in
kind.

But the Indians gave much more than they took in pots and
axes and trinkets. Their women taught the English women how
to treat the bites of lice, ticks, fleas, and mosquitoes, and through
their example the English learned that sweat baths eased the
pain of arthritis and rheumatism—knowledge that greatly
cheered Roger Bailie. Boils and bruises in the colony came to be
treated by Indian poultices, and once when Jocelyn was about to
make rags of a dress that had become infested with lice, an
Indian woman sternly took the garment from her and carried it
outside to an anthill. Jocelyn watched in honest puzzlement until
she realized that the lice were a veritable feast for an ant colony.
By the morning of the next day, the dress was free from both vari-
eties of insects.

The path between the two walled villages gradually grew
wider, and an "open door" policy soon bound the English and
Indian villages together. While the Indians were quick to pick up
basic words of the English language, Jocelyn noticed that most of
her fellow colonists were reluctant to speak the Indian tongue,
because they were quietly convinced that all things English were
vastly superior. But without the help of the Indians or a miraculous provision from John White's promised supply fleet, Jocelyn
doubted they would survive the coming winter.

According to the dictates of their Indian friends, throughout the summer of 1588 the colonists planted, harvested, and stored food for winter. The young savages taught the English boys how to build weirs to trap fish in the river, and the English women learned how to build "hurdles" of sticks, from which they hung pieces of meat or fish to smoke over a smoldering fire.

With Regina securely tied onto her back in the Indian manner, Jocelyn visited Pauwau, the wife of the werowance, and learned that this aged woman had saved her life during the travail of childbirth. During her first awkward visit with Pauwau, she sensed that the Indians did not care for effusive thanks but preferred to receive gratitude in the form of respect and an attentive ear. So Jocelyn became Pauwau's student of sorts, and from the older woman she learned much. As the summer sun slowly encouraged their crops to bloom into ripeness, she sat at Pauwau's feet and learned to make coiled clay cooking pots even as she prayed for an opportunity to bring light into the Indians' spiritual darkness.

Though she did all she could to aid the colony's survival, Jocelyn tried to remember that she and Thomas were primarily responsible for ministering to and evangelizing the Indians. In her time with the women of the Indian village, Jocelyn talked often of God the Father, Creator of the world. One afternoon while she helped several Indian women make buckskin, she told them that the Creator Father had made deer for man's use.

The women nodded. "We know of this god," Pauwau said, nodding gravely. "He is Mantoac and is older than the earth."

Jocelyn paused, her fingers deep in the sudsy mush that resulted from boiling deer brains and liver. "I suppose it matters not what we call him," she said, nodding, "as long as we serve him. But do you know of his Son, Jesus, the Christ?"

The women shook their heads as they pounded the sudsy animal skin with their fists. "Mantoac has many sons," Hurit spoke up. The pretty woman was Pauwau's daughter-in-law. "He made other gods to help his work. The sun, the moon, the stars. These are lesser gods, and they have made all creatures."

Jocelyn held up a disputing finger. "No, my friends, the sun, moon, and stars are mere creations. Jesus, the Christ, is the only Son of God."

Wide-eyed but uncomprehending, the women only stared at her as they worked the hide. Jocelyn sighed. It would have been better if they had known nothing of God at all; then they would have welcomed the news of a loving Creator. But their culture had merged God's truth with paganism's deception, and she knew only patience and gentleness would help her untangle their confused ideas.

▼▲▼▲▼ Close association with the nearby Indian tribe weakened previously inviolate English standards, and for weeks Thomas used his sermons to address the evils of heathen morality. Though they all knew, Thomas said, that the heathen practice of giving young girls for a night's pleasure was an abominable practice, there were more subtle evils of which the English had to beware. The Indian dances, he warned, were not to be imitated or practiced, their songs were not to be sung, the games of the Indian children not taught to English children. The Indian women who went without shirts or cloaks in the hot days of summer were not to be allowed into the English village without proper and modest clothing, and though Indian poultices and salves could be used for healing, they had to be made in the English village, so the colonists could be assured that no heathen incantations had been uttered as the medicine was being prepared.

The colonists bore Thomas's restrictions without comment. Except for Beth Glane and the doctor John Jones, who were forever peering through bushes and eavesdropping at windows to report on the sinfulness of their neighbors, most colonists were too busy with their work to participate in games and dances and music. The women were only too happy to learn how to make poultices and salves themselves, for it was much more practical to have the natural recipe than to journey to the Indian village every time someone was injured or required an ointment.

But as the hot days wore on and John White's supply ships did not arrive from England, one standard of civilization slipped irreparably: clothing. In June's blistering heat, the men began to go without their worn-out doublets, wearing shirts while in camp but frequently going shirtless while fishing. The women also began to economize on their clothing by shortening their skirts and removing layers of petticoats. But the lowering of these standards, Thomas proclaimed from his pulpit, was the beginning of a slow slide into paganism.

Jocelyn had to laugh when she considered her own wardrobe. In her hurry to pack Jocelyn's trunk, Audrey had thrown in an odd assortment of clothing, none of which was really practical for the wilderness of America. If she were in London, Jocelyn would have been well prepared. To dress, she would have donned a smock and French farthingale with its ridiculous hoops to hold the skirt away from her hips and abdomen, then a series of petticoats, then her kirtle. Audrey used to require ten minutes just to fasten the row of hooks down the left side of the bodice Jocelyn wore atop the kirtle, and another ten to pin the bodice's hem to the kirtle's waist at front and back. Still another ten minutes were required to pin the sleeves to the bodice, if perchance they had been unpinned when Jocelyn had last worn the dress.

All of these pieces—smocks, farthingales, pins, and an assortment of kirtles, bodices, nightgowns, and half a dozen sleeves, two of which did not match—lay in Jocelyn's trunk, yet in the colony she wanted to wear nothing but a kirtle and bodice. Sometimes a petticoat, if the day were cool.

It was no wonder that English women looked enviously at the Indian women in the heat of June and July. Buckskin was wonderfully soft and moved easily, but it was too hot and heavy to wear in a skirt to the ankles.

Ignoring Thomas's admonitions, Rose Payne, Joyce Archard, and Margaret Lawrence made themselves midcalf, one-piece dresses of buckskin and wore them to church one Sunday morning. Jocelyn saw them and held her breath while Thomas looked over his congregation. Rising from his chair, he stood before the lectern and solemnly proclaimed that the City of Raleigh was on its way to hell.

"Buckskin is buck*sin!*" he ranted. Jocelyn blinked at the ferocity of his attack but did not dare turn around to see how Mistresses Payne, Archard, and Lawrence were handling the news. "Buckskin is immodest, it is a waste of God's resources, and it harkens to the heathen, pagan community which spawned its use. No decent, godly woman should wear it, and no woman in buckskin will enter into this house of God!"

The three women filed quietly out of church that afternoon with almost-tangible clouds of guilt over their heads, and Jocelyn wondered what her husband would do if John White did not come soon. For until they found a plant suitable for weaving into cloth, buckskin and furs would be the only materials available for dress, immodest or otherwise.

▼▲▼▲▼ In the late summer evenings Jocelyn nursed Regina by the hearth while Thomas pored over his prayer book. Her hope that the baby would soften his heart had thus far proved futile, for with the advent of summer and the planting season, Thomas had joined in the work with the other men and had little time for family life. While other men came home and rested or enjoyed their families, Thomas went straight from the supper table to fetch his Bible and prayer book. When Jocelyn had cleared their supper dishes away, he returned to the board and scratched his sermons out on parchment with a quill pen, often working until Jocelyn and the baby had fallen asleep.

One night Thomas came home in a foul mood and wore a look of stern displeasure throughout supper and even as he worked on his sermon. After Regina fell asleep, Jocelyn added another log to the fire and crawled up into her bed. Noting his persistent frown, she took her battered copy of Marcus Aurelius from her trunk and began to read aloud:

> "Begin each day by telling yourself: Today I shall be meeting with interference, ingratitude, insolence, disloyalty, ill-will, and selfishness—all of them due to the offenders' ignorance of what is good or evil. But for my part I have long perceived the nature of good and its nobility, the nature of evil and its meanness, and also the nature of the culprit himself, who is my brother; therefore none of those things can injure me, for nobody can implicate me in what is degrading. Neither can I be angry with my brother or fall foul of him; for he and I were born to work together, like a man's two hands, feet, or eyelids, or like the upper and lower rows of his teeth. To obstruct each other is against Nature's law—and what is irritation or aversion but a form of obstruction?"

"What are you reading?" Thomas's tone was sharp with annoyance.

Jocelyn lifted her eyes from the book. "Marcus Aurelius."

"Why do you read that section aloud?"

She paused. In truth, she had been thinking that the passage might do him good. He did not work well with others—not with Ananias, or with the Indians, or with her. Though they were married and had a child, never had she felt that they toiled together as a man and wife should. She labored in what she considered a form of ministry with the women as Thomas worked with the men, but never did they discuss the other's endeavor. Indeed, rarely did they speak at all. The slight affection he had shown her since arriving at their new home had vanished, and now he regarded her with open disaffection, seemingly loath to touch her as they slept, reluctant to meet her glance across the board as they ate.

"I know not why I read it," she hedged. "It just struck me."

"Marcus Aurelius believed that a spark of the divine resides in all men, and nothing can be further from the truth. As a minister's wife, you should not read such things."

"Think you that I should close my mind to the thoughts of others? Marcus Aurelius had much good to say!"

"So do the heathen Indians who dwell at our side, yet they are not counted among the sons of God. Aurelius said that philosophy, and it alone, had the power to guide and guard a man's steps. And such a philosophy, Jocelyn, will doom a man's soul to hell for eternity, and doomed also will be those who read such ideas."

She let the book fall from her hand to the quilt that covered her. "I cannot speak for Marcus Aurelius," she whispered intently. "But I will speak for myself. My soul is not doomed, Thomas, nor is yours, though you have read Aurelius, too. Or have you forgotten our first conversation aboard the *Lion* and the many discussions we had following about this very author. Nor was my father's soul doomed, and he was a philosopher of great renown as well as one who loved God and his fellowman. In my father's house I read Aurelius, and Ovid, and Euripides, and Aeschylus—yet, by grace, still I am accepted by God!"

"You will not read such things here."

Jocelyn managed a laugh. "Unless God in his mercy sends John White to us soon, I will never have such books again! But the words of the great poets are hidden in my heart. Surely you have read them—"

He turned from her and bent over his books on the table. "I wish to devote myself to Scripture."

"But you have read Greek poetry."

He lifted his head slightly, and Jocelyn knew his silence was an affirmative answer.

"Then how can you deny the beauty of Aeschylus?" She sat up, engrossed by the memories that flooded her heart. "My father used to playact with me. In one of my favorite scenes, I acted as one of the Furies, and my father played Orestes, who prayed for mercy as the Furies sang their binding song."

"'Tis nothing but folly," Thomas muttered, bending over his sermon. "Your father was but a foolish old man."

Ignoring his remarks, Jocelyn closed her eyes and swayed gently with the beauty of the poetry and the memory of her eloquent father reading from the thick book. As a child, she had memorized the powerful passage and played her part dramatically, swooping around her bookbound father as he tried not to smile.

She recited the words that came easily to her even now:

> "Come then, link we our choral. If a man can spread his
> hands and show they are clean, no wrath of ours shall
> lurk for him. Unscathed he walks through his lifetime.
> But one like this man before us, with stained hidden
> hands, and the guilt upon him, shall find us beside him,
> as witnesses of the truth, and we show clear in the end
> to avenge the blood of the murdered."

"Stop!" Thomas roared.

She blinked as he hurled his precious prayer book across the room, missing her head by inches. "Such things are of the devil!" The prayer book fell to the floor with a thud as Jocelyn stared at her husband in mute astonishment.

His face paled and he opened his mouth as if to speak, then abruptly turned and slammed the door as he stormed outside.

▼▲▼▲▼ The creaking of the latch woke her a few hours later, and she heard him quietly reenter the house. He shed his doublet, removed his boots and leggings, and slid carefully beneath the blankets, trying, she knew, not to wake her.

She did not stir, but kept her back to him. Why had God brought her to such an unreasonable man? In the beginning Thomas had seemed a towering rock of strength. Now his solid qualities served only to frustrate and confound her. He was stubborn, immovable, implacable, and totally without understanding. She wondered if even a tiny spark of compassion existed in his soul.

So why did her heart break each time she looked at him?

For a long time they lay awake, their backs to each other, neither moving, neither speaking, until the dawn came and the baby stirred them with her crying.

Richard Taverner

He was cut off out of the land of the living:
For the transgression of my people
was he stricken.

Isaiah 53:8

John White felt the bow of the *Ark Royal* rise under his feet as the sleek flagship of Her Majesty's Navy headed out to sea. A marvel of engineering, the magnificent galleon had been built by Sir Walter Raleigh, then presented to the queen. The ship had two gun decks, a double forecastle, a quarterdeck, a half deck, and, above the half deck furthest aft, a poop deck. The innovative gallery, a balcony mastered by Raleigh's designer, Matthew Baker, ran forward from the stern on either side of the half deck.

All in all, the *Ark Royal* was a ship built for conquerors, with decks aplenty for captains and admirals to supervise the progress of a battle at sea. A twinge of bitter regret struck White as he thought of Raleigh's dedication to the splendid vessel, and he resolutely turned his face out to sea so that none aboard the ship might guess at his thoughts.

Raleigh could have devoted the funds invested in this ship to rescue my daughter, he thought, cynicism battering his brain. *But no, he chose instead to buy greater favor with the queen.*

The low and elegant galleon moved confidently across the surface of the waters. From his position on the poop deck, Lord Charles Howard of Effingham, chief in command against the approaching Spanish Armada, shouted orders to his scurrying crew. Howard had agreed to allow White on board as a favor to Raleigh and probably had no idea that White waited for the outcome of the sea battle for more than patriotic reasons. If the British faced defeat, White knew his chances for returning to Roanoke would evaporate like smoke from a ship's cannon. But if the English fleet decimated the Spanish Armada, the seas would once again be safe for exploration.

"God in heaven," White prayed quietly, squinting into the July sun as Portsmouth slipped away beside him, "the Holy Scriptures say you have spread out the heavens and tread upon the waves of the deep. You divide the ocean with your power; you have dominion from sea to sea. Trusting in your power; I trust that you will return me to Roanoke. May victory be ours in this battle, and may your grace provide me with a safe passage to my friends and loved ones."

▼▲▼▲ After two years of preparation to outfit the greatest armada the world had ever seen, Philip II of Spain awarded command of the massive fleet to the Duke of Medina-Sidonia, Alonzo Perez de Guzmán. Philip's ambition extended to more than victory at sea. Inspired by the exhortations of his priests, he determined to conquer the rebellious island of England and silence forever the voice of heretical Protestantism.

Philip's plan, carefully orchestrated over the past months and finally ready for implementation, involved a two-pronged attack. The Armada would break the lines of English resistance at sea, and once the English navy could no longer protect the country's vulnerable shores, an army of thirty thousand Spanish soldiers, waiting with the Duke of Parma in the Netherlands, would cross the Channel and invade the shores of England.

On the nineteenth day of July, 1588, Philip cracked his knuckles in nervous anticipation as Medina-Sidonia bowed before him. He quickly pressed his hand upon the admiral's head to impart a royal blessing. Beside him, the king's counselor murmured a Latin prayer, and Medina-Sidonia lifted his head and smiled in confident pleasure.

"We have been thwarted before, my king," he said, referring to the disastrous attempt to launch the attack three months earlier. The fleet had been scattered by a gale and required nearly a month to refit and regroup in La Coruña. "But now, sire, we are ready."

Philip lifted his hand in a silent, regal salute, and Medina-

Sidonia swirled away to board his ship. When the room had cleared of all but his counselors, Philip rose from his throne and went to the window. The harbor teemed with life. One hundred and thirty-one great and small warships awaited their commands, and upon their decks eight thousand sailors and nineteen thousand soldiers had armed themselves for battle. It was the most impressive fleet ever assembled in history, and his Armada would surely be invincible.

Philip's counselor pointed with a long finger to the admiral's ship. The sails of Medina-Sidonia's galleon snapped and filled first; then the harbor bloomed with canvas. Philip glanced toward his Father Confessor for a sign of approval, but the priest crossed himself in prayer and made no promises.

▼▲▼▲▼ The booming of cannon from a lookout ship to the south brought the activity aboard the *Ark Royal* to a momentary halt.

"So it begins, then," John White muttered, scanning the southwestern horizon. Lord Charles Howard glanced up toward the seaman in the crow's nest. "Ahoy, Captain!" the seaman cried out, pointing southward. "Hither come fifty, mayhap sixty ships. I can't count them, sir!"

Howard snapped his attention to the officers standing near him. "Time to show the poxy Spaniards what we Englishmen are made of," he said, nodding stiffly. "Every man to his station and ease up the main sheets. We will not let them one league nearer to England than they are right now!"

White felt his mouth go dry as his heart began to pound. Many of Elizabeth's courtiers had brashly predicted that Philip would never actually dare to attack. Yet Spanish galleons had claimed the horizon, and the armored fleet was sailing inexorably up the English Channel toward them.

God in heaven, what will this day bring?

▾▴▾▴ Amid the explosions of gunpowder and the furious splash of cannon fire, the English fleet got to windward of Medina-Sidonia's Armada. With the wind full in their sails, the English pressed their smaller, more agile ships away from the Spanish, while their superior guns battered the Armada mercilessly. The English cheered every time a Spanish ship was struck, but on the flotilla came, a seemingly impenetrable cluster of towered ships that moved relentlessly up the Channel.

In a tight formation, the Armada moved as a gigantic shark through the water, and only the ships on the perimeter were exposed to direct contact with English guns. In three major engagements the English were unable to do major damage, but then the *Ark Royal* and her fellows drove the Spanish fleet into the Calais roadstead, where the Spanish ships anchored. The roadstead was not as enclosed and protected as a harbor, but Howard did not dare attack the Spanish while they lay at anchor off the coast of France. He determined to wait, a clever, sly mouse awaiting his confrontation with an arrogant, clumsy cat.

▾▴▾▴ On the evening of July twenty-eighth, John White stood on the deck of the *Ark Royal* as her sailors worked in silent darkness. Eight small shallops, collected from the *Ark Royal* and several other English vessels, were tied together in a single line and filled with rotting, oil-soaked canvas. At Howard's command, the shallops were towed by a crew of seamen to the mouth of the Calais roadstead, then ignited.

The pregnant silence of the night erupted into cheers as the tide propelled the fire ships toward the sleeping Spanish fleet. White heard the long, slow chuckle of Lord Charles from the deck above as the burning shallops drifted to the immobile Armada, and pandemonium ensued. Unclothed men, rousted from sleep, frantically climbed the tall ships' rigging, and Spanish sails jerked upward from yardarms atop the masts as cables were cut and anchors abandoned.

One burning boat nudged a sizable warship, and a stream of

sparks flew up into the night and ignited oil on the deck. Within seconds, huge tongues of flame leapt into the air, and men scrambled to vault overboard in the fire-tinted darkness.

Aboard the *Ark Royal*, Lord Charles Howard stopped laughing and gave the order to make sail in pursuit of the frantic Spanish.

▼▲▼▲▼ Had a violent storm not sprung Howard's carefully set trap, the entire Armada might have been captured. But heavy winds and bucking waves allowed many of the enemy vessels to escape. The English pursued the Spanish warships into the early morning hours. As soon as dawn rendered it possible to positively identify targets, the boom of cannon resounded over the waters and a fierce gun battle ensued. By keeping his ships out of range of the floating Spanish arsenals and using his long-range guns effectively, Lord Charles managed to put five principal ships out of action. Aboard other English ships, Howard's officers utilized the maneuverability of the low English galleons to outrun the hulking Spanish vessels that dared to pursue them. By sailing quickly and turning at the last moment, English captains ran two of the Spanish ships aground.

John White saw Lord Charles kiss his fingers in delight when a sudden change in the wind threatened to drive the Spanish fleet onto the Ruytingen Shoals, but the wind shifted again, and Medina-Sidonia escaped in a headlong flight to the North Sea. The *Ark Royal* and a dozen other ships followed the remnant of the disabled Armada as far as the Firth of Forth, then broke off their pursuit outside the Scottish bay.

Exultant in victory, Lord Charles clapped White on the back and invited him to the captain's cabin for a celebratory drink. White accepted, his own heart filled with gratitude to this clever captain. As they lifted their glasses of ale in a celebratory toast, the bosun burst into the tiny cabin, a list in his hand. "In ten days," the officer said, barely suppressing a cocky grin, "our enemy has lost sixty-three ships."

"And we?" Howard asked, turning to the bosun. "Tell the good governor how many ships we have lost."

"None," the officer replied.

While Lord Charles pompously propped his boots on the desk and lifted his mug to toast his victory, White breathed a silent prayer of thanks. If Her Majesty Queen Elizabeth had lost none of her galleons and had won the naval battle of the century, there was no reason a fleet would not be soon available for renewed journeys to America.

▾▴▾▴▾ "The Honorable John White, Governor to Her Majesty's Colony at Roanoke Island, Virginia, begs an audience with the Queen of England, Wales, and Ireland."

White felt his stomach tighten as his name echoed through the throne room of Richmond Palace, but he stepped obediently forward, drawn by the sight of the diminutive red-haired queen in the chair by the window. The circle of courtiers and counselors inclined their heads in polite interest as he approached. Only the eyes of the queen remained aloof.

Before her, he knelt on one knee and bowed his head. "Your Majesty. I have a boon to ask of thee."

"Rise, John White."

He felt as awkward as a schoolboy before her, the Virgin Queen, who had just conquered the world. Her dark blue eyes were upon him now, as clever as a terrier's. Her delicate hand paused on a bauble that hung from a gold chain about her neck, and she lifted her chin slightly. "What would you ask of us?"

"Permission to sail." He should not have been so blunt. He felt the dark, disapproving glance of Sir Walter Raleigh fall upon him. Elizabeth had to be courted, he had been told; she must be flattered and warmed to the subject at hand. Those who succeeded with her acknowledged her beauty, purity, devotion to God and the reformation of the church. . . .

But John White was no diplomat. "Your Majesty, last year I left my daughter and granddaughter on the shores of Virginia in order to hasten here and accrue supplies for the English venture at Roanoke. The colonists are depending upon me, and I must return to them shortly. I pray you, I beseech you, let me return to them with a fleet of well-supplied ships."

The small hand paused on the bauble, and her pale skin colored slightly. "The costs of colonization are high," she said, her voice falling carefully upon dozens of intently listening ears. "'Twas my understanding that private investors were to finance this venture."

"They are, Your Highness, but only you can grant permission for the fleet to sail. I had assembled a fleet in March, but your order from the Privy Council forbade my ships to sail—"

"Think you that I should have left England defenseless against the Spanish?"

"No." He hung his head in what he hoped was an attitude of humility. "But I have been aboard the *Ark Royal* with Lord Charles Howard, and I have seen the Spanish defeated. You are victorious, my queen, and I—"

The hand upon the bauble lifted; the index finger wagged in a gentle warning. "The Spanish have disappeared along the Irish coast. I need Sir Richard Grenville, Sir Walter Raleigh, and Lord Charles Howard to maintain their vigilant watch. What if the Spaniards capitalize on Irish disaffection for this throne? I cannot risk another attack, John White. At this time, I cannot grant this liberty for your venture."

She nodded in curt dismissal and White bowed again, his face burning in humiliation and defeat. If he could not convince Her Majesty the Queen to remember and care for her abandoned colonists, he would have to find a way to provide for them himself.

▼▲▼▲▼ The English queen and her captains did not realize how little they had to fear from the Spanish. As the Duke of Medina-Sidonia attempted to reach Spain by circumnavigating the British Isles, severe storms battered the crippled remnant of the Armada along the rocky Scottish, Irish, and Norwegian coasts. Storms broke up fully half of the remaining fleet, and only a handful of ships limped back into Spanish harbors.

Philip II heard even worse news soon after his defeated sea captains came home. Sickness and disease had struck his army in the Netherlands, and of the thirty thousand men he had stationed there in anticipation of the English invasion, only seventeen thousand returned alive to Spain.

Overwhelmed by defeat, Philip lay prostrate on the carpet in front of the private altar in his chapel. Conqueror of Portugal and colonizer of America and the Philippines, he had gathered gold from the four corners of the earth and built the greatest naval fleet in history. How could God have allowed this ignominious destruction of his Armada by Protestant English rebels?

The colonists at the City of Raleigh had no idea that the world's two greatest civilizations battled for supremacy on the high seas, nor did they know that their fate and the naval battle were inextricably intertwined. England celebrated her supreme naval victory well into the fall of 1588, but the colonists at the City of Raleigh spent their time bringing in the harvest and preparing for winter. With each passing week they thought less about John White and the promise of English reinforcements and depended more upon the kindness and wisdom of their Indian neighbors.

And as the English and Indian cultures became more interdependent, Thomas Colman preached longer and harder against the sins of the colony.

When he first preached against buckskin, Indian beads, and dancing, most of the colonists had silently agreed with him. But as months passed and the villagers learned to appreciate the beauty and practicality of Indian ways, Jocelyn began to overhear complaints from her husband's congregation. Torn between a desire to be loyal to Thomas and the urge to be reasonable, she decided to approach him with her concerns.

She waited until after supper one night, then put Regina into her trunk. The baby stood up, clutching the edge of the trunk for support, and her wide blue eyes followed every movement Thomas made as he sat at the table. A shining splotch of drool hung from her chin as she babbled at her father.

Suppressing a smile, Jocelyn pulled up a stool at the board while Thomas studied his Bible. After a moment, he looked up at her, his handsome face darkened by shadows thrown by the dim lamp.

"Thomas, I would speak with you."

"Yes?" His voice was cool and detached.

"It's about what I hear the others say." She paused and bit her lip. How could she say these things without offending his sense of honor? "I fear you won't like to hear this."

"Tell me, Jocelyn. Faithful are the wounds of a friend." His eyes fell from her face. "If you are my friend."

His words cut her heart. How could he say such a thing? "I am, Thomas, and I don't mean to hurt you. But is it possible that you are putting too much emphasis on . . . unimportant things?"

He folded his hands over his Bible and gave her a calm smile. "Unimportant things, Jocelyn? Speak plainly."

She waved her hands helplessly. "Dancing. Singing. Wearing proper clothing. We did these things in England, Thomas, and never thought them sin. Why should they be sinful here? As long as a heart is pure before God, why does it matter if a man sings or a woman dances? Are we not commanded to make melody in our hearts? And did David not dance with joy before the Lord?"

His face flushed, but his expression did not change. "Have you anything else to say?"

She shook her head, feeling miserable.

"Then I must thank you for your insight," he said dryly, lifting his hands from his Bible. "But God has burdened me with the spiritual oversight of this colony, and I must direct matters as I see fit. And I bid you good night."

Without saying another word, Jocelyn left him and went to bed.

▼▲▼▲▼ The next Sunday morning, Thomas stood before the crowd of sober-faced colonists and thrust his hands behind his back. "It has come to my attention that there are those among you who feel I am too strict about sin," he said, his voice carrying well beyond the crowd. "I have given some thought to this matter and would like to read to you the thoughts of a sec-ond-century Christian who desired to follow God above all else."

He pulled a book from the lectern and opened it. "'Give up colored clothes,'" he read. "'Get rid of everything in your wardrobe that is not white. Stop sleeping on a soft pillow. Sell your musical instruments, and don't eat any more white bread. You cannot, if you are sincere about obeying Christ, take warm baths or shave your beard. To shave is to lie against him who created us, to attempt to improve upon his work.'"

Several people in the congregation snickered, and Jocelyn had to admit that Thomas had used a clever illustration. But to what purpose?

"Have I asked you," he said, putting the book back on the lectern, "to give up black, green, blue, or even red clothing? Have I asked you to toss out your mattresses of grass and straw to sleep on the ground instead? Have I asked any one of you to burn your harps or reed flutes, even those upon which you play praise to God? Have I asked any of you men—" he pointed to several of the men who were clean-shaven, as he was—"to surrender the blades with which you shave? Shall we all grow our hair long like the heathen so we will not bring the blade of scissors upon the hair that God has created? No! I have not asked any of these things."

He opened his Bible. "But these are the words of God, and these are the things God asks of you: 'When thou art come into the land which the Lord thy God giveth thee, thou shalt not learn to do after the abominations of those nations. There shall not be found among you any one that maketh his son or his daughter to pass through the fire, or that useth divination, or an observer of times, or an enchanter, or a witch, or a charmer, or a consuler with familiar spirits, or a wizard, or a necromancer. For all that do these things are an abomination unto the Lord: and because of these abominations the Lord thy God doth drive them out from before thee. Thou shalt be perfect with the Lord thy God. For these nations, which thou shalt possess, hearkened unto observers of times, and unto diviners: but as for thee, the Lord thy God hath not suffered thee to do so.'"

Thomas closed his Bible and looked up at the congregation.

"We are to be entirely obedient to the Lord," he said, his dark eyes sweeping over the gathering as if he weighed the purity and thoughts of every soul present. "The heathen savages that surround us shall be swept from the land, driven out before us. And we shall not adopt their ways, lest we, too, be destroyed before the awesome power of the Lord."

Abruptly, he sat down, and after a few moments of silence, the chastised congregation began to file out the door of the church. Jocelyn sat still on her bench, her cheeks burning with the shame of conviction. Had she been wrong? Was her spirit too free in this place? Though she had won many friends among the women of the Indian village, converts to Christianity had been few. Had she not been strong enough in her approach?

Laden with guilt and misgivings, Jocelyn left her husband alone in the church and followed the rest of the chastened congregation out the door.

▼▲▼▲▼ The next morning, after breakfast, Jocelyn said a meek farewell to Thomas as he left for his work, then bundled seventeen-month-old Regina on her back. She was deep in thought when she left the house, still considering whether or not her actions had been appropriate in the eyes of God, and scarcely noticed when Audrey fell into step with her outside the village.

"Well met, Jocelyn," Audrey said, her voice unusually cheerful for such an early hour of the morning. "Where are you bound?"

"Good morrow," Jocelyn said, waving her hand distractedly. "I'm on my way to the Indian village. Pauwau and Hurit promised to help me spin today. We think we can make thread from *wisakon.*"

"What?" Audrey crinkled her nose.

"That," Jocelyn said, pointing to a common variety of milkweed growing by the path. "If Thomas is bound that we shall not wear buckskin—"

"You mean buck*sin?*" Audrey giggled. "Sure, Jocelyn, and you don't think it is truly a sin—"

"I don't know." Jocelyn stopped in midstride and turned to face her friend. "I was sure it wasn't, but now I don't know. I want to please God, Audrey, and my husband. One day a thing seems right to me, then Thomas reads from the Holy Scriptures, and suddenly I'm sure it's wrong."

"Thomas read yesterday about witchcraft and the like," Audrey said, shifting her basket from one hip to the other. "But buckskin is not witchcraft, nor is anything else you've ever done, Jocelyn."

"No, it's not," Jocelyn allowed. She closed her eyes and blew the wisps of hair from her forehead. "Beshrew this confounded confusion! I don't know what to do anymore!"

"You've been doin' well enough," Audrey offered as they began to walk again down the trail toward the Indian village. "And you haven't asked me how I've been doin'."

"Oh?" Jocelyn turned inquisitive eyes toward the girl. "How are you doing, Mistress Bailie?"

Audrey blushed and looked down at the trail. "A wee bit better than I'd hoped, for certain. Y' know, for months I thought the old man married me because he wanted another servant—or worse, if you take me meaning," she said, rolling her eyes. "But he doesn't treat me like a servant at all. And he didn't come near me, either, in that way . . . until I said he could."

"You said he could?" Jocelyn lifted an eyebrow.

"Aye," Audrey answered, raising her chin. "He treats me as a lady, Jocelyn, not a servant. In the four months we've been married, he's never commanded me to do anythin'. On my first night in his house he told me he wouldn't require anything of me, but I cook and clean because I am grateful for his goodness." Her voice gentled. "He's kind, too, and sweet. He tells me stories and has promised to build me a big house as soon as 'tis safe to move outside the palisade."

"In truth?"

Audrey nodded and lazily twirled a strand of hair around her finger. "William keeps after me, of course, but y' know, he's not nearly as nice as Master Bailie, though I have to admit he's more than a wee bit handsomer. But last week I saw William flirting with Emme Merrimoth, who's thirty if she's a day, and Master Bailie would never do that, not if a hundred Emme Merrimoths passed by aflappin' their eyelashes at him!"

She ended her speech by raising her hand in a flourish of triumph, and Jocelyn had to smother a smile. "So you like your husband now?" she asked.

"He's tolerable, mind you," Audrey answered, tilting her head. "And last night—I let him kiss me. And one thing led to another, and, well—" She blushed prettily, and Jocelyn felt a stab of envy. Audrey had taken the same chance at marriage that Jocelyn had taken, but it would seem Audrey had gained a husband who cherished her.

Jocelyn quickened her pace. "We ought to hurry," she said, nearly breaking into a run. "I want to be home in time to take Thomas his dinner."

▼▲▼▲▼ The gates of the wooden palisade around Ohanoak were open as Audrey and Jocelyn approached, and Jocelyn nodded soberly to the braves who stood watch at the gate. Though the Indians had lived in peace with their neighboring tribes for years, security was never taken lightly, and one of the most grievous sins in the Indian catalog was "living carelessly." Caution was a continuous exercise, and Ananias and the council had been much impressed by the Indians' natural carefulness.

Jocelyn led Audrey to the grass hut where Hurit and her husband, Chogan, lived. Chogan stepped out as the women approached, gave them a slow nod, then walked away. Audrey gawked at the sinewy muscles in the Indian's back until Jocelyn yanked forcefully on her arm and drew the girl inside the hut.

Hurit gave them a sincere smile as they entered. Pauwau was present, too, her leathery brown face seamed with the passage of more than fifty summers, and Jocelyn bowed slightly in respect to the older woman, then took a seat on a grass mat next to Hurit.

Jocelyn had not learned much of the Indian language, but she was amazed how quickly the Indians learned English. "Good morrow," Hurit said, carefully enunciating the words.

"Good morrow," Jocelyn answered, crossing her legs under her long skirt as Audrey did the same. "I pray God will bless you."

"I pray God will bless you," Hurit answered, her dark eyes lighting in a lovely smile, and Jocelyn wondered again if she had done enough to share God's love with the Indian woman. Did Hurit understand the significance of the words she casually repeated?

Hurit called to her five-year-old son, Mukki, who brought over a large basket filled with broken seed pods and stems of the milkweed plant, or *wisakon* as the Indians called it. Hurit dipped her hands into the basket and pulled out a handful of the greenery, and Jocelyn did the same.

"Will this really make thread?" Audrey asked, taking a handful of the plant materials and watching Hurit and Pauwau as they pulled flaxen strings from the stems.

"I don't know," Jocelyn admitted, imitating the actions of her hosts. "But we have to try something. Our clothes are wearing thin, and we must find an alternative, unless we want to wear . . ."

"Buckskin," Audrey finished, her eyes squinting with amusement.

As they worked, Jocelyn tried to make casual conversation with her Indian friends. Pauwau had little to say, as always, and Hurit spoke shyly. At one point in the conversation, Hurit called Jocelyn "Kanti."

"Kanti?" Jocelyn asked, pinning Hurit with a questioning glance. "What does that mean?"

Hurit lowered her eyes in embarrassment, and Pauwau answered for her: "'She who sings.' You are called Kanti in this village."

"Sings?" Jocelyn frowned, thinking of what Thomas would say if he heard of it. "But I don't sing. Except in church."

"You do." Pauwau nodded gravely. "In the forest. The children have heard you. At first they said the song was the spirit of the wind, but then they saw you. From that day you have been Kanti."

"Do they have names for all of us?" Audrey asked, her eyes bright with curiosity.

"Only those who visit often," Hurit said, smiling in relief that Jocelyn hadn't been offended by her slip. "Kanti, her husband—"

"Thomas? What is he called?" Jocelyn asked.

Hurit blinked. "Etelooaat."

Audrey laughed. "Such a long name. What does it mean?"

Hurit and Pauwau ignored the question.

Curious, Jocelyn bent down to look into Hurit's eyes. "Hurit, what does Thomas's name mean?"

After a moment, Hurit met Jocelyn's gaze. "'He who shouts.'"

"But Thomas does not shout," Jocelyn said thoughtfully. "His voice is powerful, but even in his sermons, he rarely shouts."

"One can shout in a whisper," Pauwau added cryptically.

Jocelyn glanced back at Hurit, who made no comment but went on with her work.

▼▲▼▲▼ Audrey and Jocelyn left the village with a basket of crushed milkweed fibers and made their way along the trail back to the village. The shorter days of autumn had begun to work their magic in the forest, and the trees gleamed with gold, yellow, and orange, edged by the plentiful evergreens. Dry leaves underfoot crackled and whispered as the women walked, warning the deer that humans were present. Jocelyn slowed her steps and tried to imitate the silent walk her Indian friends had perfected. She just couldn't manage it.

As they walked, Jocelyn couldn't help but smile when she remembered her name: Kanti. In truth, she had often taken advantage of the private walk on the trail to sing, for Thomas frowned on her singing in the house, and music was considered a frivolous waste of time by most people in the village. In her wildest dreams, she never imagined that the Indian children had heard her—and listened.

Maybe music will reach their souls, she thought, deliberately blocking the stream of idle gossip that poured from Audrey. *While they refuse the gospel, the truth of God may reach them in a melody.* She quietly resolved to sing more often while in the forest and made a mental note that for this justifiable reason she would ignore the colony's rarely enforced prohibition against walking alone in the woods.

"Jocelyn, you haven't been listening!" Audrey fussed.

"I'm sorry, what did you say?"

"I said," Audrey sighed, "wasn't it sweet of Mukki to make us these necklaces?"

"Yes," Jocelyn agreed. Her fingers played with the simple beaded shells Mukki had strung on dried bear gut and slipped over her head. "He's a handsome little boy."

"I'm thinkin' he may be a bit in love with you," Audrey teased. "Or maybe he'll grow up to marry Regina some day."

"Oh, Thomas would love that," Jocelyn laughed, then suddenly unsmiled as a sobering thought hit her. In this cloistered corner of the world, whom *would* Regina marry?

▼▲▼▲▼ Thomas was seated at the board when she came in, and she gave him a quick smile as she slipped the baby from her back and put Regina in her trunk for a nap. "I didn't expect you'd be here," she said, hurrying toward the hearth where a stew pot waited on the embers. "But 'tis just as well. If you're hungry, there's plenty of pottage—"

"What is that around your neck?"

Startled by his abruptness, Jocelyn glanced down and fingered the strand of shells. "This? Mukki made it for me. It's just pierced shells, Thomas."

"You must take it off."

She looked at him, unable to believe he was serious. "Why?"

"Why?" He did not raise his voice, but spoke more intently as he stared at her in piercing concentration. "Because such things are heathen, and the people of God should not wear them, least of all my wife. Take it off, Jocelyn. Now."

Her hand tightened around the shells. "A five-year-old boy made this necklace, Thomas, not a witch doctor. There were no incantations said over it, no spells, no divination—"

"A naked heathen child has stolen your good sense," he said, standing to his feet. "Take the symbol of paganism off."

A spark of defiance deep in her soul flared into rebellion. "No."

With two broad strides he was in front of her, his hands gripping her elbows so tightly that she winced in pain. He hadn't stood so close to her in months, and in a bizarre flip-flop of emotions she rejoiced that he held her, even though she could not deny the snap of powerful anger in his eyes.

"Jocelyn," he whispered between clenched teeth as his eyes pleaded frankly, "for the love of God, remove the heathen thing from around your neck."

She cowered before the power of his gaze, but still her hand held the necklace and would not let go. "'Twas a gift given in love, Thomas," she whispered, taking pains to keep her voice low so that passing eavesdroppers outside might not hear. "There is no sin in it. There is no sin in a gift from a loving little boy, because there is no sin in love, not even . . . in ours."

He released her and stepped back as if she'd slapped him, but she refused to free his eyes, holding him to her like a magnet. She could almost feel his thoughts, understanding his struggle, and she let go of the necklace only to entwine her arms about his neck. "Can't you see, Thomas?" she whispered, moving toward him as she pulled his head down to look directly into his eyes. "Why are you afraid? There is no fear in love!"

A ragged gasp escaped him as he trembled in her arms, and in his weakness she found hope and courage. She drew him to her, lifting her lips to his. After a moment of resistance, he drank of her kisses like a parched man who has been stranded in a burning desert for far too long. Wrapping his arms around her, he crushed her to him until she was conscious only of his nearness, and in her arms he relaxed, responding to her tender touch.

His hand swept to the back of her neck and pulled the pins from her hair; then he entwined his fingers in the tumbling mass as he pulled his lips from hers. "Jocelyn," he sighed, his breath warm in her ear, "you are a torment to me."

Her laughter, warm and husky, rose to mock his words. "Was Eve not a torment to Adam?" she whispered as she felt herself flowing toward him. "He ate of the fruit to follow her into sin, yet they both were promised redemption."

Breathing heavily, Thomas sighed again, but he did not release her. He laid his forehead against hers and managed a vain protest: "I want no more children."

"Why not?" she whispered, lightly running her finger over his shoulder. "Walter Raleigh would be pleased if we populated this place. Today's babies must marry someone."

He groaned and lifted his head from hers to stare at the ceiling while Jocelyn trailed her lips over his throat, courting his senses with gentle persuasiveness. He had dared to come near her, to hold her, and she would not let him get away.

"It's the middle of the day," he protested again, but his arms tightened around her.

"That is of no importance," she breathed, cradling his head and drawing it to hers. "I have waited a year for you to kiss me again. Think you that I should wait another hour?"

"You are a torment," he said again, lifting her into his arms.

"No," she answered, her heart overflowing as his lips blazed a trail of fire across her throat. "I am your wife."

▼▲▼▲▼ Jocelyn ignored the sounds of activity outside the house as she dressed and brushed her hair. Thomas lay without speaking on their bed, yet she could feel his hungry eyes upon her as she moved through the room. Turning suddenly, she saw an inexplicable, lazy smile sweep over his face as he surveyed her. Mayhap at long last, she thought as she stooped to plant a quick kiss on his forehead, he would be free to be the husband she had always known he could be. And if she had conceived another child this day, he might even rejoice in his fatherhood and learn to cherish his children.

Someone rapped at the door, and Jocelyn laughed at Thomas's embarrassed discomfiture. He dashed into his clothes as if all the devils were after him while Jocelyn opened the door.

Beth Glane stood outside her house, and her strained smile melted into disapproval when she saw Jocelyn with her hair undone. "I must speak to the minister," Beth said, her black eyes bright beneath her bonnet. "Audrey Bailie has come back from the heathen camp wearing beads, and the minister has expressly forbidden them."

"You mean—" Jocelyn smiled and pulled the string of shells from beneath her own bodice—"beads like these?"

Beth stepped back in agitation, her face frozen in a horrified expression of disapproval. "Y-y-yes," she stammered.

Raking his fingers through his hair, Thomas came up behind Jocelyn and nodded to Beth, who surveyed him from head to toe without speaking. "Mistress Glane is upset that Audrey Bailie wears a string of shells like mine," Jocelyn said, giving her husband a conspiratorial smile. "What shall we tell her, my husband?"

"Those beads are not allowed," Thomas said, his voice grave. "They are heathen, and you were right to come to me. I'll have Mistress Bailie's husband speak to her."

"But your wife—," Beth said, pointing to Jocelyn.

"My wife will not wear them either," Thomas said. While Jocelyn blinked in astonished silence, he reached for the string around her neck and yanked it sharply, spilling the shells over the floor of the house.

Jocelyn's eyes filled with angry tears, and she turned away from the door as Thomas thanked Beth Glane again for her vigilance.

When he had closed the door, Jocelyn turned on him in fury. "You had no right to do that!"

"You must obey me, Jocelyn, as your husband and your minister."

"How could you—!" She glanced pointedly at the bed on which they had just lain and then waved her hands at the shells scattered over the floor.

Thomas shook his head and lowered his voice. "One has nothing to do with the other. And this afternoon was not only my doing, was it?" He waited for her reply, and when she could not speak, he drew his lips into a tight, dignified smile and left the house.

▼▲▼▲▼ His legs moved automatically, stiffly, and the weight of his guilt pressed hard upon his shoulders. Thomas paused in the shade of a pine tree and put a hand against it to steady himself. What had he done this day? How could the resolutions of a lifetime vanish with one touch of the girl's lips?

He had to be alone; he had to think. Mindful of the eyes of the village upon him, he left the palisade and took the trail that led to the river. The fishing crew on the bank waved to him. He smiled automatically and returned the wave, then moved along the bank until he could no longer see the fishermen.

Finally alone, he dropped onto the wet sand and hid his head in his hands. *God, where are you?* his thoughts cried out, but then he chastised himself that God had had nothing to do with this afternoon. Surely the fault was his, not God's. He had fallen prey to the most basic instinct of man, unable to restrain himself even in the heat of the day. And he had loved being with her! For a few moments he had felt himself fully a man, complete and whole, both a conqueror and blissfully conquered.

How can such a wonder be a sin? The question struck at him, and he pushed it away, ashamed.

If he and Jocelyn were on an island, or even alone on a ship, then their love would be free, but God had placed him in a colony of both righteous and sinful colonists, and both groups expected him to live as the moral and spiritual example of the community. And God, once again, had tested his resolution and found him woefully lacking.

Something gleamed through the sand at his side. After scraping the sand away, he picked up a tiny shell much like those in Jocelyn's necklace. He clenched it until the sharp edge bit into his palm. Was it for righteousness' sake that he had demanded she remove the necklace, or had he acted out of prideful jealousy? For months he had been working alongside the savages, but nary a gift had he received. He had seen the women welcome Jocelyn with open arms and wide smiles, while he was merely tolerated. Worse still, too frequently Thomas had the impression that the savages laughed behind his back.

Father, Father, have mercy on me! I have failed you! I am a woeful sinner who is not worthy of your regard. Forgive me. Forgive me. . . .

Thomas stepped from his clothing and splashed into the frigid waters of the river, swimming until his skin shriveled and his teeth chattered. Such discipline would keep his conscience clear and banish thoughts of his wife from his mind. God was a hard taskmaster, but Thomas Colman could and would prove worthy to his task. He would not let himself be distracted from his work again.

He would put this day behind him as though it had never happened.

▼▲▼▲▼ Crazily furious and confused by her husband's behavior, Jocelyn asked Eleanor to listen for Regina's crying, then she slipped toward the house of John and Alice Chapman. Though he said little of his former life now that he and his wife had made their home in the City of Raleigh, Jocelyn knew that John Chapman had been the rector of a church in Suffolk and therefore hoped he could give her advice on how to deal with the confounded minister who was her husband.

She found John Chapman under a spray of golden orange oak

leaves at the back of his house. He sat on a stool, whittling, and did not seem surprised to see her, nor did he raise an eyebrow when she began to unburden her heart. He merely kept whittling, nodding occasionally, and when she had finished airing her grievances, he slipped the knife into a leather sheath and folded his hands as if for prayer. "Blessed are the poor in spirit, for theirs is the kingdom of heaven," he said, his face bearing the wrinkles of his age with serenity. "Blessed are they that mourn, for they shall be comforted. Blessed are the meek, for they shall inherit the earth. Blessed are they which do hunger and thirst after righteousness, for they shall be filled. Blessed are the merciful, for they shall obtain mercy. Blessed are the pure in heart, for they shall see God. Blessed are the peacemakers, for they shall be called the children of God."

He looked up at her as if he expected a reply, and Jocelyn waved her hands in confusion. "I don't understand," she whispered. "Can't you help me?"

"All the help you need is to be found in those words," Chapman answered, taking the knife again from its sheath. "There is treasure there, if you will seek it, Mistress Colman."

"But the church . . . Thomas's harshness will drive people away. Surely you can do something; meet with those who find Thomas too hard—"

"No." He squinted up at her, and in his eyes she saw a gentle rebuke. "Thomas Colman is God's man for this hour in this place, and God has called me to be a peacemaker, not a shepherd."

He began whittling again, and after a moment he smiled and wished her a good day.

▼▲▼▲▼ Finding no help in John Chapman's words, Jocelyn left the village and followed one of the Indian trails through the woods. When she was certain that no one had followed her, she crept into a thicket of greenery, sat in a huddle, and put her head on her knees.

"Father God, I have made a mistake," she whispered, her heart overflowing with remorse. "I thought I could win my husband's love and instead I have become a—strumpet! He does not love me, respect my ideas, or hear my pleas. I should have refused his proposal, for it would be better to be unmarried in this place than married to him. I thought a diamond lay underneath the coal, but now I wonder if I shouldn't have married one of the other men, any one of whom would be more kind than this hard-hearted minister. . . ."

Her words ran together after a while, but still she prayed, pouring out her heart and cries to God until her plea had been diluted to a simple, "I cry you mercy, God. Change my husband's heart or kill the love I bear for him, for I cannot love him and live with this pain much longer."

She did not know how long she wept and prayed, but the sun had begun to set in the west when she finally stirred from her hiding place. If she did not leave soon, the men of the village would search for her, and it was dangerous for them to carry muskets in the dark when they were lief to shoot each other.

Stiffly, she moved out to the trail and made her way home. God had not spoken, nothing had changed, but Jocelyn knew in her heart that she could not wait forever. In time, if God did not answer her prayer, she would leave Thomas Colman.

"If Thomas so wants to be alone, perhaps he should be," she muttered grimly.

Five months later, on the twentieth of March, 1590, John White stood at the bow of the *Hopewell,* a flagship of one hundred fifty tons, twenty-four guns, and eighty-four able seamen. In her hold the ship carried artillery for the fortification of a post on Chesapeake Bay, and her captain was the experienced Abraham Cocke. The *Hopewell's* consorts were the *Little John,* a ship of over one hundred tons, loaded with one hundred seamen and nineteen guns; and a pinnace, the *John Evangelist.* White had learned well the dangers of traveling with a poorly armed convoy. These three ships would bravely stand and fire against any who might accost them on the open sea.

Though his original plans had been thwarted, as always White still had high hopes for this venture. Originally, White had planned to bring nearly a hundred new colonists aboard the *Hopewell,* many of them women. But in February, when White and his intending settlers came down to the docks where the ships were about to sail from the Thames, Abraham Cocke had refused to accept the settlers and their equipment. He agreed to give White passage, doubtless thinking that it would be advantageous to have a Virginian colony's governor on board, but he told the colonists to wait for passage on the *Moonlight,* a ship captained by White's friend, Edward Spicer, which was scheduled to sail in May.

Fighting another wave of bitter disappointment, John White settled into his quarters on the *Hopewell* and considered that he was finally about to fulfill his promises and return to the colony. Though the privateering of Abraham Cocke would certainly try his patience, he would wait and hope to see the colony by July.

In the heat of early July 1590, Ananias called for volunteers to visit the men on Croatoan Island, and Thomas Colman was among the first to sign on for the journey. Jocelyn knew her husband wanted not only to check on the spiritual health of the men but also to escape her. The strained situation between them had continued for months, and the brief passion they had shared seemed only to reinforce Thomas's belief that she was a dangerous temptation and a threat to his ministry.

There had been talk of rotating the thirty men on Croatoan home to the City of Raleigh and selecting another twenty men to hold the outpost on Croatoan, but it was difficult to imagine the integration of thirty new men into what had become a tightly knit community. Besides, Ananias argued before the council and assembly, the men on Croatoan had grown fond of their home there, and many had spoken of taking wives from the neighboring Indian village.

"Surely 'tis better to let them marry than to turn a blind eye to the temptation of immorality," John Sampson pointed out. "I say we should allow these marriages."

Ananias shook his head. "But if the governor returns with more colonists—"

"John White has tarried for nearly three years," Roger Prat pointed out. "What if, perchance, his ship never made it back to England? We could wait forever for ships that will not come."

Suddenly Eleanor stood up in the assembly. She lifted her head and folded her arms tight as a gate. "My father is alive," she said, looking around with something very fragile in her eyes.

"I'd know it in my heart if he were dead. He's alive, I tell you! And he's coming back for us!"

The assembly of colonists craned their necks as if to measure the level of Eleanor's distress until Agnes pulled her back into her seat.

"Of course, Mistress Dare," Ananias said, soothing his wife. "We know the governor will be back. But until then—" He shrugged. "What indeed could be the harm in allowing our men on Croatoan to marry Indian women?"

"I'll tell you the harm," Thomas said, standing to his feet. Jocelyn lowered her eyes and lifted her hand to cover her face. It was not time for a sermon, yet she knew they were going to get one.

"The Indians are a heathen people," he began, but Roger Prat raised his hand at the council table.

"Many of the Croatoan have converted," he said. "Manteo and Towaye were able to explain the gospel in a way they could understand. Many have already been baptized."

The comment was an indirect slap to Thomas's methods and teachings, for during his many months of work, the minister had not baptized a single Indian convert. Jocelyn saw the back of her husband's neck redden, but he did not hesitate to continue. "Even if they convert," he said, lifting his Bible from the empty bench next to him, "does not the Word of God tell us to refrain from intermarriage with strange peoples?" He flipped through the pages: "In Genesis: 'Thou shalt not take a wife unto my son of the daughters of the Canaanites.'"

"'Pon my soul," John Sampson said loudly, looking at Ananias. "When did the Indians become Canaanites?"

A light snickering fluttered through the crowd, but Thomas merely flipped through the pages of his Bible again. "Deuteronomy: 'Neither shalt thou make marriages with them; thy daughter thou shalt not give unto his son, nor his daughter shalt thou take unto thy son.'"

"To whom do the Scriptures refer in that passage?" Roger Bailie asked, peering up at Thomas.

"The foreigners in the Promised Land," Thomas answered.

"And in the book of Joshua, the Lord God said, 'Else if ye do in any wise go back, and cleave unto the remnant of these nations, even these that remain among you, and shall make marriages with them, and go in unto them, and they to you: know for a certainty that the Lord your God will no more drive out any of these nations from before you; but they shall be snares and traps unto you, and scourges in your sides, and thorns in your eyes, until ye perish from off this good land which the Lord your God hath given you.'"

No one snickered at these words. Thomas had often preached that Virginia was like the Promised Land, and the analogy seemed to fit. The English needed God to drive out the unfriendly enemies who would certainly stand in the way, and the danger of perishing in the land was all too real.

Jocelyn felt rebellion stir in her soul. By all that was holy, was her husband determined to strangle love wherever he found it? What gave him the right to defile the happiness of lonely men on Croatoan Island? She rose to her feet, only dimly aware of the ripple of consternation that passed over the assembly as she stood.

"Have you anything to add to your husband's words, Mistress Colman?" Ananias asked, arching his brows into triangles.

"Not to add. To refute," Jocelyn said, clenching her hands at her side. "If our men cannot marry whom they choose, should we then consign them to a life of loneliness? Surely if the English marry Christian Indian women, there is no harm—"

"Mistress Colman!" Thomas interrupted, dark flames in his eyes.

"Where is the harm?" she demanded, raising her hands as she faced him. "Tell me, if you can. If the women have converted, why should they not marry and find happiness? We have scores of unmarried men in Virginia, Thomas, and if we are to make a place here, we must have marriages, and families, and children—"

"Sit down!" Thomas commanded, his voice rumbling like thunder through the room. Stunned into silence, Jocelyn obeyed.

Thomas left the bench where he had been sitting and walked to the front of the church. "We must not intermarry with infidels," he said, glaring at Jocelyn as if, in that minute, she had proved to be one. "We must have faith that God will send John White and additional colonists. He who comes to God must come in faith, believing that he is—"

"But we've waited for three years," John Sampson interrupted.

"Three years are nothing to God," Thomas answered, pacing with brittle dignity across the front of the room. "Neither is a decade. Neither is a lifetime. We are nothing; our petty wants are nothing. We should be grateful that God considers our guilty, unworthy lives at all."

"Yes, Reverend Colman, we know this," Roger Prat said, rapping his knuckles against the council table. "But we have to make a decision regarding our men at Croatoan. I, for one, believe they should marry."

"No!" Every eye turned again toward the minister. "Does not the Bible tell us that the apostle Paul said it is good for a man not to live in marriage with a woman?" Thrusting his hands behind his back, Thomas surveyed the entire assembly, daring any to refute him. "Then, I say, let the men on Croatoan remain unmarried, even as I!"

Jocelyn stiffened. Though many might think Thomas was still quoting the apostle Paul, in her innermost heart she knew he spoke of himself. Despite their marriage vows and all that had happened between them, despite their child, in the most basic part of his soul Thomas considered himself unmarried. They had never become one.

In an obvious attempt to ease the tenseness in the room, Ananias chuckled. "Welladay, Reverend," he said, standing to face Thomas, "how can the men on Croatoan remain unmarried like you when you yourself are married to Mistress Colman?"

Thomas closed his eyes as the men and women around him chuckled. Jocelyn knew in that moment that he fully realized his mistake, and when he opened his eyes to look at her, her expression told him that she understood what he had meant.

His countenance fell. "I have spoken what I ought to say," he said, his voice strangely toneless.

"Then each man on Croatoan shall search his own heart and act according to his own beliefs," Ananias said as the other assistants nodded in agreement. "It is decided."

"But I shall speak to them first," Thomas interjected. "They shall make their decision after the Word of God has been refreshed in their minds."

The assistants looked at one another, whispered in consultation, and then Ananias turned to the minister. "Agreed," he said simply.

▼▲▼▲▼ After the pinnace bound for Croatoan pulled away from the shore, Jocelyn went to her house, packed her trunk, locked it, and dressed Regina in warm clothes. If Thomas was not married in his heart, she had no right and no reason to live with him. Without saying farewell to anyone, she slipped her arms through the soft leather harness that held Regina to her back and walked out of the house.

It was late in the afternoon when she entered the Indian village, and Hurit and Pauwau seemed surprised to see her. "I need a place to sleep," Jocelyn said, ignoring the blush that burned on her cheek.

Without question or complaint Hurit moved aside so Jocelyn could enter her hut.

▼▲▼▲▼ Though Richard Taverner knew the perfect attendance probably had more to do with the long-awaited funeral for William Berde than with any spiritual hunger, he was glad to see that all twenty-eight of his men had assembled under the oak trees to hear the minister's sermon. Poor William had drowned in a treacherous undertow while swimming the month before. Taverner and the others had buried him and said a few words from the *Book of Common Prayer,* but now it was up to the minister to properly send poor William off to heaven.

The minister seemed to have other things on his mind, though, and after an hour of preaching about righteous living before a holy and angry God, he abruptly closed his Bible and thrust his arms behind his back. With his dark eyes searching the faces of the men before him like a searchlight, he told his listeners that God considered sexual immorality the basest of all sins and that those in the body of Christ had no reason or cause to ever join themselves with harlots or infidels.

Taverner squirmed uncomfortably. At least six Indian women lived now in their little village. They had been converted to the Christian faith and married to their English husbands in a simple ceremony performed by Manteo. Taverner himself had lately been much taken with Chepi, a beautiful Croatoan girl who waited even now in his hut, for he had planned to ask the minister to perform a proper Christian wedding after poor William's funeral.

But the mood of the gathering grew solemn as the minister stood before them. Thomas Colman had changed in the months since Richard had last seen him. His mouth was angrier; a cold, pinched expression lay on his face; and his glittering dark eyes seemed to have found hard answers to the world's most difficult questions.

No one interrupted or dared to ask a question as the minister opened his Bible and read the Scriptures forbidding intermarriage. "Unless you want a great wave from the sea to cover this place," the minister said, his hand trembling in awe as he pointed to the water beyond the beach, "you will live rightly before God. Unless you want the great monsters of the deep to pitch themselves forward onto this island and devour you in the middle of the darkest night, unless you want the wrath of God to be poured out in a storm unlike any you have ever seen, you will obey the Word of the Lord and restrain yourselves from this kind of immorality."

The minister's face was strained with fatigue, but seemed

lighted from within as he held his Bible to his breast. "The council of assistants has directed Ananias and me to tell you that you may do as you think best regarding the marriage of yourselves with the heathen savages in this place. But I could not let you surrender yourselves to immorality and unholy marriage without first hearing the Word of God."

He swept his long arm over the gathering, and his voice thundered through the whisper of the ocean breeze. "Judge for yourselves, and weep over the folly of your thinking."

▼▲▼▲▼ When the sermon was done, the company followed the minister to the small stretch of beach where William Berde lay buried, but Richard hung back and waited for an opportunity to discreetly tug on Ananias Dare's sleeve.

"What is it?" Ananias whispered, lingering behind.

"It's what he said," Richard whispered, nodding toward the spare, dark form of the minister. "In truth, Ananias, half a dozen of the men are already married. I was hoping to gain a wife myself, this very day."

Ananias pressed his lips together. "Will the men heed the minister's words?"

Richard nodded. "I believe they will. Not one man among us wants a wave to sweep the land, or a sea monster—"

"I see." Ananias crossed his arms. "Richard, you're the leader here. My advice—and the council's—is this: Say nothing to the minister about your wives. When we have departed, take up the matter among your own men, and do as you see fit. Let those who wish to marry do so, and those who wish to remain unmarried shall do so as well."

"Aye," Richard mumbled, not much comforted.

Ananias leaned closer and whispered in his ear, "This girl you want to marry, is she beautiful?"

Richard thought of Chepi: dark, lustrous eyes, gentle mouth, soft skin, her face like gold in the fading light of sunset. She had stolen his heart the moment he had seen her in the Croatoan village, and it had taken Richard six long months to gather the courage to even speak to her.

"Yes," he whispered, drawing a ragged breath. "She is beautiful."

Ananias grinned. "You fortunate fool. I'd marry two of the heathen beauties had I the chance."

He slapped Richard on the back and together they walked to hear the funeral of poor William Berde.

▼▲▼▲▼ After the pinnace had departed, Richard called a meeting of his men to relay Ananias's message. "So those of you who wish to remain married shall," he said in summary as hot water-scented winds blew across the clearing where the men had gathered. "And those of you who wish to put away your wives shall not be bound by the law."

Hugh Pattenson leapt to his feet. "I wouldn't want to risk calling down God's wrath," he said, his voice an awed, husky whisper. "I won't keep a heathen wife. But what shall I do with her?"

"And I?" Richard Shaberdge stood, his face edged with anger. "Why didn't you tell us, Taverner, that we shouldn't marry infidels? I believe I never would have married had I known this would happen."

"I'll send my wife back," Henry Rufoote said, leaping from his place. "Her and all her heathen things. 'Tis only right. And who knows what sort of beauty the governor will bring me?"

"In truth, you have a point," Charles Florrie said, standing. A blue flame of defiance burned in his eyes as he walked toward the hut where his Indian wife waited. "I'll send my wife back to her people this very day. These savages have no idea what marriage means anyway. There's no harm in putting a wife away."

Richard felt control slip from his grasp like seawater as the entire company moved toward the huts to watch what would happen. Though the air was heavy with impending rain, snatches of their conversation reached his ears:

"I'faith, the women are worthless heathens. Let's take 'em back!"

"But not without showing 'em a good time, eh?"

"So if she's not your wife anymore, you won't mind me spending time with her—"

"Stop, stop, stop!" Richard called, but his words were snatched by the bawling winds and flung back in his face. Angry and ugly, the men ran from hut to hut, pulling out startled women, and Richard watched in helpless horror as Chepi, her eyes round with fear, was carried from his hut kicking and screaming. With no regard for her outstretched arms or pitiful pleas, her abductor threw her down upon the sand with the others.

Lightning cracked the skies apart as Richard sprinted forward. "Don't you touch her!" he cried. He flung himself into the widening circle of men, his ears ringing with the screams of the women and the hooting of the wild, wet wind. He could feel his panic rising as all signs of decency and restraint fled from the faces of his men; then they fell upon him and the women. His arms pummeled whatever resistance he encountered, and once he felt a jawbone give way beneath his fist. Then one man held his arms and another produced a blade that shimmered and curved and finally bit into the soft flesh between his ribs.

Lightning ripped the storm cloud overhead, thunder rolled over the low island, and Richard Taverner pitched forward upon the sand where his blood mingled with the rainwater and the tears of seven women.

Thomas was not entirely surprised to learn upon his return that Jocelyn and Regina had left the village to live with the Indians. "I'faith, her mind is a wee bit addled," Audrey explained to Thomas, weeping delicately into her handkerchief as she stood with her husband outside the minister's house. "We were distressed to find her gone, but one of the savage messengers told us she had simply walked into their village, and Master Bailie sent a delegation to be sure that she hadn't been taken against her will."

"She is well?" Thomas asked, taking pains to keep his voice level.

"Yes," Audrey said, wiping her eyes. "And so is the little girl, bless her heart. They are well and happy, but—"

"'Tis enough, Mistress Bailie; we should be going," Roger interrupted, steering his wife away from the minister's frozen face.

As Audrey moved away, Roger Bailie regarded the minister with a curious look. "I can't imagine why you, of all people, should be the first to fail in marriage," he said. "But if there is anything we can do—"

"Pray do not worry yourself," Thomas answered, lifting the latch on the door to enter his empty house. He nodded at the old gentleman with the lovely girl at his side. "I give you good day, Master Bailie."

The house seemed strangely empty without Jocelyn's presence. Her trunk still lay against the wall, closed and locked, and her cooking pot lay in the fire pit, scrubbed and clean. The blanket had been neatly folded across the foot of the bed. Thomas's trunk stood unmolested, his books stacked neatly on the floor near the board.

God, where are you?

He removed his hat and hung it on the nail by the door. The space looked strangely empty. Despite the summer heat, she had taken her cloak from the peg upon which it hung; the blue bonnet that perfectly matched her eyes was gone as well. He would look to spot it in the forest and gain a private word with her. Though he was not surprised that she had gone, still he wanted to hear his condemnation from her own mouth. Torture, after all, demanded that the guilty one suffer to the fullest possible extent.

A pain pounded behind his eyes, and his skin burned from its exposure to the sea and the July sun. He lay down on the empty bed and closed his eyes, willing himself to sleep.

▼▲▼▲▼ Three days later, at dawn, the lookout in the tower let out a cry. "Canoe on the river," he called, the alarm ringing over the village. "Croatoan from the looks of it!"

Ananias ran out of his house, still chewing his breakfast. A Croatoan canoe! Did the savages bring news of John White?

"Who comes?" Ananias called, shielding his eyes from the morning sun as he squinted toward the man in the tower.

"It's Manteo!" the lookout called. "I'faith, it's Manteo himself!"

The noise and the news brought colonists scurrying from all the houses, and when Manteo and his companions stepped onto the shore, they were caught up in joyful embraces and questions.

Manteo said nothing, however, until he stood before Ananias. "I will speak in private with the council," Manteo said, his dark eyes grave with some secret knowledge.

A tangible hush fell over the crowd, and they parted wordlessly as Ananias gestured to the other council members and led the way to the church.

▼▲▼▲▼ Thomas Colman was praying in the church when the group of men entered. Ananias asked him to leave.

"No," Manteo said, putting his hand across Ananias's chest. "The man of God will stay."

The council members looked at one another, then led the way to the table in the front of the room. They took seats, but Manteo stood, his stalwart companions a constant shadow behind him.

"The English men of Croatoan took wives of my people," Manteo said, raising his eyes to the minister in a swift, keen look. "The English men of Croatoan misused the women and killed them. One woman, Chepi, had only lived fourteen summers, but she was taken by the English and killed. Chepi—" Manteo paused, suddenly a dark and vigilant presence in the room— "was my sister."

Ananias felt the room swirl slowly around him. Thomas Colman paled visibly. "How can this be?" the minister asked, placing his hands upon the table. "We were just with the men, and they agreed not to take Croatoan wives."

"They had been married many moons," Manteo answered. "After you—" he pointed abruptly to Ananias and Thomas— "came, the women were no longer wanted."

"I talked to Richard Taverner," Ananias said, raising his hand. "Surely something went wrong. He told me that the men had married and agreed that the women would be returned safely to their village if the men no longer wanted their wives."

"Taverner is dead, too," Manteo answered, sending a chill up Ananias's spine. "Do you not understand? If a man does not treasure a thing of great worth, he will despise it."

Thomas Colman cleared his throat to speak. "Then he will be punished, for God will always punish the wicked."

Manteo ignored the minister. "Alawa, Sokanon, Wikimak, Nijlon, Nattawosew, Kimi, Chepi," he said. "Their mothers and sisters weep for them. Their fathers and brothers cry for vengeance."

"God help us," Ananias replied reflexively.

"Though the other Indian nations urge us to make war

against our English brothers, we will not," Manteo said, his eyes clouded with hazy sadness. "But we will not give our daughters and sisters to be married to the English."

The other council members regarded Manteo in silent shock, but Ananias nodded slowly. "'Tis well done, Manteo," he said, nodding in agreement. "We will not ask for your daughters."

With the dignity and power of a great buck, Manteo turned silently and left the church, his companions following. The council members stared at one another for a moment; then John Sampson thrust his fist into Thomas Colman's face. "See what you have done! If you had said nothing, this tragedy would not have happened."

God, God! Thomas's heart cried. *I thought I was doing what you wanted! How can this . . . this evil be your will?*

Even as his weary heart protested, he met Sampson's angry gaze without flinching. "I am not to blame for the base impulses of evil men. If they had followed the Word of God, none of this would have happened. And now, despite their evil, right has been restored."

Roger Bailie had watched the entire scene with no comment, and now he tented his fingers before his face. "In my dealings with the savages, sirs, I have learned that what they don't say is oft more important than what we hear. Manteo said the Croatoan would not war against us, but what of the Roanoac? Or the Chesapeakes? The Croatoan have been a voice in our favor for these many months, but the other tribes would seize upon any excuse to destroy us. In days to come, will the Croatoan support us as ardently as they have in the past?"

Ananias chewed his lower lip thoughtfully. The old man had a point. Though they had not made an enemy in this harsh action, they had lost powerful friends. It would be better to punish the erring Englishmen and restore the Croatoan's goodwill than to do nothing.

"Have ten men make sail in the pinnace on the morrow," he said, standing. "We have yet another mission to accomplish on

Croatoan. And you, sir—" he pointed at the minister—"this time, you shall remain here."

▾▴▾▴▾ The pinnace sailed easily down the coast and anchored off Croatoan, but Ananias felt his stomach churn and tighten into a knot as the shallop was lowered into the water. It was the first time no lookout had run forward to greet them.

"All ashore," Ananias called with a confidence he did not feel.

Within ten minutes, the handful of men stood in what remained of the lookout village at Croatoan. Only smoldering ashes and blackened poles remained of the huts, and in the center clearing a heap of fly-covered bodies lay bloating in the sun.

"The savages!" John Sampson muttered under his breath. "Did Manteo lie to us?"

Ananias shook his head and pointed to a battle-ax that lay halfway buried in the back of an Englishman's skull. "I have seen those markings before, on the day George Howe was murdered," he said, iron in his voice. "It was the Roanoac. Manteo and his people are not to blame."

"What do we do?" Henry Browne asked, his bright blue eyes wide with horror.

"We bury them," Ananias said, sheathing the dagger he had automatically pulled from his belt. "And then we visit the Croatoan village. And any five of you who are willing," he glanced at the men on the beach, "may remain with Manteo's people, for someone must still post a lookout for John White."

▾▴▾▴▾ The flashing eyes of Ananias Dare greeted the minister when Thomas opened his door. "I give you good day, Reverend," Ananias said, stepping forward as if he would push his way into the minister's house. "I have a story to share with you."

"A story?" Against his better judgment, Thomas stepped aside.

Ananias entered and tossed his hat onto the pile of books covering the board. From the expression of disgust on his visitor's face, Thomas knew the man had noticed the stale and dank smell of the house. The hearth fire was cold; the dishes on the board, dirty.

But Ananias said nothing about the house. "Yes, a story. Of an island where twenty-and-eight men have been buried, murdered in their sleep by the Roanoac."

Thomas swallowed against the unfamiliar constriction in his throat and forced a lighthearted note in his voice. "Would you joke with me, Ananias?" he said, sinking onto a stool.

"I am not joking."

Thomas felt his hands begin to tremble.

"Our destruction has begun, Thomas. The peace we have labored so mightily to protect has been compromised because you insisted that the heathen weren't good enough to marry—"

"I preached nothing but the Word of God!"

"You preached your own opinions! The Indian women on Croatoan were converts. They believed more in the grace of God than you ever have, *Reverend* Colman!" Ananias's voice carried through the open windows, and from the corner of his eye Thomas saw two women outside stop and stare at the small house.

"Lower your voice!" he hissed. He stood to his feet and clasped his hands behind his back. "I preached only what I believe to be true. I must stand by my convictions."

"Then tell me this, Reverend. If your convictions are so pure and holy, where is your godly wife?"

Thomas felt his mouth go dry. "You know she is with the savages."

Ananias nodded. "You forget, sir, by marriage I am a kinsman to your wife and I know her well. I know she is a devout woman, one who knows and loves God, and yet she could not live with you. And though I know you think me nothing but a lecher and a sinner, let me tell you that at least I recognize my sin. I made a mistake once. I have an illegitimate son in England,

and I am forgiven. I admit it freely now. I don't care if the world knows!"

The anger in Ananias bubbled as a living thing, and he came closer, bringing his face within inches of Thomas's. "So why, sir, am I, a sinner, happy with my wife while you, a perfect minister, drive yours away? Can you answer that question?"

Thomas blinked and pulled his face away even as Ananias's words rang in his head. *The man is furious, crazy with fear, worried that the savages will attack . . .* , he thought, seeking any defense he could against the terrifying truth that seemed to ring in Dare's words.

"I think you are confused," Thomas answered tightly, maintaining his dignity with difficulty. "My wife has nothing to do with your sin, and you are wrong to boast of it so openly in this village—"

Ananias turned and, in three steps, left the house, slamming the door as he went. The space where he had stood seemed to vibrate gently, and a remnant of his wrathful presence remained in the room, a palpable afterimage that faded only after some moments had passed.

Thomas fell weakly onto the bed, burying his face in his hands. Cold terror lay in the pit of his stomach, fear that Ananias's words might be true.

God! God! Where are you?

All reason left him, and for the first time in his life he could neither pray, read, nor think. He curled into a tight ball, drawing his knees stiffly before his chest, and waited for the darkness to claim him.

Aboard the *Hopewell* in the Western ocean, John White sighed impatiently. The ship on which he traveled had been chasing Spanish treasure ships since April, nearly losing its cargo and its crew in the process. Edward Spicer and the *Moonlight* had rendezvoused with the *Hopewell* during the early days of July, but Captain Cocke had not seemed inclined to turn toward Virginia until nearly the end of that month.

Unfortunately, as White had tried to warn the captain, July and August meant rough weather at sea, and the *Hopewell* and the *Moonlight* began to encounter the dark winds and rain of hurricane weather as they worked their way up the Florida coast. White dipped his pen into an inkwell and scratched an entry in his journal:

> On the very first of August the wind scanted and from thence forward we had very foul weather with much rain, thundering and great spouts, which fell round about us nigh unto our ships.

The bad weather continued until the ninth of August; then a calm enabled the two vessels to anchor off the shores of a narrow, sandy island west of Wococon. On the morning of the twelfth, the ships found their way to the long tongue of shoals that extended outward from the barrier islands, and toward the evening of the fifteenth White was able to report that they were about three leagues off Port Ferdinando.

White stood at the rail in the twilight and squinted his failing eyes beyond the barrier islands. At least two columns of smoke rose from the direction of Roanoke Island, and White felt his heart begin to beat faster. They were alive! And they had waited for him!

Because he could not risk setting even a shallop into the treacherously shallow waters in darkness, Captain Cocke promised they would venture inland at the morning's first light.

▼▲▼▲▼ At sunset in the Croatoan Indian village, Manteo walked to the hut where the five Englishmen lived. Quiet and surly, they had done little in the two weeks since their arrival to ingratiate themselves with the people of his clan. They seemed to live in fear that the Indians would yet take revenge for the deaths of the seven women.

He stood outside the doorway, and the Englishmen's fire lit him against the black night. "One of the children saw two ships on the sea this afternoon," he announced, crossing his arms.

The Englishmen inside the hut looked at one another; then Henry Browne, their self-appointed leader, stood to face Manteo. "How do we know you are telling the truth?" he asked, his eyes glinting with the light of hostility. "What if we go to the sea and find the Roanoac there to ambush us?"

Manteo did not blink. "Go or stay," he said, backing away. He didn't trust these men enough to turn his back on them. They were like the long guns of the English: loud, smelly, and apt to explode at the wrong time.

"He may speak the truth," another Englishman interrupted. "That's why we're here. We're supposed to be watching the sea."

"Yes," Browne answered. "Or Spanish ships may roam the shore, and Manteo and his people want us to be taken to Spanish dungeons or serve as slaves upon one of their galleons. I'd as lief be killed by Roanoac than taken by the popish Spaniards."

"But what if the ships were sent by Gov'nor White?"

Browne squatted on his knees and stared at the man who dared dispute him. "You don't truly believe he's coming back, do ye?"

Standing outside in the darkness, Manteo listened until their protestations grew too foolish to be believed; then he turned and left them alone.

▼▲▼▲▼ "Ahoy, John White!" a voice called from the *Moonlight* the next morning, and John looked across the water to see the gleaming blonde hair of Edward Spicer aboard the *Hopewell*'s consort. "Do you think your pretty daughter will give an old sea hound a kiss?"

"Ahoy, Edward!" White answered, feeling almost like a schoolboy in his glee. "If the sea hound is you, I'll send you to the devil before I'll let you near my daughter! But the wee one might give you a peck on the cheek!"

Edward waved and disappeared into the crew milling on the *Moonlight*'s deck, and White turned to join his own landing party. He checked the revolver in his belt, then paused to study his reflection in a small looking glass he carried in his doublet pocket. He was heavier than when he had left this place, his beard grayer, his hair thinner, and crescents of flesh bagged under his tired eyes. But he would have changed little compared to little Virginia Dare, who had grown from an infant to a toddler. What must his granddaughter look like now?

He climbed into the shallop and held tightly to the side of the boat as the last of the landing party boarded with him. Aboard the *Moonlight*, Spicer was lowering his shallop as well.

"You've arranged to fire the guns, right?" White called up to Cocke, who chose to remain aboard his ship.

"We'll fire them," Cocke promised. "Every hour."

"Good." White straightened himself in the boat. The sound might even reach as far south as Croatoan, but would surely alert the colonists at Roanoke. Nothing signaled the arrival of a fleet so well as cannon fire.

The first cannon boomed as the shallops set out along the coast of the island of Hatarask and passed the high sand dunes White knew as Kenricks Mounts. A great plume of smoke rose suddenly from behind the dunes, and White motioned toward the beach, commanding the landing party ashore. If the colonists had moved this far south and heard the *Hopewell*'s guns, this fire was a sign to divert him.

They landed and marched south to Kenricks Mounts, but could find nothing. The heat of the day pressed upon them like ocean waves, and the continual breeze from the sea served not to cool them but only to make them thirsty. "We must have fresh water," one of the seamen complained, but White ignored him and surveyed the blackened sand where the fire had burnt itself out. There was nothing left, not even the brushwood which must have lit from natural causes.

"There is nothing here," White mumbled to himself. "Nothing at all."

Dead tired and dripping with sweat, White and his men marched back to the beach, where White showed the seamen how to dig in the sand and find fresh water in the dunes. Once they had quenched their thirst, White announced that they would press on, but Edward Spicer put out a restraining hand.

"The day is far spent, John," he said, glancing toward the brightening western horizon. "We will start again on the morrow."

White reluctantly agreed, and the two shallops returned to their ships.

▼▲▼▲▼ The *Hopewell* and the *Moonlight* used the scant remaining hour of daylight to move northward within two miles of the Outer Banks. The next morning, the shallop from the *Hopewell* set out at daybreak as a wicked northeaster blew directly onto the barrier islands and churned the waters at the narrow funneling inlet which led to Roanoke Island.

Captain Cocke, John White, and a crew of men held onto the small boat as it whipped into the fierce current and tossed in the tide. The shallop overturned just after it passed through the inlet into the waters off Roanoke, but a fierce undertow and crashing waves made swimming difficult.

Struggling with all his might, White swam with the men to shore. After resting to regain their breath on the beach, they waded in the shallow water to gather the few provisions that had been with them in the boat, noting with disappointment that their food, matches, and gunpowder had been totally ruined.

Cocke gave the order to haul the boat onto shore, and White helped the men spread their wet provisions on the sand to dry. "Ho!" one of the seamen called, pointing to the stretch of sea beyond the bar. "The *Moonlight*'s crew!"

White and the men with him stood on the beach to watch as Captain Spicer's boat made for the bar. "The wind has picked up since we came through," White said, his expert eyes studying the sea. "Perhaps they should not undertake the risk. Shout out, Captain, and tell them to turn back."

Captain Cocke waved his hands toward the boat, but the crew aboard the *Moonlight*'s shallop were too busy to pay attention to the landing party. The strong and fierce waves pounded the land at the north and south of the inlet, and Spicer's steersman, Ralph Skinner, handled the boat well until she had nearly passed the bar.

Suddenly a rough wave overswept the shallop and tossed it like a child's toy, throwing the men into the water. Most of them clung to the boat as she bobbed upside down in the tide. A few tried to wade ashore but were knocked down and swept away by the angry sea. White could see Captain Spicer and Skinner hanging on to the boat, but as the waves continued to pound and toss the craft, soon both men disappeared.

Only four of Spicer's men—good swimmers who got safely into deeper water off Roanoke—were in a position to be saved. Captain Cocke and strong swimmers from his boat rowed out to pick up the four who waited in deep water, and when he returned with the survivors, a deep gloom had settled over the entire company.

"We were eleven," one of the shivering survivors said, crossing his arms around his wet doublet. "Seven are missing."

"Seven are drowned," Cocke answered, glancing toward the treacherous sea. "Who were they?"

A second survivor, a boy probably only sixteen years old, spoke up. "I don't know all of the men, sir," he said timidly, burying his feet in the sand in a vain effort to warm himself. "But the captain was aboard—"

"We knew him," White interrupted, his mind still reeling from Spicer's loss.

"And the surgeon, a fellow called Haunce," the first survivor inserted. "And there was a fellow by the name of Edward Kelley—"

"I knew him as well," White said, catching Cocke's eye. "He was one of the Lane colonists at Roanoke. A good man."

"And a boy about my age called Robert Colman," the boy added. "He was a son of one in the colony here."

Robert Colman, White thought. *Surely the lad was Thomas Colman's son! Had he come to seek his father?*

"And the others?" Cocke asked.

"Ralph Skinner, Thomas Bevis, Edward Kelborne," the boy answered, ticking the names off on his fingers. "They were seamen, sir, like us. Hands of the crew."

"Aye." Abraham Cocke stood and watched the shore. "We'll wait until the bodies surface, if they do. They deserve a Christian burial."

▼▲▼▲▼ They waited six hours and buried three bodies, one of whom was Edward Spicer. John uttered a brief and sincere prayer over the grave of his friend, and marveled that so many had died in such a short time. In his entire year at the colony under Ralph Lane, they had not lost even one man, yet on this morning they had lost seven in a single hour. Such was the treachery of the sea.

It had taken every bit of his persuasiveness to convince the men on shore that they must go on. Shaken by the violence of the sea and the loss of their captain and comrades, neither Cocke's crew nor Spicer's men had any further inclination to look for the colony, but White persisted. To his surprise, Abraham Cocke supported him, and an hour before sunset, the nineteen men climbed into the two shallops and rowed their way up Roanoke Sound.

At first the place seemed a deserted Eden, but then through the trees on the north end of the island they saw a great fire burning. Afraid to risk going ashore in the falling darkness, they beached their ships on a sandbar in the harbor and sounded a trumpet to alert whoever moved on shore to their presence. At White's suggestion, through the night the men sang familiar English songs to reassure the inhabitants that they were friendly, but no one answered.

After spending an uncomfortable night in the boats, the two parties went ashore at dawn and found that the fire had been only a grass fire, probably ignited by lightning from the storm that had so agitated the ocean. They walked westward through the woods to Croatoan Sound, directly across from Dasemunkepeuc, then worked their way eastward toward the place where White had left the colony. Several times the party spotted Indian footprints, probably made within the last twenty-four hours, but there was no other sign of human life.

As they walked, John White could not help but think of the irony in his situation. It was August eighteenth, Virginia Dare's third birthday, but they had found no trace of his granddaughter on the island of her birth. It was almost as if the child had never existed.

But as the explorers neared the site of the old fort and village, White gasped in delight as he spied a tree that had been carved with the fair Roman letters "C-R-O."

"Why is the word incomplete?" Captain Cocke asked, running his finger over the carving.

White smiled confidently. "No more is needed. This signifies the place where I will find the planters. This a secret token agreed upon between them and me at my departure."

He pressed forward toward the village and soon found the place where the colonists' houses had stood. White noted with pleasure that the houses had been taken down and the village enclosed with a palisade of great trees. On one of the chief posts at the entrance, the bark had been removed, and five feet from the ground the word *Croatoan* had been fully engraved.

"Did I not say so? They have moved to Croatoan," White said, glancing around the houses to make sure no life stirred. A thorough examination of the fort indicated that the colonists had left heavy equipment but had taken at least one mortar and firearms. White went to the creek where the shallop and pinnace had been anchored, but there was no sign of a vessel either on or under the water.

"Governor White!" the young sailor from Spicer's ship ran up, his face glowing. "We found English trunks! Come and see!"

A frown settled upon White's forehead as he followed the boy into the ruins of the village. Had the colonists reason to leave in such a hurry that they would bury their possessions rather than transport them?

The boy pointed to a trench which had been opened for some time. Five trunks lay broken amid the dirt, and the articles from the trunks had been rifled by human hands and ruined by the weather. To White's chagrin, he discovered that three of the trunks were his own, and the books that lay rotting in the rain were his own sketchbooks and journals. His armor, left behind in the safekeeping of the planters, lay rusting under a nearby tree.

White paused and leaned his hand against an oak. One voice in his heart whispered that the colonists were safe at Croatoan, but another voice muttered darkly that they had fled into the unknown, caring little for their governor or his promise to return.

He felt a hand upon his back. "There is no more we can do here," Abraham Cocke said, jerking his head toward the beach. "Come, Governor, we must go."

White protested weakly but followed the captain to the beach where they had left the boats. The wind had freshened, and a dark cloud loomed over the ocean. "Row, men; make haste," Cocke called, settling himself into the shallop. The men obeyed instantly, recognizing the danger in the heavy storm clouds, and it was only with difficulty that the two small boats made it back to their ships.

▼▲▼▲▼ At dusk on the same day, Manteo appeared again before the hut of the Englishmen and forced a smile as he spoke. "A distant thunder sounded today from Roanoke," he said, jerking his head toward the north end of the island.

"A storm," Browne said quietly. "'Tis storming even now."

"No," Manteo answered. "Not a storm. Big guns."

The English looked at each other again. "A sea battle?" one of them said. "I told you there were Spanish about!"

"If there are Spanish about and they're firing cannon, there must be English about, too!" Browne's face lit up in a grin. "Manteo, did you speak truly about the ship?"

Manteo didn't dignify the question with an answer. But after a moment, the one called Henry Browne grinned. "That's it, then. On the morrow we go to the beach and lay low. We'll wait until we see the ship, make sure she's flying the blessed British flag, then light our signal fires!"

"God bless the Virgin Queen and John White!" another man said, grinning toothlessly. He lifted his mug in Manteo's direction. "And we'll be thanking you for your hospitality, Manteo, but we're on our way home."

Manteo turned and left them to their celebration.

▼▲▼▲▼ The fierce and insistent wind pulled at the ships and strained the cables through the night. White sat in the captain's cabin and watched Cocke's face, afraid that at any minute the captain would give the order to set out to sea, where they could better weather the storm. When the bosun shouted that an anchor had broken loose in the storm, White steeled himself for the inevitable bad news, but Abraham Cocke looked at him with a glance of mingled understanding and pity.

"We have two other anchors, Governor," the captain said, idly fingering the compass on his table. "The wind should die down on the morrow."

No man aboard ship slept that night, and the winds did calm in the morning. Cocke sent a message to the *Moonlight*, now commanded by her master, John Bedford, that the ships would raise anchor and sail south to go ashore at Croatoan, where John White was certain he'd find his colonists living with Manteo.

But as the seamen on the *Hopewell* raised her anchor, the cable that was wound round the capstan broke. With only one anchor to hold her, the ship lay at the mercy of the waves. Watching the surf relentlessly propel his vessel toward the treacherous shallows, Captain Cocke shouted furious orders while John White prayed for help. As the ship drifted past Kenricks Mounts toward the dangerous underwater shoals, all hands on deck braced themselves for the inevitable wreck. But at the last moment, Cocke recognized the dark color of deep water and skillfully steered the ship into a channel. From there he raised the sails and managed, through the grace of God, to take the ship out to sea.

▼▲▼▲▼ Henry Browne and his four companions lay low in the sea grass on the northernmost beach and listened for the rumble of cannon. Sounds from the sea should have carried easily to them, for the wind blew strong in their faces, but all they heard was distant thunder from the heaven full of gray scud.

"I think that savage was lying," Robert Little muttered, turning to recline on his elbows in the sand. "And one of us ought to be watchin' our backs. What if the Roanoac come? Can we be forgettin' the sight of those other men? I believe I'll never forget—"

"There it is!" Browne cried, leaping to his feet. A blessed, glorious sight passed before their eyes, a magnificent English galleon cutting through the waters offshore, the bright British flag flying from her foremast. "Ahoy!" Browne screamed, his voice muffled by the strong wind.

"Light the fire," Little called, scrambling toward the brush they had piled against a sand dune. Frantically the men struck the flint over the brush, but the wind snuffed every spark as it hooted and jeered at their efforts.

"Hurry!" Michael Bishop called to his companions, waving his arms uselessly as he jumped up and down on the beach. "She's moving southward. She's not stopping!"

The other four men made a wall with their bodies and breathlessly coaxed one spark into a tiny tongue of fire. When at last it rose from a sprig of straw to lick a dried leaf, the men stood back as the wind caught the blaze and set the brush to burning in earnest. But when they turned in triumph toward the sea, the English galleon had disappeared.

▼▲▼▲▼ With only one anchor and no supplies of fresh water, the *Hopewell* was forced to head south to pick up stores. Captain Bedford, speaking for the *Moonlight,* begged to take his "weak and leak" ship back to England. He had lost too many hands to safely continue.

Cocke and White reluctantly agreed that the two ships should part company, and the *Moonlight* and the prospective colonists aboard her set sail for England. The *Hopewell* sailed southward for two days, but contrary winds kept her from making good time. On the twenty-eighth of August, Cocke decided to head northward for water.

Jocelyn laughed as Regina toddled by holding Mukki's hand. Her fair-skinned daughter stood out among the young ones of the Indians, but skin color apparently made no difference to the people of the Chawanoac tribe. They accepted Regina as easily as they had accepted Jocelyn, allowing her to work and live and laugh among them without criticism or comment.

What an easy, simple life, she thought, watching the women take turns as they stirred the clay cooking pots and helped each other prepare meals. *Mayhap these savages are more like Christians than we English are. Is that why Thomas distrusts them so?*

She imitated her hosts and squatted by the fire as she considered the notion. It was perfectly possible that Thomas was jealous of the Indians, for though he preached his gospel continually among the English, the community was still peppered with jealousy, covetousness, greed, and distrust. Here, though, where the people had only creation itself and the natural law of conscience to guide them, selflessness, sharing, and loyalty abounded.

True, they were lost, and she had heard enough stories to know that Indian brutality could be quick, severe, and senseless. But peace reigned in quiet Ohanoak, and for the first time in months, Jocelyn's conscience cleared, her bitterness eased, and she was able to lift her thoughts above the confusion and frustration she felt whenever she thought about her husband.

She left Regina with the older children and wandered into the quiet hut she shared with Hurit, Chogan, and Mukki. The hearth fire in the center of the hut had been allowed to burn out; the sleeping mats lay neatly rolled in a corner of the house.

Jocelyn sat on a grass mat and placed her head on her knees.

"Father God," she prayed, "you have said that if a man lacks wisdom, he should but ask. Shall the same hold true for a woman? If so, heavenly Father, I beg you to show me what I must do. Shall I remain here among the Indians? I could work here, Father, and show your love consistently. I may even win several to the gospel. In the English village I am nothing, only one women among several, a wife scorned by her husband, who will certainly not want me to come back. . . ."

She waited in silence. Children laughed outside; women called to each other in the rapid Indian tongue; birds twittered overhead in the trees. She felt her eyes grow heavy in the stillness of the afternoon. She must not go to sleep, for there was work to be done. . . .

Go back.

Jocelyn jerked her head upright. The voice had spoken in her ear, but she sat alone in the hut. The hairs on her arm lifted. Had God actually spoken?

"Go back?" she whispered, looking over her shoulder to make sure no one had slipped in while her eyes were closed. No one was there. She bowed her head again. "But Thomas will hate me for leaving. He will say I have humiliated him before the entire village."

Go back.

She glanced over her other shoulder; she was still alone. "I will go back, on the morrow—"

Go now. I will give you strength when the time comes.

What time? She shivered and swiveled to face the back of the hut. No human was in the room with her, but the place seemed to tremble visibly with an unseen presence, a power that could not be denied.

Go—boldly, faithfully, successfully. . . .

"I'll go," she whispered, then stooped under the passageway to fetch Regina.

William Clement

God shall likewise destroy thee for ever,
He shall take thee away,
And pluck thee out of thy dwelling place,
And root thee out of the land of the living.

Psalm 52:5

When Agnes Wood saw Jocelyn coming through the gates of the palisade, her broad face erupted into a toothy grin. "'Pon my soul, I thought I'd never see the day you would come back to us," she said, clomping toward Jocelyn in man-sized shoes. "But I'm thanking God to see you, I am. Miss Eleanor's not well, Miss Jocelyn, and I'd like to take ye to see her—"

"I'll visit her as soon as I'm able," Jocelyn said, placing Regina into Agnes's outstretched arms. "But now I must see my husband." She glanced around the village, where several other colonists peered up from their work to watch her. She lowered her voice. "Is all well here, Agnes?"

Agnes shrugged and ran her heavy hand over Regina's curls. "As well as to be expected, I'm sure. There has been no news from Croatoan since the horror of the slaughter, and most folks are busy about their business. We've the harvest to get in, you know—"

"I know," Jocelyn answered. She walked forward into the circle of houses, and the sight of her own small home made her pause. "Will you watch Regina for me?" Jocelyn asked, turning to Agnes. "I'd like to talk to Thomas."

"Aye, with pleasure," Agnes answered, taking Regina to the house she shared with Eleanor and Ananias.

Jocelyn smoothed her hair, then lifted her chin and walked to her house. *You fool*, she thought, *he's probably not even here. Since when has Thomas been home in the middle of the afternoon?* But the voice had been insistent, and she had hurried home. . . .

She lifted the iron latch on the door and stepped inside. The room was dark, since the shutters were closed, and it took a moment for Jocelyn's eyes to adjust. The board was laden with Thomas's books, the bench strewn with his papers. A nauseating stench rose from the pot that lay atop the cold and blackened logs in the fire pit.

A groan shattered the stillness of the room, and Jocelyn drew the bed curtains. Drawn up into a dark knot, Thomas lay there, his long arms wrapped around his body and his knees drawn to his chest. "Thomas!" she whispered, drawing closer. "I've come home."

He did not reply, and when she pressed her hand to his stubbled cheek, his skin burned with fever. "Thomas!" she said, shaking him. "Can you hear me?"

Trembling with fever, he groaned in reply. Jocelyn sprinted back through the door for help.

▼▲▼▲▼ After extracting a bowl of blood from his patient, Doctor Jones said the sickness was probably ague. "These spells," he said, pointing to Thomas's fevered trembling, "are brought on by the ague cake. I can feel the swollen organ through the flesh of his abdomen. The disease is oft reported in the summer months in marshy lands."

"I'faith, I'm glad I came when I did," Jocelyn whispered as she watched Thomas's suffering. "What can I do to help him?"

The doctor pulled his mouth in at the corners. "Ague has a hot stage, a cold stage, and sweating stage," he said, slowly gathering the bloody tools of his trade into a leather pouch. "Make him as comfortable as possible in each condition." He stared at Jocelyn in severe concentration. "The minister will doubtless be weak for many months. Are we to assume that you will take care of him, Mistress Colman, or are you planning to rejoin the savages?"

Jocelyn crossed her arms and met his granite gaze. "I will not leave. This is my place."

The doctor nodded abruptly. "Good. Let me know if his condition worsens. The bleeding today should rid his body of whatever morbific matter is causing this trouble. I'll come by tomorrow to see if purging will be necessary."

"Thank you," Jocelyn whispered, following the doctor to the door. She fastened the latch after he left and, leaning against the wall, slowly slid to the floor and curled into a knot. She had managed to keep her wits about her as she ran for the doctor and even as he had drained much of her husband's lifeblood, but now she let herself bury her head in her hands and weep.

▼▲▼▲▼ Over the next few days a steady stream of colonists made their way to the minister's house to offer their prayers for a quick recovery. Beth Glane, a vigilant and persistent presence, came each morning and sat praying in the corner of the room until Jocelyn asked her to leave at sunset.

Jocelyn had the feeling that Beth held an unshakable belief that she was more suited than Jocelyn to the role of a minister's wife. And because Jocelyn knew Beth had been among those quick to criticize her husband, she was amazed that in the helpless state of illness, Thomas had achieved a status akin to sainthood in the pious woman's eyes.

Though many of the maidservants had taken husbands from the single men, Beth devoutly refused to marry, choosing instead to render her service to Henry and Rose Payne, her master and mistress, and to God. And part of her service to God, she informed Jocelyn one morning, was to minister to the Reverend Thomas Colman.

Jocelyn willingly accepted the villagers' prayers and gifts of food, for between nursing Thomas and caring for Regina, she had little time to rest. Regina, now a rambunctious two-year-old, demanded her constant attention during the day, and Thomas shivered and moaned as his fever rose throughout the night.

He had not spoken directly to her since she came home, yet his eyes were often open, and she frequently spied him looking at her as though he did not know her. More often, though, he tossed in delirium, sweating profusely, and Jocelyn was hard pressed to keep his bedding clean and dry.

One day just before sunset, Thomas moved and mumbled something. Jocelyn rose from the table where she had been feeding Regina, and from the dark corner where she sat praying, Beth Glane leaned forward in the vaguest of movements, a shifting of shadows.

"Did you speak, Thomas?" Jocelyn asked, placing her hand on his fevered forehead.

"Anna," he mumbled, shaking his head from side to side. "Anna—don't."

Jocelyn could feel Beth Glane's triumphant smile and knew the story would be spread throughout the village by morning. *Of course I knew that girl was not a fit minister's wife,* she could hear Beth saying. *Why, even in his sleep the minister calls out for someone else, a woman called Anna.*

"The sun is setting, Miss Glane," Jocelyn said, pulling the blanket to Thomas's chin. "Mayhap you should take your leave now."

Beth said nothing, but slipped from the house, and yet her spiteful presence seemed to linger in the corner she had occupied. Jocelyn sighed but turned to her daughter and began to wipe the remains of pottage from Regina's chin. "For this God sent me back?" she asked as her daughter smiled innocently. "To nurse a man who cares nothing for me and to endure the hateful glances of a woman who would take my place?"

Blessed are the merciful, for they shall obtain mercy.

The words rang in Jocelyn's memory as she put Regina to bed.

▼▲▼▲▼ The fever worsened that night, and Thomas writhed in pain. Jocelyn sponged his brow and chest with fresh water, but the damp cloths grew hot within minutes of applying them to his burning, red skin. He spoke often as he tossed, repeating broken phrases about Anna, his guilt, and God.

"What about Anna?" Jocelyn asked, not expecting a reply. She wet his hair and ran her fingers through it to keep the damp tendrils from his face.

"Anna," he repeated again, moving restlessly under her ministrations. Then: "God forgive me."

Genuine pathos echoed in his words, and Jocelyn felt a whisper of terror run through her. What had happened to Anna? Who was she, and what had she to do with Thomas? A sister? A friend? A niggling fear rose in her mind: his first wife?

She wanted to hold him, to find the source of his apprehension and smooth it away, but he was too hot to be comforted by her touch and too restless to relax. After sponging his fevered body through the long hours of the night, Jocelyn put her hand on his forehead and sighed deeply, discovering his fever had broken. Exhausted, she lay on a blanket on the floor and fell instantly asleep.

▼▲▼▲▼ "Mistress Colman."

Someone tugged on her sleeve, and Jocelyn opened her brick-heavy eyelids to see the round face of seven-year-old William Wythers. "Yes, William," she said, pushing herself into a sitting position on the floor. "Is anything amiss?"

"Aunt Wenefrid sent me with this loaf of corn bread," the boy said, pointing to an oblong bundle in his hand.

"Thank you, William," Jocelyn said, struggling to keep her eyes open. She glanced up at the bed. Thomas slept deeply, his arms flung across the mattress, his face pale. The bright red flush of fever had vanished.

"Aunt Wenefrid," William persisted, not leaving, "would have me ask if there is anything I can do to help you."

"No," Jocelyn replied automatically; then she spied Regina standing upright in her trunk. The baby, at least, had slept well and was ready to be fed and entertained.

"Well, there may be one thing," Jocelyn said, smiling at the eager boy. "Regina loves to play, and she needs her breakfast. Do you think your Aunt Wenefrid would mind feeding another baby this morning?"

"No," William said, his eyes bright. "Can I take her home?"

"Yes, and thank you," Jocelyn said.

She watched as William carefully lifted Regina from her trunk, then held the baby's hand as she toddled double-time to the boy's longer steps. Jocelyn felt her heart soften when William reached out to touch Regina's auburn curls. "She's beautiful," he said gallantly, still holding her baby hand in his. "Much more beautiful than my aunt's new baby."

"Thank you for saying so," Jocelyn said. "But I wouldn't say anything about that to your Aunt Wenefrid. I'm leaving her in your care until I come to fetch her."

"I'll take care of her," William promised, herding Regina through the doorway. Jocelyn lay back down on the floor and was asleep again before the door had closed.

In the islands of the Azores, John White discovered that Abraham Cocke was unwilling to return south to Croatoan Island. Once again, privateering and the temptation of treasure distracted the captain's interest from the planters in Virginia. After four weeks of chasing treasure ships to no avail, on the first of October, 1590, the *Hopewell* turned for England.

John White made a last entry in his journal:

> On Sunday the twenty-fourth, we came in safety, God be thanked, to anchor at Plymouth.

Audrey Bailie smoothed her new buckskin skirt and adjusted her bodice, a worn garment that would not last many more months. From across the room, her husband took a long look at her legs and smiled appreciatively. "You are a sight in that skirt," he said. "But I wouldn't wear it to church, my dear."

"I'faith, I'm not that thick," Audrey said, laughing. "I wouldn't even wear it to the minister's house, except that I hear he doesn't notice who visits. And if he doesn't know who's standin' over him, he's not likely to know what a body's wearing, is he now?"

She gave her husband a smile and slipped out of the house. Now that the harvest was nearly done, Roger had promised to build her a kitchen, an entirely separate room from their bedchamber, and Audrey was thrilled by the thought of living in the biggest house in the village. Let Eleanor Dare and Rose Payne pride themselves on their status as gentlewomen. Audrey Bailie would show them what a wise marriage and a doting husband could do for a woman's status.

The clearing in the center of the village stood empty at this midmorning hour, for most of the women were busy in the fields and most of the men had gone to their duties on the river or in the forest. A group of men came out of the storehouse, however, and Audrey recognized the hoarse voice of William Clement. Ducking quickly behind the shadow of the Joneses' house, she took a tortoise-shell comb from the leather bag at her waist and pulled it through her hair in quick strokes. There. A girl didn't have to look like a hurried housewife if she didn't want to.

She lifted her chin and stepped back into the clearing. If she could reach Jocelyn's house without attracting attention. . . .

But she had no such luck.

"Hey, Audrey, me love, where are you goin' in such a hurry?" William called, pulling himself away from the men as they dispersed to their work.

"Can you be thinkin' that I should take the time to talk with you?" she said, pouting prettily. "After I saw you yesternoon walkin' close as you please to Jane Pierce?"

"Aw, Jane's as good as married to William Browne," Clement answered, leaning against the wall of a nearby house to block Audrey's path. "And her eyes don't sparkle as devilishly as yours do, girl."

Audrey pursed her lips and pretended to be angry. "I believe I don't know what to think of you, William," she said, planting her arms akimbo. "You ask me to marry you and then tell me to marry Roger. You pledge your loyalty to me, then sport with the other women—"

"Beshrew the other women," William said, moving dangerously close. Audrey could smell the lusty odors of earth and sweat, and the jolt of desire in William's eyes forced her to look away.

"I must go see Miss Jocelyn," she said, the playfulness gone from her voice. "Pray let me pass, William."

"Why?" he asked, reaching out for her. The touch of his hand ran up her arm, and her senses throbbed with the awareness of him. It was dangerous, this. If anyone saw them, if anyone read the hot blush on her face—

She tore herself away. "Later, William," she cried, running in the opposite direction. I'faith, she'd go around him from now on. Any girl who played with fire would surely be burned sooner or later.

▼▲▼▲ William remained where he stood, leaning against the house with one hand, the other confidently cocked on his hip. He watched Audrey's flustered retreat with an appreciative grin, which vanished when James Hynde broke his concentration.

"When will you leave that dolly alone?" James said, carrying a basket of fish from the river. "She's happy with the old man, can't you see it?"

"She may look happy with that shrunken bag o' bones," William answered, pausing to spit casually on the ground at James's feet. "But she doesn't know what she's missin'. When we're married, then she'll know real happiness."

"You are wasting your time," James said, shifting the basket he carried from his arms to his hip. "Why spend so much time and energy on a married woman? I hear Jane Pierce is eager and willin'. Or the savage women—the men trade the unmarried ones like candy. Go do some favor for the chief, and he's lief to reward you with his daughter—"

"The devil can take the savages, for all I care," William said, his eyes narrowing. "I've my eye set on that red-haired girl, and nothing else will do. The time's coming, my friend, when the old man will drop, and I'll be free to claim her as my bride. Then I'll have the house, the goods, everything. If I take a savage woman, what'll I have? Nothing, except a case of the pox."

James giggled, and William suddenly unsmiled. "'Tis not funny, my friend. When I'm married to Audrey and living in Roger Bailie's house, I'll be able to take his place on the council, too. Power, possessions, and a bonny redhead with legs that could stretch from here to England—those things are worth waiting for."

▼▲▼▲▼ Audrey sat uneasily on the small stool in Jocelyn's house and battled her guilty conscience. Only a few years ago it had been her job to clean, cook, and help Jocelyn, but now Jocelyn treated Audrey like visiting royalty. The minister lay under a pile of blankets in the bed, pale and quietly sleeping. He seemed not to care that his young wife had dark circles under her eyes and had lost at least twenty pounds from her already-thin frame.

"You ought to let me help you," Audrey protested, standing up for the fifth time.

"No," Jocelyn said, cocking her hands on her slender hips. "Think you that I should forget that you are a married woman now? You served me oft enough. Sit back and let me bring you some water and bread. Little William Wythers brought me a loaf of corn bread just this morning—"

"William Wythers." Audrey shivered. "Every time I see that boy I think of the day of his whipping. Do you recall it, Jocelyn? 'Twas soon after we landed on Roanoke, and I thought for certain that you had married a monster—"

"I remember," Jocelyn interrupted, placing a slice of corn bread on a plate before Audrey. She gave the girl a fixed, polite smile, and Audrey knew it would be best to change the subject.

"So," she said, daintily breaking off a piece of bread, "how is the minister faring? I see the praying priestess hasn't come today."

"Faith, she did come early this morning," Jocelyn answered, cutting a slice of the bread for herself, "but I turned her away."

"In truth?" Audrey nearly choked on the bread. "I cannot imagine her leaving without a fight."

"I told her I had stripped my husband down for a bath," Jocelyn said, her eyes sparkling with merriment, "and that the sight was unfit for virgin eyes. She left as quick as she had come."

Audrey dissolved into a gale of giggles, and Jocelyn gave a short laugh touched with embarrassment. "I did not lie, I promise. The man has not had a bath in months."

Audrey threw back her head and laughed again, and Jocelyn lifted her cup of water in a silent toast.

▼▲▼▲▼ The two women talked for an hour, and during the conversation Audrey saw Jocelyn wipe her husband's brow, lay her hand tenderly upon his forehead, and place his

Bible on the bed where, every so often, his hand sought the comfort of the leather binding. "He rests better when it lies beside him," Jocelyn said, without smiling.

"I would have thought he would rest better with you beside him," Audrey said, half-joking, but she bit her lip when Jocelyn did not smile in return. "Welladay, what's this?" Audrey whispered.

"He loves me not," Jocelyn said, one thin shoulder lifting in an elegant shrug. "I knew it when I married him, yet I hoped he would learn to care for me. But we are both of hard heads and harder hearts, and each time I think we might be joined together in love, something pulls us further apart."

"I have wondered," Audrey admitted, "but after the baby came, I thought he had learned to be a proper husband—"

"He keeps me at arm's length," Jocelyn answered. "We have learned to live in such a way that we are . . . compatible."

Audrey felt a wave of compassion stir her. Her young and delightful mistress deserved a prince among husbands, one who would cherish and adore her high spirits, not a grim, gray, distant person like Thomas Colman. Surely if Jocelyn had not been frightened and grieving for her father when the minister proposed, the marriage would never have taken place.

"Faith, how do you do it?" Audrey asked, spreading her hands wide. "Come with me, Jocelyn, and put aside this man. Beth Glane and the other women would gladly nurse him. Why kill yourself for a man who loves you not?"

"Because blessed are they that mourn, for they shall be comforted."

Jocelyn's voice was so low Audrey thought she had imagined the answer, but then she looked up and saw the light of love shining from Jocelyn's eyes as she looked at her sleeping husband. "I tried to leave," she went on, her voice as light as a thistle bloom that falls into silence without a sound, "but God brought me back. For some reason, God has placed love for Thomas in my heart, and I cannot deny it."

"Love must be fed to survive," Audrey quoted blithely,

remembering the first time William had told her this as he begged for a kiss.

"No," Jocelyn whispered, "true love gives and waits. For as long as it takes . . ." She tiptoed to the bed and lifted the Bible from beneath Thomas's hand. "Know you what grace is, Audrey?" she asked, flipping through the pages.

Audrey thought a moment. She had often heard sermons about it, but remembered little save that grace kept believers from hell and that sinners did not deserve it.

Jocelyn didn't wait for an answer. "Grace comes from the Hebrew term meaning 'to stoop,'" Jocelyn explained. "God gave us grace because there is nothing we can do to deserve his mercy. For many months I thought God wanted me to show love to Thomas, but what God wanted most of all was for me to show forth his grace."

Jocelyn lifted the Bible and read, "'For by grace are ye saved through faith; and that not of yourselves: it is the gift of God: not of works, lest any man should boast. For we are his workmanship, created in Christ Jesus unto good works, which God has before ordained that we should walk in them.'"

"So God wants you to stoop?" Audrey asked, not understanding. "By serving this hard-hearted minister?"

"Yes," Jocelyn answered, smiling as she looked at the sleeping man. "Love that reaches up to God is worship. Love that reaches out to a husband is affection, and that wasn't enough for us, Audrey." Her voice warmed, and she took Thomas's hand and held it to her cheek. "But love that stoops to give—that is grace."

Audrey felt the corner of her mouth fall in a derisive smile. "I'll see how well you are stooping when he wakes up," she said, lifting her chin. "And then, if you are ready to leave, you and the baby will be welcome in me house."

▼▲▼▲▼ Audrey was still shaking her head in disbelief when she left Jocelyn's house, but she stopped to talk to Agnes Wood and Eleanor Dare as they returned from the fields.

Together they carried a heaping basket of pumpkins and gourds, and Eleanor's delicate forehead glistened with perspiration.

"Ho, now, a fine basket, that," Audrey said, stopping to admire the produce. "Is there more to gather?"

"Aye," Agnes answered, not slowing her pace, but Eleanor abruptly dropped her handle of the basket and stopped to talk. "There is much work yet to be done," she said, fanning herself. "Papa will be pleased with our crop." She dimpled as she looked at Audrey. "And you, Audrey Tappan, you are a naughty girl! Does Jocelyn know you are out here? You should get home to your mistress before she knows you are gone!"

Audrey cast a questioning look toward Agnes. The older woman's eyes narrowed in pain and an unspoken plea to remain silent. Audrey hesitated, then said, "There's no gainsaying that. I'll see Jocelyn soon . . . I promise."

"Good," Eleanor said, lifting the handle of the basket again. "Tell my papa, when you see him, that we're having fish and hominy for supper. And tell Ananias to hurry home!"

"Name of a name," Audrey murmured as the two women continued past her. "Eleanor has lost her reason." A mixed group of Indian and English children skipped by; behind them, struggling to keep up, ran four-year-old Virginia Dare.

Audrey felt a sharp pang of sorrow when she heard Eleanor's words: "I'faith, can't those children be still? But that little one is a lovely child. Whose is she, Agnes?"

▾▲▾▲▾ Doctor Jones followed one guiding law of medicine: As long as a patient's fever stayed down, bleeding was not necessary. So Jocelyn rejoiced that Thomas's fever remained low during the daylight hours, and through the weeks of November and December he gradually regained his strength. The fever and chills returned at night, but they no longer frightened Jocelyn. She either sponged Thomas or held him in her arms until he lay quiet and still. And so, day by day, the minister of the colony began to be healed.

He had very little to say during his weeks of convalescence. He never reproached Jocelyn for leaving, never questioned why she had returned. He seemed to accept her presence, but whether as a penance or a blessing Jocelyn could not tell. Often she felt his eyes upon her as she fed him, cleaned the house, and cared for the baby. After nearly a month of such constant surveillance, she dressed Regina in warm clothes and demanded that her husband get out of bed.

He stared at her as if she had lost her mind, but then he managed to ease his way into a shirt and pair of leggings. When he lowered his painfully thin legs onto the floor and tried to stand, Jocelyn saw his difficulty. She supported him with one shoulder while she led him and Regina out of the house and into the sunshine of a small clearing just outside the palisade.

The December breeze blew cool, but Jocelyn spread a grass mat on the ground in the sun and heaped blankets around Thomas's shoulders. He sat down, obeying her without complaint; then Jocelyn placed Regina in his lap. "I must air out the house," she said, turning on her heel, "and you must spend time with your daughter."

She left them there, not knowing what would happen, but she thought of them often as she threw open the shutters and swept the floor. She dragged the old, sweat-soaked mattress from the house and sewed a new cover from woven grass, then stuffed it with dried straw and pleasant-smelling herbs. The project took nearly half the morning, and at any moment she fully expected to hear Beth Glane's righteously indignant complaints that the sick minister had been left to die outside the village.

But no one bothered her as she worked. When the mattress had been refreshed and the house aired, she packed bread and some dried slices of meat into a leather pouch and set out for the sunny spot where she had left her family. She walked confidently until she reached the edge of the grassy clearing; then her heart skipped a beat as she glanced toward the mat. Thomas lay motionless on the ground and the baby sat on his chest. Had something happened? She sprinted toward them, her heart in her throat, then stopped abruptly as she heard Thomas's quiet voice: "So they came, you see, two by two. And God preserved their lives and shut them in upon the ark."

Smothering a smile of relief and gratitude, Jocelyn slipped onto the mat beside them and spread out the lunch she had brought. Without speaking, she observed the tender bond that had formed between father and daughter, and when lunch was done, she bundled up the mat, the blankets, and her baby, and led her husband home.

▾▲▾▲▾ The weather accommodated many such outings in the weeks that followed, and Jocelyn thanked God for a mild winter. The sunshine and brisk winds seemed to do Thomas good, for color had begun to return to his haggard cheeks, and she could no longer count the ribs in his back when she changed his shirt. On the few days when winter gales kept them inside, Thomas would pull Regina up into his lap as he read his Bible at the board, and enunciate slowly as his slender finger pointed out the words.

Fearful that her praise would stifle his new feelings, Jocelyn said nothing, but continued her work. Often she felt as though she served as the hands of God, ever silent, but always working toward some end she could not see. God had promised her that he would give strength when the time came—was this the time for which God had sent her back? She began to think it was.

One afternoon as she walked to join her family at lunch, she spied the dark form of Beth Glane in the clearing. Beth sat on a blanket next to Thomas, one arm extended in his direction, her black bonnet bobbing with the urgency of her complaint as if it were part of her head. Jocelyn sighed in exasperation. For weeks she had done all she could to shelter her husband, but apparently the business of the ministry would follow him everywhere.

Jocelyn approached from behind Beth.

"I caught them myself," Beth was saying, her hands trembling as she gestured emphatically. "Boys and girls! Savages and

English! Swimming together in the river, they were, without regard to holiness and without clothes of any kind!"

Thomas turned his dark eyes toward Beth. "How old were these children, Mistress Glane?"

"Well," Beth huffed, "in truth, what does it matter how old they were?"

"In truth," Jocelyn interrupted, noting with satisfaction that Beth's bonnet jerked in honest surprise at the sound of her voice, "they were no more than babies. Audrey and Hurit told me themselves that they took the young ones to the river to splash. And, as I recall, it was many months ago and no harm was done."

Thomas smiled genially as Beth sputtered in confusion. "You were sick, of course, Reverend, and I wouldn't have bothered you when you were ill. But if we don't stop communal bathing with the babies, how can we stop it with the youngsters? Or the maidens?"

The image of Beth Glane bathing in the river forced Jocelyn to press her lips together to keep from laughing. And, she was pleased to note, the righteous zeal that in days past would have sent Thomas rushing to rebuke babies had dimmed to a steady glow. His voice was calm and eminently reasonable as he answered Beth Glane's hysteria: "I think we have concerns of more importance than naked babies, Mistress Glane."

The bitterly cold breaths of February and March slashed at any settler who dared venture out in those months, but April dawned bright and beautiful. Jocelyn led her family to the greening meadow each morning with a light step, rejoicing that Thomas now considered his time with Regina as a part of his daily routine. His strength had returned to the point that he no longer needed Jocelyn's assistance, and often he walked with Regina perched high on his shoulders. The sight brought a lump to Jocelyn's throat as memories of her own father came crowding back.

She continued to bring them lunch, and after relaxing for a brief while in the meadow, they would return to the house. Thomas gradually resumed his duties of visiting the sick and praying for those who requested prayer, but Doctor Jones advised that the minister not visit the Indian village nor work in the hunting, fishing, or building crews until his health had been fully restored.

Day by day, Jocelyn continued to rejoice and thank God for his goodness. God himself had told her to return; he had shown her the secret of grace. Her willingness to stoop had made all the difference in the world. While Thomas had not yet professed his love for her, the new gentleness in his eye and his devotion toward Regina signaled a fresh tenderness in his heart. In time, Jocelyn was sure, that tenderness would turn to her.

▼▲▼▲▼ One afternoon in late April, Jocelyn and Thomas lounged on the blanket in the meadow and watched

Regina chase a butterfly through the tall grasses. The little girl had spent the last hour peacocking in a scarf Jocelyn had made from the lining of one of Thomas's worn doublets, and the air rang with her happy squeals. Thomas's eyes were lit with laughter as he watched his daughter, and Jocelyn sighed in contentment.

"I saw your cousin yesterday," he said, his eyes still following Regina. "We must pray for her."

"I know," Jocelyn said, a shadow falling upon her heart at the mention of Eleanor. "She is not well. She believes that Uncle John is among us."

"She cannot accept that he has not returned," Thomas said, turning to Jocelyn. His voice was heavy with compassion. "In her mind the year is still 1587."

Jocelyn bit her lip. "Think you," she said, hesitating. "Think you that Uncle John is coming back? It has been so long, nearly four years—"

"What do I think?" Thomas murmured. He rolled onto his stomach and propped himself on his elbows, earnestly searching her face. "I will tell you what I think, Jocelyn, and I have not spoken of this to any other man or woman. I believe that John White never made it to England."

"'Tis not inconceivable," Jocelyn said, studying his face. "I have oft heard it suggested that his ship was lost—"

"No, there's more to consider," he said, holding up a hand. "When we left, Spain and England were ready for war. The Catholics were determined to stamp out the glorious work of the Reformation and the true gospel. They stood ready at any moment to raid our ships and to invade England. They were prepared, Jocelyn, and mayhap they were able to do it."

Jocelyn drew in a slow breath as the full impact of his words struck her. England and Spain in a full-blown war? And if, perchance, the Spanish had won . . .

She opened her mouth, but no words would come.

"Yes," Thomas said, noting her expression. "The gospel we knew may now be buried under a sea of popish teachings. And

John White, if he lives at all, is surely in chains for professing his belief in the true gospel. All Protestants are imprisoned, surely, for the Inquisition continues to this day."

Jocelyn felt her heart thump against her rib cage. She had heard of the infamous Inquisition, in which imprisonment and torture were used to coerce "confessions" from those who followed Protestantism.

"Even this Bible," Thomas laid his hand on the book at his side, "if found on a ship seized by the Spaniards, will earn a man a trip to the inquisitors' chambers. Before we left England, I heard of a cook aboard the English ship the *Elizabeth*, which was searched while anchored in a Spanish harbor. This poor man, Henry Gottersum, was burned alive for admitting that he was a convinced Protestant."

Jocelyn's mouth went dry as she struggled to speak. "Surely my uncle—"

"I know not, Jocelyn. But I believe our purpose here might be far broader than our English investors ever imagined. If silenced in England and other free countries, the true gospel now resides solely with us. And it is our responsibility to carry it to the world."

He rolled onto his back and thoughtfully folded his hands on his chest. "God's will is surely being worked here, Jocelyn. We must remain true to the faith and to his calling."

▼▲▼▲▼ Thomas resumed his pulpit on the first Sunday in May and told his astonished audience that it was their responsibility to carry the gospel to the world. "Though it be a heavy obligation," Thomas said, looking more grave than ever with strands of silver in his hair, "God has called us to duty. We are to be holy lamps, fit for the light of his gospel, and we must purge our lives and hearts of any uncleanness." He paused. "In the weeks of my absence I have heard much of immorality in the camp."

Several men who had been cooling themselves with palmetto

fans abruptly ceased moving, and Jocelyn saw several women flush. "There has been a fair-haired baby born to an Indian woman who is not married," Thomas went on, holding his hands behind his back. "And there has been talk of things which ought not to be mentioned in a place where Christ is the sole author of law and the arbitrator of our actions."

His face lengthened, and bale fire seemed to glow in his eyes. "We must chastise our hearts and our minds to set things right," he said, bringing his hands before him in a gesture of prayer. "The council will join me to enforce what is right, and you, my friends, must commit yourselves to righteous living and holiness."

Convicted by their minister's words and fervency, as one body the congregation dropped to their knees and prayed for forgiveness and spiritual cleansing. And carefully, through the spaces of her fingers, Jocelyn knelt in prayer and watched her husband, praying that in his spiritual cleansing he would not purge himself of the gentleness he had shown in the past weeks.

▼▲▼▲ The next morning, Thomas directed Jocelyn to renew her work with the Indian women of Ohanoak, for he would begin catechism classes for the Indian men. Obediently, Jocelyn packed food and water for lunch and took Regina's hand. Thomas had set out for the Indian camp immediately after breakfast, but Jocelyn slowed her pace and sang a hymn as she and her daughter left the village and followed the trail to the camp.

Spring had worked its magic over the newly budding trees, and the early gold of the leaves had only recently turned to green. Wildflowers frilled themselves in mottled patches of sunlight, and for a moment an enormous flock of passenger pigeons flew overhead and darkened the sky. Jocelyn walked slowly, enjoying the sights and sounds around her as she sang, and suddenly realized that not once in four years had she missed the crowded, stale streets of London.

She heard Thomas long before she saw him. His voice carried above the walls of the palisade around the Indians' grass huts, and Regina giggled and pointed toward the sky when she heard her father's voice. "Yes, dear one, your father speaks," Jocelyn said, nodding at the lookout who stood outside the village.

Thomas stood in a clearing past the cook fires. A group of men sat on mats around him, listening intently to the fervent man who gestured and moved before them like a dark streak of lightning. Jocelyn shook her head gently and turned into the house where Hurit lived.

The five Indian women inside Hurit's house sat around a pot on the fire in the center of the hut. "*Hau,*" Jocelyn said, releasing Regina's hand into the custody of Mukki. The young boy smiled in delight and led the baby outside while Jocelyn settled onto a mat near the fire.

"It is good to see you, Kanti," Hurit said, her dark eyes glowing. "We heard that your husband was sick."

"God has brought him back to the land of the living," Jocelyn answered. "And the great Father God who knows and sees all has sent me to you today. I have great news about a Savior."

Hurit's smile crinkled the corners of her eyes. "You have spoken of him before," she said, stirring the pot. "The son of the Manitou—"

"Let me tell you, then, about Queen Elizabeth," Jocelyn said, praying that a different image might take root in the women's imagination. "When I was small, of not more than five or six summers, I heard much about Queen Elizabeth. How could one woman be so powerful and so rich, I wondered. Then my father took me to see the queen. She was beautiful, in her way. She wore long ropes of pearls and had bright red hair and skin even more pale than my own. I had often heard about her, but for the first time, I saw her. And then I knew she was real."

Jocelyn looked at the circle of expectant faces. "Do you believe that the great English queen lives across the ocean?"

Hurit glanced for a moment at the somber face of Pauwau,

then turned back to Jocelyn and nodded. "You do not lie," she said simply. "I believe that the English queen lives as you say."

"Good," Jocelyn answered. "As I grew older, I learned that Queen Elizabeth wants the best for her people. She has made laws to protect the poor and to punish those who steal and kill. Her ways are right. Her laws are for our good. Do you understand?"

Without hesitation, Hurit nodded. "It is as you say."

Jocelyn took a deep breath. "Now I am grown, and I tell you that the great queen has sent us to this place so that we might tell you about the only true Son of God, Jesus the Christ. If we find ourselves in trouble, our great queen Elizabeth cannot rescue us from the wrath of the Roanoac, or the storm, or the freezing cold of winter. Only God can do that, and I place my trust in him.

"You see," she said, leaning closer to the women, "I believe Queen Elizabeth lives beyond the wide ocean just as I believe God the Father created all things. I believe the queen cares for her subjects just as I believe God the Father loves his people. But I do not believe the queen will send help to save us should an enemy attack tonight. Even so, I do not fear, for God the Father has already given his Son to taste death for me. Therefore I do not fear the Roanoac or the storm or starvation."

Hurit stopped stirring the stew. Pauwau stared at Jocelyn and idly ran a finger down her wrinkled throat.

"How can God taste death?" Hurit asked, her eyes blurred with indecision, and Jocelyn knew then that God's Spirit had begun to work.

▼▲▼▲▼ All five of the women in Hurit's hut chose that day to follow the Son of God, and as Jocelyn walked home she felt as though she walked on air. Surely Thomas was right! God *had* sent them to this place to spread the gospel in an alien land. It mattered not that they were alone and abandoned. As long as they had each other and followed the true light of God, the colony would survive and thrive. It was God's will.

Greatly encouraged, Jocelyn startled a flock of birds from the trees with her song of praise:

All people that on earth do dwell,
Sing to the Lord with cheerful voice;
Him serve with fear, His praise forth tell,
Come ye before Him and rejoice.

The Lord, ye know, is God indeed;
Without our aid He did us make;
We are His flock, He doth us feed,
And for His sheep He doth us take.

O enter then His gates with praise,
Approach with joy His courts unto;
Praise, laud, and bless His name always,
For it is seemly so to do.

For why? The Lord our God is good,
His mercy is forever sure;
His truth at all times firmly stood,
And shall from age to age endure.

▼▲▼▲▼ Thomas felt the exhaustion of illness overtake him in a sudden wave, and he collapsed on the roots of a gnarled oak. He had given these men the best he had, but not once did the light of understanding flicker in their eyes. After an hour of patient listening, most had walked away to gather their bows or fishing nets. Only two elders with nothing else to do had stayed to listen.

And, the voice of doubt sneered in Thomas's soul, *those two were probably deaf, for they responded not at all.*

He rested his hands upon his knees and hung his head, gathering his strength for the walk home. He would come again on the morrow, and again, until the gospel burst through the hardness of the Indians' hearts. He would be like a tidal wave, pounding and pounding until his words broke through, and then the gospel would sweep forth in a cleansing rush over the camp, obliterating the idols and the temple which held the bodies of the dead chiefs. . . .

A shadow fell across the ground, and Thomas looked up. Chogan stood before him, a proud warrior whose dark, piercing eyes reminded Thomas of the blackbird for whom the savage had been named. Thomas remembered that Chogan was Hurit's husband and, therefore, a friend of Jocelyn's.

"*Hau*," Thomas said, covering his eyes from the glare of the sun as he looked up at the warrior.

"My wife has chosen to follow the son of the great god," Chogan said, crossing his tattooed arms.

"She has?" Thomas asked, scrambling to his feet. A wave of energy pulsed through his veins as he dusted himself off. "How can this be? Did she hear my speaking this morning?"

Chogan shook his head. "No, Etlelooaat. She and all the women with her have chosen the way of the son of the great god. When the sun rises on the morrow, Hurit will speak to the men of the village."

"Hurit will speak—" The words caught in Thomas's throat, and he raised a questioning brow. "Hurit will speak?"

The Indian nodded solemnly. "The werowance and the others want to hear the words of the women."

For one dark moment jealousy writhed like a coiled and angry serpent in Thomas's soul. The leader of the tribe would hear a *woman* before listening to him? A woman who had spent the morning cooking with his wife?

But then the hand of reason steadied him. It was no secret that God worked in mysterious ways. And God often used smaller, weaker vessels to proclaim his truth. After all, did not even Balaam's donkey speak?

Ultimately, however, God relied upon his prophets to spread the truth of righteousness.

▼▲▼▲ By the time of the June harvesting of the first corn, every Indian soul of an age of understanding had been converted and baptized. At Thomas's insistence, the *kiwasa*, idols placed in the temples to watch over the bodies of dead chiefs, were removed from the village and the bodies of the dead chiefs buried. Save for an occasional ancient incantation murmured by the old priestesses, the pagan practices Thomas had despised gradually evolved into Christian rituals.

Thomas could not explain the miracle of the natives' sudden understanding and desire to know the things of the true God, but he attributed the conversions to his fervent prayers. It was a sign from God, he reasoned, that America would thenceforth be the lamp to shine forth the light of the world. These savages would tell others as they journeyed to hunt and trade, and many would travel through the wilderness of Virginia to seek the truth in the City of Raleigh.

Though the people of Ohanoak had converted, Thomas was not entirely happy. Though they now cavorted around their campfires in praise to the true God, they refused to give up their dancing in favor of a sedate worship service. And though the women had donned sleeveless mantles to cover the nakedness of their upper bodies, still they wore provocative slit skirts that troubled Thomas. He had ceased to preach against buckskin, for since their landing in Virginia, no suitably strong material had been found to replace the clothing the colonists had brought from England. Buckskin, it seemed, was a necessary evil. Thomas knew he would just have to be vigilant to make certain that the women covered themselves modestly in the heavy material.

Despite their newly found fervent love for God, Thomas thought the Indians were still too superstitious. He had taught them about God's Holy Word, the Bible, and was impressed by their reverence for the book until it became clear they considered it a powerful talisman. Men sought to touch it before hunting; women asked permission to rub it on their swollen bellies as their time of childbirth neared.

Their superstition extended even to prayer. They seemed not to understand that they had the privilege of praying themselves, for they often asked Thomas to pray that God would strike their enemies or bring a good harvest. Once, after Thomas had given what he knew was a stirring sermon about the miraculous feeding of the five thousand, the Indian werowance, Abooksigun, folded his arms and legs and declared that the people of Ohanoak would hunt and plant no more, for God would feed them. It had taken Thomas nearly half a day to convince the chief otherwise.

Despite Jocelyn's joy and his private relief when the Indians converted, Thomas feared that his converts were not genuine. Had they, he wondered, been so awed by the advanced civilization of the Englishmen that they adopted his religion as easily as they aped his tongue? He had heard the savages marvel that so many Englishmen got along without women. Others had freely suggested that the English settlers were spirits risen from the dead.

It would take time and trial to prove their faith.

Eighteen months passed. Roger Prat died after contracting a
bloody flux during December of 1592, and his eighteen-year-old
son, John, replaced him on the council. Young George Howe,
now seventeen, was also deemed of an age to assume his
father's vacant seat. In January 1593, Ananias Dare and the other
assistants held a council meeting and invited, as a special guest,
the minister Thomas Colman.

Ananias stood and extended his hand in greeting as Thomas
Colman took his seat before the council table. "You must have
had a tiresome day," Ananias said, noting the lines of exhaustion
on the minister's face. He made a determined effort to be
friendly. As Eleanor's mental condition had progressively deteri-
orated over the past few months, Ananias had come to appreciate the prayers of the minister and his wife.

"Yes," Colman said, nodding politely to the other assistants.
"Chogan and I have been discussing the wisdom of visiting the
other savage tribes. From what I can gather, there are many heathen tribes north of this place. Thirty and four are ruled by the
mighty chief Powhatan."

"I have heard of him," Ananias said, frowning. "The Indians
say he has a brave heart and fears nothing."

"Every man fears something, my friend," Colman said, leaning forward as he rested his arms upon his knees. "Now—what
brings me before your council table?"

"The council wanted you present tonight," Ananias said
evenly, looking to John Sampson and Roger Bailie for support,
"because it has come to this: We have been here six years, and
the men God has spared—including our own young George

Howe and John Prat here—wish to marry. We need more children to populate the colony."

"Have we not children enough?" Colman asked, lifting an eyebrow. "It seems my wife is forever visiting new babies and women in confinement."

"The men deserve wives," John Sampson inserted, cracking his knuckles as he leaned forward. "Though I left a wife in England, come May it will be seven years since I've seen her, and the English courts will declare me dead. She will be free to marry again. Why shouldn't I marry as well?"

"You would commit adultery, knowing full well that you are married already?" the minister asked, suddenly unsmiling.

"I *don't* know that I am still married!" Sampson roared, fire flashing from his eyes. He slammed his fist down upon the council table. "How do I know my wife does not lie in a churchyard grave? And my son has grown from a boy of twelve into a man, and he needs a wife."

"All our women but Beth Glane and Agnes Wood have already married," Thomas pointed out. "Who, then—"

"You know who," Ananias interrupted, facing the minister straight on. "The Indians live among us now, Thomas. They are as Christian as we. The werowance has often proposed the idea of intermarriage to me, and I cannot offend his honor much longer. Our refusal to take Indian wives has caused the Indians to doubt our friendship. We tell them they are our brothers in Christ—"

"We have been through this before," Thomas interrupted. He reached for his Bible as if it were a weapon.

Ananias saw the gesture and shook his head. "You were not invited here, Reverend, to give an opinion or read to us from the Word of God. We know what God told the Israelites, but we are not Israelites." He sighed. "I am not sure we are Englishmen anymore. But we *are* citizens of Raleigh, and we must live according to new laws. The council has decreed, Thomas, that Indian-English marriages will be sanctioned by the civil government, whether or not you approve."

"Civil marriage." The minister spat the words. "There is no

true marriage if a man and woman live apart from the blessing of God—"

"So say you," Ananias answered, lifting a hand. "And so we have made provision. Though John Chapman has not spoken a sermon since your illness, he is a clergyman still, and he has agreed to pronounce any willing man and woman married in the sight of God."

The minister flushed to the roots of his hair, glared at the council for a silent moment, then stood and left the church.

▼▲▼▲▼ Jocelyn jerked in alarm when the door slammed behind her. When she turned, she saw Thomas standing motionless in the room, his hand pressed to his forehead. "Does your head ache?" she asked, stirring the embers of the fire so the room brightened.

"They know not what they do," he said, taking a seat at the board. He rested his elbows on the table and pressed his palms to his forehead.

"What has the council done, Thomas?" Jocelyn whispered, mindful that Regina slept in the attic. "Mayhap it's not so bad as you think—"

"They have cowed John Chapman into marrying Indian women and English men," he said, his fingers knotting into his hair. "They were not content with civil marriage, but now heathen and Christian will be united alike in the holy ceremony of marriage before God."

Jocelyn reached across the table to him. "The Indians are heathens no longer. The idols are gone. They are as Christian as we are."

"Are they?" Thomas's eyes were bold and defiant as he looked at her. "I do not know for sure, Jocelyn, for they dance and sing in words I cannot understand—"

"Do they understand your Latin or Greek?" Jocelyn asked. "No. They trust you, and you must trust them." She picked up a skirt of Regina's that she had been mending. "And it is a good thing, this. Already some of our men have gone to live in the Indian village to be with the women they love, so now they can be married."

"You would excuse their fornication?"

Jocelyn could feel his glare from across the table. "No, I'll not excuse it," she said, looking him straight in the eye. "But even God allows a man to marry if he chooses. You have forced thirty men into celibacy, Thomas, and it is not natural."

His face was like granite as he stared at her. "Lustful thoughts can be curbed," he finally said, speaking slowly. "Men do not require women to live."

"You've proved that well enough in this house," Jocelyn answered, turning from him to her mending, determined that he should not guess how deeply she cared. "And think on this, Thomas. Which is the greater sin? A man who loves a woman without the benefit of marriage, or a man who marries a woman and refuses to love her? Even the Bible has commanded husbands to love their wives as Christ has loved the church."

He did not answer, and Jocelyn did not look up from her mending. After a moment, she broke her thread and lowered her voice. "I am not surprised that you are silent, for both are sin, Thomas, and both are wrong. And until you can stand honestly before God yourself, why judge your brothers so harshly?"

She stole a quick glance at him—his eyes were fixed on the leaping flames of the dying fire. "I must preach against sin," he finally replied, his voice a toneless whisper.

"Yes, and you shall. But it is the Word of God that convicts sinners, sir, not you. And if you refuse to show grace to your fellow men, soon you will drive them all to the Indian village. Who will hear your preaching then, Thomas?"

He stared at the fire without a word, and Jocelyn finished her mending, then slipped out of her bodice and kirtle and into her nightgown. As was her habit, she knelt at the side of the bed and tented her fingers as she prayed: "Father God, have mercy on us, but especially on my husband, Thomas." Then she climbed into bed and studied the orange glow of the fire until she fell asleep.

From the small house he had taken at Kilmore Quay in Ireland, John White sat at his desk and idly tapped his pen on the sheet of blank parchment before him. How could ink and parchment contain the fullness of the emotions he wanted to express?

Outside his window, the tumbling roar and release of the ocean intruded steadily upon the quiet of the night shadows. He liked the sound of the sea, for often he comforted himself with the thought that his family lay just on the other side of the water. . . .

He dipped his pen into the inkwell.

John White to Richard Hakluyt, 4 February 1594:

To the worshipful and my very friend, Master Richard Hakluyt, much happiness in the Lord.

Sir, for the satisfying of your earnest request, as well as for the performance of my promise to you, I have sent you the true discourse of my last voyage into the West Indies, and parts of America called Virginia, taken in hand about the end of February, in the year of our redemption 1590. There were at the time three ships absolutely determined to go for the West Indies, but when they were fully furnished, and in readiness to make their departure, a general stay was commanded of all ships throughout England. I presently acquainted Sir Walter Raleigh, that by his endeavor it would please him to procure license for those ships to proceed on their determined voyage, that thereby the people in Virginia might speedily be comforted and relieved.

Whereupon he by his good means obtained license of the Queen's Majesty, that the owner of the three ships should transport a convenient number of passengers, with their furnitures and necessaries to be landed in Virginia. Nevertheless, that order was not observed. Commanders of the ships denied to have any passengers, or anything else transported, saving only my self and my chest, no, not so much as a boy to attend upon me.

Thus both governors, masters and sailors, regarding very smally the good of their countrymen in Virginia, determined nothing less than to touch at those places, but wholly disposed themselves to seek after purchase and spoils, spending so much time therein that summer was spent before we arrived at Virginia. And when we were come thither the season was so unfit and the weather so foul that we were constrained to forsake that coast, having not seen any of our planters, with loss of our ship-boats, and seven of our chiefest men: and also with loss of three of our anchors and cables, and most of our casks with fresh water.

I would to God it had been as prosperous to all, as noisome to the planters, and as joyful to me. I would to God my wealth were answerable to my will. Thus committing the relief of my discomfortable company the planters in Virginia, to the merciful help of the Almighty, whom I most humbly beseech to help and comfort them, according to his most holy will and their good desire, I take my leave from my house at Newtowne in Kylmore the fourth of February, 1594.

Your most well-wishing friend,
John White

It was a lovely green day in early May when Jocelyn and Regina were interrupted on their regular walk to the Indian village.

"Jocelyn!" The shrill scream made Jocelyn pause on the forest path, and for a moment her heart stopped beating. Had something happened to Thomas?

Audrey ran up the trail, a vision of flying skirts, tumbling red hair, and crimson cheeks. When at last she reached Jocelyn, she clung to her friend's hand and struggled to catch her breath.

"Is something wrong?" Jocelyn asked, taking Audrey's shoulders. "Is it Thomas? Or Master Bailie?"

"No," Audrey answered, panting. She bent forward with her hands on her knees, breathing deeply, then laughed and patted five-year-old Regina on the cheek. "Don't let me frighten you, ladies, but I have good and terrible news!"

"Pray, tell us then," Jocelyn said, more than a little irritated that Audrey had alarmed her so. "'Pon my soul, I thought John White had appeared on the riverbank—"

"I'm with child." Audrey stopped panting and patted her stomach while Jocelyn stared in surprise.

"So you say! In truth?"

"Aye." Audrey dimpled and took Regina's hand as they continued their walk along the wide path to Ohanoak. "I didna know for sure, but it's been two months since me last time of bleeding. Pauwau felt my stomach yesternoon and told me to expect a son in the winter."

"A son?" Jocelyn gazed at Audrey in delight. "But how does Pauwau know?"

Audrey lifted her shoulder in a shrug. "Who can say? But

Master Bailie is absolutely beside himself with delight. And while I don't know how William will handle the news—"

Jocelyn stopped and regarded her friend with a stern gaze. Mindful of Regina's tender ears, she mouthed her next words: "Did William—"

Audrey gave her a quick, denying glance. "No! And he'll not say so, either, for I have never given him more than a kiss, and not even that in the years Master Bailie and I have been married. 'Tis Master Bailie's child, in truth, and he knows it."

"Good." They walked in silence for a moment; then Jocelyn squeezed Audrey's hand. "So if that's the good news, what's the terrible?"

"That's me problem," Audrey said, wringing her hands. "The news is both good and terrible. I never thought I'd have a child, so when Master Bailie dies and I'm free to marry William, what will I do? Proud as he is, William won't want to raise another man's son."

Jocelyn patted the girl on the shoulder. "I wouldn't worry about that now," she said, smiling. "'Tis time to think about your husband and your baby. The morrow will take care of itself."

▼▲▼▲▼ Several weeks later, William Clement and James Hynde lay facedown on broad rocks overhanging a slow-running stream, their hands thrust into the cold water. A large trout moved only inches away from William's hand, and though the frigid water had nearly numbed all sensation in his fingers, William kept his hand still and limp, like a mere extension of the sea grasses. The nosy trout moved closer and curiously nudged a finger. William held his breath, willing the animal to turn, and when the creature did, his fingers closed around the silver scales, and he flipped the fish out of the water, struggling to keep it in his grasp as the fish flopped in a frantic struggle to escape.

"There's five for me," William said, rolling down his sleeve in a vain effort to restore warmth to his arm. "Mark me, James, you are too slow."

"Not I," James said, his arm floating freely beneath the surface of the water. "According to what I hear, you are the slow one."

William turned at the sound of derision in James's voice. "What do y' hear?"

James's mouth tipped in a faint smile. "I hear that old Master Bailie's gone and made himself a child. The fair Audrey will have his baby come winter."

William felt his face burning. "Egads, do you believe everything you hear? It's not possible. Not only is the old goat past his prime, but Audrey would never—"

"Judge for yourself, next time you see her," James answered, turning his face back to the water. "'Tis as plain as the nose on your face. Either Master Bailie's made himself a brat, or some other bloke—"

William gave his companion a killing look and swallowed a hysterical surge of angry laughter. "'Tis of no importance," he said, again rolling up the sleeve of his jerkin.

He noisily thrust his hand into the water and smiled in pleasure when James swore softly. "I cry you mercy, Wills, I almost had one before you splashed 'im away."

"If there is a brat," William said, breathing deeply so he could relax long enough to catch a fish, "when old Bailie dies, I'll send the kid to live with the savages. Or I may make him a servant, since Bailie's made one of me all these years."

His smile deepened as he thought of it.

"You wouldn't do it," James said, lowering his voice for the sake of a five-pound trout that nosed his way up the stream. "Oh, you are a fine one with the ladies, my friend William, but you've been talking for years about doing away with old Master Bailie while the man grows younger every day and makes a child to prove it! Yet on you talk and fret and fume, all the while doin' nothing."

"You want me to do something?" William said, pulling his arm out of the water. He sat up and drew the back of his wet hand across his sweaty brow. "I'll do something, or my name isn't William Clement." He crossed his legs and searched the woods as if for an idea. "It might be a hunting accident, a drowning, or the misfire of a musket," he said softly, leaning back upon his elbows. "But mark my words, James, Master Bailie will never live to see the birth of his brat."

▼▲▼▲▼ Roger Bailie paused from his work in the fields to wipe his brow. The sun was uncommonly hot and the corn plants withered, and he knew he ought to be worried about drought. But in the weeks since Audrey's incredible news, he hadn't had the inclination to allow a single sorrowful thought to cross his mind.

Several of the other planters approached to ask his opinion about where to place the large kegs that would water the fields, and Roger answered them pleasantly, but breathed a sigh of relief when they moved on. Lately he had found himself torn between a hysterical urge to laugh and the desire to sit and thoughtfully prepare for the months and years ahead.

Strange that a man of sixty and six years would want to think about the future. Last winter they had buried Master Prat, who had lived to the ripe old age of sixty and two, and the Indians spoke of a hundred-year-old werowance who lived in the mountains. In his younger days Roger had thought he would be well satisfied to live sixty years or sixty and five, but now he felt as if he could endure to be a hundred and still yearn for more life.

It was Audrey who had brought him new life. The babe was only a symbol of his happiness. He had admired the girl's spirit since the first time he had seen her aboard the *Lion,* and like a stern father he had witnessed her dangerous flirtations with William Clement. Often he had slipped into alcoves aboard the ship or hidden behind the houses of the village to watch the two of them together, and it was only of necessity to save the girl from certain heartache that he had proposed the ridiculous marriage arrangement.

He had not really planned to love her; he wanted to keep her on a shelf, safe and protected from the ruffians of the world. But she had inched her way into his heart as surely as an ant finds the honey jar, and nothing in the world could compare to the way she made him feel when she snuggled on his shoulder.

And now she would bear him a son! True, he had little faith in the Indian woman's prophecy and knew the child could be a daughter, but what harm lay in imagining that a new, young Roger Bailie would pick up the thread of life after he had been called to heaven?

▼▲▼▲▼ William Clement finally decided upon his plan. For three weeks he had considered various options: A hunting accident was improbable because Master Bailie rarely hunted. Likewise, an accidental drowning would not be believed, for Master Bailie did not swim for pleasure and hated fishing. All Bailie did was spend his days overseeing the corn fields, and what harm could come to a man in a field of corn?

But harm could lie in other, more innocent pastimes, and after careful consideration William Clement decided to poison Roger Bailie.

One night he visited the hut of Pauwau, the old Indian priestess, and asked for an herb that could make a man sleep. She regarded him impassively with the unblinking black eyes of a shark, then her gnarled finger drew in the sand. "The red fruit of this tree will make a man sleep forever," she said, drawing the likeness of a tree with needle-covered branches, "but the wood bark, leaves, and seeds will make a man sleep deeply for the space of a night. A woman who drinks of the juice from the berries will lose an unborn child." Her eyes narrowed slightly as she looked up from the ground. "How long do you want to sleep, William Clement?"

He gave her an impertitent grin. "Not long, old woman," he said, rising to his feet. "Not long at all."

As he walked home that night, William congratulated himself. He would find that tree and brew two cups of tea, one for

Audrey and one for his master, and rid himself of two complications in one evening.

▼▲▼▲▼ "A fine meal, my wife," Master Bailie said, placing his hand over Audrey's. Audrey felt herself blushing, but she didn't pull away. Her blooming belly and her husband's open affection had been growing alongside each other, and she did not know how to discourage Master Bailie without hurting his feelings. Nor, indeed, was she so sure she wanted to discourage him.

"I am happy you liked it," she said, pushing her chair away from the board. She removed their plates and stacked them on the ground, then attempted to turn the heavy board against the wall. Her husband leapt to his feet to help her, and when the board had been eased out of the way, she timidly smiled her thanks.

"You are looking very well," Master Bailie said, taking a seat on the bench near the fire. Audrey looked down. She wore one of her old bodices, newly dyed bright blue in an Indian dye pot and refitted to cover her expanding shape, and a wrap skirt of the softest suede. Her dainty ankles peeped forth at the bottom of the garment, and she caught her husband peeking at the bit of leg that showed between the edge of her skirt and the top of her moccasins.

Let the minister rave about the evils of Indian clothing, she thought, watching her husband light the pipe he had been given by one of the men. *I find savage garments quite comfortable.*

She scraped the dinner dishes into the compost jar and glanced out the window. A sudden moving shadow caught her eye, and she paused for a moment as a dark premonition held her still. What business had anyone to be about at this hour? But after a moment, nothing else moved, and Audrey resumed her clattering work with the dishes.

When she had finished, Master Bailie took her hand and pulled her onto the bench next to him. "Would you like some cider?" he asked, his smiling eyes two bright points in a battle-field of wrinkles. "Is there anything I can get for you?"

Audrey jumped as a loud rap sounded at the door. Master Bai-lie sighed and opened it, and his annoyance deepened into irrita-tion when he discovered that William Clement had disturbed him.

Audrey held her breath. What possible reason could William have for disturbing the master's privacy? He knew better than to visit at night!

"I give you good evening, Master Bailie," William said, bow-ing carefully after he entered the house. He carried a wooden tray upon which were two steaming mugs. "I thought you might like to have some tea. Pauwau recommends it."

For an instant Audrey thought she saw William wink at her; then he looked solicitously toward his master. "I know the day was hot and long. And Pauwau has promised the tea is very soothing."

"Tea," Master Bailie said, glancing toward Audrey. "In truth, tea does sound good—"

"No, Master Bailie," Audrey whispered. A niggling doubt rose in her mind and would not be silent. She rose from her seat and placed a restraining hand on her husband's arm. "In truth, I would prefer cider."

"The cider jug is empty," William said, his cold blue eyes snap-ping. "And this tea is good. Pauwau told me how to brew it."

"It does have a nice cherry color," Master Bailie said. He took one of the mugs and passed it under his nose, inhaling deeply. "Ah, this is nice indeed. Here, Audrey, have some. Thank you, William, for your thoughtfulness."

Audrey took the mug her husband offered and gazed thought-fully at William. If, as she suspected, he intended her husband harm, then did he plan to harm her, as well? If she drank, would he leap forward to dash the cup from her lips?

She raised the cup and pretended to sip it, but William did not move. Her husband raised his cup to sample the brew, but Audrey threw her arm against him. If his mug contained poison, she would never forgive herself.

"Hold, sir," she said to her husband; then she turned to the man she had thought she would love forever. "William," she said, her tone artificially bright, "why not join us in a cup of tea? We must raise a toast to my soon-coming child."

"I am not thirsty," he said, his brows rushing together in a frown.

"Nevertheless, you shall drink with us," she answered lightly, placing her mug on the bench near the fire. She hastily grabbed a clean cup, filled it with hot water from the kettle in the fire, and handed it to William.

He paused, his eyes blue and questioning, and she lifted an eyebrow. "Have you no more of the delicious herb?" she asked. "We will not drink without you, William."

"No, my man," her husband interjected. "A generous gesture, dear wife."

"I have no more of the berries," William said, his voice even and calm. "But surely the same taste is acquired through the leaves." He tossed his tray onto the ground and pulled from his pocket a handful of needles, which he crushed in his fist and dropped into the hot water. Stirring the mix with his finger, he lifted his cup toward Master Bailie's outstretched mug.

"To your child," he said, his eyes steady upon Audrey.

She brought her mug from the bench and touched it to the other two. "To my child," she whispered, and all three drank deeply.

When they had done drinking, William bowed and left them.

As she undressed for bed, Audrey laughed at her worries that William had poisoned them. The tea warmed her belly and made her feel deliciously light-headed, and she snuggled willingly into the arms of her husband as they both fell into a deep and dreamless sleep.

▼▲▼▲▼ William Clement did not go to his house immediately, but danced through the village in celebration. On the morrow he would be master of Roger Bailie's wife, house, and possessions. As heir to the wife, he would also inherit the master's seat on the council. People would bow before him with the respect they had awarded the generous old fool, and James Hynde would finally stop chiding William for his lack of gumption.

He had done it! Even now the old man probably drew his last breath, or his vile seed had already passed from Audrey's womb. How brittle she had been with him when he offered her the tea! But she had always been softhearted and protective of the old man. That was one reason William loved her, for silly Audrey had always been unduly concerned about the helpless.

Exhausted from his frantic dance, he collapsed under a tall oak tree in the center of the village and laughed. All would be finished on the morrow, and no one would suspect a thing. As Master Bailie's servant, he would naturally be the first person to visit after sunrise, and he would clean up the mugs and put them away. Audrey would be there, in bed, alive but weak, and he would call frantically for the doctor and midwife even as he carried the cold corpse of Roger Bailie from the house.

He laughed again and the sound rolled eerily through the night, then seemed to halt against a wall of silence. Clement abruptly stopped laughing. Rectangles of yellow-and-orange light gleamed from a few of the houses as nighttime fires died down, and above him the moon sailed across a sky of deepest sapphire, casting bars of silver shadow across his hands and feet as he sat under the tree.

Suddenly the silver bars gained density and weight, and William gasped in awe as they became actual silver ingots. He held his breath, afraid to move lest the bars shift from his body and fall immaterial into the darkness. What riches, and here, upon his body! He had sailed to America in hope of finding silver and gold, yet all one had to do was lie in the moonlight and wait for Nature to cast her spell. . . .

William frowned. A sense of foreboding descended over him with a shiver. This vision, and the numbness that seemed to be overtaking him, was but the herb. Hadn't Pauwau said it would make him sleep? Struggling to mask his fear, he painted on a stiff smile, but still the moon poured heavy silver upon him. The weight of the ingots pressed upon him now, driving the breath from his body. His legs and feet were immobile beneath the burden; even his hands could not move. The witch of an Indian had tricked him! The *bark and leaves* were lethal, not the berries!

Terror stole his breath; his forehead gleamed with perspiration despite the cool evening air. As cold as lead he was, and about as helpless. Above him, insects and animals sent their calls through the night, and the stars washed the sapphire heavens in brilliance until William Clement's soul left his body and nothing remained under the oak tree but the poisoned corpse of a would-be murderer.

▼▲▼▲▼ It looked, Thomas told Jocelyn, as though William simply sat down and gave up the ghost. Roger Bailie reported that William had brought them tea just after darkness had settled, then had wished them a good night and left as if nothing whatsoever was wrong.

Thomas had found berries and needles from a yew tree in William's pocket and had taken them to the Indian village. Pauwau had listened to the story of William's death in silence, then studied the berries and needles without expression. "The tree is death," she said simply when Thomas had finished. "If the man used these, it is God's justice that he is dead."

And so at William Clement's funeral, Thomas had nothing to tell the village except that a man had died, and God alone knew what had happened.

▼▲▼▲▼ In January 1594, Audrey Bailie gave birth to a son. When the baby was one week old, Jocelyn and Regina visited the happy mother and father. "Oh, Audrey, he is beautiful," Jocelyn said, taking the baby into her arms. "I'm certain there hasn't been a prettier baby in all the colony."

"He takes after his mother, of course," Roger Bailie said, proudly sitting behind his wife on the big family bed. "Though he certainly did not waste time being born, I can promise you that!"

"Roger caught the baby himself," Audrey added proudly, smiling at her husband. "There was no time to call you, Jocelyn, or even Pauwau. One minute I had a pain in me back; the next minute I was on the floor with a baby between—"

"He's lovely," Jocelyn interrupted, remembering Regina's curious ears. "Have you named him?"

"Fallon Roger Bailie," Audrey said, lightly running her hand across the wisps of fuzz on the baby's head. "Fallon means 'ruler' in Gaelic."

"Fallon Bailie," the proud father repeated. "The best boy in the village, and no doubt!"

▾▲▾▲▾ Four weeks later, Roger Bailie caught pneumonia and lay near death. Audrey allowed Jocelyn to take care of baby Fallon while she nursed her husband. As Roger's strength ebbed, Audrey knelt by the side of the bed and held his hand.

"Mistress Bailie," he whispered, struggling for breath, "are you there?"

"I'm here, dearest," she said, leaning closer to him. "I won't leave you, Roger."

He licked his dry lips and struggled to speak. "Can you forgive an old man for desiring your youth? Though I know you loved William Clement, I couldn't bear to see you waste your beauty—"

"Don't fret, me husband," Audrey said, shushing him. "Save your breath so you can get better."

"No, Audrey," he whispered. His eyes darkened with the love he had long ago stopped trying to conceal, and she bent to kiss him. His hand tightened around hers as she lifted her head. "I am sorry if I made you unhappy."

"Unhappy?" she whispered, surprised out of her calm ministration. "Faith, Roger, how could you make me unhappy? You lifted me from a life of servitude and made me your wife. You honored me with respect and liberty, and you have made me fruitful and given me a son. God knows I never expected to have any of these things, my dearest Roger, and I owe them all to you."

Gently, she lifted his hand to her cheek. "Don't you see, dear? I love you, Master Bailie. And I have known nothing but kindness from you in all our days together."

As she pressed her lips to his hand, Roger Bailie closed his eyes. She heard him inhale—once, twice, thrice—then he paused and exhaled for a long moment to breathe no more.

Audrey blinked back her tears and continued to hold his hand. "So you've gone, have you now, Master Bailie?" she called, lifting her eyes toward heaven. "Go in peace, me love. I'll take good care of your son. I'll give me life for him, if I have to."

Outside, a cold wind blew past the house with soft moans. Inside, pillowed by her husband's hand, Audrey Bailie slept.

Ocanahonan

*I will walk before the Lord in the land
of the living.*

Psalm 116:9

Eight years passed. The graves of Roger Bailie and William Clement sank into the marshy land, as did the graves of others who breathed their last on Virginian soil, but life continued in the way it had since the beginning of time. The City of Raleigh and the Indian town of Ohanoak merged and became known in the region as Ocanahonan. Jocelyn marveled that there had ever been two distinctly different villages, so completely had the colonists and Indians become one people. It was a society of mutual benefit: The Indians taught the English the secrets of hunting, fishing, and planting; the settlers taught the Indians how to build multistory, permanent buildings and work iron and metal. Together they mined copper from the hills further inland, and together they traveled through the nearby region on hunting expeditions.

The Weapemeoc and Tripanick tribes were taken aback by the sight of their dark-skinned brothers in such close alliance with the "clothed people," as the English were called, and despite Thomas's high hopes, they did not accept the gospel readily when they chanced to visit Ocanahonan. Most Indian tribes were too set in their ways and too wary of the English to eagerly embrace a foreign religion. Jocelyn often found it necessary to remind Thomas that they must be patient—they had worked for years before the first Indians had converted to Christianity.

One spring day in 1602, however, emissaries from a band of the Mangoak tribe approached the ever-expanding palisade. With their hands open to declare their peaceful intentions, their chief—a tall, solidly built Indian called Rowtag—approached the gate and asked through an interpreter to address the elders of the village. In response, Ananias called a meeting of the council, which now included the minister and two Indians: Abooksigun, the aged werowance of the Ohanoak clan, and Chogan.

The Mangoak chief stood before the council with an indolent, tomcat grace and spoke to Abooksigun in a voice of careful restraint. His muscles bulged and slid under his bronzed skin, and the sight of his hard jaw, tendoned neck, and deep, painted chest struck the other men speechless.

"I hope the man is on our side," Ananias jokingly whispered to John Sampson. "I would as lief battle the devil himself as this savage."

When the stranger had finished speaking, Abooksigun nodded and translated for his English friends. "Rowtag leads fifty people in a tribe that used to number one hundred," the werowance said, enunciating carefully. "A Powhatan war party has killed many of the tribe, and there are not enough hands to plant crops. Many of his people are children under the age of ten summers."

"What does he want us to do?" Ananias asked.

Abooksigun interpreted the question, and Rowtag replied, opening his hands in an expansive gesture.

Abooksigun spoke again. "He and his people have heard of the greatness of the town of Ocanahonan. They have heard of the god who rules this town and would know more of him. They would like to bring their children, their warriors, and women into this place to live and work and worship this god."

Ananias glanced at the minister, who sat speechless at the end of the council table. "It seems, Reverend Colman, that news of your work has preceded you," he remarked dryly. He smiled at the tall newcomer. "Pray tell Rowtag that he and his people are welcome in Ocanahonan, the City of Walter Raleigh."

▼▲▼▲▼ Dark and fair-haired youngsters began to be numbered among the many at Ocanahonan, and Jocelyn watched the rainbow children play in the shallows of the river and wondered what her father would say if he could see his four-teen-year-old granddaughter shepherding the children safely from the river to their homes. Regina had grown tall and lovely, as slim and dark as her father, but with Jocelyn's startlingly blue eyes. She spoke the Indian tongue more fluently than Jocelyn, and her quick smile warmed the hearts of even the most stoic Indians.

Soon after her fourteenth birthday, in the late spring of that year, Regina's menses began. On that morning Jocelyn had been surprised to see Hurit and the ancient Pauwau coming toward the house. Wordlessly, Pauwau beckoned to Regina and led her outside the town to a hut on the riverbank, motioning for the girl to go inside.

"She must stay inside until the bleeding has stopped," Hurit explained to Jocelyn, who had followed out of curiosity. "She has become a woman today."

"Thomas won't like this," Jocelyn said, twisting her hands. "It's too heathen—"

"Does your husband not go alone into the woods to pray?" Hurit said, cocking her head. "This is the same. Regina needs time to think and pray, for she must put away the things of children and put on the things of women."

After the Indian women had gone, Jocelyn peered inside the hut and called anxiously to her daughter. "I am well, Mama," Regina called back, her voice strangely mature. "I will see you soon."

And three days later, when Regina returned from the river-bank, hungry and pale, she walked with a proud assurance that Jocelyn had never seen before. William Wythers, who had always been Regina's favorite playmate, followed the girl like an entranced schoolboy. Thomas, too, watched his daughter wistfully, doubtless remembering the chubby child who used to climb onto his lap. Jocelyn sighed, knowing that those days were gone forever.

Gone forever, too, were the settlers' regular visits to Croatoan. Manteo reported that the five men Ananias had left there dis-

appeared one day and simply never came back to camp.
Whether they were drowned in the sea or met with mischief,
Manteo could not tell.

So Ananias and the council members tied the pinnace to a
dock on the river and left the boat slowly to rot, using the more
maneuverable shallop whenever they had to journey on the
water. And every afternoon, Eleanor Dare left her maid and her
daughter and walked to the dock, watching the horizon for signs
of a ship that never appeared. In public, Eleanor referred often to
her father, who was always around the corner or in the next
house, and Jocelyn knew that her cousin had now slipped fully
back to a more comfortable time because she could not accept
that her father had abandoned her in the wilderness of Virginia.

▼▲▼▲▼ "Hurry, Jocelyn, the feast is about to begin,"
Audrey called through the minister's window as she led eight-
year-old Fallon by the hand. Jocelyn picked up a ribbon and tied
her hair at the base of her neck, then studied her reflection in a
bowl of water on the table and smoothed the curly tendrils that
escaped to frame her face. She looked neat and prim in her worn
English outfit, hopelessly out of style by Ocanahonan standards
and not at all like a woman on her way to the biggest celebration
of the year.

From behind a stack of books, Thomas looked up at her. The
silvery gray strands, which had first appeared in his hair after
his illness, had multiplied, and dignified furrows lay at the sides
of his mouth and upon his forehead. At forty-five, he looked his
age, but Jocelyn thought he had never looked more handsome.

"Are you sure you won't go with me?" she asked, picking up
a bundle of bread. "Regina's there already, and she'd love for
you to sit with her, Thomas."

"You have lost your mind," he answered smoothly, running
his finger over the pages of his book. "Go without me. You
always do."

Jocelyn took two steps toward the door, then turned to face

him again. "It is not a pagan feast, you know. Mayhap it used to be, but now we see it as an occasion for rejoicing, a time of forgiveness—"

"Go without me," Thomas urged again, and because she knew she was wasting her time, Jocelyn left the house.

The July sun's blistering heat had already passed overhead as Jocelyn walked past the cornfields. The last sowing of corn had grown tall and ripe, and soon the villagers would begin to bring in the crop.

But the feast of the green corn was more than a celebration of the coming harvest; it was also a time to put away evil and old quarrels. The young boys of the village had been busy visiting the houses of the village since morning. At each home, they ceremonially extinguished the hearth fire to symbolize the death of old jealousies and grudges. Tonight, after the feast, new fires would be kindled on every hearth.

On every hearth, Jocelyn thought with a wry smile, *but mine.* Thomas would have no part in what he considered pagan symbolism.

Her stomach growled, and Jocelyn happily sniffed the aromas of roasting venison and pork. To whet their appetites for the great feast to come, every villager had fasted throughout the day. After the feast and prayers of thanksgiving to God for a good harvest, men who had anything against another would be reconciled; women would embrace and forgive petty quarrels. After making peace with one another, the entire village would celebrate with a circling dance around the leaping fire in which the dried stalks of corn blazed and smoked.

And as the fire burned down and the sun set, the villagers of Ocanahonan would hold hands and sing the hymn that had done much to unite the Englishmen's love of God and the Indians' love of nature:

> *All creatures of our God and King,*
> *Lift up your voice and with us sing*
> *Alleluia, Alleluia!*

Thou burning sun with golden beam,
Thou silver moon with softer gleam,
O praise him, O praise him,
Alleluia, alleluia, alleluia!

Thou rushing wind that art so strong,
Ye clouds that sail in heav'n along,
O praise Him, Alleluia!
Thou rising morn in praise rejoice,
Ye lights of evening, find a voice,
O praise Him, O praise Him,
Alleluia, alleluia, alleluia!

Thou flowing water, pure and clear,
Make music for thy Lord to hear,
Alleluia, Alleluia!
Thou fire so masterful and bright,
That givest man both warmth and light,
O praise Him, O praise Him,
Alleluia, alleluia, alleluia!

And all ye men of tender heart,
Forgiving others, take your part,
O sing ye, Alleluia!
Ye who long pain and sorrow bear,
Praise God and on Him cast your care,
O praise Him, O praise Him,
Alleluia, alleluia, alleluia!

Let all things their Creator bless,
And worship Him in humbleness,
O praise Him, Alleluia!
Praise, praise the Father, praise the Son,
And praise the Spirit, three in one,
O praise Him, O praise Him,
Alleluia, alleluia, alleluia!

Jocelyn hurried to the clearing where the great fire had been laid, then squeezed into the circle between Hurit and Audrey. "See how William Wythers follows your Regina?" Audrey said, elbowing Jocelyn in the ribs. She smiled impishly. "Such a handsome boy, William. Are you thinking to marry your daughter soon?"

Jocelyn made a face. "At fourteen?"

"My people believe fourteen is a good age," Hurit said, a shy smile upon her lips. "If a girl is a woman, what is the point of waiting?"

"She's just a child," Jocelyn said, waving their comments away. But as the flames leaped higher in the darkening sky and she watched her daughter dance with the slim but powerfully built youth, Jocelyn realized with an uncomfortable start that William Wythers was no longer a child. At nineteen, he was well of an age to be married. And there was no denying the mutual attraction between this young man and her daughter.

"May heaven help me," Jocelyn choked, clutching Audrey's arm in feigned alarm. "I'm going to lose my baby!"

"Don't sit and cry about it," Audrey said, her eyes on the impressive form of Rowtag as he led the men in a circle around the fire. "Life is for the living! Let's get up and dance!"

And while Jocelyn sputtered in protest, Audrey and Hurit lifted her from the ground, and together they joined in the women's dance of praise and thanksgiving to the God of the harvest.

▼▲▼▲▼ Hiding in the shadows, Thomas Colman skirted the party and walked with his hands behind his back, surveying the ghastly scene with a disapproving frown on his face. The huge central fire played over the dancing figures like a demon of light, its caressing fingers of smoke and heat swirling amid the thud of drums and the whine of a harmonica. Thomas stiffened in horrified surprise when he saw that all of the dancers, his wife and daughter included, had painted their faces in bold red designs.

"Is this what you have brought me to?" he questioned, glaring up through the smoky sky to the heavens above. "There was a time when I thought you had called me to spread the gospel, but now my own people, the chosen ones, have been reduced to pagan practices. My own wife, my own daughter . . ."

Blindly, he plunged into the forest, ignoring the trail. Sprawling vines, heavy with the growth of summer, clung to him as he passed, but he pressed through, ripping himself from the thick undergrowth that would hold him captive.

A fallen tree stopped his progress. "And now," he whispered, breathing heavily as he leaned upon the tree, "I am the only righteous soul in this place. All others have intermarried with the evil ones. They have sold their souls for comfort and in the name of peace. Like Elijah, I cry to you, God, that I, even I only, am left. Though you had seven thousand priests in Israel with Elijah, there are not seven thousand men of God here. And so with Elijah, I say, it is enough; now, O God, take away my life."

There was no reply save the whisper of the wind through the trees. Dejected and exhausted beyond words, Thomas turned from the raucous noise of the feast and walked toward the silence of his dark house.

▼▲▼▲▼ The answer came to him in the night, and on Sunday morning Thomas addressed his mixed congregation of English and Indians with new zeal in his heart.

"We will take missionary journeys like Paul and Silas," he said, pounding the table before him in a burst of energy. "I have been wrong to expect the savages to come to us. A dangerous spiritual apathy has settled over this place, and we must take the gospel into the wilderness."

"Can we hunt while we preach?" one man shouted, and the congregation laughed until Thomas held up a hand.

"No," he said, frowning. "If we do less than undertake the journey for the cause of Christ alone, we weaken our purpose. Did Jesus the Christ think of feeding or clothing himself as he carried the cross to Calvary? Did he worry about the wheat in his field or the stores in his barn? No. He was single-minded, as we shall be. In a week, when the crops are in and our families are settled and prepared for the winter, I will lead whomsoever is willing into the wilderness, where we shall fish for the souls of men. Whosoever will may join me."

He gave the benediction to dismiss the congregation, but every man, woman, and child froze in place when Ananias Dare stood and held up his hand. "It's passing strange that the minister spoke today of a journey," he said, managing a smile that did not reach his eyes. "But the council has decided that one last attempt should be made to reach England. Our pinnace is rapidly deteriorating, and before she is totally useless, I'm willing to sail her back to England. My wife will go with me, and I'll need a crew of twelve men. If God wills, we will return, so I would advise all volunteers to leave their wives and children safely in this place."

A barely perceptible murmur wound through the crowd, and Ananias cleared his throat for silence. "There's no gainsaying that this will be a difficult journey," he said, rubbing his beard. "I'm no sailor and no pilot, but my wife has her father's charts and a few things that might help us. So if you are willing to try for England, go home, discuss the venture with your families, and speak to me later in the week."

Ananias saluted the minister. "I give you good day, Reverend."

▼▲▼▲▼ "So you see, Jocelyn and Thomas," Ananias said, idly turning his hat in his hand as he stood inside their small house, "as you are our closest relations, we've no one else to ask for this favor."

"We'd be happy to watch over Virginia," Jocelyn said, her heart filling with compassion as she gazed at Ananias's tortured face. "But are you sure you must go?"

Ananias gripped his wife's hand, and Eleanor smiled vacantly. "Papa will be so pleased to see us," she said, her smile a ghostly imitation of true pleasure. "He told me we should meet him back in Portsmouth. We simply must go, Jocelyn. There's no question."

Ananias met Jocelyn's gaze. "Perhaps she will recover her wits at home," he said, lowering his voice. "Besides, the time has come to contact the Crown about our fate. And if, perchance, John White does wait in England—"

"In Portsmouth, dear," Eleanor interrupted, patting his hand. "He's in Portsmouth, in the little house. Do you remember?"

"Of course," Ananias said with a pained smile.

"We understand, Ananias," Thomas said, his deep voice cutting through Jocelyn's fears. As always, he was in control. "And we'll care for Virginia—"

"Not too closely, for I wouldn't want her husband to think you are intruding," Ananias said, smiling.

"Of course not," Thomas answered.

Jocelyn listened with a vague sense of unreality. Fifteen-year-old Virginia Dare was to marry Ahanu, Abooksigun's youngest son. Somehow it seemed fitting that the first English child born in Virginia should marry one born on the same soil as she, but Jocelyn had been shocked beyond belief when Thomas had agreed to allow the wedding to be held in the church. He was yet unwilling to perform the ceremony, nor would he allow a couple of mixed marriage to visit in his home, but Jocelyn knew his heart had softened if he would permit John Chapman to use the church to marry Virginia and Ahanu.

"We will see you at the wedding, then," Ananias said, nodding to Jocelyn. He pulled Eleanor with him, and she gave Jocelyn another imitation of one of her old smiles. "Farewell, sweet Coz," she called as she and Ananias stepped out into the night.

"I can't believe they're actually leaving us," Jocelyn whispered as she and Thomas stood in the doorway and watched them go. "Will we ever see them again?"

"It will be as God wills," Thomas answered.

▼▲▼▲▼ Resplendent in his bright red paint and heavily tattooed as befitting the son of a werowance, Ahanu stepped out of his grass house and presented a gift of suede and fur to his bride. In return, following the custom of the Indians, Virginia Dare gave her new husband an embroidered belt and quiver. Then the newlyweds put their gifts aside and held hands as they walked to the church.

John Chapman was waiting for them, and the assembled guests filed quickly into the rough benches to witness the ceremony. "Ahanu," Chapman recited when the guests had been seated, "before God and these witnesses, do you take this woman to be your wife?"

Ahanu nodded. Chapman squinted with his failing eyes and, convinced that Ahanu was in agreement, continued. "Before God and these witnesses, do you, Virginia Dare, take this man to be your husband?"

"Yes," Virginia whispered. From where she stood at the back of the church, Jocelyn felt a stirring of envy in her breast. Love for Ahanu had brought a flush of beauty to the girl's cheeks, and Jocelyn wondered: *Did I look like that on my wedding day? That was fifteen years ago, and it's hard to remember.*

"I therefore pronounce you man and wife before God," John Chapman finished.

Triumphant Indian yells rent the air as the English applauded and cheered, and Virginia Dare fell into the strong arms of her young groom. From across the room Jocelyn saw Abooksigun stand from his place and wave his arms in victory. Ananias wiped tears from his eyes, but Eleanor stared blankly ahead, her head cocked to one side as if she wondered whose wedding she had just observed.

The crowd streamed to the loaded tables outside for the wedding feast, but Jocelyn hung back with Thomas, who seemed reluctant to participate in a wedding of which he could not approve. "I think," he said slowly, watching the revelers, "that I shall leave on my missionary journey on the morrow."

"So soon?" Jocelyn asked, alarmed.

"The harvest is in, and I have ten willing men," Thomas answered. He looked again at the party, then nodded resolutely. "On the morrow, then," he said, leaving her.

▼▲▼▲▼ A light frost covered the ground on the November morning when Thomas rose before sunrise, dressed in his worn black doublet and leggings, and wrapped a loaf of corn bread in a square of cloth. "I do not know when I will return," he told Jocelyn casually, as if he had decided to wander in unknown and dangerous wilderness every day of the year. "But pray that God will preserve us."

"I will," Jocelyn whispered, clutching her shawl around her shoulders in the chill of the room.

"Thomas, may I ask . . . ?" She paused, uncertain how to proceed with the question that had haunted her for days.

"What?"

"Why do you have to leave?"

He sighed. "I thought I had explained myself in church. I have heard God's call to carry the gospel into the wilderness—"

"Not that." She waved his words away and stepped closer, studying his face. "Why do you have to leave *me?*"

For a moment his face twisted, and she saw guilt, pain, and some indefinable longing flash through his eyes. Then the veil of reserve fell into place. He shifted toward the door and gave her his customary smile. "You knew you were marrying a minister," he said, shrugging slightly. He paused, and when he spoke again Jocelyn's heart broke at the flat, almost hopeless tone in his voice. "I belong to God first, to the colony, to the mission field. What I—what you want—can't change the demands of God on my life."

He combed his wiry silver hair with his fingers, paused at the board, and looked around to see if he had forgotten anything. For a moment she thought he might kiss her good-bye, but he only nodded abruptly in her direction. "Tell Regina farewell for me when she awakes," he said, pointing to the attic, where Regina slept. Abruptly, before she could reply, he left the house.

It was after noon on that same day that Ananias's party loaded food and supplies aboard the pinnace. Ananias and his men had spent the past week recaulking the leaky ship with tar and pitch, and John Prat, a cooper like his late father, had fashioned several new barrels and casks to hold fresh water, vegetables, and stores of dried meat. The men also loaded pine planking, since wood was a valuable commodity in England, and in a leather satchel Ananias carried letters from the planters to wives, children, and friends who waited in England.

Jocelyn had written no letters. She had no ties to anyone in England, for her entire world now existed in Thomas, Regina, and the ever-expanding town of Ocanahonan.

She stood on the dock and watched Eleanor move lightly over the deck as the men wrestled with piles of canvas and twisted cables. "Ahoy there, Cousin," Eleanor called down, spotting Jocelyn, and for a moment Jocelyn thought her cousin's wits had returned. "Have you come to wish us Godspeed?"

"Yes," Jocelyn called, waving a square of cloth toward the vessel. "I'll miss you, Coz!"

"Father's in his cabin, or he'd come out to say farewell, too," Eleanor said, looking fragile and delicate as she clung to a cable of the rigging and leaned over the edge of the boat.

Jocelyn hid a thick swallow in her throat. "Give your papa my love, then," she called, her voice cracking. "And take care, Eleanor. My love and prayers will go with you."

"Thank you," Eleanor called. She turned prettily and descended belowdecks, and within an hour the pinnace unleashed her cables and raised her rusty anchor. A gentle breeze filled the oft-mended main sheets, and Ananias Dare and his brave sailors stood on the deck and waved tearful farewells to their friends, wives, and children who would wait in Ocanahonan.

Two weeks later, Jocelyn met Audrey on the path to the well outside the palisade. The chill afternoon air, bathed in the burnished sunlight of autumn, carried faint hints of coming winter days. "Since Thomas and Ananias have both seen fit to rid the camp of men, 'twas surely God who sent Rowtag and his people to us," Audrey grumbled, trudging next to Jocelyn as they carried water from the river to the village.

"At least Thomas and his men will be back soon," Jocelyn said, pausing a moment to rest her arms. She lowered her buckets to the ground and rubbed her callused palms. Often she felt like cursing Thomas's missionary work, for though the harvest was in, there was still much work to be done to prepare their house for the winter. If Thomas didn't return soon, Jocelyn and Regina would be working alone. In addition, there was the matter of William Wythers, for the boy had dropped broad hints that he'd like to marry Regina soon, and he would have to talk to Thomas first. . . .

Audrey followed Jocelyn's example and lowered her buckets, but sat on a tree stump and tossed her free-flowing hair over her shoulder. "'Tis nothing but good, the arrival of Rowtag and his people. I couldn't believe it when they all wanted to be baptized in the freezing autumn water. When wee John Chapman tried to lift Rowtag out of the river by himself—" She giggled and rolled her eyes. "Well, even a saint such as you, Jocelyn, would have to admit that Rowtag's uncommonly handsome, or haven't you noticed?"

"Yes," Jocelyn said, indulging her friend with a sidelong smile. "I've noticed."

"He's a man of strong mental faculties, too, for his people follow him without complaint. They'd all be perishing with hunger now if he hadn't brought them here, though we've profited, too. Why, his men put the men of the Chawanoac tribe to shame in their huntin'. Just last week Rowtag's braves brought in three bucks, ten swamp hogs—"

A hulking shadow fell across the path, and Audrey shut her mouth and gaped at the towering image before her. Even Jocelyn stepped back, surprised by the stealth with which Rowtag had approached. Had he heard—or understood—their conversation? In six months, just how much English had he learned?

"You," he said, pointing to Audrey.

"Me?" she asked, blushing to the roots of her red hair.

Rowtag nodded without smiling, then took Audrey's hand and pulled her up. "You come with Rowtag." He pointed to her, then to himself, then toward the grass hut he had recently erected inside the palisade.

Audrey threw a question over her shoulder: "'Pon my soul, Jocelyn, do you think he wants to show me his house?"

"I don't know," Jocelyn answered, amazed. She laughed at the look on Audrey's face. "Go with him and see what he wants."

Audrey nodded and let the Indian lead her to his house. Jocelyn left their water buckets in the path and followed at a distance as Audrey kept up a steady stream of foolish chatter, probably none of which the Indian understood.

At the threshold of his house, Rowtag dropped Audrey's hand, then reached inside the opening of the doorway and brought forth a lush beaver fur, which he presented to Audrey with gentle dignity. Audrey smiled, looking up at the chief, but called for help. "Jocelyn! Fetch someone who can help me understand what he wants."

Jocelyn hurried farther into the village and met Hurit's son, Mukki, now grown tall. "I need you, Mukki," she said, taking his hand. She led him to Rowtag's house, then placed her hands on the young man's shoulders and looked up to whisper in his ear. "Can you tell us what is happening here?"

Perplexed, Audrey stood with the heavy beaver fur spread across her upturned hands. Rowtag was speaking in the Mangoak tongue, pointing occasionally to himself, then to Audrey, then to the hut. Mukki turned to Jocelyn and grinned. "It is simple, Mistress Colman," he said, his eyes sparkling in merriment. "The chief wants to marry the widow Bailie."

"*Marry* her?" Jocelyn said, incredulous. "But she wouldn't—"

"Oh, yes, I would!" Audrey broke in. Without hesitation she dropped the beaver fur and threw her arms around Rowtag's neck. Jocelyn blinked in astonished silence, and Mukki grinned again.

"I'll fetch John Chapman," he said, smiling conspiratorially, then he sprinted toward the old cleric's house.

"I hope he hurries," Jocelyn mumbled as Rowtag swept Audrey off her feet and carried her inside his house.

▼▲▼▲▼ Jocelyn knew Thomas would rant for hours if he knew how unconventional was Audrey's wedding, but John Chapman, standing at the door of the grass hut without daring to look in, recited the proper vows of matrimony and pronounced that Rowtag and Audrey Bailie were husband and wife in the eyes of God and the people of Ocanahonan. After the ceremony, which had been witnessed only by Jocelyn, Mukki, and the cleric's wife, Alice, Jocelyn silently walked home, beset by worry. Had Audrey made a terrible mistake?

▼▲▼▲▼ Two weeks into the wilderness, Thomas Colman sat on a rock and paused for breath. His doublet was uncomfortable and totally unsuitable for the wilderness, but dignity demanded that he wear it on such a holy mission. The men around him had often lost their tempers and their zeal for the journey, for after two weeks of difficult wandering without encountering a single receptive Indian village, they were ready to turn southward for the comforts of home and family.

God, are you there? Thomas prayed, fighting the feelings of desperation that constantly threatened to overcome him. *Surely you had a purpose for sending us into the woods!* "Show me, Father," he whispered fiercely. "Show me what I am to do and I will obey! Show me what you want of me. . . ."

"*For by grace are ye saved through faith; and that not of yourselves; it is the gift of God: not of works, lest any man should boast.*"

Thomas frowned in confusion. *Is that to be my answer? You make no sense, God!* He closed his eyes hopelessly. *So be it, Lord. If you will not guide me, I can only go on, for I will not turn back until I have discovered your purpose.*

Suddenly, behind Thomas, Anthony Cage grunted in surprise. "There," he said, lifting his hand toward the horizon. "Smoke. Do you see it?"

Energy surged into Thomas. At last! Now he could act on the Lord's behalf. "I do," he answered, standing. He adjusted his doublet and turned to give his men a smile of encouragement. "You see, men, what happens when we trust God? Like the pillar of fire he sent the Israelites of old, he has shown us today the direction in which we should go."

Turning smartly, he changed their course and walked toward the trail of smoke and whatever lay ahead.

▼▲▼▲▼ Out on the Western ocean, Ananias studied the heavy compass in his hand and struggled to make sense of the reading. The wind had freshened considerably in the last few hours, and the boat sailed surprisingly well, moving at breakneck pace toward an eastern destination only God could name.

"What do you say, Ananias?" John Starte called down from the crow's nest. He had left an Indian wife and three sons at Ocanahonan. "Are we moving north or south of due eastward?"

"I can't tell," Ananias said, thumping the compass with his fingers. The protective glass over the compass had cracked, and moisture from the sea air had affected the needle. He looked up at John. "In truth, I know not where we're going."

Richard Darige, a veteran of many ocean voyages, popped up from belowdecks. "I hate to disturb you, Ananias," he said, his eyes on the darkening sky to the south, "but this approaching cloud is no mere storm. I'd lower the main sheets if I were you."

Ananias's frustrated temper cracked. "You are not me!" he shouted, raising his voice to be heard above the winds that had begun to shrill over the deck. "And the wind moves us quickly, does it not?"

"Ananias!" Eleanor rose from the companionway and came toward him, her hair tangled by the wind. "Darling Ananias, Papa says that you should—"

"Name of a name, your papa is dead!" he shouted as the high arc of the bow dipped and rose, sending a stinging splash of spray over everyone on deck. Eleanor blinked back tears, and Ananias staggered under the heavy hand of guilt. "Go below, Eleanor," he said, placing a hand on her shoulder. "Your papa is waiting for you." He turned her toward the companionway and motioned for Richard Darige to take her below.

"Lower the sheets," Ananias called reluctantly. The men scrambled to obey as the foul winds blew and a strangling rain fell from the heavens to strengthen nature's assault.

▼▲▼▲▼ Back at Ocanahonan, Jocelyn felt a subtle increase in the wind and motioned to Regina. "Help me gather in the last of these corn shucks," she said, throwing her arms around a pile of the dried leaves they had been using to stuff mattresses. "The wind's picking up. If we don't get these inside they'll be blown to wherever your father is."

"Mother," Regina called as she lifted an armful of the dried shucks, "William has gone fishing in the shallop. Will he be all right?"

"He's a grown man," Jocelyn answered as the wind blew harder. Then she found herself repeating Thomas's favorite phrase: "It will be as God wills." She paused to murmur a quick prayer for Thomas's safety, and when she opened her eyes, Regina was smiling and pointing toward the riverbank.

"Oh, never fear, I see William now," she said, her love for the boy shining clearly on her face. "He's tying up the shallop."

"Welladay, let's hurry then," Jocelyn said, teasing her daughter. "William is safe, so surely all is right in the world."

▼▲▼▲▼ The rising wind pressed upon the small pinnace like a mighty hand as the men climbed like monkeys over the worn cables. Ananias stared in horror when one cable snapped, and wind and momentum thrust Richard Arthur into the churning sea. All hands rushed to the bulwark to search the waters, but they could see nothing other than storm-tossed waves.

"Eleven men," Ananias whispered, trying not to think about poor Richard Arthur and his family back at Ocanahonan. "Can a ship be sailed with only eleven men?"

It was impossible to walk on the deck without slipping on the wet surface, so Ananias sent all but one other man belowdecks to ride out the storm. He and Morris Allen lashed their bodies to the main mast with stout cable and steeled themselves to endure the rain, sharp as a lance against their skin. The wind slashed and shoved the pinnace against the surface of the deep while the men prayed.

Suddenly Morris Allen began to shout the words of a psalm: "God is our refuge and strength," he called, his reedy voice cutting through the roar of the gale, "a very present help in time of trouble. Therefore will not we fear, though the earth be removed, and though the mountains be carried into the midst of the sea!"

The mainmast cracked above their heads, the splintering sound spiraling down around them as the crow's nest snapped off and tumbled into the sea. The pinnace listed severely, then righted itself as the broken beam groaned and slid from the ship.

"Though the waters thereof roar and be troubled, though the mountains shake with the swelling thereof," Allen continued to shout. "There is a river, the streams whereof shall make glad the city of God, the holy place of the tabernacles of the most High!"

A crumpled sheet of canvas on the deck ballooned into life and covered the men like a second skin, threatening to suffocate them. But another gust blew the canvas free, and Morris Allen continued his praise as the wind shrieked in fury around them: "The Lord of hosts is with us; the God of Jacob is our refuge. Come, behold the works of the Lord, what desolations he hath made in the earth!"

Ananias let his head fall back upon the splintered wood of the mainmast. In that moment he knew it was not important that he reach England. All that mattered was that he stand before his Maker with a clear conscience. He would come to God as a child with dirty hands, but it was enough to know that God was a father whose love would wipe away every stain.

"Be still, and know that I am God," Morris Allen continued. Ananias wondered where the man found the strength. "I will be exalted among the heathen, I will be exalted in the earth. The Lord of hosts is with us; the God of Jacob is our refuge."

Then Ananias saw the rogue wave that would spell the end of the pinnace and all aboard—and his last thought was, *It is enough.*

▼▲▼▲▼ The hurricane's gale-force winds moved inland, snapping trees along the Virginian coast like kindling and wreaking havoc in Ocanahonan. Many of the English houses were knocked from their foundations; the few grass houses were obliterated as easily as a child blows a dandelion into the sky. Rising river waters carried the dock away. Winds lifted the sturdy shallop and smashed it against the toughened and gnarled oaks on shore.

After the storm, the villagers ventured out to assess the damage and to salvage what they could. Much of the stored corn had been spoiled, and not a single family had a dry mattress upon which to sleep. The shallop was a broken mess far beyond repair, and Jocelyn knew that from this day forward the colonists would build and use the portable canoes favored by the Indians.

But she breathed a prayer of thanks that no one had been killed. And despite the loss of the corn, they could always eat fish from the sea and wildlife from the forest. And perhaps it was a blessing that the pinnace, the shallop, and the dock were gone from the riverbank. The colony's last links to England and painful memories had vanished as utterly as shadows at noonday.

North of the hurricane's path, Thomas and his band of missionary men walked boldly from the forest to a clearing before the high palisade from which the column of smoke had come. A double line of savages stood at the gate as if they had expected visitors, but Chogan pointed to the west where another band of savages approached. These warriors, dressed only in breechcloths despite the cool of autumn, had painted their faces and chests bright with the red tints of war. They carried stone axes and clubs, and wore embroidered quivers of arrows over their shoulders.

Thomas held up his hand, signaling his men to stop. The leader of the approaching war party spied the English and stopped, too, though the double line of savages outside the village howled in impatience.

"What are they doing?" Thomas asked Chogan.

Chogan stepped forward and crossed his arms. "A victorious war party returns home," he said, nodding gravely toward the approaching warriors. "See? They carry the heads of their enemies and have a captive."

Thomas squinted. Bloodied heads hung from the hands of several warriors, and a young girl in buckskin walked between them, her hands bound behind her. An ugly purple bruise lay upon her cheek, and a bloodstain ran down the length of her tunic.

"What will they do to her?" Thomas asked quietly.

Chogan nodded to the double line outside the village. "She will walk the gauntlet," he said. "See the clubs they carry? They will force her to walk between the lines and receive their blows. When she reaches the village, she will be tortured until she dies."

Thomas felt his gorge rise. "I had heard of such barbarism," he said, shaking his head, "but I never thought to see it."

From fifty paces away, the leader of the war party studied the missionaries intently. He was a tall and thick man of about forty summers, with long black hair plaited with many feathers. His features were handsomely sculpted of straight lines at his mouth, eyebrows, and nose, and his eyes shone dark and wary. After a moment, the warrior lifted his bow and notched an arrow, and Chogan stepped forward and held up a restraining hand.

"What will you do, Reverend?" Chogan called over his shoulder, his eyes never leaving the approaching warrior's face. "You must do something."

Thomas gave a nervous jerk on his doublet and stepped forward to meet the warrior. "We will talk to him," he said, grateful that Chogan walked by his side as he advanced to meet the war party.

The savages in the lines of the gauntlet quieted to watch the confrontation. Too bewildered to pray, Thomas looked to Chogan. "Tell him we have come to trade," he said, remembering the savages' love of gifts. "Tell him we have much to offer."

Chogan spoke easily in a tongue Thomas had never heard, and the warrior lowered his bow. Interest flickered in his eye, and he gestured to the men behind Thomas.

"He wants to know if the men behind you are for trade," Chogan said.

"No," Thomas answered, nervously raking his fingers through his hair. "Tell him—in heaven's name, Chogan, what do we have that these savages would want?" He pressed the back of his hand to his forehead. "Muskets?"

"You have no powder and the long guns are broken. You would offend his honor if you gave him a worthless musket."

"Then what?" Thomas asked.

Chogan briefly considered. "The boat."

"The pinnace?" Thomas shook his head. "Ananias and the others—"

"The shallop," Chogan corrected. "I will tell him you have a big wooden boat for fishing, a boat that can sail the sea more easily than a bark canoe."

Thomas nodded while Chogan interpreted. When he had finished speaking, the savage warrior gave Thomas a look of bright eagerness mixed with strong indecision.

"He will want to know what you want in exchange," Chogan said, his eyes darting to Thomas.

"Why, the girl, of course," Thomas said. Chogan gave him a quick, half-accusing look, and Thomas quickly amended his statement. "We will give her freedom, Chogan. Surely you don't think God would have us leave her here to die."

Chogan shrugged, considering, and proposed a trade of the boat for the girl. The warrior lifted a finger to his face as he thought, then angrily slammed his fist into his hand.

"Why is he angry?" Thomas asked.

"He wants to know whom you will leave as hostage until you return with the boat," Chogan interpreted. "If you take the girl, he will have nothing."

Thomas sighed. "Tell him we can't bring the boat. He'll have to come get it himself. But the boat will be ready, and if 'tis not, well then—"

"A life for a life," Chogan said, raising an eyebrow. "One life must be forfeit if you do not give the boat."

Thomas hesitated, then studied the young captive. Surely she was not more than thirteen or fourteen—Regina's age. God would want him to love this girl as much as he loved his own daughter, and if a life must be forfeit, it would be his own.

"Tell him we agree to the exchange," Thomas said, nodding toward Chogan. "He may come for the boat at our village on the river, and if we do not surrender it as promised, a life will be forfeit. But he must give us this girl now."

Chogan translated, and the war chief nodded toward his warriors, who thrust the girl forward so roughly that she fell onto her knees. Thomas advanced and gingerly lifted her.

The savages in the gauntlet wailed in disappointment as Chogan and the party of Englishmen turned and walked back into the wilderness.

▼▲▼▲▼ In the storm-tossed village of Ocanahonan a fortnight later, Thomas told Jocelyn and Regina the story. "It was necessary to keep the girl bound for two days," Thomas said, eating supper with his family in their newly repaired home. "She would have run into the woods had we not. Chogan said it was likely her entire village had been slaughtered, so she had nowhere to go. In time, she came to trust us."

"Poor dear," Jocelyn murmured, remembering how surprised she had been to see the missionaries return with a teenage girl. "But Hurit will know how to take care of her. Hurit is a great comforter."

"Aye," Thomas said, his eyes resting affectionately upon Regina. "And on the way home, Chogan told me that the war chief we met was none other than Opechancanough, brother to the great chief Powhatan."

"I have heard much of this Powhatan," Jocelyn said, refilling Thomas's bowl with corn mush. "The Indians say he is wise and brave."

Thomas made a face. "He's a pagan, Jocelyn, and no doubt. When I heard what they were planning to do with that girl—" his eyes darkened, and he stared morosely into his bowl—"I thought of Regina and I knew I could never allow her to remain behind. She was the reason God sent us to that place. And then we encountered the rainstorm and wondered if we would ever see this place again. . . ."

He paused to playfully stroke Regina's cheek, and she rolled her eyes and looked away. "Papa!"

Thomas laughed, then took a bite of mush and swallowed.

"All we must do now is give Opechancanough the shallop when he comes, if he comes at all. He may never find our village."

"The shallop?" Jocelyn's hand froze at her throat. "Thomas, you promised him the shallop?"

"Why not?" he said. Then a sudden, cold thought struck him. "Jocelyn, the storm did not take the shallop?"

"Yes," she whispered, sinking onto the bench across from him. "There is no shallop. What will you do with this war chief if he comes?"

Thomas's eyes filled with dread, but he would not answer her. Abruptly, he rose from the table and went out into the night, slamming the door behind him.

▾▲▾▲▾ For seven days Thomas prayed that Opechancanough would not find his way to Ocanahonan, but on the wind-whipped morning when he saw villagers scurrying through the clearing like birds before a cat, he knew the war chief had come for his prize.

With the Indian girl safely hidden away, Thomas slipped alone out of his church to face the formidable Opechancanough. Chogan surprised Thomas by smoothly stepping out of the shadows. Had he known the war chief was coming? But there was no time for conjecture.

Opechancanough had not come alone. With him were at least thirty fiercely painted warriors armed with battle clubs, and Thomas suspected that probably at least that many were hiding in the woods around the village.

Thomas and Chogan stepped forward to meet the chief, and the bustle of the village stilled. Shutters were silently and discreetly closed, the laughter of children abruptly ceased, and women hid themselves behind closed and barred doors.

Opechancanough made a speech, and Chogan listened intently, then turned to Thomas. "He is impressed by the size and strength of your village and compliments you for your bravery. He says if you will point him to this large boat, he and his men will take it now."

"Tell him I do not have the boat," Thomas said, his arms thrust behind his back. "The storm destroyed it."

Chogan translated, and the war chief nodded in mute acceptance, then proclaimed another declaration.

"Opechancanough says he will choose his prisoner, then," Chogan translated, drawing himself up to his full height. He wrapped his fur mantle closer around him. "I will go, Reverend. It was my idea to offer the boat."

"No, tell him I am his prisoner," Thomas said, stepping forward. He walked to within five feet of the chief, then abruptly thrust his hands out in front of him, ready to be bound.

▼▲▼▲▼ From inside their house, Jocelyn and Regina watched the scene in silent horror. Thomas had not told them what would happen if the savage chief did not receive the promised boat, but it was all too clear by Thomas's action what he intended.

"Father God, help us," Jocelyn breathed, watching Thomas stand unarmed before the savage chief.

A sudden sound distracted her, and before Jocelyn could move, Regina had flung open the door. "Papa!" she cried, the sound tearing Jocelyn's heart.

Regina skimmed lightly over the sand, then threw her arms around her father's waist and fell to her knees. "Don't do this. Don't let him take you! I won't let you go!"

Jocelyn reflexively feel to her knees in the doorway. "Please, God, no . . . ," she cried, her eyes glued to the appalling sight before her.

▼▲▼▲▼ Opechancanough had entered the village warily, awed by the strong palisade and the strange tall buildings. But he had not been impressed by the casual atmosphere of the few people he had startled with his presence, nor was he pleased when the tall man in black thrust his arms out in a gesture of surrender. No warrior surrendered willingly. This man would die a coward's death, meekly accepting his torture. It was not a fair trade.

His musings were interrupted by a heart-stopping scream and the sight of a young woman who rushed forward to cling to the dark, unsmiling man. Opechancanough's eyes narrowed in interest. The girl had shown more bravery than the man and was a suitable trade for the captive girl.

Opechancanough gestured toward the sobbing blue-eyed girl and spoke to the Indian who served as interpreter, "I will take her."

▼▲▼▲▼ "What's he saying?" Thomas asked, trying unsuccessfully to pry Regina from his ribs. "What's he saying, Chogan?"

Chogan's dark eyes filled with compassion as he turned to Thomas. "He will take your daughter. A girl for a girl. It is an even trade."

"No!" Thomas protested, pushing Regina away with all the force his arms could muster. She flew to the ground, crying, and Thomas stalked forward until he was within an inch of the warrior's face. "You will take me!" he said, thumping his chest and roaring as though the savage were deaf. "You cannot have her! Take me. *My* life is forfeit!"

Opechancanough showed no response, but gestured abruptly. Two of his warriors moved forward and lifted Regina from the ground.

"No!" Thomas shouted, running to his daughter's side. He made an effort to dislodge one of the warriors' arms, and without hesitation the warrior drew back his club and brought it down on Thomas's skull.

He spun and fell in the sand. Dazed with pain, he tried to rise, but the earth heaved beneath him and sounds echoed crazily in his head: Regina screaming, Chogan whispering earnestly, Jocelyn wailing in the distance. Warm blood trickled from his ear, and Thomas wearily swiped at it as he struggled unsuccessfully to rise to his feet.

Another voice protested fiercely, and through his cloud of pain Thomas saw William Wythers spill from the doorway of his uncle's house and run toward the savages. He did not get far, though, because a group of village men sprang forward and held him tight. They carried him, kicking and screaming, back inside his uncle's house.

"Chogan!" Thomas cried, crawling through the sand on his hands and knees. "You must convince them. Have them take me, not my little girl. They can have me, but they must not touch her."

Chogan did not move, and, apparently satisfied that no others would be foolish enough to charge him, Opechancanough nodded and led his warriors out of the village as Regina's cries echoed among the barren treetops.

"*Why, God, why?*" Thomas wailed, sprawled in the dust.

Looking down, Chogan's eyes were wet with compassion. "Have you not said," he asked gravely, "that all will be as God wills?"

Gilda

When I shall bring thee down
With them that descend into the pit,
With the people of old time . . .
I shall set glory in the land of the living.

Ezekiel 26:20

A group of men brought Thomas into the house. Doctor Jones examined the gash across Thomas's scalp and pronounced that it was not serious, but that Thomas should go to bed. Beyond pain, Jocelyn watched the tableau unfold before her as she sat wordlessly by the fire in a devouring gulf of despair. She felt as though a section of her body had been torn away as Hurit, Chogan, and Agnes Wood wiped their eyes and touched her shoulder and murmured comforting words that never reached Jocelyn's soul.

Her baby lay in the hands of brutal savages, and she was powerless to help. Where was God when Opechancanough took Regina? Why had her heavenly Father led Thomas from the village to exchange their daughter's life for a savage's?

When the outsiders had gone, Jocelyn looked at her husband. After fifteen years of loving him in silence, loneliness had carved a hollow inside her soul, and now she crawled inside it, feeling no love, no pity or compassion for Thomas. He lay in the bed, racked by sobs, and she wanted nothing more than to tell him to go to the devil. Such a spiritual giant! If he had been content with life in the village, he would not have felt compelled to go out and save the entire wilderness from damnation. In his efforts, he had brought a demon of perdition to them all, for now Opechancanough knew the location of the town, he knew its strengths and weaknesses. . . .

A rap sounded at the door, and Jocelyn automatically rose to answer it. Every muscle of her body ached under the heavy load of grief she bore. But she bore it silently, unlike Thomas, who sobbed over losing the daughter he had never wanted in the first place.

Agnes Wood stood outside, her face lit by a sliver of December moon. "Miss Jocelyn, I thought I ought to tell you," she said, glancing furtively about her in the darkness.

"What is it, Agnes?" Jocelyn asked.

"It's William Wythers. His uncle knew William would go plumb crazy about Miss Regina, so they tied the boy's hands and put him in the attic to sleep. But it appears he got loose and busted through the roof. Anyway, they're afraid he's gone after those savages, Miss Jocelyn." She paused to blow her nose into a handkerchief. "I thought you ought to know."

"Thank you, Agnes," Jocelyn said and felt the corners of her mouth lift in a habitual smile. By all that was holy, how could she smile when a rock had fallen through her heart? She closed the door and stared at her sobbing husband.

At least William Wythers loved Regina enough to risk his life to find her.

▾▲▾▲▾ Two days passed with no word from William or Regina. Thomas and Chogan had organized a search party the day after Regina's abduction, but the trail left by Opechancanough's warriors did not proceed in the direction of his village. After a while, Chogan and his scouts lost the trail and led Thomas home.

Jocelyn had never seen her husband so helpless. He did not read his Bible, kneel in prayer, or go to the church to fuss and fume. Instead, he sat alone in the house with the shutters closed and pondered thoughts that he would not share.

On the third day, Jocelyn came home from the storehouse and threw open a window.

"Close the shutters, please," Thomas said, his voice low and quiet in the room. He lay on the bed, fully dressed, his hands folded on his chest like a corpse laid out and ready for burial.

"No," Jocelyn said, gritting her teeth as she went about her work. "You talk of faith, Thomas. Now it's time to practice it."

"I have lost my daughter. Have you no respect?"

"I have lost my daughter, too!" Jocelyn whirled around and sat on the bed, leaning over him so he could not move away. "Think you that I do not know what grief is? Think again, Thomas."

"I was ready to go with them," Thomas replied dully. "Why didn't they take me?"

"You *wanted* to go with them," Jocelyn answered, lowering her head until her nose was a scant inch from his. "You've been trying to kill yourself ever since we landed here. In hunting parties, search parties, on expeditions. 'Take me, God. I'm not happy here.' Isn't that what you've been saying for these many years?"

He did not answer, and Jocelyn shook her head. "How thick-headed can you be, Reverend? God doesn't want you! He wants *us* to have you, but you won't let your wife love you; you fought the love of your daughter for years; even the church people and the Indians must measure up to your inviolate standards before you will accept them. Well, you placed yourself on the altar one time too many, Thomas, and God threw you back. It's no sacrifice to give what you don't want yourself."

He seemed to cower before her words, and Jocelyn took a deep breath to calm herself. "You may not care for yourself, Thomas, but I once did," she whispered, sitting upright. "For years I've wanted you to be a husband and father, but you kept yourself from me. You wanted to sacrifice something for God. Well, now you've done it. You've lost your beloved daughter, and I hope God thanks you mightily for it."

His head bowed as her words poured over him, and when she had finished, she heard his broken sobs again. Frustrated beyond tears, she climbed into Regina's attic room and curled up in her daughter's bed, pulling the tattered blanket over her as if it could protect her from the overwhelming loneliness of their house.

▼▲▼▲▼ Rowtag led a handful of warriors silently through the forest, following the movements of Opechancanough's men easily. It was as he suspected. Opechancanough did not intend to carry the captive English girl back to his own village, but moved instead toward the town of the great chief Powhatan, his brother.

As elusive as shadows in the forest, the warriors dogged the enemy party as Rowtag considered his strategy. He knew that Chogan had taken the minister on a purposely futile hunt for the trail. The man of God was weak and frightened, and would prove to be a liability should a battle arise. But William Wythers, who had burst out of the village in a blaze of insane fury, had found Rowtag's party. The Indian had tried to convince the young man to return home and wait, but William had refused. In an effort to save time and the girl's life, Rowtag had reluctantly allowed him to accompany his scouts.

On the trail, Rowtag stopped abruptly and his men froze behind him. In the distance, he could see that Opechancanough's party had circled around a temporary camp, probably of hunters from Powhatan's village. They would feast together, then light a campfire and relax as evening wore on.

Rowtag turned to his men and motioned for them to get down. Catching a glimpse of the impassioned fury in young William's eyes, Rowtag shook his head. "We must wait until dark," he said firmly.

Clutching their spears, Rowtag and his scouts crawled forward on their bellies until they lay just outside the enemy camp. Three temporary structures had been set up at the north end of the circle, but most of the warriors sat around the fire smoking and eating in pleasant relaxation. Five or six women had been present when Opechancanough first arrived, but they had disappeared into one of the huts. Rowtag could not see the English girl.

Someone pulled on the sleeve of his garment, and Rowtag jerked around, his hand on his dagger. "Please," William

Wythers begged, desperation shining in his brown eyes. "Can you see Regina? Why can't we go in there and get her?"

"We are six," Rowtag whispered, turning to stare again at the camp. "They are sixty. Are you ready to die?" William did not answer, and when Rowtag turned again, the boy had crept back to his hiding place.

The ground grew cold underneath Rowtag's belly as the sun sank lower in the west, but at sunset the women appeared in the circle, leading the English girl by leather straps wound around her wrists. Regina's long brown hair had been plaited in the Indian fashion, and her face and arms had been painted in bright strokes of yellow and blue.

Rowtag drew in his breath. This was no ceremony of torture.

The women twittered nervously as the English girl blinked in fear, then a tall brave stepped from another hut across the circle. His arms were folded across his chest, his hair long and free in the wind, and despite the cold of December, he wore only a breechcloth and leather boots. Rowtag raised an eyebrow when he recognized the brave: Kitchi, son of the mighty chief Powhatan.

Opechancanough stood between the girl and the young man, and uttered a few words. The braves in the circle whooped in glee, the women clapped their hands, and Opechancanough took the leather thongs that streamed from the girl's wrists and gravely handed them to Powhatan's son. Nodding severely, Kitchi led the girl into his hut.

Rowtag bowed his head. It was a marriage, of sorts. If Kitchi found the girl pleasing, he would accept her as his wife.

Apparently he was not the only observer who understood the significance of the events in the circle, for suddenly William Wythers burst forth from his hiding place in the brush and charged the camp, screaming at the top of his lungs.

Alarmed, Rowtag gave the signal for his men to retreat. Opechancanough's braves would undoubtedly search the area, and if they were found, all would be dead by morning.

▼▲▼▲▼ Rowtag allowed five hours to pass, then returned to his place outside the circle. The leaves and limbs where he had lain had been disturbed, but apparently Opechancanough's men had given up the search for intruders and returned to the warmth of their campfire. In the fire-tinted darkness Rowtag could see William Wythers tied to a stake, his face red with blood. Rowtag's lips thinned. He could not save the boy from the tortures that awaited him, so he prayed William's sacrifice would not be in vain.

His gaze slid to the hut where the girl had disappeared and waited. After a space of time, the warrior Kitchi appeared, a relaxed smile on his face. He approached his warriors who sat around the fire, and they shared a laugh. Then one of the braves used a shell to scoop a burning coal from the fire pit and solemnly offered it to Kitchi.

Rowtag looked away; the torture was to begin in earnest now. The Powhatan clan had devised many methods of punishing their enemies, and the warriors would be busy in their devious activity at least till morning or until the boy died. But as long as they were occupied, the girl could be spirited away.

Rowtag motioned for his men to watch carefully as he slipped to the back of Kitchi's hut.

▼▲▼▲▼ Rowtag moved soundlessly toward the enemy camp. When he had reached the back of Kitchi's hut, he lifted the grass mat that covered the framework of timber. Regina sat inside, her eyes wide, her face smudged with paint and dirt. She made no sign of recognition when she saw Rowtag, nor did she move when he urgently motioned to her.

Outside the hut, William Wythers shrieked in pain, and Regina opened her mouth in a silent scream and covered her ears. As softly as a shadow, Rowtag crept in, grabbed the girl's bound wrists, and dragged her out through the narrow opening at the back of the hut.

▼▲▼▲▼ A knock woke Jocelyn in the darkness of night, and she rose to answer the door as her brain swirled in a vague half-sleep. Chogan and Rowtag stood outside the house, and Rowtag carried Regina in his arms, dazed and painted, but alive!

"O Father God, thank you," Jocelyn whispered, opening her arms to her daughter.

From the bed where he slept, Thomas rose and stumbled toward them like a drunken man. "Regina?" he mumbled, reaching for her. "Regina!"

Chogan nodded soberly. "Let her tell you what has happened," he said; then Jocelyn left the warriors in the dark as she turned to help Regina into the house.

The girl's teeth were chattering, but whether from fear or the cold Jocelyn could not tell. She slipped her own tattered blanket about Regina's shoulders and helped her daughter sit on the edge of the bed. "Are you all right?" Jocelyn asked, running her hands over Regina's arms and legs.

"Yes," Regina whispered, clutching the blanket about her. "But William—"

"Don't speak of it," Thomas whispered, slipping his arms around his daughter's shoulders. He comforted her while Regina cried, then, as the sun rose in the east, Thomas helped his daughter upstairs to her room and tucked her into bed.

At the first light of dawn, Jocelyn left Regina sleeping and went to Audrey's house. Rowtag, his face lined with exhaustion but otherwise expressionless, opened the door and bade her enter. After Audrey had served Jocelyn a steaming drink, Rowtag sat on a grass mat by the fire and asked if Regina had spoken.

Jocelyn shook her head. "Thomas wanted her to rest," she explained. "But you must tell me what you know, Rowtag."

Without embellishment or theatrics, Rowtag then told such a story of horror that Jocelyn wanted to cover her ears and scream for him to stop. But she didn't. She just sat woodenly until Rowtag had told the entire tale. When he had finished, Jocelyn stared at him in horror.

"A bride for Powhatan's son?" she whispered, clutching her shawl about her. "My Regina?"

"At least she did not have to face a gauntlet," Rowtag said. "And Powhatan's son, Kitchi, is a brave warrior."

A distant bell rang in Jocelyn's memory. *Kitchi.* Where had she heard that name? Long ago, in the woods, a young boy had thumped himself on the chest and called himself by that name. . . .

"Praise the Lord that you have your daughter home again," Audrey said, smiling. She sat beside Rowtag and draped an arm over his broad shoulder. "Surely God has worked in this."

"Yes," Jocelyn whispered, standing to her feet. She thanked Rowtag for his bravery in returning Regina, then went home to tell Thomas what she had learned.

▾▴▾▴ "She was given to this . . . Kitchi . . . as a bride," Jocelyn explained as Thomas sat at the table. His face had tightened into a mask of rage, and she feared he would explode at any minute.

"It is no matter. She is home now," Thomas said, his hand clenching into a fist.

"But—" Jocelyn shuddered and put her hand over her eyes, unwilling to think of her virgin daughter in the hands of a savage. "Thomas, what if she bears a child?"

"She will not," Thomas said abruptly. "They were together only once—"

"Think again, Thomas, for Regina is the result of one night," Jocelyn whispered fiercely. "And what if this savage comes back for her?"

"He does not know where she is," Thomas said, staring at the ashes of the fire. "We will hide her for as long as we must. She can remain in her room. We must keep the news of her return even from the others, so no wayward rumor can reach Powhatan—"

"But what will we say of William?" Jocelyn asked, leaning her head on her hand. "We have to tell his folks what happened. We cannot let them hope he will come home. . . ."

Thomas's eyes hardened. "Would you tell them how he died? How he was tortured? It is evil enough that our Regina witnessed the sight of the heathen devils' work—"

"But William was so brave, bursting into the camp to save her! Surely we should tell his aunt and uncle that he gave his life—"

"We will not speak of William Wythers, or of Powhatan, or his son," Thomas cut her off firmly. "We will pretend this has never happened. Regina will forget. She will marry another, in time. God's will must be done."

Jocelyn stared at him, frowning, and knew that he did not perceive the irony of his words. Yesterday he would not consider that Regina's abduction might be part of God's will, but today God's will had been restored. Did God's will not include both peace and suffering?

She rose and left him at the fire while she went upstairs to check on their sleeping daughter.

▼▲▼▲▼ Jocelyn and Thomas did not need to worry about hiding Regina. She slept through the day of her homecoming, never stirring, and when she awakened the next morning, she stared blankly at Jocelyn and did not speak; neither did she make any effort to climb down from the attic.

Audrey's eyes widened in horror when Jocelyn visited and confided in her. "I'll be wantin' to help you, of course," she said, reaching for Jocelyn's hand across the table in Audrey's kitchen. "If there's anything I can do—"

"You will soon have more than enough to worry about," Jocelyn said, pointing delicately to Audrey's thickening waistline, "since you are with child."

Audrey blushed prettily. "Still, if I can come and talk to Regina, she may rouse herself. And in time, we can bring her down and take her about the village."

Jocelyn nodded her thanks. "We will see," she said simply, fighting back tears of helplessness. "And we will continue to pray."

▼▲▼▲▼ Despite the prayers and hopes of her parents, Regina's dreamlike state continued for weeks. One spring day Jocelyn looked at her daughter's body and realized that her worst fear had come to pass: Regina would give birth to a grandchild of the savage chief Powhatan.

Thomas refused to believe Jocelyn at first, but six months after the abduction he had to admit that his daughter's body carried a child. And on a hot September morning when the baby was born to a mother who neither spoke nor screamed nor cried, Jocelyn caught the infant in her hands and noted that the baby girl had hair as stiff and black as a raven's wings and skin the color of raw honey. "I think we'll call her Gilda, for she has such lovely golden skin," Jocelyn said, wiping the baby clean. "What do you think, Regina? Do you like the name?"

Regina's wide eyes seemed not to have noticed that a living being had come from her womb. Jocelyn wrapped the baby in clean cloths and carried her downstairs, placing her in the same trunk that had held Regina as an infant. Thomas sat at the board with his books, watching the scene with undisguised aversion in his eyes. Jocelyn called a warning as she climbed the attic stairs. "Don't touch my baby," she said, carefully lifting her skirts as she climbed. "Regina's in no condition to raise the child. If you don't want her, Thomas, the baby will be mine alone."

Regina's eyes were mirror brilliant as Jocelyn knelt by her side. "Let me cool your forehead," Jocelyn said, wringing a cloth in a basin of water. But the clammy skin under her ministering hand was cool, and Jocelyn uttered an indrawn gasp when she saw that Regina's lips were blue. A scream clawed in her throat as she pressed her head to Regina's chest and listened vainly for a heartbeat.

As tears of sorrow fell, Jocelyn sank to the floor and buried her face in the mattress upon which her only child lay.

That afternoon, while Thomas wept and prayed over the body of their daughter, Jocelyn wrapped the baby in a blanket and left the house. She walked quickly, avoiding the glances of curious passersby, and rapped upon the door of the house where Audrey lived with Rowtag, Fallon, and her newborn son.

Audrey's cheerful smile flattened when she saw the seriousness in Jocelyn's face, and she gasped at the sight of the bundle in her arms. A mewling wail rose from the baby, and Audrey understood immediately why Jocelyn had brought her.

"She needs a nurse," Jocelyn said simply, handing the child to Audrey. "Since your own Noshi is still at the breast . . ."

"Certainly, I'll be happy to nurse this little one as well," Audrey said, taking the baby as Jocelyn followed her inside the house. Audrey's son, a chubby, dark-haired infant with pale green eyes, lay in a cradle by the fire while nine-year-old Fallon played with wooden toys on the floor.

Audrey said nothing as she unfastened her bodice, but when the baby had begun to suckle, she looked up at Jocelyn. "How fares Regina?"

Dry-eyed, Jocelyn lifted her head. "Regina is dead."

Audrey closed her eyes and pressed the baby closer to her. Jocelyn studied Fallon and Noshi and considered that her own family had become as racially mixed as Audrey's. Though Thomas hated intermarriage, he was now the grandfather of a black-haired, blue-eyed girl who had direct ties to the most powerful chieftain in the land.

"Her name is Gilda," Jocelyn offered, breaking the silence. "I told Regina so, at the end."

"'Tis a fitting name," Audrey whispered, running her finger over the baby's delicate brow. "And a beautiful baby."

"Yes." Jocelyn stood to her feet. "I must return to Thomas, but mark me, Audrey, the baby will be mine."

"Surely." Audrey shifted the tiny mewling bundle to her other arm. "I'll bring her to you when she's fed."

"No—keep her tonight, and maybe tomorrow, until after we bury Regina." Jocelyn turned toward the door. "And Audrey," she called, not looking back.

"Yes?"

"Thank you."

Jocelyn pulled the door open and stepped out into the September sunlight.

▼▲▼▲▼ Jocelyn refused to go to the funeral service, and Thomas accepted her wishes without comment. Afterward, when the confused colonists had dispersed from the grassy field where the dead were buried, she slipped from the house and made her way to the graveyard in silence. A fresh mound of earth lay among the graves, and Jocelyn knelt to brush the crumbled soil with her fingers.

Regina lay under her hand. Flesh of her flesh, the miraculous result of a lovely mingling of her body with Thomas's. Regina had inherited Thomas's spirit, Jocelyn's hair, Thomas's dark skin, Jocelyn's laugh, and Thomas's hands. But the girl who had embodied their union breathed no more, and the mental and spiritual fusion that had given her life had long since disappeared.

Jocelyn stood and drew her shawl closer about her as a cool breeze caressed her cheek. Another daughter would inhabit their house in the years to come, born of the union between Jocelyn and Thomas and the barbaric world in which they had hoped to make a difference.

"Our Gilda will certainly fare better than we," she whispered, suddenly feeling much older than her thirty-four years. "For we,

Father God, are yet aliens in the untamed world outside our palisade. But children like Noshi and Gilda may bridge the sea of difference that lies between us and the savages."

Finding comfort in that thought, Jocelyn murmured one last farewell to her daughter and began the long walk home.

For more than thirteen years Sir Walter Raleigh received impassioned letters from John White, begging that another ship be sent to search for the planters in Virginia. But Raleigh's fortunes as well as his favor in the eyes of Queen Elizabeth had dwindled considerably. He had invested heavily in the exploration of Guiana and Cadiz, and most of his investment had disappeared.

Nevertheless, in the early months of 1603, Raleigh was able to dispatch two ships to explore the vicinity of Chesapeake Bay in hopes that the lost colony of planters might be found. But when Elizabeth breathed her last and James of Scotland assumed the English throne, Raleigh, who had never wooed James's favor, was arrested and charged with treason.

At the end of September, Raleigh sat in his cell in the king's Tower of London and heard a report from Henry Shute, a sailor who had been aboard the fifty-ton ship the *Elizabeth*. Under the command of Bartholomew Gilbert, the vessel had failed to find the entrance to Chesapeake Bay. Shute reported that the captain and many of the crew had gone ashore north of the bay and stumbled upon an Indian war party.

"We found 'em the next day," Shute said, a grayish pallor under his skin as he told the tale. "All of 'em dead, sir, not a one left alive. Me and the boys ran for the ship, and the eleven of us brought her home to the Thames."

Raleigh thanked the man for coming and nodded silently as Shute wished him well. The jailer led his visitor away, and Raleigh pondered a rumor he had heard earlier. Samuel Mace, the captain of the second ship, had apparently kidnapped Indians from the Virginian shore before his return to England, for the

Tower buzzed with the story of a Thames wherry towing an Indian canoe and savages to the landing place leading to Lord Cecil's house in the Strand. It was said that the savages willingly gave demonstrations in canoe handling for the gentlemen and the king's court in Hampshire.

Raleigh rubbed his hand over his beard and picked up a pen. He had reached the end of his abilities. As a prisoner condemned to die, there was nothing else he could do for John White except report that his two ships had brought back much news of Indians, but no news of the colonists.

In a vast Indian camp northwest of the river Chowan, the great chief Powhatan sat in council with the elders of his tribe. The fierce chief had a lean face, pitted and scarred from his youth, with thick eyebrows and carbon black eyes that never failed to awe his followers. His sinewy arms and chest had been tattooed with emblems signifying his bravery and his office, and he wore his long black hair loosely tied at his neck.

For the last twenty summers Powhatan had been building his authority in the lands along the two mighty rivers that flowed to the great sea, and tribe after tribe had either submitted to his power or been massacred. To date only the Chickahominy, a tribe on the north bank of the southern river, had successfully resisted paying him tribute, and he had heard rumors that the Chickahominy tribe had sent certain of its clans to trade with a group of clothed people who lived on the bank of the river Chowan and spoke in a strange tongue. He had also heard disturbing reports that clothed people in a large ship had taken several of his warriors aboard their boat and sailed away across the sea.

"Clothed people," Powhatan said, speaking to the group of werowances who led his subordinate tribes. "What have they to do with us?"

Matchitehew, Powhatan's chief priest, inhaled deeply on his pipe and offered his thoughts: "A prophecy has come to us, great Powhatan, in dreams. From the mouth of the Chesapeake waters a nation will arise which will give end to your empire. We have dreamed this three nights in succession. A great bear will rise from the sea to devour Powhatan and his people."

The chief stiffened. Into the flames of the fire before them, Matchitehew threw a powder that produced red smoke. Then the aged priest drew deeply on his pipe and passed it to Powhatan.

The chief inhaled and kept his eyes thoughtfully on the fire.

In the town of Ocanahonan, Jocelyn relished her new role as mother. At Regina's birth she had subdued her maternal instincts under Thomas's stony disapproval, but now that Thomas had completely shut himself away, Jocelyn determined to love Regina's baby so fiercely that the girl would not miss the love of a father.

She knew she had incurred the wrath not only of her husband but of certain devout men and women in the colony who thought it unsuitable for a minister's wife to raise the illegitimate half-breed daughter of a savage. One afternoon Beth Glane and Rose Payne made a point of stopping Jocelyn at the well and pointedly suggested that Jocelyn give the baby to one of the Indian women to raise.

"We know it grieves the minister to have such an emblem of sin in his house," Beth said, her eyes narrowing in pious concern. She held her arms out for Gilda. "It is affecting his ministry, which affects the entire town."

"If you love God and if you love your husband," Rose inserted, "you'll want to set things to right. So if you will just give the child to us—"

"Good ladies," Jocelyn said, turning so that Gilda lay out of the women's reach, "I decided long ago that I must live to please God, without regard to whether my life pleases you or my husband or the town. And since God has brought this child into my life, ladies, until he tells me to surrender this child, you must forgive me if I continue to raise her myself."

She painted on a smile and walked away, but Beth's harsh

parting words gave her pause. "Can you say that you are proud of that child of sin?"

Jocelyn thought a moment, then turned to face the pair of women. "I'm not proud of her conception or the sorrow we bore the day she came into the world," she said, her eyes misting despite her resolve. "But I accept what falls into my life, provided it comes at the hand of God. And of this beautiful creation of God's, yes, ladies, I am proud."

Turning on her heel, Jocelyn left them in the dust and took Gilda home, muttering as she went, "Blessed are the meek, for they shall inherit the earth."

▼▲▼▲▼ As months passed, Gilda grew to be a favorite in the village. She and Noshi seemed to symbolize the best of the English and Indian cultures, and Jocelyn and Audrey often took Fallon and the babies down to the river to play. Like the Indian mothers, they indulged the children whenever possible, but began training them at age three for life in the wilderness. In the spring of 1606, Rowtag proudly gave Noshi his first bow and arrow, and Jocelyn bit her lip and said nothing while Rowtag took a long bone needle and tattooed the arms of both his sons with the mark of the Mangoak tribe.

Rowtag took a firm hand in the raising of his children, and since Thomas steadfastly refused to acknowledge Gilda's presence, Rowtag stepped in as a substitute father for her. Jocelyn and Audrey did not object when he bade the children to run from one end of the village to the other with a mouthful of water they were forbidden to swallow. Jocelyn did protest once, albeit feebly, when Rowtag took Fallon, Noshi, and Gilda to the river on a chilly spring morning and bade the children swim to the other side and back, but the warrior merely shrugged and said that children must be strong and unafraid if they were to survive in the forest.

To illustrate the importance of bearing pain without complaint, one afternoon Rowtag bade the children watch while he stood with crossed arms for the space of an hour upon a bed of stinging ants. As impassive and solid as stone, he neither moved nor flinched as the insects covered his legs and trunk.

What would the people of London say if they saw this? Jocelyn wondered, watching from the window of her house. *How could I make them understand? The Virginian wilderness will demand more than iron guns and mighty ships if we are to survive here. It will demand strength of heart, body, and—*

Her eyes fell upon her husband, who stopped to upbraid the silent Rowtag for indulging in yet another heathen practice.

—strength of spirit.

▼▲▼▲▼ Miles away, Powhatan nodded a greeting to his brother, Opechancanough, who followed a string of captives into the village. Forced to run the gauntlet, the bruised and bloodied captives bolted haphazardly from one side of the camp to the other until Powhatan's warriors rounded them up. As women and children sang songs of victory, the captives were tied to stakes in the center of the camp while the serious art of torture began.

Powhatan pulled Opechancanough from the sight and led him into his hut. Grunting, the great chief seated himself upon a mat and took up his pipe. Inhaling deeply, he fanned the smoke into his face, then passed the pipe to his brother. Opechancanough inhaled as well, then released the smoke in a steady stream through his nose and mouth and waited for his brother to speak.

"Matchitehew dreamed again last night of the great bear from the sea," Powhatan said, taking the pipe from Opechancanough. He paused to inhale.

"Is the great chief worried about this bear?" Opechancanough asked, knowing full well that Powhatan had been enraged by the priest's persistent prophecy.

"I do not worry," the chief answered, passing the pipe again. "But I would be rid of this bear." He took a deep breath, inhaling the smoke in the hut, allowing the magic of the pipe to calm his fury. Closing his eyes, he spoke again to his brother. "What do you know of the clothed people?"

Opechancanough resisted the urge to smile. His great brother rarely asked his opinion, but Powhatan knew little of the clothed people, whereas Opechancanough had been to their village and brought one of their own women to Powhatan's son. It mattered little that the girl had run away, for one of the clothed men had remained behind in exchange for the life that was owed. The clothed man had survived the night of torture and died at sunrise.

"It is said that Ocanahonan, the City of Guater Ralie, is mighty," Opechancanough said, speaking slowly as if reluctant to part with such valuable knowledge. "Their village is rich in hard goods and stores. But their men are weak. One gave himself up to me freely, so I did not take him. The girl screamed like a baby. The one who came for her defied us to the end, though he did not sing a death song. We ate his heart to do him honor."

Powhatan rested his hands upon his knees. "I have posted warriors along the sands of the great sea to watch for the ships which bring the men with long guns. If they come near, we will destroy the clothed men at Ocanahonan."

Opechancanough nodded. "You have spoken well, but why not destroy them now?"

"There is time," Powhatan answered, enjoying his pipe. "I will know when the time has come."

▼▲▼▲▼ The sky darkened with restless thunderclouds one hot afternoon in early April 1607, and Jocelyn left the cornfields where she had been planting and made her way to the river. The village canoes lay neatly upturned on the bank. Three men who were busy stretching bark across a wooden frame greeted her politely as she splashed her arms and face with the cool river water. She was about to turn for the village when she spied a trio of familiar childish bodies farther down the bank.

"Fallon, Noshi, and Gilda!" she called, half-scolding. "How did you get out here? I thought we told you not to go past the guard at the gate!"

"We didn't," Gilda answered, her thumb in her mouth. Wordlessly, she pointed to a section of the palisade near the water's edge, and Jocelyn could see that the ground had eroded underneath the wall. "Ah, I see a hole just big enough for three children," Jocelyn said, teasing. "But did you think we would not see the mud on your arms and faces?"

Gilda responded to her mother's gentle scolding by throwing her filthy arms around Jocelyn's neck, and Jocelyn returned the muddy hug without complaint. Fallon and Noshi stood nearby, their faces dark with guilt until Jocelyn held her arms open to them, too, and Noshi giggled and joined in her embrace. Thirteen-year-old Fallon hung back, smiling shyly.

After a moment, the young children squirmed away and went about their playing. "What are you building?" Jocelyn asked, sitting nearby on the sand. She slipped out of her moccasins and lowered her feet into the water. Gilda pointed a stubby finger to a mud house she'd built while four-year-old Noshi held up a tiny canoe he had fashioned from bark sewn with pine needles.

"You truly have the gift of your father," Jocelyn exclaimed, eying the boat. "'Tis excellent work, Noshi."

"And I," Fallon said, moving timidly toward Jocelyn. "Have I the gift of my father, Mistress Colman?"

Jocelyn felt her heart break as she looked at the copper-haired boy. "You are most fortunate," she whispered, reaching out for him. He took her hand and sat next to her, and Jocelyn leaned to whisper in his ear. "You are blessed because your first father, Roger Bailie, gave you life. He was a good man and well respected. And now you have Rowtag, a father to teach you the things you must know to be a man. And through it all, you have the love of your heavenly Father, who will watch over and protect you always."

"Always?" he said, looking up to her with bright eyes.

"You will never be out of his hand," she whispered, giving him a hug. "You and Noshi and Gilda. You are much loved."

Satisfied, Fallon ran to join Noshi at the water's edge. A ray of sunlight broke through the overcast sky and caused the ring on Jocelyn's finger to gleam. Absently, she twirled the ring around her finger, and Gilda splashed through the muddy water and picked up Jocelyn's hand.

"What a pretty ring, Mama," she said, pulling Jocelyn's palm so close to her face that her eyes crossed. "Can I wear it?"

"My ring?" Jocelyn answered, laughing. "I think not, love. It belonged to my mother and will be Regina's—"

Her words caught in her throat. Often it was difficult to believe that Regina was no longer with them.

Gilda gave her a dimpled smile. "Please, can I wear it?"

Jocelyn paused only a moment. Why not let the child have it? It was rightfully hers, after all. "Here, dear one," she said, slipping the ring from her wet finger. "'Tis too big for you, but maybe we can find another way for you to wear it." She took a string of dried bear gut from the leather pouch at her waist and threaded it through the ring, then knotted it and slipped it over Gilda's head. "It is yours now. Promise me you'll never lose it."

"I promise," Gilda replied solemnly, then in a trice she turned to follow Noshi, who was chasing minnows in the waters farther downstream.

"*Fortiter, fideliter, feliciter,*" Jocelyn murmured, recalling the ring's inscription as she watched the children play. "Boldly, faithfully, successfully. Have I been bold, faithful, and successful here, Father God? With Gilda, yea. With Regina, I could have done better. But with Thomas . . . every day he is more of a stranger, Father, and my efforts to love and serve him have come to nothing. If there is anything you can yet do . . ."

She sighed. If love between them had been meant to be, it certainly would have blossomed long before this.

▼▲▼▲▼ Rowtag's hunting party returned to Ocanahonan the next week with ten deer, four wild hogs, and a captive Powhatan with a frightening story to tell. The young brave, little more than a child, had wandered away from his scouting party and panicked, rushing as mindlessly as a frightened animal into the midst of Rowtag's warriors.

"For five days he had been without meat," Rowtag explained to the council upon his return. "And when we shared our food, he opened his heart, and his tongue began to loose a tale you should all hear."

"What tale was this?" Thomas asked, a trace of amusement in his eyes.

Rowtag did not smile in return. "He says that Powhatan is collecting a war party to destroy this city. He awaits a sign. Then he will cover this forest. Like an avenging fire, he will wipe the citizens of Ocanahonan from the earth."

The minister frowned, and the other members of the council stirred uncomfortably. "How do we know this child speaks the truth?" John Sampson asked. "He is a Powhatan, and they are our enemy. If we take time to make weapons, we'll never get our crops planted. We can't hide in the palisade when the fields have to be tended. I think this savage chief is afraid of us, and he would like nothing better than for us to starve next winter and die as a result of our own cowardice."

"I believe the story," Thomas said, his eyes deadly serious. "The face of Opechancanough is hatred distilled to its essence. He is Powhatan's brother." His eyes met Rowtag's. "I believe the boy. What can we do to prepare?"

Rowtag closed his eyes. "We men must make weapons. The women must make ready. And every citizen of Ocanahonan must pray."

John Prat's hand slammed upon the table. "Sampson is right, I daresay. How can we risk our entire crop on the word of a frightened boy? You have been tricked, Rowtag, but we will not fall for this charade. Life must go on, and we will not risk a panic. Our children cannot fear to walk in the forest, our women must be able to go to the fields for planting, and we must continue to hunt as usual. We are the clothed people, and Powhatan fears us."

"Say nothing of this to the others," John Sampson warned, his eyes boring into Rowtag's. "For twenty years we have been unafraid, and we must continue as always."

Rowtag said nothing, but looked at the minister. In Thomas Colman's eyes he saw fear . . . and regret.

▼▲▼▲▼ Jocelyn stood at the fire when Thomas came home and stared in surprise when he ignored his usual ritual of greeting and fell onto the bench at the board. Without meeting her eyes, he told her everything Rowtag had said to the council.

"Did the other council members believe the boy's story?" she asked, not taking her eyes from the pot she stirred over the fire. There was no sense in upsetting the entire city if the boy was exaggerating.

"I believed him," Thomas answered. "We are doomed, Jocelyn. If Powhatan attacks, there is nothing we can do to defend ourselves against so many."

"Shhh, don't talk of it now," she said, tapping the spoon on the rim of the pot. "We'll eat first, then talk when Gilda is asleep."

The dinner was a quiet one for the adults, though Gilda babbled and crowed and told a never-ending story about the adventure she'd had in the woods with Fallon and Noshi. When the supper dishes had at last been put away, Jocelyn washed Gilda's grubby hands and face, rocked her for a while, then placed the girl in her little bed and turned to light the lamp. When the glow filled the room, she was startled by the mindlessly blank look upon Thomas's face.

"Thomas," she whispered, tucking Gilda's blanket under her chin, "if this incredible story is true, we will pray tonight for a miracle. Surely God would not have brought us here if we are all to die. Since the will of God brought us here, he will sustain us. There is nothing to fear—"

"God's *will?*" Thomas spat the words as if they were distasteful, and the blankness of his expression mutated into a look of intense hatred.

Jocelyn left Gilda and turned to face him. "Surely. Everything that happens comes to us through the hand of God."

"How, woman, can you say this is God's will? I could not tell the others the truth, but this is my fault and mine alone. God has nothing to do with it."

"Your fault?" A sharp pang of compassion pierced her heart. "Thomas, surely you can't blame yourself for this—"

"Have you forgotten, Jocelyn? Our daughter was the bride of Powhatan's son. He will bring his armies to bear upon us in retaliation for her escape."

"That was four years ago! And Powhatan did not know Regina found her way home. Even most of the villagers did not know she returned to us."

"Then God alone will bring this to pass." Thomas rested his head upon his hands as he sat at the board. "He will punish me yet again because I have borne bitterness in my heart against him for allowing Regina to die. God could have spared her. He could have taken the life of this half-breed child instead—"

Instinctively, Jocelyn moved to shelter Gilda from the torrent of hate in his words, and Thomas turned in his chair so suddenly that she jumped. "Do not fear for the child. I do not blame God for Gilda. The fate of our city was sealed on the day I stood before Opechancanough, and for that I blame myself."

"You must not." Jocelyn put her hand to her head; her temples had begun to pound. "Thomas, you cannot blame yourself. I saw you try to give yourself to that savage. It was not your fault that he chose Regina instead."

He slammed his hand on the table with such force that a stoneware platter jumped to the floor and shattered.

"It is all my fault!" he roared, standing. He clenched his fists as if he would pound an invisible foe. "How can I make you see? I've been telling you since the day we married that I am cursed! I cannot love. I should not have had a child! I knew something dreadful would happen, for the hand of God is intent upon my chastisement and correction. All that I love, everything that I place before God, is destroyed."

Stunned by the sound of honest desperation in his voice, Jocelyn stood in a paralysis of astonishment as Thomas lowered his head. "I loved you," he said, tears rolling down his sculpted face. "On the ship, I fell in love with your spirit, your intellect, and your beauty. I knew then that God would command me to marry you, because the most rigorous test in life I could endure would be to have you as my wife and yet not love you, not touch you. . . ."

"Why should God demand such restraint?" Jocelyn whispered, trembling at his confession. She took a hesitant step toward him. "Thomas, I wanted nothing more than for you to love me, but I thought you resisted me because you mourned for your first wife. I had hope that love would grow, but—"

Thomas raised his hands as if to shield himself from her words, then backed away to the wall behind him and slid to the floor. He drew his knees to his chest. "I loved you always," he said in a husky whisper, "but I dared to hold you in my arms only twice. The first time begat Regina, and I resisted loving her because I knew God would take her away. His harsh hand of judgment waited until I grew to love her, then waited longer until I relaxed. I grew overconfident in my work. I prided myself as a missionary. But God unmasked my vainglory when he took my daughter and made her a harlot to the savages I had thought to win."

"No, Thomas, you can't believe that," Jocelyn whispered. Her heart stirred with sympathy as she knelt on the ground beside him. The walls that had forever separated them were tumbling down, but why had he resisted so long and through so much pain?

Thomas covered his eyes with his hand. "Everything I touch, God destroys. I left my son, Robert, in England because he had come to fear and despise me. For twenty years I have prayed for him, but God has kept me in exile, unable to write a letter or send word. Before I left, I sent a letter inviting him to join me here in Virginia, but not a word has come from England . . . and in my innermost heart, I knew it would not."

"Surely your son does not hate you, Thomas," Jocelyn said, placing her hand upon his. "Why shouldn't he love you even though you are far away?"

"He cannot love me because I am guilty. I could not love you because I am guilty. Regina was taken—because God has not ceased to punish me."

"For what?" she asked, alarmed by the desperate note in his voice.

Thomas closed his eyes and leaned his head against the wall. "'For we are consumed by thine anger, and by thy wrath are we troubled,'" he quoted. "'Thou has set our iniquities before thee, our secret sins in the light of thy countenance.'"

"What do you mean, Thomas?" Would he never stop speaking in riddles?

He opened his eyes and looked at her, and his eyes shone with an honesty she'd never seen before. "My secret sin. God has punished me because I killed my first wife." The words slipped away like steam from a kettle, and he laughed, a broken, hollow sound that reverberated throughout the house. For a moment Jocelyn was certain his mind had snapped.

"It was in a fit of anger," he went on, his voice calm and quiet in the room. "My wife had put on a red dress, and I protested, knowing that certain folk of my parish would object to a clergyman's wife dressing in unsuitable silks and colors. I told her to change the dress, and she refused. I attempted to force her and we struggled."

The light vanished from his eyes, and his face stiffened with the horror of the memory. "I pushed her and she fell, hitting her head on a brick of the hearth. The sheriff said the death was an accident, but my son saw everything and told the story to my wife's sister, who came and took the boy away. Naturally, being the murderer of his mother, I did not protest."

"You are *not* a murderer!" Jocelyn said, taking his hand. The wounded look in his eyes eased somewhat, and Jocelyn remembered her father's belief that confession was good for the soul. She cast about for a new avenue of conversation. "Is that why you left England?"

He nodded slowly. "In part. In time, the people of my parish heard the rumors that I had killed my own wife, and though nothing was ever proved against me, I knew I was guilty. If a man is angry in his heart, he is guilty of murder."

Jocelyn made a weak sound of protest, but he shook his head and continued. "I knew that God had chastised me by taking my wife and son, and so I fled to America, booking passage on the *Lion*. I determined to get here any way I could." Icy anger edged his voice. "Like foolish Jonah running from God, I fled to Virginia and discovered that no ocean is too wide for God's wrath to cross."

"And the payment for your passage was marriage to me," Jocelyn said, lowering her eyes.

"Mark me, I didn't want to marry you," Thomas repeated, and the suddenly gentle expression in his eyes brought the color rushing into her cheeks. "I hoped that you'd refuse me, and I could be free of God and serve your uncle. I wanted to leave the church behind, for I was embittered toward God and all that had to do with him. But though I should never have asked, when you agreed to marry me, I had not the strength to protest. I knew if I didn't marry you, your uncle would give you to some other man, and I couldn't bear that thought. . . ."

Jocelyn wound her arms around his neck and pressed her lips to his hair. How wrong she had been! For twenty years she had lived and labored under the false assumption that he had no feeling for her while in truth, his love lay buried under guilt.

"Thomas," she said, cradling his head on her shoulder, "God forgave you long ago! The past is forgotten! And it is not too late for you to live. You have been bound, Thomas, not by God's wrath but by guilt, and the truth of God sets men free! You have struggled to live, think, and dress according to a harsh set of laws, but God would have us move and live and think in freedom."

"In freedom!" he protested, pulling away. "Without God's laws, sin will abound and ruin this place—"

"God's laws are love," Jocelyn corrected, holding him tight. "God is not chastising you; you are struggling under a self-imposed burden! You have labored so long and carried so much that freedom will feel strange to you—"

"Strange?" Thomas rolled his eyes in amused disbelief. "There is no freedom in the ministry, Jocelyn. Of all people, you should know this."

Jocelyn put her finger across his lips. "I have known total freedom, Thomas, except where you and your rules have constrained me. And your rules are useless, for there is nothing we can do to deserve God's grace. We can't be good enough, pray hard enough, or keep our lives clean enough. But God has set us free. We can clothe ourselves in his goodness, because he is good, not because we are."

"If only you were right," he whispered, his head falling against hers as he relaxed in her embrace. "To live just one day without fear of God's retribution—"

"There is no fear in love," she whispered. "Not in God's love, for it is perfect, and perfect love casts out fear. If you love God, Thomas, you do not need to fear your Father's hand."

His strong jaw worked as he searched for words. "But I am so . . . unworthy."

"What did Martin Luther preach?" she asked, lifting her head to look at him. "Salvation by grace, not by works. Luther himself said that no one can be good and do good unless God's grace first makes him good, and no one becomes good by works." He seemed to gobble up her words, hungry for truth. As he gave himself to her voice, Jocelyn felt her heart stirring as if from a long, deep sleep.

"No one," she whispered, "deserves grace. But in his sovereign mercy God has chosen to give great grace to imperfect, ill-deserving individuals like me, and Rowtag, and Audrey, and Regina, and Gilda." She rested her head against his and tightened her embrace around his shoulders. "His grace flows to you, Thomas, in spite of, and in greater measure than, your guilt."

A shuddering sob shook Thomas, and he clung to her and surrendered to the unrelenting love of his wife and the irresistible love of God.

▼▲▼▲▼ Two weeks later, on April twenty-fourth, an English expedition under the command of Captain Christopher Newport eased into the waters of the Chesapeake region. Newport's three ships, the *Susan Constant*, the *Godspeed*, and the *Discovery*, had been chartered by the Virginia Company a year earlier to establish a permanent English colony on Chesapeake Bay.

From the trees along the shores, Indian scouts spied the ships and sent runners racing to Powhatan.

After hearing the scouts' reports, Powhatan sent runners to the towns he controlled, and his allied villages began to prepare for war. The clothed people, Powhatan told his council, would bring guns of thunder, medicine stronger than any seen in the land. Within hours, a force of more than eight hundred warriors journeyed to Powhatan's village.

Proud to play a major role in the upcoming drama, the warriors wore body armor made of strong reeds. They made paints of fine clays mixed with bear grease and strung their bows and lashed sharpened arrowheads to fresh arrows. Others brandished heavy clubs of wood spiked with the antlers of deer or the teeth of animals.

Finally, as the warriors from far-flung villages poured into the camp, Powhatan's men hung magical feathers from their wooden shields and painted the surfaces. When each warrior was sure his shield was certain to inspire terror, he swathed it with a grass mat to keep the magical motif's power from leaking away.

The night before the war party was to depart, Powhatan stood in the center of his village before his men. His body, richly adorned with copper beads and brilliant strokes of red paint, gleamed from its coat of bear grease. He had shaved his head from forehead to crown, and the long hair that remained hung freely down his back so its power might be fully released. On the chief's right hand, the old priest stood ready to superintend the war party's relationship to the gods, and on Powhatan's left stood the younger conjuror, the white-eyed mystic who, though blind to the things of earth, could see things of the spirit. A small green-and-yellow snake had been pierced and attached to the conjuror's ear, and the reptile writhed and wrapped its tail around the blind man's neck as Powhatan raised his arms for silence.

"The time has come!" Powhatan cried, turning slowly to face the circle of people around him. "We will prove our hearts on the field of battle! Then shall the other nations say that the Powhatan have much courage. We are not afraid of the big guns of thunder. We are not afraid of the clothed people's strange medicine and strange god. We will approach like foxes, fight like lions, and disappear like birds. We shall show the great bear from the sea that we do not fear him and the clothed people have no place here!"

Fearsome and terrible in their battle paint, the warriors raised their clubs and let loose their war cries. Even the women and children of the village were caught up in the frenzy that followed. Drums began to beat in rhythm, and Powhatan raised his war club and danced around the post in the center of the village, striking it at will. One by one, other volunteers joined him, hitting the post with their weapons as they moved in and out of the circle, until the entire camp danced and screamed in exhilaration and anticipation of the victory to follow.

When the hysteria reached its peak, Powhatan broke off and led the warriors to a pile of leather pouches on the ground. He took a pouch, fastened it to his belt, and picked up his shield. Each man followed his example until a single line of warriors walked out of the camp, each man following in the footsteps of the man before him so that an enemy could not guess at the size of the war party.

Mumbling prayers to the gods of wind, rain, and fire, two young warriors lifted the pole on which hung the sacred medicine bundle. The bundle had to face toward the enemy at all times, could not touch the ground, and had to be hung at night between supports of forked sticks.

As the warriors filed out of the chief's village, the torches were extinguished and the singing silenced. Under cover of darkness the war party proceeded, each man carrying nothing but his weapon and his shield. A bow and quiver hung across each man's back, and at his waist hung a leather pouch of parched maize flour that had been pulverized and combined with dried berries and maple sugar. When mixed with water, a single handful could sustain a warrior for an entire day, and Powhatan and his party carried enough maize to last more than a week.

▼▲▼▲▼ Three days later, Powhatan and his war party spied the high wooden palisade around Ocanahonan, the village of the clothed men. Moving like shadows in the woods, Powhatan's warriors spread themselves around the camp, surrounding it on all sides. For most of the day they hid themselves in trees, in the brush, and along the riverbank to learn as much as possible about the enemy before striking.

What Powhatan saw did not impress him. The clothed people, most of whom were Indians, lived with little caution, moving easily in and out of their walled palisade with no apparent concern. They did not scan the treetops or listen for unusual sounds. When they walked through the woods, they tramped casually and made so much noise that Powhatan and his people did not worry about being heard themselves. One of the clothed men walking outside in the heat of the day passed so closely that Powhatan could have slit his throat with one swift slice of his stone dagger, but the chief restrained himself. He favored night assaults and dawn attacks, when the medicine of the gods was strongest.

Powhatan saw no sign of the long guns of which he had heard much. Two large iron guns, stouter than a man, sat poised on the riverbank, but vines had partially covered one, and the other was coated in a dull layer of orange rust.

▼▲▼▲▼ Audrey peered out the window of her house and saw Rowtag standing in the courtyard, his hands alert at his side and a troubled look upon his brow.

"Rowtag," she called, a teasing note in her voice. "Why stand you lonely out there? The children are playin' elsewhere. This be our time together . . . *alone.*"

Rowtag held a finger to his lips, then turned and seemed to study the trees. Audrey sighed and slipped out of her apron. If the mountain would not come to her, she would have to go to the mountain.

She crept out of the house, stopping the door with her palm so that it made no noise, and purposely planted her feet heel-toe, heel-toe, so that she moved soundlessly over the sandy ground. With her husband's broad back to her and no one else in sight, she waited until she caught the wonderful earthy scent of him, then threw her arms around his chest.

"Caught you!" she squealed.

He turned sharply and drew back his hand as if he would strike her. Audrey blanched and pulled away as Rowtag paled. "Do not startle me," he said, an apologetic frown on his face. "I could have hurt you."

"I was teasing," Audrey mumbled. She felt herself blushing like a scolded child.

"Something . . . ," Rowtag said, scanning the treetops outside the palisade again. "Something is not right."

"Did you hear something?" Audrey asked, her stomach tightening as fear brushed the edge of her mind.

"It is what I do not hear," Rowtag answered. He stood for a moment more, his muscles tense, and Audrey couldn't stand the suspense.

"Come home with me," she said, taking his hand and pulling him toward the house. "What you don't hear is the sound of two busy little boys, and we must take advantage of the silence, me husband."

▾▲▾▲▾ The sun dipped gradually into the west, and Powhatan slowly uncrossed his arms and legs. Around him, imperceptibly, other warriors readied themselves for the assault.

▼▲▼▲▼ Of all the hours in the day, Thomas Colman liked dusk best. He fervently believed that it was the duty of each Christian to walk with God in the twilight hour to review the day's deeds and words to see if anything could be improved. And this day, he reflected, smiling, could not have been bettered in a single respect. He had awakened in Jocelyn's arms, kissed her passionately as she woke, and clung to her for a long minute before dressing. He felt foolish, as silly as an adolescent school-boy, and wondered that such feelings could still reside in the heart of a man his age. For the first time in his life, he felt free to love his wife with every ounce of his emotion, mind, and body.

"'Thou hast ravished my heart, my sister, my spouse,'" he quoted, willing for the first time to believe that the Song of Solomon had anything to do with the literal expression of love, "'thou hast ravished my heart with one of thine eyes, with one chain of thy neck. How fair is thy love, my sister, my spouse! how much better is thy love than wine! and the smell of thine ointments than all spices! Thy lips, O my spouse, drop as the honeycomb.'"

He smiled, thinking of the woman who had brought his world to life. She was stubborn, rebellious, independent, and beautiful, so why hadn't he discovered her sooner? His eyes had followed her for so many years; the very sound of her breath was as familiar to him as his own; and yet he had not really understood her vulnerability until he took her into his arms. When they had finally become one as God intended, Thomas realized the mystery of marriage, the depths of love, and sacrifice that bound two souls together.

The snap of a twig broke his concentration, and Thomas turned to see the aged John Chapman approaching, rocking on his hips as if they were stiff. "Hallo, Thomas!" John called, waving his hands. "Your wife sent me to fetch you in. She told me to tell you," the old man's eyes twinkled, "she wants you."

Thomas grinned shamelessly. Had the entire town seen the change in their relationship over these last few weeks? He lifted his hand to wave a response, but he froze in horror when an

arrow hissed from nowhere and pierced John Chapman's forehead. Thomas stared in hypnotized disbelief as the old man fell
into a patch of engulfing vines without even blinking.

Quickly, Thomas looked around him, his eyes scanning the
woods for a brief moment. From where had the arrow come?
What enemy lurked in the woods?

Then, instinctively, he ducked, his hands lifting to cover his
head, just as another arrow thunked into the tree behind him.
His heart slamming against his ribs, Thomas raced for the gates
of the palisade, thundering his wife's name in a frantic warning.

▾▲▾▲▾ The enemy poured out of the woods. At least a
dozen of Powhatan's warriors managed to enter the village
before Thomas had roused the guards to close and bar the gates,
and furious hand-to-hand fighting ensued. Totally unprepared,
the Englishmen and Indians who had been strolling through the
courtyard fell like Christians before the lions, and families rose in
panicked confusion from their supper tables as the roofs of their
homes were set ablaze. The men of the city scrambled for their
swords and pikes, for not a single musket was usable. The gunpowder had long been gone, and the twenty-year-old guns had
rusted in the humidity.

Jocelyn was sitting on the bed with Gilda in her arms when
Thomas burst into the house. "In the name of God, tell me what
has happened!" Jocelyn whispered, cold terror pulsing through
her veins. "Are we to die tonight?"

"Not if we can help it," Thomas said, throwing open his old
trunk. Flinging books onto the bed, he lifted a leather scabbard
from under a stack of parchments and pulled from it an eight-
inch dagger.

"Thomas!" Jocelyn exclaimed, amazed. She had never known
him to carry a weapon and had never dreamed he owned one.

"They have killed John Chapman," Thomas said, opening the
door. He cast a backward glance toward her and gave her a fleeting smile. "They will not get far."

Alarmed at the fear in their voices, Gilda began to cry, and Jocelyn drew the child closer. Thomas left the house promising that God would watch over them.

▼▲▼▲▼ The battle raged inside the compound for an hour. The men of Ocanahonan were quick to defend their families once the danger was fully apparent, and the dozen of Powhatan's warriors who had invaded the city were finally subdued. As a rain of burning arrows continued to fly over the rim of the palisade into the village, members of the council dodged the missiles and ran to the church. Afraid to be alone in the house, Jocelyn crept with Gilda into the back of the chapel.

"It is Powhatan, then," Thomas was saying, his eyes darkly intent upon Rowtag. "You are sure?"

Rowtag nodded. "I am. Two of the dead bear the mark of his tribe. The woods are full of his men, for the birds were silent today. Without a doubt, we are surrounded."

"How do we fight them?" young John Sampson asked, his long nose pinched with fear. "We have posted guards around the palisade to prevent them from scaling it—"

"They will scale it, in time, or they will burn it," Rowtag answered, his arms folded tightly across his chest.

"We have no guns," Thomas pointed out. "The gunpowder's gone, the cannons are useless—"

"A lot of good they've done us," Sampson snapped. "Cannon to blow away Spanish ships that never came."

"What will Powhatan do next?" John Prat leaned forward toward Rowtag. "You know how he fights. Tell us what we should do."

Jocelyn could feel her heart knocking as Rowtag gravely regarded his companions. She knew he had anticipated this attack. By all rights he should have muttered, "I told you so," and stalked from the room. But he didn't.

"He will wait until morning," Rowtag said, looking carefully at each man, one by one. "His warriors will breach the palisade.

They will burn our houses, kill, and take captives. They will plunder our storehouses and carry away whatever they desire."

"Could we slip away in the darkness?" John Sampson asked. "Dig a tunnel and canoe down the river to another place—"

"We don't have canoes enough for everyone," Thomas pointed out. "How, then, would you choose to divide those who will live from those who will die?"

Jocelyn felt her frightened heart stir with pride when Thomas stood to his feet and placed his hands upon the table. "We have lived here for twenty years, and I say we stand and die here, if God leads us to do so. And if, perchance, God chooses to spare us, the victory and glory will be his. And if he chooses to take us to heaven, are we not ready to go?"

For a brief second, Thomas's eyes sought Jocelyn's; then he turned again to the council. "Let each family draw together tonight for prayer. Let each man fight on the morrow for his life. And let us be confident that in this, as in all things, God's will must be done."

John Sampson pressed his tented fingers to his lips, John Prat drummed the tabletop with his fingers, and Rowtag nodded gravely and spoke for all of them: "So be it."

With Gilda on her hip, Jocelyn followed Thomas back to their house as the other council members went home to be with their families. Though smoke still drifted over the camp, the burning houses had been doused, and for the moment the deluge of arrows had stopped. But Jocelyn knew from the eerie calm of the night that Powhatan and his men were still outside the walls. Powhatan was but resting, reserving his armament for the coming morning.

Thomas took Gilda from her as she entered the house, and as she mechanically went about tidying up the supper dishes, he sang a soft, funny lullaby to the child until she slept. When Gilda was safely asleep, Jocelyn turned to Thomas and patted her apron helplessly. "What do we do now?" she asked, tears blurring her sight.

"Ah, my dear," he said, standing to enfold her in his arms. "First we pray, and then we hold each other. I shall tell you again how much I love you, and you shall tell me what a rascal I am."

Despite the tremor of fear that shook her heart, she laughed and tilted her head up toward him. "My darling rascal," she whispered, winding her arms about his neck, "my heart is right with God, so kiss me first. We have all night ahead of us."

"You're right," he answered, bending down. His breath was warm in her ear. "And we have years of lost time to redeem."

His hands spanned her waist and drew her to him. With a soft sigh he settled his mouth on hers, and with exquisite tenderness he lifted her from the floor. A small sound of wonder came from his throat as she gave herself freely to the man she had loved for twenty years.

▾▴▾▴▾ Later that night, Jocelyn drew her shawl about her shoulders and stepped into the vast and endless plain of evening. Lights burned in several houses, and from her doorway she could see the quick, restless movements of the men Rowtag had stationed as sentries along the palisade. From one house she heard the sound of frightened weeping, from another, insistent prayer. But in her own house, all was silent.

Thomas slept as easily as did Gilda, his face as innocent and fresh as the child's. After a time of heartfelt prayer, he had rested in Jocelyn's arms and fallen asleep as though he had not a worry in the world.

But Jocelyn walked through the darkness and thought about the morrow. She could face death if she had to, for the foremost struggle of her life had ended weeks ago. At last, she and Thomas were one. And whether they shared another month or another lifetime, she knew nothing would separate them again.

But the children deserved a chance to live. Pacing in the moonlight, Jocelyn prayed for inspiration; then a voice from her past spoke again: *"I will give you strength when the time comes."*

"The time has come," she cried, lifting her eyes to the dark heavens. "What can I do, Father God?"

A silence, thick as wool, wrapped itself around her; then a memory ruffled through her mind like wind on water: Gilda at the river's edge, muddy and streaked with grime, because she and the boys had slipped from the village through a hole under the palisade wall. . . .

Jocelyn hurried to Audrey's house.

▾▴▾▴▾ "It may be the only way," Jocelyn said, leaning toward Audrey and Rowtag in her eagerness. "Let us send the boys and Gilda to the river. They can take a canoe, and they're so small they can lie in the bottom, covered by a canvas or a mat, and drift downstream. When this battle is done, we will seek them among the Indians further south."

Rowtag put his hand upon Fallon's head. "This boy is wise already. He will know how to survive in the woods."

"But, Papa—," Fallon protested.

"Listen to your papa," Audrey said, her voice sharper than Jocelyn had ever heard it. "You will take Noshi and Gilda and hide in the canoe like Jocelyn has said. You will not make a sound or lift your head until the canoe is far, far away."

She reached for the hands of her firstborn son. "Fallon, everythin' will depend upon you, but God will go with you. And when this is over, we will find you, of that you can be certain. You will not be alone."

The boy's eyes flickered to Jocelyn. "God holds me in the palm of his hand?" he asked, his voice quavering uncertainly.

"He does," Rowtag answered, stepping forward. Placing his broad hand again on the boy's copper-colored hair, Rowtag managed a sober smile. "And today you have become a man, my son."

"There is one other thing I must ask of you," Jocelyn said, pressing her hand against her forehead as her lips reluctantly formed her request. "Gilda is the granddaughter of Powhatan and daughter of Kitchi, his son. You must tattoo her with whatever emblems are necessary, Rowtag, so that if something happens, all the savages will know who she is."

Rowtag paused. "You are certain of this?"

"Yes," Jocelyn whispered. "But it must be done quickly."

Audrey pulled Fallon to her and glanced for a moment at Noshi, who slept on a fur by the fire. "When must they go?" she whispered.

"The morning will be too late," Jocelyn ventured.

"They must go now," Rowtag said, stepping toward Noshi. He lifted the boy, fur blanket and all, and his steel gray eyes gentled at the sight of the child in his arms. "It is well you are named Noshi, for you will be the father of many. Go in peace, my son, and God go with you."

Noshi stirred and rubbed his eyes, and Jocelyn stood up from her stool. "I'll bring Gilda," she said, stepping again into the darkness.

▼▲▼▲▼ She woke Thomas and explained the plan. Together they dressed Gilda in a warm suede dress. Jocelyn paused when she saw her ring still looped through the string of bear gut at the bottom of Gilda's trunk; then she resolutely slipped it over the sleepy girl's head. "Rowtag will tattoo you with many colors to mark you as the daughter of a great Indian chief," she whispered to her beloved child. "But this ring will mark you as mine."

"What, Mama?" Gilda asked, rubbing her eyes.

"You are going on an adventure trip with Fallon and Noshi," she explained, kneeling so that she could look directly into Gilda's startled blue eyes. "Remember how you crept through the hole under the wall of the palisade? You will do it tonight, too. Fallon and Noshi are waiting for you now."

Gilda did not seem surprised and trustingly took Jocelyn's hand as they started from the house. And in mute testimony to the love that had bloomed between Thomas and his granddaughter in the past weeks, she thrust her other chubby hand toward Thomas. Smiling at her tenderly, he took it, and the three of them moved silently through the velvet darkness to Rowtag's house.

Audrey, Rowtag, and the two boys were waiting. Rowtag's needle and dyes were ready on the table in the kitchen, and Jocelyn marveled that Gilda did not protest as Rowtag deftly applied the needle and marked her as a daughter of Powhatan's tribe.

When all was done, Fallon led the way through the village to the opening under the palisade. It was a tiny hole, much too small for an adult, but perfect for the children.

"Shall we not enlarge it so that others may escape as well?" Thomas whispered.

Rowtag shook his head. "One canoe may slip away unnoticed, but two would draw attention from Powhatan's braves. To send others would mean certain death for all who ventured out."

Jocelyn took Thomas's hand, afraid for a moment that he would argue with Rowtag, but he only bent to kiss the top of

Gilda's dark head. "Go with God, little one," he said, his voice breaking as he ran his finger lightly down the length of her nose.

Jocelyn fell to her knees and pressed the child's body into hers, breathing deeply to absorb the scent of the little girl. She ran her fingers through the girl's hair, held her face between her hands, and embraced her one last time. "Always remember the ring," she whispered into Gilda's ear. "And know that I love you. And God will go with you always."

"I will remember," Gilda promised solemnly.

Audrey and Rowtag drew their boys to them one last time; then the four adults stood silently while Fallon slipped through the hole. Noshi followed, his brow furrowed with worry, and Gilda paused at the wall and flashed Jocelyn a bright smile. "I'll see you again, Mama," she called, stepping into the hole. She giggled. "Fallon's got my feet."

"Go with him, darling," Jocelyn called, and Gilda clenched and unclenched her hand in a childish wave, then slipped from sight.

Rowtag pressed his ear to the wall of the palisade. "They are running toward the canoes," he said, his voice low. "They will be all right."

Jocelyn and Audrey embraced; then both couples turned toward their homes to wait for the attack that would come in the morning.

"Will we find the children again?" Jocelyn asked as she walked beside Thomas. Her voice trembled in the darkness. "Will we know them . . . when we see them again?"

"Of course we will know them," Thomas answered, slipping his arm about her waist. "We will know everyone in that place. And when we arrive, I beg you to set aside a bit of eternity for me."

"Why?" she asked, looking up at him.

Bending down, he lightly pressed his lips to hers. "I want to get to know you all over again."

Running across the dark sand of the riverbank, Gilda felt the
ring thump rhythmically against her chest. It was a strange game
for the middle of the night, but the wind playfully caught her
hair, and tiny glimmers of moonlight upon the river blinked at
her like a thousand friendly eyes.

Fallon had already slid a canoe into the water when she
caught up with the boys, and she clambered into the boat and
lay flat on the floor as Fallon instructed. Noshi climbed in beside
her, pressing his slender frame against hers, and Fallon climbed
in beside Noshi, drawing a grass mat over them.

Gilda could feel the current tug at the boat, and after a few
moments of resistance, the current soundlessly carried the canoe
into the river. Gilda dared to whisper, "Why are we covered with
the mat?" Fallon whispered back, "We are playing a hiding
game. No one must know where we are."

After a long time of being very still, Gilda yawned and closed
her eyes to sleep as the gentle river current rocked the children
and gurgled a soothing lullaby.

EPILOGUE

At Ritanoe the werowance Eyanoco preserved seven of the
English alive, four men, two boys, and one young maid, who
escaped and fled up the river of Choanoke. . . .

From a 1610 report by William Strachey from a friendly Indian